The Fabulously
Fashionable Life of

*Isabel
Bookbinder*
x

Holly McQueen has wanted to be a writer ever since discovering that the nuns at her junior school would let her off maths homework if she wrote a story instead. After unexpected detours via law, magazine journalism, and even musical theatre, her first novel, *The Glamorous (Double) Life of Isabel Bookbinder* was published by Arrow in 2008. Holly lives with her husband in London. She still avoids maths.

Praise for *The Glamorous (Double) Life of Isabel Bookbinder*:

'The ultimate beach novel . . . McQueen is a good writer who knows her audience and weaves together a tale that'll have you giggling' *Daily Mirror*

'Like catching a snippet of gossip in the girls' loos and deciding you want to carry on listening' *Daily Mail*

The Fabulously Fashionable Life of

Isabel Bookbinder

x

HOLLY McQUEEN

arrow books

Published by Arrow Books in 2009

2 4 6 8 10 9 7 5 3 1

Copyright © Holly McQueen 2009

First published in Great Britain in 2009 by
Arrow Books
Random House, 20 Vauxhall Bridge Road,
London SW1V 2SA

www.rbooks.co.uk

Addresses for companies within The Random House Group Limited
can be found at: www.randomhouse.co.uk/offices.htm

The Random House Group Limited Reg. No. 954009

A CIP catalogue record for this book
is available from the British Library.

ISBN 9780099524649

The Random House Group Limited supports The Forest Stewardship
Council (FSC), the leading international forest certification organisation. All
our titles that are printed on Greenpeace approved FSC-certified paper carry
the FSC logo. Our paper procurement policy can be found at
www.rbooks.co.uk/environment

Typeset by SX Comping DTP, Rayleigh, Essex
Printed and bound in Great Britain by
CPI Cox & Wyman, Reading, RG1 8EX

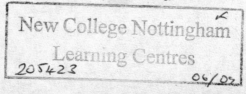

To my parents, with love
And for Josh, as ever – TD

Acknowledgements

I am enormously indebted to the fabulously fashionable Frances Bentley and Verity Parker at *Vogue*, who provided every assistance and answered every ridiculous question with careful thought and enthusiasm. Any errors in the representation of life on a fashion magazine are mine alone.

Huge thanks to all at Arrow, especially Louise Campbell, Claire Round and Louisa Gibbs for their endless hard work, their truly imaginative flair, and for their delightful company at lunch. And of course huge thanks to Rob Waddington, Oli Malcolm, Jay Cochrane and Trish Slattery for their creativity, their total commitment to getting my book 'out there', and their near-equal commitment to sampling Snow Kittens in cutting-edge cocktail bars.

In particular, thanks to Vanessa Neuling, who manages to combine enviable serenity with talent and passion, and is thus a Holy Grail of editors, and of course to Kate Elton – Publishing Goddess, constant source of advice and encouragement, and proud owner of the best sense of humour in town (well, she laughs at my jokes).

And thanks to Clare Alexander, my agent in shining

armour, who is as warm as she is witty and witty as she is wise, and to Patrick Janson-Smith, without whom there would be no Isabel.

In the Beginning

God, I feel inspired.

I woke up with the dawn this morning. At least, I thought it was the dawn. I've just bought one of those super-intelligent artificial-daylight alarm clocks that wake you up exactly like a natural sunrise. Much better than being woken by a horrible unnatural alarm clock. It does all kinds of clever things to your metabolism, and your brain chemistry, and something called your Arcadian rhythms, and you jump out of bed feeling all calm, and well rested, and ready to face the day ahead.

I must have read the instructions wrong, though. The stupid thing started glowing radioactively at eighteen minutes past two, which only made me feel furious, and sleep-deprived, and ready for absolutely nothing. I couldn't make the horrible orange light fade back down again so eventually I staggered into the bathroom, dumped it in the bathtub, and covered it with two large bath sheets. I think I must have gone back to sleep somewhere around half past three.

When I woke up again just now, nice, proper *natural* daylight had started streaming through the blinds. I do a couple of energising yoga-type stretches, which ought to sort out my metabolism and my Arcadian rhythms very nicely, then I head into the kitchen to make my first strong black coffee of the day.

Now that I'm going to be a Top International Fashion Designer, strong black coffee is probably going to form the cornerstone of my diet. It's very important to start as I mean to go on.

It's quite difficult to actually *enjoy* strong black coffee, though. I did try to get into it once before, when I was going to be a best-selling Novelist, but all I ever ended up doing was drinking lovely yummy mochaccinos instead. But this time I'm going to be seriously disciplined. When I'm the public face (and figure) of my own fashion label, I won't be able to get away with any extra poundage. My ideal customer – I just call her The Woman I Design For – is extremely discerning. Whatever will she think of me if I go about the place looking a little bit on the chunky side, simply because I can't resist the temptation of a delicious frothy coffee?

I have to say, though, I think the Woman I Design For would be a bit of a cow if she wouldn't even overlook *one* little mochaccino a day.

I mean, here I am, thinking of nothing but how I can make her look fashion-forward and fabulous, and she's getting all uppity about a measly little two hundred calories of caffeine and sugar I need to kick-start my morning.

Actually, only a hundred and eighty-three calories, according to the sachet.

You know, I think the Woman I Design For is just going to have to get over it. I'll go for a jog round Battersea Park this evening. That ought to placate her.

Mug of yummy mochaccino in hand, I head back to the bedroom to get on with the most important part of my day so far: assembling my Signature Look.

I mean, where would Donatella Versace be without the leopard skin and the Tango tan? Or Stella McCartney without the snazzy little tailored trouser suits? And look at Vivienne Westwood, with all that punky hair and distressed tartan. If I'm going to make it as a Top International Fashion Designer, the right Signature Look is absolutely vital.

OK. Well, obviously, I don't own any leopard skin. My wardrobe is pretty thin on snazzy little tailored trouser suits, too. I think I have got a tartan skirt lurking in here somewhere, one that Mum ordered for me from the Boden catalogue several years ago, but it's not distressed. Though I was pretty distressed when Mum gave it to me, if that counts. I mean, it had 'Fun' coloured buttons, for heaven's sake.

Hang on a moment. Maybe Fun Buttons could be my Signature Look?

. . . *Stunning Isabel Bookbinder dazzled at her close friend and mentor Valentino's birthday party, in a black lace gown accessorised with her Signature Fun Buttons* . . .

. . . *high priestess of style Isabel Bookbinder looked cutting-edge as ever at this year's Glastonbury,* working denim hot pants and a vintage panama trimmed with her Signature Fun Buttons . . .

Hmmm.

Perhaps not.

What I'm really after is something elegant and fabulous. Something that expresses my fashion personality. Something The Woman I Design For would sell her granny to buy. Some classic black trousers, perhaps, and this little stripy T-shirt, for easy Parisian chic? Then some high-heeled loafers, a long string of beads and, for that final twist of Gallic *je ne sais quoi*, this navy-blue beret I picked up from Comptoir des Cotonniers last winter.

But when I turn to look in the mirror, I don't look chic and Parisian at all. Shove a baguette under one arm and I could be on my way to audition for an ill-advised remake of *'Allo 'Allo*.

OK. Back to the drawing board. I suppose I could try mixing Designer, Vintage and High Street. It's what all the fashion magazines are always saying you should do. I'll team my Stella McCartney pistachio-green silk pleated skirt (the Designer bit) with an off-white Karen Millen blouse (the High-Street bit) and this gorgeous rose-pink brocade duster coat with bracelet-length sleeves that *looks* like it's Vintage but is actually brand new from a mother-of-the-bride shop in Shepton Mallet. Well, if The Woman I Design For is anything like me, she'll be too scared to go into proper vintage shops, too, so it's a perfectly valid solution.

I love it. It's cool, it's cutting edge, and I'm pretty sure it's got more fashion personality than you could shake a stick at!

Signature Look cracked, for now at least, I take a few mind-clearing yoga-style breaths, sit down at the writing desk in the corner of the bedroom, and reach for my Mood Book.

You see, I've remembered this article I once read about John Galliano. I think he talked about his 'Process' a lot, and his 'Fashion Vision', but the most useful thing I recall was that he collects all his ideas for his new collection on something called a Mood Board. What he does is, he starts out with a single word that sums up what he wants the Collection to reflect – *Cabaret*, say, or *Tranquillity*, or *Brothel*. Then he just gathers together all the things that inspire him and bungs them up on a piece of cork-board in his airy Parisian studio. Lines of poetry, scraps of fabric, pictures torn out of magazines, that kind of thing.

Well, obviously this is perfect for my Process, too! I've got poetry books rattling about the place some-where. And I've got loads of unwanted clothes given me by Mum that I can hack up for scraps of fabric. *And* I tear things out of magazines *all the time*. It's perfect!

I've gone one better than John Galliano, though, even though I say so myself. I mean, corkboard is all very well, but it's not the most exciting thing you can buy. And seeing as I'm not yet in possession of my own airy Parisian studio, or any studio for that matter, I thought I'd need something a little bit more portable.

Smythson don't actually do formal Mood Books – I did check – but they do have these really gorgeous little pocket notebooks that say *Fashion Notes*, which is perfectly suitable for the time being.

I open up my brand-new pink notebook, which is sitting on the desk in front of me.

Right. So. What one, single word sums up everything I want to say in my Debut Clothing Collection? I mean, one word is easy-peasy, isn't it? Not like trying to write a whole novel, or something, where you have to write tons and tons and tons of them.

I pick up my special propelling pencil.

Then I put it down again.

Then I pick it up again.

God, I feel inspired.

I mean, really, really inspired.

Now all I need is a Debut Collection.

IN THIS WEEK'S *HIYA!* MAGAZINE, TOP INTERNATIONAL FASHION DESIGNER ISABEL BOOKBINDER SHOWS US AROUND HER STUNNING CHELSEA APARTMENT, AND TELLS OF HER EXCITEMENT AT THE LAUNCH OF HER EXCLUSIVE NEW FRAGRANCE.

Stunning Isabel, 27, opens the door to welcome us inside. Clad only in a silk dressing gown that skims her skinny size six figure, Isabel is only just out of bed after last night's fabulous launch party for her brand-new perfume, ~~Isabel no 5~~ ~~Acqua d'Isabel~~ Isabelissimo. Stocked exclusively at Harvey Nichols in London and Bergdorf Goodman in New York, waiting lists for the Top International Fashion Designer's first fragrance have already run into the thousands. We settle down in her fabulous living room where, over strong black coffee, Isabel opens her heart about her fabulously fashionable existence.

HIYA! So, we hear it was quite a party last night! All your Top International Fashion Designer friends were there to support you – Stella, Marc, ~~Miu Miu Miucer~~ Mrs Prada, and Valentino, of course . . .

IB Dear Val. He's such a great friend and mentor.

HIYA! This was all to launch Isabelissimo – a wonderful mix of ~~frangipani and white musk~~ ~~patchouli~~ ~~jasmine~~ ~~flowers and green~~ scents. Tell us, Isabel, where did you get your inspiration for the fragrance?

IB Well, as always, I found myself truly inspired by The Woman I Design For. I feel like I know her so well – ~~a~~ ~~strong sassy free-spirited~~ an independent woman who isn't afraid to be ~~feminine alluring sexy~~ glamorous.

HIYA! And who also isn't a miserable old body fascist.

IB That too. Absolutely.

HIYA! Fragrance may be your latest exciting venture, but clothes were where it all began for Isabel Bookbinder . . .

IB That's right. ~~I was just a girl with a portable Mood Book and a dream~~ I don't think I knew, when I started work on my first-ever Collection that sunny September morning in a one-bedroomed flat in South London, just how big my brand would become.

HIYA! But now your label Isabel B is feted by the fashion cognoscenti and worn by A-listers all over the world, while your newer diffusion line, Izzy B for Isabel Bookbinder, is finding a whole new generation of fans in Harvey Nichols and Selfridges!

IB Yes, it is quite good, isn't it?

HIYA! Could you talk us through a typical day in your glamour-filled life?

IB As a Top International Fashion Designer, there's no typical day! I might be auditioning models for my latest catwalk show, meeting an Oscar hopeful to discuss her awards-show gown, pounding the streets of Manhattan to find the perfect Fifth Avenue location for my new boutique . . . Of course, wherever I go, I'm always thinking about my latest Collection, jotting down a single word here or a single word there in my handy portable Mood Book. That's a very important part of my Process.

HIYA! Goodness, it sounds much harder work than we'd thought! Now on to your private life, if we may . . .

We've all heard the rumours about you and Daniel Craig...

IB Daniel and I met when I chose him to be the face and body of my new ~~underpants~~ menswear Collection. We're just good friends.

HIYA! So you won't comment on the photographs of you two breakfasting on his hotel terrace at Cap Ferrat?

IB (blushing) I'm afraid not. The paparazzi can be very intrusive, and my Daniel is a very private man.

HIYA! So, Isabel, what's next for your luxury-goods empire?

IB Well, I have three brand-new Emporio Bookbinders opening worldwide later this month, so there are lots of launch parties to arrange. I'm also hard at work coming up with a name for another diffusion line – at the moment, we're thinking Iz by Isabel Bookbinder or Izzy B by Isabel Bookbinder. And if I have the time, I'll design the bottle for another new fragrance, which will be an exotic blend of ~~tuberose~~ ~~vanilla~~ ~~lemonbalm~~ ~~and~~ scents.

HIYA! While still hard at work on your new couture clothing Collection, of course!

IB Of course. I've started assembling a new Mood Book already.

HIYA! Isabel Bookbinder, thank you for your time.

IB Thank *you*. It was a pleasure.

Chapter 1

Well, this isn't quite what I was expecting.

I mean, I don't know about you, but I'd have thought Central St Martins would have a really swanky reception area. Gleaming black lacquer on every surface, perhaps, with an original 1970s disco ball suspended from the ceiling, and hot-pink velvet-upholstered chesterfield sofas to lounge on. Or if not that, then maybe something fabulously art deco, with deep leather armchairs and little mirrored cabinets. Or at the very least, minimalist white walls, floor and ceiling, with tiny little Scandinavian balsa-wood chairs that look like they'll crack if anyone without a life-threatening eating disorder so much as hovers above one.

But Central St Martins' waiting room has none of the above. What it does have is the following:

1) grey carpet tiles, peppered with little blobs of decades-old chewing-gum;
2) walls papered with a yuck-yellow version of that horrible nubbly wallpaper you find in old people's homes; and
3) those Day-Glo orange plastic moulded chairs that make your bottom sweat if you sit on them for longer than two minutes.

As I've been waiting for my interview here for nearly half an hour already, there's some serious nether-region perspiration going on. I know this will have played havoc with the pleats in my Stella McCartney silk skirt. All I can hope is that there isn't an extremely embarrassing damp patch there, too.

Because frankly, my outfit is embarrassing enough already. Here I am, in my off-white blouse, my pistachio-green skirt and my rose-pink fake-vintage duster coat, and *everybody else* is in black trousers and a black V-neck sweater, almost like it's a uniform or something.

Oh, God.

It isn't a uniform, is it?

'Excuse me?' I lean over to the bespectacled girl on the Day-Glo chair beside me.

She looks up, startled, from her copy of *Pop* magazine. 'Yes?'

I lower my voice. 'I'm sorry to disturb, but I was just wondering – there isn't some sort of uniform requirement at Central St Martins, is there? Perhaps something they mentioned on the application form?'

She blinks at me from behind her glasses. 'Um. I don't think so.'

'Well, then, is there some sort of uniform requirement for fashion designers in general, do you know?' I nod round the waiting room at everyone in their near-identical outfits. 'Something laid down by the . . . er . . . British Union of Fashion Designers? And

Framework Knitters,' I add, because that's definitely something union-y I've heard of before.

She just blinks at me again. 'Well, I can't speak for everybody else. But personally, I wear black so I can blend into the background, and put my fashion personality into my own designs.'

'Oh.' Clearly, I should never have tried to actually *wear* my fashion personality. 'Well, thank you.'

I sit back in my seat again, trying hard to look calm and collected. But inside, I'm churning with embarrassment. I feel like such a hick from the sticks. And I *look* like a gaudy Neapolitan icecream in a room filled with earnest single espressos.

You know, I bet there really is a uniform requirement on the application form. A fact I'd know if I hadn't been too scared to fill the application form in. It was ever so long, with big spaces where you were meant to write down all your previous fashion-related degrees and relevant work experience. Given that I have none of either, I thought it was best to just avoid the blank spaces altogether.

Or maybe it really wasn't on the form, and it's just something you're expected to *know*. Well, if you have connections, like I expect everyone else at St Martins does, then it's the kind of thing you probably would know. But I don't have connections. I don't have a rock-star dad, and an ex-model for a mum. I mean, look at that boy right opposite me – the spitting image of Trudie Styler, if ever there was one. And now I come to think of it, the bespectacled girl next to me has a distinct air of Art Garfunkel about her.

I haven't got a hope in hell, have I?

The thing is, I know it's a little bit ambitious, applying to Central St Martins for a Fashion Master's. Especially when I haven't even studied fashion Minors before. Not to mention the fact that they've already filled up almost the entire course for the year, and there's just a couple of last-minute places left for us latecomers. But this was really the only fashion course that appealed to me. Every other course I investigated seems to be filled with the most incredibly fiddly, tedious stuff. How to hem a skirt. How to make a sleeve. How to sew a seam. Whereas what I'm after is the really interesting and important bit. How to get your clothes stocked by Harvey Nichols. What to name your fragrance. How to persuade Keira Knightley and Daniel Craig to star in your worldwide ad campaign. That sort of thing.

Because at the end of the day, anyone can hem a skirt or sew a seam, can't they?

Well, I mean, *I* can't, obviously.

But the point is that I'll be more than happy to pay other, better-qualified people to do so, when I've got my own label. If I'm the one coming up with all the genius ideas, I don't think I can possibly be expected to deal with all the boring stuff like manufacturing, too. I mean, I very much doubt Kate Moss does any of that stuff for *her* clothing Collection. And Sarah Jessica Parker doesn't look like she'd be too handy with a needle and thread, but she's designed a fashion line of her own. Not to mention all those footballers' wives who keep popping up all over the place with a jeans brand here or a bikini collection there. So I honestly don't see it as what my boyfriend Will would call a *barrier to entry*.

Anyway, there's one other very big reason why Central St Martins is my fashion college of choice. Which is that I've sort of told my family I've got on this course already.

This wasn't my plan, by the way. Fibbing to people about my career has caused me so many problems before, I'd honestly intended never to do it again. In fact, when I decided I was really going to go for this fashion-designing dream of mine, I even made myself a bit of a vow – to tell the truth, the whole truth, and nothing but the truth. But then, when I actually plucked up the courage, last weekend, to mention to my family that I was giving up novel-writing to concentrate full-time on becoming a Top International Fashion Designer, they didn't take it too well. By which I mean that my dad didn't take it too well. We were all gathered for a Sunday lunch to celebrate my older brother Marley and his wife Daria getting pregnant. In amongst the general sense of excitement and celebration, I thought it might be a good time to . . . what do they call it? Bury bad news. Well, the only thing that nearly got buried was me. Dad shouted so loud that he frightened Daria, who ran off to be sick. Then Marley got very upset, and Mum started crying, and the only way I could calm everything down was by pulling something big out of the bag. Dad being a headmaster, I knew the only thing that might placate him was the solid respectability of a recognised degree course.

And it did a pretty good job of placating, I must say. I mean, Dad wasn't exactly *thrilled*, but at least it stopped all the yelling. And Mum, actually, *was* thrilled – she whispered so in my ear before I got the train home that evening, anyway. I think she'd really been thrilled from the first moment I made my announcement, to be honest, but she finds it difficult to admit to being thrilled about anything without Dad's express permission to do so.

So here I am. Waiting for my interview for a place on the world-famous Fashion Master's at Central St Martins.

Waiting a very, very long time, it must be said. I'm actually getting a tiny bit bored. I'd really like to get this week's *Grazia* out of my handbag, but Art Garfunkel's daughter is still buried in her *Pop*, and one particularly smug girl is even holding up a copy of *Madame Bovary*, though I don't think she's turned a page in twenty minutes. Several people are leafing through the copies of *anothermagazine* that are lying about on the plasticky coffee table, so I pick one up, too, and start flicking. I raise my eyebrows knowingly at a very long article about Japanese Harajuku style, then make fascinated-sounding noises at a rather disturbing picture of slightly fleshy people parading along a catwalk wearing what looks like cling film.

Actually, I think I'd much, much rather read my *Grazia*.

I'm just about to give up and display my lowbrow credentials – I mean, I'm already the odd one out in this outfit – when suddenly a woman calls out my name.

'Isabel Bookbinder?'

A rather dumpy woman in black (natch) is standing in the doorway of the waiting room, smiling pleasantly in my direction.

'Yes! I'm Isabel!' I pick up my bag and hurry towards her, hoping nobody's noticed the damp patch on my squashed skirt. 'Nice to meet you.' I stick out a hand and try to look quietly confident, the way you're meant to at interviews.

'Diana Pettigrew.' She shakes my hand back before leading me a few feet along a hallway and ushering me through a door into a small, dimly lit office. 'Have a seat. I hope we haven't kept you waiting for too long?' She points me towards another – terrific – orange plastic moulded chair.

'Thank you!' I beam at her, to show her I'm easy-going and laid-back, just the kind of student any right-thinking teacher would be thrilled to have on their course. 'Not at all. It gave me the chance to sit and think,' I add, hastily, before she gets the idea I'm too easy-going and laid-back to take her course seriously. 'Thinking is an extremely important part of my Process.'

'Right . . .' She looks a bit confused, and starts to

leaf through a pile of thin cardboard folders on her desk. 'Now, just one little admin issue . . . we don't seem to have received your application form yet.'

'That's right.'

She glances up for a second. 'Er – is there a reason for that?'

'Well, I didn't want to rely on the post. Things go missing so much these days.'

'But applications are done online.'

Shit. 'Oh, well, I don't trust technology either.'

Diana Pettigrew's forehead is creased into a frown. 'So . . . you've brought the form with you now?'

'Not exactly.' I can feel my palms starting to sweat along with my bottom. 'You see, I didn't really feel the application form represented who I am.'

This is completely true. This is not breaking my nothing-but-the-truth vow.

'I have a very unorthodox approach to fashion,' I go on. 'I don't like to be constrained by have-tos and should-haves. Which is why I feel so very well suited to life at Central St Martins,' I say, smoothly. 'After all, if you can't be creative and individual here, where can you be?'

'Ms Bookbinder.' Diana Pettigrew's lips are set in a rather irritable line. 'I have taught John Galliano. I have taught Alexander McQueen. Not even they were too creative and individual to fill out our application form.'

'Well, you did an excellent job on both of them,' I say, meekly. 'Congratulations on that.'

There's an odd silence for a moment, then she lets

17

out a sigh. 'Well, we are where we are. You can always fill out an application form later. For now, why don't I have a little look at your portfolio?'

'Oh, absolutely!' This is the bit I've been really excited about. I get my gorgeous pink Mood Book out of my bag and hand it over.

Her eyebrows shoot upwards. 'You don't have a standard artist's portfolio?'

'Well, that depends on what you mean by a standard artist's portfolio.'

'We *mean*,' Diana says, 'the sort of thing you'll have seen all the other applicants with. A collection of your clothing designs. Your sketches. Some photographs of items you've actually *made*.'

Ah. So that's why everybody in the waiting room was clutching a large black folder as though their lives depended on the contents.

'Oh. Well, that's not quite the way I work. I tend very much to start things out at the conceptual stage . . .'

'Well, everyone *starts out* at the conceptual stage!' Diana Pettigrew snaps, staring down at my Mood Book like it's a whiffy old sock in her teenage son's bedroom. 'What on earth is this?'

'It's my Mood Board! Well, my Mood *Book*, really, because it's so much more portable than a great big piece of corkboard . . .'

Diana has opened up the book at the front. 'You've written the word *Pretty*.'

'That's right!'

18

'In French as well as in English.'

'Well, I do hope to become a Top *International* Fashion Designer.'

She ignores me. 'You have glued in a piece of pink satin . . .'

'Which *is* Pretty, I'm sure you'll agree!'

'. . . and stapled on a photo of Keira Knightley wearing Valentino couture on a red carpet.'

I smile at Diana. 'Keira would be the ideal Woman I'd Design For. And I've got the most amazing idea for an Oscar dress for her . . .'

'A dress you have sketches of somewhere else?'

'Well, no, not exactly . . . I find actually *drawing* clothes quite difficult, to be perfectly honest. But, I mean, that's not that big a deal, is it? I mean, when you're actually a designer, you can just *pay* someone to do the drawings and . . . you know, sew stuff together. Make the sleeves. Can't you?'

'You *can't make a sleeve*?' Something about the horror on her face tells me I've made a fundamental error here.

'I wouldn't say *can't*. It's more that I've never really tried.'

'Well, how's your sewing?'

'Oh, you know . . . so-so!' I laugh. Diana doesn't. 'But can Sarah Jessica Parker sew?' I ask, rhetorically. 'Can Victoria Beckham?'

She sits back in her seat and folds her arms. 'Can you cut a pattern?'

'Well . . .' I shift, uncomfortably, in my seat. My

bottom is getting sweatier than ever. I'm starting to have some really serious regrets about my nothing-but-the-truth vow. 'That all depends on the kind of pattern you're after. I mean, I could probably do a square. Maybe a triangle . . .'

'All right. Stop.' Diana Pettigrew holds up a hand. 'Isabel. Help me out here. You've neglected to fill out a proper application form. You seem to have no idea about the most rudimentary elements of garment-making. You've come to an interview with nothing but a so-called *Mood Book*, and your greatest design role models appear to be Sarah Jessica Parker and Victoria Beckham.' She leans across the desk. 'What is it you feel you have to offer Central St Martins?'

I take a deep breath. 'OK. I'm going to be completely honest with you here.'

'That would be helpful.'

'I don't have all the experience some of your other applicants have got. And I'll admit – I don't have any rudimentary knowledge of garment-making. In fact, the only garment I've ever made was a screen-printed T-shirt in Year Nine. And even that didn't come out like it was supposed to.' This is completely true, by the way. Somehow I managed to get the screen-printing equipment the wrong way round, so in the class photo all the other girls are wearing T-shirts saying *Babe* and I'm wearing a T-shirt bearing the inexplicable *ebaB*.

'Then why on earth are you applying for the toughest Fashion postgraduate course in the country?'

'Because I think I'd be really, really good at this, if

you'd give me the chance!' I lean forward. 'Honestly, Diana . . . I mean Ms Pettigrew. I'd work incredibly hard. And I've got big plans for the future – I mean, how many other students do you get who are *already* working on their fragrance line?'

'I don't think we've ever had a single one,' she says, rather faintly.

'Exactly!'

'I'm sorry, but you are manifestly underqualified!' Diana Pettigrew is standing up. 'Letting you on this course would be an insult to my other students and, quite frankly, a cruelty to you.'

'But I don't mind about that!' I want to grab her hands, but I have a feeling she's already thinking of summoning a security guard to eject me. 'Look, the course doesn't even start for another three weeks – I'll make sure I learn all the rudimentaries of dressmaking before then, I promise . . .'

Diana stands up and goes to the door.

'. . . and this is the only way my family will take me seriously.' My voice has suddenly got a lot smaller.

'Look, Ms Bookbinder . . . Isabel . . .' Her face softens, ever so slightly. 'I can't give you a place here just so that your family will take you seriously. All I can suggest, if you're really serious, is that you reapply . . .'

'When?' I grab my diary out of my bag. 'Is there another late round of applications?'

'. . . in three years' time.' Diana opens the door. 'In the meantime, I would suggest that you take a basic

Fashion degree, get some decent work experience and try putting together a sensible portfolio that does not simply revolve around the word *Pretty*.'

I'm not about to argue with her. Not with the entire waiting room listening ten feet away.

I pick up my bag, put my Mood Book back inside, and, with the very little dignity I have left, walk out of her office.

Chapter 2

Well, I don't have time to feel sorry for myself. I've got to get to Mortimer Street to meet my friend Barney, and thanks to Diana Pettigrew, I'm already half an hour late. The buses are backed up all the way along Southampton Row, so I bite the bullet and jump in a black cab.

A cab I can't possibly afford now that my dreams of becoming a Top International Fashion Designer are in danger of heading down the toilet.

The thing is, it wasn't *only* because of Dad that I wanted to get into Central St Martins. I wanted to be able to prove something to my boyfriend Will, too. There he is, heading off at six o'clock every morning to his high-powered, well-paid job in a City law firm. And all I've been doing since I moved in with him three weeks ago is sitting around the flat with my Mood Book, tearing things out of magazines and looking up possible inspiration words in the dictionary. I mean, *I* know that's all part of my new job. But I'm not sure Will does.

He's not *said* anything, of course. In fact, there's a small part of me that's getting a tiny bit worried that he actually rather likes the idea that he goes off to work all hours while I, in his eyes, do nothing. I have a sneaking suspicion that it makes him feel a little bit Master of the Universe-y. You know, one of those tall, broad-shouldered, pinstriped men who pay for their wives' tennis lessons, and leave fifty-pound notes by the toaster in the morning for 'treating yourself to a manicure', and expect you to be able to do fancy knots in their tie while you gaze at them adoringly and send them out of the door with a cheery wave to earn pots of money and have it away with their secretary.

I'm not suggesting, by the way, that Will is having it away with his secretary. Apart from anything else, I'm pretty sure he's actually terrified of his secretary (I know I am). Anyway, Will really isn't the cheating kind. I mean, he *does* happen to be tall, and broad-shouldered, and occasionally even a little bit pinstriped (a *very subtle* pinstripe that I picked out for him half-price in the Selfridges sale, which, if he wears it with a crisp white shirt, makes him look slightly like a Hugo Boss ad), but that's one of the many reasons he's quite so fanciable. And I've always thought Will understands that I'm not the stay-at-home, Stepford Wife sort, either. I mean, all right, I wouldn't have a fundamental objection to a fifty-pound note by the toaster, and I could probably learn to do a fancy knot in a tie if I really had to. But I draw the line at tennis lessons. The madness has to stop somewhere.

Anyway, since moving in with Will last month, I've found all these feminist principles that I didn't even know I had. So I'm not just giving up on my career at the first hurdle. All right, so Central St Martins don't want me. There are tons of other options I can explore! Nobody ever got anywhere in life without setbacks and hard graft. I'll enrol for all kinds of courses at some down-at-heel community college, if I have to. Then I'll sit up into the wee small hours, possibly beside a guttering candle, if I can find one, sewing hem after hem until my fingers bleed and my eyesight fails. I'll learn how to make a damn sleeve! I'll make nothing *but* sleeves, until I can make sleeves in my sleep. I'm going to set about this the sensible way. No short cuts, no easy options. Just good old-fashioned hard work.

I don't think I'll tell Mum and Dad I didn't get into Central St Martins, though. I mean, I think it's best for everybody if I let them carry on thinking I'm enrolled on that nice respectable degree course that calmed everyone down the last time.

In the meantime, I'll have to make some serious headway on the actual designing front. Because surely if I could tell Mum and Dad I'd had my entire Debut Collection snapped up by Harvey Nichols, say, or what's-her-name from Brown's, the importance of a nice, respectable degree course would diminish quite a bit.

I grab my Mood Book from my bag, open it to a fresh page and look around for an inspiring word to get me going.

Traffic? . . . *Hubbub*? . . . *Bendy Bus*? . . . No, that's two words. Ooh, I know, how about *City*? Yes, that's not bad! *Isabel Bookbinder's Debut Collection, City, is filled with gritty, urban pieces like . . .*

Well, *like . . .*

Actually, gritty, urban pieces aren't that much fun. That would have to be all microfibre T-shirts and combat trousers, wouldn't it? Can't see The Woman I Design For being too happy about that.

OK, so what about . . . *Shoppers?* Or *Tourists?* Or . . .

Suddenly my phone vibrates with a text: *How did it go?* It's from my best friend, Lara. She's been away for the last two weeks, holidaying in Florida with her dad, current stepmum, and their brood of small children. We've texted back and forth, but I haven't actually spoken to her since a couple of days after I moved in with Will. Now she's back, it'd be great to hear her voice.

I call her office, and she picks up almost instantly. 'Dr Alliston speaking.'

'Isabel Bookbinder speaking,' I echo, in her solemn work voice.

'Iz!'

'Am I disturbing? You're not with a patient?'

'Client,' Lara corrects me. She's a clinical psychologist, which means her entire day is spent talking to barmy people. Sorry, barmy *clients*. 'No, no, I'm just catching up on paperwork. It's so great to hear your voice!'

'So, how was Florida?'

'It was great. I've got an amazing tan! And the kids

26

were sweet, of course. I taught Claudine, Marcus and Harry to swim!'

I don't know if it's because she's got a PhD in psychology, or just because she's an incredibly nice, well-adjusted person, but Lara handles her enormous, non-nuclear family with amazing ease. At my last count, her mum and dad had clocked up six marriages between them, and Claudine, Marcus and Harry are only a tiny fraction of the multitude of complicated half- and stepbrothers and sisters Lara has to buy presents for every Christmas. When I ask her how come they all get along so well, she's incredibly blasé about it being nothing more than Good Communication, and Respecting Boundaries, and Learning to Compromise, but I'm not so sure. I think after a career of listening to her patients – sorry, clients – spout on about malevolent mothers and spiteful sisters, Lara has learned to be grateful for what she's got. Either that, or far-flung families really are the way to go. I mean, look at my family. We're so nuclear we're practically toxic.

'But I'll tell you all about it later,' Lara goes on. 'I want to know how it went at St Martins.'

'Well, remember that time I went for an interview at Morgan Stanley?' This, by the way, was the brief (very brief) period when I quite fancied becoming a Top Businesswoman, in an Armani suit and a slash of crimson lipstick. 'Quite a lot like that.'

'Oh, God. Oh, *Isabel*.'

'Yes.'

There's a long, rather bleak silence. I have to say, it's a tiny bit disheartening.

'God, I hope you don't react like this with your patients!'

'Clients,' Lara corrects me, automatically. 'Sorry, Iz.' I can almost hear her gathering her forces for an encouraging onslaught. 'Well, I actually think this is a good thing.'

This is why it's so great to have a clinical psychologist as your best friend. She knows all these clever, cognitive-behavioural tricks that mean you can make anything sound good. Like, say your husband has run off with the Swedish au pair. Lara will tell you that instead of sitting around wondering if your head will fit in the oven, you really ought to be congratulating yourself on never again having to pretend you actually enjoy 'Dancing Queen'. It's called cognitive restructuring, apparently, and it's extremely effective.

'Why is it a good thing?' I settle back in my seat, preparing myself for some nice, soothing, cognitive restructuring.

'Well, I'm just not sure you were ever really cut out to be a fashion designer, Iz.'

'What?' This doesn't sound very reconstructive.

'I was reading this article in *Atelier*, on the flight back from Orlando . . . oh, hold on, I've still got it in my handbag . . .' Lara rustles around on the other end of the line for a minute. 'Yes, here we are . . . "Twenty-four Hour Party People? Behind the Scenes with the

28

Fashion Aristocracy". Ugh – Fashion Aristocracy! Well, that's got to put you off, for starters!'

'Yes . . .' Though actually, I'd quite like to be in the Fashion Aristocracy.

'Anyway, they interview all these top designers, Stella McCartney, Lucien Black, Alexander McQueen . . . and it doesn't sound like fun at all. Actually, it just sounds really, really hard work, Iz. High stress, endless hours. I mean, you'd never get to see Will.'

'I never get to see Will anyway.'

'Oh?' Lara's professional antennae have clearly shot up, and are aimed in my direction. 'Is everything OK?'

'Yes, yes, everything's fine!' I reach forward to open the taxi window, because it's suddenly feeling quite warm in here. 'Everything's brilliant. I mean, he's incredibly busy with work at the moment.' This is true. He's got these horrible, difficult clients who are trying to buy an oil pipe somewhere and pay no tax, or something. Will calls them his Dodgy Kazakh Businessmen. Anyway, dodgy or not, they've taken over most of his life for the last two months. It's just unfortunate that things suddenly got even busier as soon as I moved in. 'But that's why it's so great we're living together now,' I go on. 'Even when he's really busy, at least we know we'll see each other at some point during the day. Or night,' I add, thinking of all the times in the last week that Will's crawled into bed beside me in the early hours.

'Right . . . Iz, are you *sure* everything's OK?'

'It's fantastic! I've never been happier!' I don't think

now is the time to mention all these feminist thoughts that have suddenly crept up on me. Or my fears about the tennis lessons. 'You know, I think we've moved into a very adult, mature phase of our relationship,' I say, hoping Lara will be impressed enough to get off my back. 'We don't *need* to see each other all the time. He has his work, I have mine. It's all about . . .' I rack my brains to think of the kind of thing you hear on talk shows all the time. 'Focusing on our future. Building a life together.'

'Sounds like fun,' Lara says, flatly.

'It is,' I snap. 'It's about the *quality* of time you have together, Lara, not the quantity.' This is completely true, by the way. Because even though it's sometimes two in the morning when Will gets into bed, and even though we might only have ten minutes snuggling up together, it's still the best ten minutes of my day. Drifting off to sleep again with his left arm wrapped tightly around me has this wonderfully soothing way of making me totally forget the three hours I might have spent waiting up for him earlier. 'Which is why we're having a special dinner together this evening,' I carry on. 'Bringing Back the Romance.'

'Bringing *back* the romance? Iz-Wiz, you've only been living with him for three weeks!'

'No, I don't mean it like that.' And it's true. I don't. Things with Will are wonderfully romantic when he's not so snowed under with his bloody job that we don't have the time to just . . . *be* together. I suppose really I should be thinking about this dinner as Bringing Back the Good Old Days Before a Bunch of Dodgy Kazakh Businessmen Stole My Boyfriend. 'Anyway, I thought we were talking about my career, here! Because that's what I really need to focus on. Not my incredibly romantic, successful, adult, mature relationship.'

'Well, OK, but I'm just a tiny bit concerned about you . . .'

'Don't be. Everything's great with Will. Honest.' My cab is pulling up on the corner of Mortimer Street and Great Portland Street. 'Look, I have to go. Can I see you tomorrow?'

We agree to meet near her office for lunch tomorrow, then I hop out of the taxi and pay. Barney is waving me over from the corner, as though I might not have seen where he is. Which, given that he's standing behind a large, tomato-red coffee cart, would really mean it was time for a visit to Specsavers.

This is Barney's own new career venture, by the way. He finally left the *Saturday Mercury*, where we both used to work – or, as he always put it, 'work' – and has opened up a gourmet coffee cart. It's only the one at the moment, here on Great Portland Street, just a short walk from the Portland hospital. I thought this was a great location, because of all that celeb-spotting you can do, when they come and have their babies! Anyway, once the Coffee Messiah (I know, I know, I have *told* him) hits the big time, he'll roll them out across the entire city. This is going to be terrific for me, because I'm one of the shareholders! Well, sort of. Actually, all I've done is hand over the thirty quid birthday money I got from my godmother Barbara to put towards Barney's fixtures and fittings. But in return for this wise investment, I get to be a multi-millionaire a couple of years from now, when Barney starts outselling Starbucks. It's going to be completely brilliant!

The only tiny spanner in the works at the moment is that the Coffee Messiah isn't actually selling all that much coffee. The problem isn't in the product itself. Barney's coffee is absolutely top-notch. The beans are painstakingly sourced from all kinds of exotic, far-flung places, and the coffee is made in this beautiful gleaming Faema machine Barney tracked down in an old coffee bar in Naples. The delicious creamy milk comes from a little organic farm in Devon, and the snacks on offer are brilliant, too. He's hired some fantastic little old Jewish lady in Golders Green to fry up fresh batches of doughnuts, and the croissants are baked fresh every morning by his French sister-in-law.

The trouble is that most people like to be free to choose their preferred coffee without interference. And at the Coffee Messiah this is not, in fact, possible. For example, you may feel like you're putting on a pound or two, and ask for skimmed milk in your latte instead of the specially sourced creamy Devonshire stuff. This is not permitted. You may be in the mood for an iced-coffee beverage, or even something sweet and chocolatey-flavoured. This is not permitted. In fact, the mere mention of words like *frappuccino* or *mocha* will almost certainly see you banned from the Coffee Messiah for ever. You may pop along sometime in the afternoon and request a cappuccino. This is not permitted. Instead, you will be subjected to a prolonged lecture on the right time of day to drink milky coffee, 'because they never drink cappuccino after eleven a.m. in Italy.'

I'd bet good money that neither, in Italy, do people actually go out in public wearing a tomato-red apron emblazoned with the words *Coffee Messiah* and a matching tomato-red baseball cap declaring *On The Third Day, He Frothed Again*. But Barney won't listen to a word of criticism about his uniform. I have the strongest feeling that his mother designed it.

'Well?' His round face is creased with concern as I get to the cart. 'How was it?'

'Er . . . not all that great, actually. I'm not sure I'm the kind of designer Central St Martins is looking for.'

'Oh, *Iz*.' Barney envelops me in a big, warm hug. He feels more cuddly than ever. I'm getting a sneaking suspicion that he's been snacking on the leftover doughnuts more than he actually admits to. 'I'm so sorry. You worked really hard.' He thinks about this for a moment. 'Well, you *planned* to work really hard.'

'Exactly! You've seen how dedicated I've been these last couple of weeks, Barn.'

He nods. 'I know. I mean, how many other students already have the plans in place for their own fragrance line?'

'Yes, well . . .' I don't actually want any uncomfortable reminders of my fifteen minutes with Diana

Pettigrew. 'Anyway, I've got to decide where to go from here.'

'Well, there are other fashion courses . . . or maybe you could get some work experience . . .'

'Barney! You sound just like my dad.'

'God. Sorry.'

'Anyway, there's no point in going to any other fashion school. Central St Martins was the only one I ever wanted to go to.'

Now Barney looks a bit confused. 'But I thought you only decided you wanted to be a fashion designer a couple of weeks ago.'

'I only decided to *pursue my lifelong dream* a couple of weeks ago. But I've been wanting to be a fashion designer for . . .' I don't actually want to put a specific figure on this, '. . . *yonks*.'

'Oh. Right.'

'Don't you remember all that time I used to spend at the *Saturday Mercury* reading fashion magazines when I should have been working?'

Barney frowns. 'I don't remember them being fashion magazines. I do remember you were a big fan of *heat*.'

'The *fashion pages* of *heat*,' I say, firmly. 'Don't you remember how I used to pore over them? I was obsessive! I took notes!'

I did, too. On little scraps of paper. Because there's nothing more frustrating than seeing a photo of a particular jumper you like, say, and then not remembering where it's from or how much it cost.

Oh, actually, there is one thing more frustrating. Losing the little scrap of paper telling you where the jumper comes from and how much it cost.

'Well, Central St Martins or not, you'll still make it, Iz.' Barney claps a hand on my shoulder and rubs in an encouraging way. 'I've got loads of faith in you. I mean, you didn't have the faintest clue what you were doing when you were being a Novelist, and you still almost got that big book deal, didn't you?'

This is still a tiny bit of a sore point with me. I was working as a PA for Katriona de Montfort – or *multi-millionaire children's author Katriona de Montfort*, as the papers always call her – and writing this really terrific bonkbuster, *Showjumpers*, at the same time. Then I kind of fibbed a bit to some publishers, who'd got the idea it was actually Katriona writing *Showjumpers*, and the next thing I knew, they were offering a seven-figure book deal. Offering *Katriona* a seven-figure book deal, that is.

You see why I took this vow to be more truthful. I just couldn't handle the stress of deceiving people any more.

'Anyway, what am I cooking for Will this evening?' This is the main reason I've come across town to see Barney. He's done the cooking for my bring-back-the-romance dinner with Will, and I've got to collect the dishes. I peer over behind the counter to see two carrier bags, filled with foil containers. 'Something romantic, I hope?'

'As requested.' Barney picks up the carriers and

hands them over like they contain gold bullion, or something. 'OK, I've done you a red wine risotto . . .'

'Oooh, lovely! Just like I asked!'

'Yes, well, I shouldn't really have given in.' Barney is looking disapproving. 'Risotto should never be made in advance like this, you do realise?'

I nod, trying to look suitably respectful. 'I'm very appreciative, Barn. And I'm sure Will's going to appreciate it, too. You know how much he likes your risottos.'

Barney's round face breaks into a beam, reminding me of the mutual appreciation society he and Will have always had going. 'Well, your boyfriend really knows his Italian food, Isabel, so you have to make sure you do me justice on this one. Now, I've cooked the rice incredibly al dente, so it shouldn't suffer too much, but you must *promise* to heat it properly. That means stirring it constantly – *constantly*, Iz. No getting bored and wandering off to watch Fern and Phil on Sky Plus. And a *gentle* heat, remember?'

'Yes, yes.' Barney's one of those cooks who gets unbelievably anal about techniques, and the right way to do things. Whereas I'm one of those shove-it-all-in-and-see-where-life-takes-you sort of cooks.

Actually, that might be why I have to hire Barney to cook for me.

'And there's a red-wine reduction in this little pot . . .' Barney points out a polystyrene container, 'which you drizzle over the risotto when it's ready for serving . . .'

My mouth is watering already. 'Yum!'

'Now, I know you said you didn't want a starter, but I've got you some lovely mixed antipasti from Camisa. Olives . . .' he holds up a jar. 'Peppers.' Another jar. 'Stuffed anchovies.'

'Great!' I'm not going to hurt Barney's feelings by telling him that the stuffed anchovies will be going straight down the waste disposal. I mean, has he never *had* a romantic dinner? 'And pud?'

Barney's face lights up, as it always does whenever pudding is mentioned. 'Panettone bread-and-butter pudding,' he says proudly, lifting up the foil on the pudding basin so I can have a sniff of the creamy-yellow custardy mixture inside. 'My own recipe! Now, I'll want you to tell me tomorrow, Iz, what booze you think I used. You'll *think* it's brandy,' he adds mysteriously, 'but you might be surprised . . .'

I promise faithfully that Will and I will devote at least half an hour of our romantic evening to discussing Barney's unique use of alcohol, then I try to give him twenty pounds for the food, which he refuses.

'Just come and hang out with me tomorrow and tell me all about it,' he says. 'That'll be payment enough!'

He waves me off as I start heading for the bus stop, then turns back to his coffee cart to polish up the Faema.

Isabel Bookbinder
A one-bedroomed flat
Battersea
London

John Galliano
An airy Parisian studio
Paris
France

12 September

Dear Mr Galliano,

May I begin by saying what a great admirer I am of your work. Your Fashion Vision is second to none, and what you don't know about your Process is almost certainly not worth knowing.

In fact, it is this Process I am writing about. After attending an interview today at your ~~Alma Cog almer~~ old college, Central St Martins, I find myself in some doubt about how to proceed. Though I believe I have heard that you are in the habit of using a Mood Board to gather your ideas, your former teacher Diana Pettigrew informs me that this is not, in fact, standard practice. Can you help here, ~~John~~ Mr Galliano? Having spent a not inconsiderable sum stocking up on portable Mood Books (my own invention; feel free to borrow it) at Smythson, I don't want to continue down this route if it is going to make me a laughing stock within the fashion-design community. I have already ~~buggered up~~ placed a foot wrong by not realising about The Uniform; I do not wish to make any more fundamental errors of this kind.

If I was right in the first place, and Mood Boards/Books *are* a valid part of the design Process, perhaps you could give Diana Pettigrew a quick call and tell her so? I am sure that the realisation that you, John Galliano, are a fan of this method might make her ~~wake her ideas~~ more amenable to the suggestion. Even if this saves just one Central St Martins applicant from embarrassment in the future, your efforts will not have been in vain.

Yours in admiration,

Isabel Bookbinder

PS Do you have any connection to the ebullient ringmaster in Enid Blyton's excellent children's book series, *Mr Galliano's Circus*? I've often wondered if this were the case.

PPS And I'm right about The Uniform, aren't I?

Chapter 3

The bus ride back to Battersea Park gives me really valuable career-research time, which is brilliant multi-tasking. I've stopped off to buy the *Atelier* with the Fashion Aristocracy article that Lara mentioned, so now I can settle down in my seat to read it.

And OK, maybe Lara might have a small point about the hard work and stress. Certainly those pictures of various designers (wearing black, natch) backstage at fashion shows, looking hot and sweaty with pins clenched between their teeth, could take a bit of the gloss off the glamour of it all. And all the meetings with investors don't sound too much fun, either. But obviously this article is very one-sided. Probably designed to put half-hearted types off applying to the fashion industry at all. I mean, they don't show pictures of all the fabulous after-show parties, do they? They don't show the high-level meetings with Oscar hopefuls.

The Fashion Aristocracy job that *does* look universally appealing, though, belongs to this woman who works as Lucien Black's *Muse*. I've heard about professional Muses before – isn't that posh Lady Amanda So-and-So one of them? – but I wasn't really sure what they did until now. Well, this article has cleared all that up nicely. Lucien Black's Muse is his business partner, this woman called Nancy Tavistock, who's also something called a Fashion Editor-at-Large for *Atelier* magazine itself. God only knows what a Fashion Editor-at-Large is – certainly the pictures of Nancy Tavistock, a stunning Chinese-American, make her look very far from large herself. One picture shows her sitting on a front row in between scary Anna Wintour and that mad-looking geisha woman with the big quiff from the *Herald Tribune*, and another shows her with an extremely tall, slightly smug-looking man who appears to be her husband.

Anyway, *Atelier* makes this Tavistock woman's life sound completely amazing. Basically what she seems to do is, turn up at Lucien Black's studio every now and then, pull out a bit of ropy old tweed she's found in an exclusive vintage emporium, or perhaps an opium den in Marrakesh, announce that she's really *feeling* ropy old tweed this season, and Lucien Black and all his staff fall over themselves to say how genius she is, and that his entire new Collection will be built around that exact same type of ropy old tweed. Alternatively, she might whip out her scissors and lop three inches off the hem of a cocktail dress, and Lucien Black and all his staff fall over themselves to say she's defined the Shape of the Season. Then he names a couple of bags after her – I always wondered why his bags were called things like the Tavistock and the Nancy T – and they all swan off to drink champagne and eat oysters at Scott's of Mayfair.

I mean, is that the best job you've ever heard of, or what? A bit like being a Top International Fashion Designer, but without the faff of doing any of the actual designing!

I'm so caught up in wondering how it is you get to become a professional Muse that I go past my stop, and have to walk fifteen minutes back in the direction of Will's flat with all Barney's heavy food containers.

The landline is already ringing when I finally get inside and dump all my things down on the kitchen table.

It's a withheld number, so I answer it, in case it's Will.

'Hello?'

'Iz-Wiz!' It's not Will at all. It's Mum, the only other person who calls me from a withheld line. I still can't get used to the fact that she works in an office, now, too. She writes local news round-ups for the *Central Somerset Gazette*, the first job she's had since Marley was born. 'I'm not disturbing, am I?'

'Actually, Mum, I've literally just walked in the front door . . .'

'Oh, so you're busy. Well, I won't keep you. I was just phoning to let you know that Daria had her twelve-week scan, and everything's cooking away nicely!'

This is actually lovely news. I'm really excited about the arrival of Daria's first baby – or my first niece or nephew, as I like to think of it – and it's good to hear that everything's looking fine.

'Do they know what it is yet?' I ask, sounding a bit

like Rolf Harris on *Cartoon Time*. 'Boy? Girl? Mathematical genius?'

'Oh, they can't tell that for a little while longer. Besides, Marley told me they don't want to find out. They prefer the unexpected.'

This surprises me. Both Daria and Marley are mathematicians. I thought the whole point of mathematics was that nothing is ever unexpected. In a world of change and upheaval, two plus two will always be four.

'Anyway, I don't care what they're having!' Mum sounds glowy with pleasure. 'They're having my first grandchild, is what they're having!'

Which I think is just a tiny bit self-centred. But it's nice to hear Mum so happy.

'Anyway, you know I don't want to talk about the baby till it's safely here. Tell me how things are with you, Iz-Wiz! Have you been round to Matthew's new place yet?'

My other brother, Matthew, has just moved to London with his girlfriend Annie. Both of them are starting new teaching jobs here, so given their exceptional good looks and (I'm reliably informed) sexual magnetism, I'd expect the adolescent pupils of St Dominic's to discover insatiable appetites for cold, wet field sports pretty soon.

'No, not yet. I've been ever so busy.'

'Well, of course you have! Designed anything nice today?'

'Nothing much, Mum . . .'

'Oh.' She sounds disappointed. I'm starting to get the feeling, based on the number of times she's calling me every day, that maybe her job at the *Central Somerset Gazette* is about as much fun as mine used to be at the *Saturday Mercury*. After days spent writing up church bazaars, and trying to find an interesting slant on the renovation of Yeovil town centre, I think she's probably craving a bit of glamour and excitement in her life.

'Well, I have done one . . . um . . . evening gown.'

'Oooh, really?' She's perked up, as I wanted her to. 'What's it like?'

I glance over at my *Atelier*. Eve Alexander, who's one of my favourite actresses, is on the cover, looking stunning in something eau de Nil, one-shouldered and slinky. Just the kind of thing I *will* put in my Collection, when I actually get the chance. In fact, *Slinky* is not at all a bad word to start with!

'Oh, it's just this one-shouldered, slinky thing . . . eau-de-Nil-coloured . . .'

'My favourite colour!' says Mum, which is sweet of her, as I know she hasn't got a clue what eau de Nil is, and anyway, her favourite colours are fuchsia and lemon yellow. 'It sounds wonderful, Iz-Wiz! You know, you really ought to give Barbara a call. She'd love some of your designs for Underpinnings.'

Underpinnings is my godmother Barbara's lingerie shop, in Taunton.

'In fact, I was thinking only the other day, you could do her a whole exclusive collection! You know, like

44

Designers for Debenhams. Oooh, Isabel B for Under-pinnings, you could call it! A diversification line.'

'Diffusion line, Mum.'

'Yes, yes. But that's the way all the top designers make their money, you know. I read an article all about it in *You* magazine.'

'Well, I'll think about it.' Much as I love Barbara, I'm hardly going to make any headway in top fashion circles if I limit my hopes to dressing the style mavens of Taunton.

'Oh, well, obviously, your course is the most important thing! Now, have you got any idea who you're going to get to model in your graduation show yet?'

God, I should never have taught Mum about Google. I thought it might help her with work, but I think I've created some kind of Frankenstein's monster. Her Googling of Central St Martins threw up some article about Stella McCartney, and now she's got it into her head that everyone gets über-models like Naomi Campbell and Kate Moss to strut down the catwalk for them in the end-of-course fashion show.

Which, all right, they probably do. But that's not something I'm ever going to get the opportunity to find out, is it?

'No, not yet, Mum.'

'Well, just make sure you steer well clear of that Naomi Campbell, when you meet her. Her and her phone rage.' Mum tuts. '*And* she'd be a bad influence on you. All those drugs.'

This is the other thing Mum's got into her head – that the fashion industry is so awash with banned substances that Central St Martins is selling neat little lines of cocaine alongside the KitKats in the snack bar.

'You must promise me you aren't going to go getting involved in all that,' Mum goes on. 'Because Barbara says *everyone's* on drugs in fashion – the designers, the models . . . she says even the nice lady who did that new range of knickers for Underpinnings takes an awful lot of bathroom breaks. And she has terribly dilated pupils.'

The idea that members of Somerset's small-business community are shovelling coke up their nostrils would be very amusing if it weren't for the fact that Mum actually believes it.

'Mum, you don't need to worry about drugs.'

'Well, you have such an addictive personality.'

'I do?' God, what on *earth* has Mum been Googling?

'You're a middle child . . . and with Marley so bright and Matthew so handsome, I do sometimes fear we didn't give you the security you needed . . .'

OK. Now I know for sure that Mum's even more bored at her job than I used to be at the *Saturday Mercury*.

She goes on before I can say anything, lowering her voice. 'There was that time we found those . . . pills in your things from university, remember?'

'That was ProPlus!' I shout, starting to get saucepans out of the cupboard.

'Well, I don't know the street names of these things.' Mum sounds a bit huffy.

'They're caffeine tablets, Mum! I *told* you.'

'If that's what you say, then I believe you, Isabel. Dad too.'

Yeah, right. Dad would like nothing more than to think I'm a pill-popping junkie, if only to have the satisfaction of confirming his lifelong belief that I'm an utter waster.

'Look, Mum, I really need to get going.' I'm trying to open Barney's risotto container one-handed. 'I'm cooking a special meal for Will this evening.'

'*Ohhh?*'

'It's nothing, really.' I'm already backing away from this, alarm bells screaming in my head. 'Just a nice, cosy evening in together.'

'And you don't think it's . . . anything more than that?' Mum is sounding incredibly excited.

'No, Mum, I honestly don't.'

'You're sure?' she demands. 'Because Jenni here – you know, she does the horoscopes? – was doing psychic readings for some of us the other week, and she was *quite* clear there's going to be a wedding in my life in the next twelve months.'

Oh, for crying out loud. 'Mum, that's ridiculous.'

'Isabel! She's genuinely psychic! She predicted that Nathan's sister was going to have a boy . . .'

'It's a fifty per cent chance!'

'. . . *and* that she was going to call him Joshua . . .'

'Mum, everyone calls their babies Joshua these days.'

Which is true, by the way. I read this article saying that, in London, you're never more than three metres away from a small boy called Joshua. Or that could have been rats. I read so many articles, I sometimes get these things mixed up.

'*And*,' says Mum, in the voice of someone pulling out a trump card, 'that he'd have one brown eye and one blue!'

Oh.

Well, I suppose that is quite a coincidence.

I mean, not that I have much truck with psychics. But it might be interesting to know what the chances are of a baby being born with one brown eye and one blue. Statistically unlikely, I'd say.

'All I'm saying,' Mum goes on, rather smugly, in the face of my startled silence, 'is that maybe Will's got a *special surprise* for you this evening. That's all!'

'Well, thanks for that,' I say, trying to sound uninterested and unconcerned. 'But I really think Jenni's got this one wrong.'

'Whatever you say!'

'Honestly, Mum, I really do have to go now . . .' I've given up trying to get the lid off the risotto with just my left hand. Partly because it's impossible to do it one-handed, and partly because I'm suddenly wondering if I should try to keep my left hand looking as nice as possible. I mean, however beautiful an Asscher-cut diamond *is*, you can't accessorise it with split nails and rough cuticles, can you?

Or an emerald-cut diamond with baguette-cut stones on either side.

Or a massive sparkly princess-cut *pink* diamond, surrounded by little white ones and set in platinum.

I have to catch my breath, all of a sudden, as I get an instant picture of Will, kneeling on the kitchen floor in candlelight . . . for some reason Phil Collins' 'Groovy Kind of Love' is playing on an invisible sound system . . . no, I have to do something about that: a *beautiful operatic aria* is playing on an invisible sound system . . . Will reaches into his pocket for a little velvet ring box before looking up at me with his chocolatey eyes all creased with a smile around the corners, clearing his throat and saying . . .

'Oh, before you go, Iz, I've remembered the other thing I was calling about!' Mum's voice brings me back down to earth again. 'I knew there was something else I had to tell you! I was just sorting out who's bringing what to the barbecue on Saturday . . .'

Oh, God. I've been trying not to think about Saturday. Saturday is the day of this year's Annual Bookbinder Family Barbecue, a gathering of assorted Friends of the Family plus distant relatives who I never see from one year to the next. Most of the latter are from Dad's side of the family, so naturally the day always ends in ghastly competition of some kind, either sporting or intellectual. Frequently both. Last year represented a true nadir on this front, with the inauguration of Uncle Michael's General Knowledge and Obstacle Course Contest. Dad presided as quizmaster, with far more pomposity than even I had been expecting, reading out the most difficult questions from Trivial Pursuit while two teams of increasingly fractious party guests raced around an assortment of cones and netting in the garden, pretending not to take it seriously, until Uncle Michael ran at full pelt into the conservatory windows and wouldn't let us call an ambulance because he didn't want to incur the time forfeit.

'. . . and I remembered I hadn't asked Auntie Clem if she'd do me one of her nice blackberry pavlova thingies,' Mum is going on. 'So I gave her a call, and she said she'd love to make one . . .'

I'm not sure where this story is going, but I do know I've got more important things to think about than Auntie Clem's blackberry pavlova thingies.

'. . . and I happened to mention that you'd got a place on this wonderful fashion course . . .'

'Mum! I told you I didn't want you boasting about this to people!'

'I wasn't boasting, darling! It was just nice for me to have something good to say about you. You know how Auntie Clem's always . . . *banging on* about her lot,' Mum adds, with the kind of sudden venom that thoughts of Auntie Clem, Dad's older sister, can inspire. 'Anyway, you'll never guess what? Portia is going to Central St Martins, too!'

It's a good thing I've put the risotto container down. 'Portia is . . . what?'

'Going to Central St Martins,' Mum repeats. 'She's

starting this term. Some postgraduate fine art degree, apparently. You know what Portia's like for her degrees.'

Yes, I know only too well. My cousin Portia, four years younger than me, is about the saintliest of Auntie Clem's brood of impeccably qualified daughters. Last I heard she was off in Florence, studying history of art, brushing up her already fluent Italian and making life miserable for countless perfectly blameless Florentines, probably.

And now she's coming to Central St Martins, to make life miserable for me instead.

'You know, your dad was ever so pleased when he heard Portia's going to the same place as you. Clem says it's the very best art college in the country.'

'But I'd already told Dad that!'

'Yes, darling, but you know you've had the tendency to exaggerate in the past . . .'

I lean my head against the fridge, in an attempt to curb the cold sweat that's already breaking out across my forehead. 'You know, Mum, Central St Martins is a big place . . . I could very easily not run into Portia at all, the whole time we're there . . .'

'Oh, don't worry about that! Clem's going to tell Portia to make sure she comes and finds you on the first day! It's a pity Portia can't make it to the barbecue, or you two could have chatted. But she's got some special orientation weekend for her course, apparently. I suppose you'll be doing something similar soon.'

'Er, yes . . .'

'Anyway, I should be going,' Mum is saying. 'I just wanted to tell you that nice news about Portia.'

'Yes,' I say, zombie-like. 'Nice news.'

'And we're looking forward to seeing you at the weekend! Maybe with some *more* nice news . . . ?'

'No, Mum.' Thanks to Portia and her insatiable appetite for further education, all thoughts of diamond rings and candlelit proposals are gone from my mind. 'No nice news. I really do have to go now.'

'All right, darling! Good luck with the dinner! And the designing!'

Chapter 4

Mum's phone call has spooked me so badly, it's some time before I can even get myself together to start cooking – all right, reheating – Barney's food. But eventually I put the risotto on to heat (gently) while I go and jump in the bath. I bung in about half a bottle of Aromatherapy Associates Relaxing Oil, and dig out this article I remember from an old *Marie Claire* with Top Businesswoman Nicola Horlick's six Top Tips for de-stressing. But I can't relax or de-stress in the slightest! All I can think about is snooty, superior Portia, ringing Auntie Clem after her first day at St Martins to announce that even after extensive enquiries, she can't find me on any course anywhere. And then Auntie Clem will get straight on the phone to Mum – or, more likely, to Dad – and then he'll get straight on the phone to me – or, more likely, jump into his car, speed up the M4 and drag me outside by the hair . . .

OK. This is ridiculous. *If* Mum's weird psychic friend is right and this *is* going to be the night when Will proposes, I'm not about to have it ruined by anything. Least of all worrying about the fact that my creepy cousin can expose my little fib. There's plenty of time to panic about all that tomorrow.

Anyway, if Will proposes, I might be able to get away with telling my family that I've pulled out of the course in order to plan the wedding. Yes! Even Dad couldn't whinge about that one – not now that he'll finally be getting me to drop his sacred Bookbinder name. It's perfect!

And there really would be loads to do, if we're getting married. We'd have to find a venue, for starters – perhaps a castle in Ireland, or a palazzo in Italy. We'd need to get to work on the guest list. God, I've got to get on and meet his family! Will hasn't introduced me to his parents yet, because . . . actually, I don't know why Will hasn't introduced me to his parents yet. I've met his *brother* – God knows, I've met his brother. I've even been on a *date* with his brother, but that was all a long time ago. Oh, maybe that's why Will hasn't introduced me to the rest of his family yet! He's worried they'll judge me for moving from one brother to the other. Well, they're just going to have to get over it, if I'm going to be their daughter-in-law. And hopefully when they see how much I love Will, they'll forget all about my hideously mistaken episode with their older son, and there'll be no awkward digs over the mulled wine and mince pies every Christmas for the next decade.

Oooh, maybe this wedding could even help me make headway with my fashion career while I'm at it, by designing my own dress! Something simple, but heart-stoppingly beautiful, with long sleeves (I may as well put all that sleeve-making I'll be learning to good use), possibly a little train at the back . . . I'll design a gorgeous bridesmaid's dress for Lara, too, in palest dove-grey, and a really manky one for Annie, my brother Matthew's girlfriend, because she's blonde and voluptuous, and will completely outshine me in the photos unless I take drastic action. And then I'll send the pictures in to *Brides' Boutique* magazine, and they'll be flooded with requests for all my designs, even the manky one, because everyone knows a manky bridesmaid's dress is a clever bride's secret weapon, and I'll get this amazing reputation for designing stunning clothes for real women . . .

Real Woman: The New Fragrance from Isabel Bookbinder.

Once I'm out of the bath, it's time to decide on this evening's Signature Look. This is a tough one. I want to look ravishingly beautiful, obviously, but I also want Will to be proposing to the sweet, simple girl he fell in love with. In the end I decide on proper sexy uncomfortable underwear from La Perla, then pull on my favourite jeans and a borrowed white shirt from Will's freshly dry-cleaned pile. No shoes – I'm going barefoot for that natural, carefree look.

Going barefoot and wearing white, however, are two things I can't honestly advise in the kitchen. I've barely been back in there for two minutes when I've got Barney's red-wine reduction all over the front of the shirt, and dropped burning risotto – Jesus, I thought it was heating *gently* – in between my natural, carefree toes.

I hop about trying to find a piece of kitchen roll without spreading too much stickiness over the floor – because Will's going to have to kneel down on it later, probably, if he's going to do the proposal properly – and while I'm leaning down to mop up the mess, I suddenly catch a glimpse of the digital clock on the oven.

20.13

It's eight o'clock? *Gone* eight o'clock? But Will was meant to be back at half seven. He's forty-five minutes late for our Bringing Back the Romance Dinner! But . . . this is just unacceptable. He *promised* me he wouldn't be late tonight! With a churny, furious feeling right in the depths of my stomach, I dial Will's direct line, knowing that Marie, his scary secretary, will have gone home hours ago, and won't pick up.

'Thomson Tibble Telford, William Madison's office, how may I help you?'

Damn. It's Marie.

'Hi, Marie!' I smile, because that will make me sound much friendlier. It's a trick I learned from my old boss, Katriona de Montfort. 'It's me!'

'I'm sorry, who's this?'

This is a trick I think Marie learned from *her* old boss, Satan. 'Me,' I say firmly. 'Isabel.'

'And that would be Isabel . . . ?'

'*Isabel.*' I refuse to play her little game and give her my surname. She knows exactly who I am. In fact, I think she has some kind of a crush on Will herself. She's never been anything other than foul to me, even when I tried really hard to be friends in the beginning. 'Will's girlfriend.'

'Oh, *that* Isabel.' Marie gives a little laugh. 'Whoops!'

'Right,' I say. 'Whoops.'

'Well, I'm sorry, Isabel, but he's in a meeting.' Marie sounds as if she couldn't be less sorry if she tried. 'I'm just waiting for him to get back so I can get his signature on some documents that have to go out tonight.'

'Oh.' I can't hide the disappointment in my voice. 'I thought he might already have left for the day.'

''Fraid not!' Marie sings at me gleefully. 'But he should have been back hours ago. This was only meant to be a lunch meeting.'

I check the clock again. 20.16. That's one seriously long lunch meeting. 'Well, do you know when he might be back?'

Marie sucks on the air between her teeth, like a plumber who's about to quote you three hundred quid to unblock a toilet. 'Oooh, I couldn't say. But he had lunch with Julia yesterday as well, and they weren't back in the office until . . . gosh, it must have been nearly nine.'

Julia?

Who's Julia?

Will told me these clients were dodgy Kazakh business*men*.

Are men called Julia in Kaz . . . Kazbi . . . wherever it is that Kazakhs come from? Foreign names can be

57

very different from ours. I mean, I knew a Danish bloke at university called Kristen, which is a girl's name pretty much anywhere else in the world.

The churny feeling in my stomach is being replaced by something different. Something a little chillier. Still, the last thing I'm going to do is let snotty old Marie think I might be concerned. When I'm not concerned. Not in the teeniest bit.

'Oh, Julia!' I say in my brightest, not-concerned-at-all voice. 'I *love* Julia! How is she?'

'I didn't know you knew Julia,' Marie says, after a moment.

'Well, of course I know Julia.' I'm going to be a bit sneaky here. Try and find out as much about this Julia as I can. 'Um . . . pretty? Good hair? Nice clothes?'

'That's the one,' says Marie.

Oh.

Wait, there's one last hope.

'Of course, it must be ever so difficult for her, working these long hours . . . at *her age*,' I say sadly.

Marie snorts. 'Her age? You mean thirty-two?'

'Right.'

'The youngest partner Thomson Tibble Telford has ever appointed,' Marie adds, with the satisfied air of a salt merchant at a wounds convention.

Terrific. So this Julia is some kind of international tax-law genius, as well as everything else she's got going for her.

'Well, Julia's a great pal of mine,' I carry on, determined to beat Marie at her own game. 'Has been

58

for years, in fact. Will and I are always having her round to the flat. *Our* flat. You know, the one Will and I share.'

'Really?' Marie actually yawns. 'I wasn't aware that Will knew Julia before she moved here from the Moscow office three weeks ago.'

Well, I think this conversation has reached its natural end.

'Look, Marie, could you just tell Will I called, and ask him to call me back whenever he gets the chance?'

'Sure. I'll tell him you were trying to track him down.'

'No! No, I'm not trying to *track him down*! I just . . . look, it doesn't matter. I'll see him later anyway.'

I hang up, quickly, before Marie can say anything else.

Well, this is fine. Completely fine.

Our big romantic evening must have slipped his mind, that's all.

I mean, yes, it's at least the fifth special plan he's forgotten/cancelled/postponed since I moved in last month. But this is what you get for going out with a high-flying tax lawyer who adores his job.

Adores his colleagues, too, apparently.

I mean, it's *me* that Will's in love with, isn't it? It's *me* who he used to sneak out of the office to meet for slightly-too-long lunches, where he'd always insist I have pudding no matter how much of a hurry he was in to get back to work. *I'm* the one he took on our (admittedly one and only) weekend away in that super-swanky hotel in Rome, which he'd specifically chosen not only for its absurdly romantic views but for the fact that you could choose your pillows from an *actual pillow menu*, which he knew would send me into paroxysms of delight.

It's me he's coming home to every night, no matter how late it is. It's me he's in the Adult, Mature Relationship with.

You know, I bet this Julia wears proper fur, which Will ought to disapprove of.

And I bet she calls him *darlink*.

And I bet . . .

I'm still betting when I shovel Barney's beautiful, burnt dinner into the bin, making absolutely sure I don't accidentally catch a glimpse of my left hand. The one that I thought – idiot that I am – might have a beautiful engagement ring on it by now.

And I'm still betting when I climb into bed, alone, four hours later.

Chapter 5

I wake up to the smell of slightly singed toast, and open my eyes to see Will standing over me. I notice that he could probably do with a shave, even though he looks pretty good with the little hint of dark stubble, and his eyes are bleary and bloodshot. He's already in his suit for work, and he's holding out a plate of toast and Nutella with an expression of extreme sheepishness on his face.

'I'm sorry,' is all he says.

I roll over, turning my back on him and on the toast.

'Did you get my text?' he asks, after a moment.

'You mean the one you sent at one o'clock in the morning, telling me you were on your way home? And you were sorry you'd ruined our lovely romantic evening? Yes, Will. I got that text.'

He sits down on the bed and tries to make me turn back towards him. 'It was a manic day, Isabel. I had the clients on my back from the moment I got in . . .'

'No time to, say, eat lunch, then?' I glance over my shoulder at him.

He yawns, trying to smooth his freshly washed hair so it doesn't dry into tufts. When it's wet, it's even darker than usual, which usually makes him look great but today just makes him look even more drawn and exhausted. 'Well, I had a lunch *meeting* . . . if you can call it lunch. I was there until after eleven.'

'I know. Marie told me. You know,' I add, although what I'm about to say is the most clichéd thing you could say, *ever*, 'I think I've got a better relationship with your secretary than I have with you.'

Will lets out a bark of laughter. 'Isabel, this is Marie we're talking about.'

'So?'

'So, it isn't possible to have a good relationship with Marie. Marie hates everybody.'

'Apart from you.'

'Apart from me.' Will puts a hand on my arm. 'By the way, sweetheart, there's something I have to tell you. You're going to hate me for this, but I'm not going to be able to make it to the Bookbinder barbecue this weekend.'

This makes me turn right round. '*What?*'

'The clients need me to go to the Cayman Islands. I'm heading out first thing tomorrow, and I don't know when I'll be back. Sometime in the middle of the week, if I'm lucky . . .'

'The *Cayman Islands?*' I stare at him. My heart is racing nastily. 'Do you think I'm some kind of an idiot?'

Because, I mean, really. How stupid does he think I am? He can't even be bothered to come up with some vaguely convincing lie about having to go to Brussels, or something. When in fact, he's jetting off to some white-beached paradise to sip exotic fruity cocktails through a straw while Julia (because I'm sure it's her he's going with) sashays about in a string bikini. Probably a *fur-trimmed* string bikini, which he ought to disapprove of. Probably saying things like, 'A little more coconut oil on my luscious, tanned body, please, darlink . . .'

'I don't think you're an idiot at all.' Will is looking worried. Or is that *guilty*?

'You're a tax lawyer, for crying out loud! What on earth would you need to go to the Cayman Islands for?'

Now his face breaks into a smile. 'Sweetheart, the Cayman Islands are a tax haven.'

'You mean a tax lawyer's heaven.'

'No. Far from it.' He rubs his eyes very hard, looking very, very tired all of a sudden. 'It's miserable. I'll be in meetings the whole time. The Dodgy Kazakh Businessmen will be difficult. The air con will probably be broken. And all I'll really want is to be here, at home, with you.'

Well, he talks a good talk, I'll say that for him.

'You're going by yourself, then?' I say, taking the toast from him, but sulkily, so he doesn't suspect I actually quite fancy it.

'No, there'll be a couple of us.'

'Julia going?' I ask, ever so casually.

Will gets up off the bed and starts slipping his tie over his head. 'Probably, yes, we'll need her to help us translate things for . . .' He stops. 'Have I mentioned Julia before?'

'I remember her name,' I say, vaguely, in case he suddenly gets the idea I'm checking up on him. 'That's all.'

'Oh, OK. Well, look, I'm really, really sorry about the barbecue, Iz. You know I was looking forward to meeting everyone.'

This is what makes me worried. That he can lie, just like that, so smoothly and convincingly. I suppose it's what makes him such a good lawyer.

'Can you take someone else instead?' he asks. 'Lara? Or Barney?'

'Maybe.' Over my dead body am I exposing poor Barney to the Bookbinder Family Barbecue. And Lara . . . well, Lara's been to enough of them to know how to cope. But I'm not sure *I* could cope with Lara there, mooning over my brother like a wet weekend in Scarborough.

'Christ, I really have to go.' Will glances at his watch, then leans down and kisses me swiftly on the forehead. Yes, on the forehead. The way Masters of the Universe kiss Stepford Wives goodbye. 'What are you doing today, Iz?'

'Who knows?' I shove another piece of toast in my mouth mutinously. 'Go and get a manicure, perhaps. Maybe play some tennis.'

'Riiight . . .' Will looks confused, but not confused enough to risk being late in to work. 'Well, have a lovely day, sweetheart. I'll try not to be late. I'll try not to be *too* late,' he corrects himself, before slinging his jacket over his arm and heading for the front door.

He's long gone by the time I realise he didn't even ask how things went at Central St Martins. Obviously he's got more important things to think about.

Right. Well, Will may think I'm just a timid little stay-at-home thing, no match for the mighty Julia, but I'm going to *show him*. God knows, if he's about to swap me for a newer model, I'll need to throw myself into something. Not to mention the fact that I'll be in serious need of funds, if I've got nowhere to live. I have a sudden vision of myself, wandering the streets of London with a single, battered suitcase, while Julia swanks up in a shiny black taxi outside Will's flat and starts hauling giant Louis Vuitton trunks inside. Well, I'll show her. Just wait until I open up the Moscow branch of Emporio Bookbinder. She'll come in one day with all her glitzy, fur-wearing Russian friends, and my KGB-trained, fiercely loyal security guards will single her out in the crowds and chuck her out on to Red Square . . .

Driven by this ambition, I'm up, showered and all dressed in elegant grey trousers (High Street), Kurt Geiger shoes (Designer) and my fake-vintage duster coat by half past nine. And now I'm sitting at my desk, strong black coffee in hand, raring to make some serious progress with my Collection.

Now, where had I got to? Oh, yes – *Slinky*.

I write this down in my Mood Book, in firm capital letters, and then sit back to have a little think.

Isabel Bookbinder's brilliant Debut Collection, entitled Slinky, featured a simply stunning one-shouldered dress in elegant eau de Nil . . .

Well, this is an excellent start. The fact it's one-shouldered is a stroke of genius, for one thing, because that will cut down on the sleeve-making. In fact, if I made it a sort of toga shape, I wouldn't need to worry about making sleeves at all! All I'd really need to do is get a big piece of material – something slinky, obviously – and sort of . . . *drape* it into a dress shape . . . pin it on one shoulder, perhaps with an eye-catching brooch . . . Perfect!

I have a little go with an extra-large pashmina and a couple of safety pins for ten minutes or so, until I think I've cracked it. It's extremely satisfactory for a morning's work, I have to say.

So, what now?

I pop on *This Morning* for half an hour, because *Beat the Stylist* is very important career-related research, and because it's always nice to see Fern and Phil falling over themselves at each other's double entendres. Important career-related research over, I decide to leave early for my lunch with Lara, so I can drop off Barney's food containers to him at the coffee cart on the way.

Barney is gratifyingly pleased to see me when I arrive at the Coffee Messiah. But he rapidly loses his good humour when I tell him about my disastrous evening.

'Iz, you should have called me! I'd have come over!'

'Thanks, Barn, but I was OK. I just read some magazines and went to bed . . .'

'I mean you should have called me to come and eat the food.' His normally cheerful face has darkened. 'That risotto was a masterpiece. *And* the pudding. It was grappa, *by the way*,' he adds, stroppily. 'But I'm sure your waste disposal really enjoyed it.'

'I'm sorry, Barney.' Honestly, you'd think *he* was the one with the (possibly) cheating boyfriend. 'How can I make it up to you?'

He thinks about this for a moment. 'You can watch the coffee cart for fifteen minutes while I go and check out the pastries at Villandry.'

I stare at him. 'But you've got all these amazing pastries here!'

Barney sighs. 'It's for market research. I see all these office workers to-ing and fro-ing to Villandry all day. It makes you wonder what Villandry are doing that I'm not.'

I don't want to point out that Villandry are probably doing nothing more complicated or mysterious than giving their customers what they ask for. 'No problem, Barn. I can watch the cart.'

'Great!' Barney starts taking off his tomato-red apron and baseball cap, and hands them over to me.

'Do I . . . er . . . have to?'

'Yes, Iz, you do.' He folds his arms and stares at me. 'What if a customer walks by, and doesn't know you're here to serve?'

Chance would be a fine thing, I think, but don't say.

I just put the baseball cap on meekly, then slip the apron over my fake-vintage coat.

Barney claps his hands. 'Right, let me run you through our espressos of the day . . .'

I just can't summon up the energy to pay all that much attention, but I nod attentively and scribble a few notes on an order pad, and say things like, 'Oooh, delicious, Rare Reserve Brazil Comocin Peaberry,' and 'So is that a *fruity* flavour or a *sharp* one?' and Barney seems pleased enough. He's a bit less pleased about my incomprehension of his beloved Faema, but he quite enjoys giving me the idiot's guide to how to work it if absolutely necessary. Then he makes me an extremely tasty double espresso, with instructions to sip it orgasmically every time a possible customer heaves into view, and trots off up Great Portland Street towards Villandry.

I settle down on the high stool behind the counter, and get my Mood Book out again. This single-sheet-of-material, drapey thing is triggering all kinds of fantastic ideas! I mean, it isn't just limited to one-shouldered dresses. You could do a totally strapless version, if you sort of wrapped material around somebody. Or you could *cut a hole* in a sheet of material and pop it over their head, making an elegant kind of tunic . . . And obviously, not everything has to be eau de Nil. My colour palette will give me a lot more options. All these designs could also be made in, say, *burnt sienna*. Or *café au lait*. Or *magnolia* . . .

'Excuse me? Are you serving?'

I look up to see who's just spoken. It's a tall girl with strawberry-blonde hair, an incredibly compact baby bump encased in a fine black cashmere shift dress, and . . . oh, my God, is that . . . ? Yes it is. It's a YSL Muse bag! A really gorgeous patent leather one, in a kind of blue-black colour. Well, you just know *she's* come straight from the Portland. Not a celebrity, sadly, but pretty glam nevertheless.

'I asked, are you serving?'

'Yes! Yes, we are serving! Absolutely!' This is Barney's first customer of the day – possibly, now I come to think of it, the first customer of the week. As a Coffee Messiah shareholder, not to mention as Barney's friend, it's my absolute duty to make sure she buys a cup of coffee. I mean, this Faema thing can't be that difficult to work! It's just like a giant Nespresso machine, probably.

'Good. Get me a cappuccino. Double-shot.'

I blink. 'Really? In your conditi . . .' The look she gives me silences me instantly. 'Sure! Double-shot cap! Coming right up!'

How good did that sound? I *knew* I'd be all right at this coffee-serving thing! I turn round to start firing up the Faema, while my pregnant customer flicks open a phone and stabs at it.

'Mummy?' she says, into it. 'Me again. Sorry I cut you off before. *God*, I'm having a hideous day. This *fat* man was in front of me at Villandry, buying up practically the whole shop, so now I'm getting something at this funny little place round the corner . . . I *know*, Mummy, but you know I have to keep my blood-sugar levels up.'

I press a small, relatively unintimidating button on the Faema, which suddenly makes an alarming gurgling noise, sort of like it's about to blow up or something.

'I *know*, Mummy,' my customer says again, starting to sound slightly snivelly. 'I know I've been running myself into the ground. But you know how stressed Nancy's being, especially with what happened at Fashion Week, and now this big deal going south . . .'

Oh. Well, I should have known she worked in fashion. I mean, the Muse bag, the body fascism . . . the head-to-toe black, come to think of it.

'Yes, Dr Roussos says I must stop work *immediately* . . . Well, not quite bed rest,' she's wittering on, 'but certainly lots and lots of very deep relaxation . . . yes, I was thinking maybe St Lucia too . . .'

The alarming gurgling noise is becoming a violent hiss. I turn the button off and try to open one of the steam valves before pressure starts building up. I'm beginning to sweat into my baseball cap. God, I can just see the headlines: *COFFEE NOVICE OBLITERATES FASHIONISTA, UNBORN BABY AND YSL MUSE BAG – HANGING TO BE BROUGHT BACK SPECIALLY!!!*

'All right, Mummy, I'll call you later.' My customer hangs up. 'Is there some kind of problem?' she snaps at me.

'No, not at all!' I twist open another two steam valves, which – thank God – lessens the hissing to merely sinister levels. 'In fact, I was just going to . . . um . . . talk you through our beans of the day!' Maybe if I can stall her long enough, Barney will make it back from Villandry in time to make her a delicious coffee. And hopefully she won't recognise the back of his head. 'We have a particularly good one made from peaberries!'

'Peaberries?'

'Yes, they're an extremely rare, extremely reserved . . . um . . . berry. From Brazil.'

She frowns. 'You mean like the goji berry?'

'Yes! Just like the goji berry! But even better,' I go on, suspecting this might be the way to keep her here. 'Even *more* antioxidants.'

Well, it might have, mightn't it? I mean, who am I to say, one way or the other?

'And you can make coffee out of it?' she asks, shifting her Muse bag into the crook of her arm. Her sulky face is registering a little interest.

'Delicious coffee. You're going to love it.'

'Well, am I going to love it any time in the next two minutes?' she snaps back at me. 'Some of us have actual jobs to go to, you know.'

'Yes, of course. I'm sorry . . .' I peer over her shoulder, up Great Portland Street, but there's no sign of Barney yet. 'I'm just letting the peaberries steep,' I say, 'for full antioxidant effect . . .'

Thank God, her phone is going.

'Ruby speaking,' she barks. 'Oh, Jasmine, sweetie, *hi* . . .'

I give up on the horrible spiteful Faema and pretend to be busy at the enormous grinder – another piece of Barney's top-of-the-range equipment that I've got no idea how to work. But I think I can just get away with sort of waving a cup nearby and looking as though I'm waiting for ground coffee to start pouring into it.

'No, but I haven't been at my desk all morning . . . of course I will . . . you mean the crystal meth Greta Bonneville was sending?'

Hold on a moment.

Did she just say *crystal meth*?

'No, no, I think it's just the meth,' she goes on. 'Nancy didn't ask Greta for anything else this time.'

Oh, my God. Mum was right about the fashion industry after all! Everyone really *is* on drugs.

And here's me standing with my jaw open. God, how uncool must I look? When she's chatting away about the stuff like it's Chinese takeaway or something. I pretend not to even notice what she's just said, and push a few knobs on the grinder to show how very distracted I am.

'Of course, I'll let you know the minute it comes in . . . no, no, it'll be perfectly OK for me to open it . . . I'll call you and you can come and check it out before I give it to Nancy . . . Oh, thanks, sweetie . . . Well, Dr Roussos was quite adamant I really do have to think of myself right now . . . Nancy will just have to find another dogsbody! I mean PA!' Ruby gives a little giggle, listening to what this Jaz person on the other end of the line is saying. 'Oh, I don't know, she'll just plunder the ranks at *Atelier* and find some work-experience grunt ready to cater to her every need.'

I almost drop the cup I'm holding. Because I've just worked out who this Nancy is that she's been bitching about! It's Nancy Tavistock! The woman whose fabulous life I was just reading about! Fashion Editor-at-Large of *Atelier* magazine and professional Muse to Lucien Black.

And she's in need of a brand-new PA.

Well, a new dogsbody.

But I'm not fussy. I'd be her dog's *walker*, if I had to. I'd clip the dog's *toenails*.

This is my chance to sneak in the back door of the fashion industry! Stuff all those rock stars' brats at Central St Martins, with their degrees and work experience, and sleeve-making prowess. Working for Nancy Tavistock – leading light of London's Fashion Aristocracy – would get me *right in there*.

I could be discovered by Lucien Black. Groomed for international fashion design stardom.

Or even . . . no, that's too incredible to even think about.

But, I mean, what if Lucien Black wanted to *get a new Muse* at some point in the future . . . ?

I'm actually shaking here. OK, calm down. Right now, I'd happily settle for the PA job. It's all just about seizing the opportunity.

Opportunity: The New Fragrance from Isabel Bookbinder.

'Oh, well, if there's someone you know for the job, you should call Ellie in HR,' Ruby is saying. 'She's already set up a few interviews . . .'

No! This is my job!

'OK, darling, amazing to talk to you . . . No, I may not be there when you bring the meth, I've got lunch at Café Anglais at one . . . All right, sweetie, bye now!' Ruby's face changes to thunder the minute she hangs up. 'OK. Where's my coffee?'

Oh, thank God. Not a moment too soon I see Barney hurrying towards us, laden down with Villandry carrier bags.

'Coming right up!' I say, as he slips behind the counter. 'Barney, one large peaberry cappuccino, please.'

'Oh, but it's after eleven . . .' he begins, but I interrupt him.

'That'll be two pounds exactly,' I say loudly to Ruby, who shoves a two-pound coin in my hand and then waits while Barney mutinously grinds beans and froths up milk. The whole process takes about forty-five seconds. 'Recommend us to all your friends and colleagues!' I say, as Ruby stalks away. 'Enjoy all those yummy antioxidants!'

Barney stares at me. 'Antioxidants?'

'*Peaberry* coffee, Barn. You know, you really should be marketing it as a big health drink.'

'But the peaberry is just a kind of coffee bean.'

Oh. I hadn't actually realised that.

'Anyway, look what I picked up at Villandry,' he begins, taking white boxes out of his carriers. 'And I was right! Nothing looks anywhere near as good as my doughnuts . . .'

I'm not really paying him all that much attention. I've only got a limited window of opportunity here. OK – Ruby is out to lunch from around one o'clock, which means I'll need to schedule my interview with Nancy Tavistock for then. I really don't want Ruby recognising me as the coffee-cart girl. I snatch my phone from my bag and dial 118 118.

'Iz? Who are you calling?'

'The number for *Atelier* magazine,' I tell the operator. 'Can you text me that?'

'*Atelier* magazine?' Barney is looking confused. 'What are you calling them for?'

I hold up a hand to shush him, dialling the number I've just been texted. 'Oh, hi there,' I say, in a carefully neutral voice, as someone picks up. 'Do you work with Nancy Tavistock? . . . Oh, you do! Well, this is Ellie from HR. I wanted to squeeze in a *very* important interview for Nancy, if I may . . . the name is Isabel Bookbinder . . .'

This week, Isabel Bookbinder's Top Tips on How to Become a Fashion Muse. Originally a Top International Fashion Designer herself (her Debut Collection, *Slinky*, is still regarded as a masterclass in 21st-century draping), she gave up designing to replace Nancy Tavistock as Lucien Black's professional source of inspiration. Isabel ~~is currently single~~ ~~lives with her boyfriend, Will Madison~~ ~~is currently sing~~ ~~lives w~~ divides her time between London, Paris and Milan.

1. Seize the Opportunity

'Sadly, there is no straightforward career path for the keen fashion Muse. London's eminent fashion colleges tend to focus very much on the practical aspects of fashion production (sleeve-making etc.), leaving those with different skill sets with nowhere to turn. For this reason, it is imperative that you seize any opportunities that come your way. ~~Eavesdropping on~~ Accidentally overhearing just one conversation may lead to your big break into the world of professional Muse-ing, so be prepared to act fast if the moment strikes.'

2. Be Prepared

'Spend every spare moment you have perfecting your Signature Look. Fashion Designers may be able to get away with their frankly rather uninspiring uniform of black V-necks and trousers, but as a Muse, you will be expected to work a distinct Signature Look from the very beginning. A Designer/Vintage/High-Street combination is always a safe bet, and should win you many plaudits, while head-to-toe leopard skin is inadvisable. Fun Buttons should be avoided at all costs.'

3. Be Inspiring

'Your Top International Fashion Designer has employed you for this very purpose. However, there are times when inspiration runs dry, even for the best of us. If this happens, DO NOT PANIC. Try one of these fail-safe fall-backs. Why not pull out a bit of ropy old tweed you found in a vintage store/opium den? Or, pull out a pair of scissors and start lopping things off (for safety reasons, probably better to do this before you've cracked open the champagne)!'

4. Get Yourself Properly Equipped

'See above for all ropy old tweed/scissor requirements. Other essential Muse kit should include, but need not be limited to: a portable Mood Book (bulk-buy at Smythson and maybe you can negotiate a discount); up-to-date magazines (*Pop* or *anothermagazine* are generally read in public, *heat* or *Grazia* in private); Class A drugs (of your choice); and a small photograph of Daniel Craig (or whoever it is you're trying to persuade to model for your designer's campaign this season).'

5. Refuse to be Intimidated by Scary Anna Wintour (SAW)

'You will almost certainly, at some stage in your career, find yourself seated next to SAW at a fashion show. *Show no fear.* You have just as much right to be there as she does. Dressing in spectacularly expensive clothes may help you to truly believe this, as may hiring a Personal Trainer several months before the event so that you, too, can be a skinny size ~~six~~ ~~four~~ ~~two~~ zero.'

6. Really, Seriously, Find a Way to Love Strong Black Coffee
'See Tip 5. Plus, nobody ever wanted their Muse to be a wobble-bum.'

Isabel is photographed at Scott's of Mayfair, wearing Lucien Black 'Izzie' dress, with Lucien Black 'Iz' handbag.

Next month, Angelina Jolie's Six Top Tips on How to Become a UN Spokesperson and Top Humanitarian.

Isabel Bookbinder
Battersea

Daniel Craig
~~Cap Ferrat?~~
~~On location at Pinewood Studios?~~
London

Dear Daniel,

Chapter 6

I didn't get to speak to Nancy Tavistock herself, but that's probably just as well. Anyway, Lilian, the girl I *did* speak to, who seems to be some kind of office administrator, managed to find fifteen minutes in Nancy's schedule at one fifteen today. There were a couple of nasty moments when she started moaning at me – or rather, at Ellie from HR – about how unco-operative the boys in the post room are, and how she'd really appreciate it if I could have a word with their supervisor about their attitude. I promised I'd do my very best, and then hung up just as she started saying how uncooperative Technical Support were this morning, and maybe it was time to have a word with their supervisor, too . . .

But the first hurdle is cleared, at any rate. And it was pretty instructive. I mean, quite obviously I'm going to have to take a temporary time-out on this honesty vow. Which I'll reinstate, just as soon as possible. Honestly.

Well, it'll be worth it. This job with Nancy Tavistock is *perfect*. For starters, it gets me on a fast track into the fashion business. Because at the end of the day, what would any sane person prefer: years learning how to make sleeves with Diana 'standard artist's portfolio' Pettigrew, or leaping right into the deep end with Nancy 'Fashion Aristocracy' Tavistock? And it's really going to help me solve the problem of how I explain to Mum and Dad why Portia can't find me at Central St Martins. Because now I can say that actually, my first term is based around a special, *highly prestigious* internship at a Top Fashion Magazine! And then, thanks to the fact I'm on a fast track into the fashion business, it should only take a couple of months before I've got my own label up and running, which will be so impressive that even Dad won't be able to cause a fuss about me abandoning the rest of my course. It's brilliant!

Once he's stopped being all moralistic about my Ellie from HR impersonation, Barney's incredibly supportive. He even shuts the coffee cart down to come along with me to Starbucks so we can sort out my hair in the bathroom, and then he very nicely offers to run all the way to the Marylebone High Street Boots and back for emergency Frizz Ease. My outfit, thank God, is acceptable enough. All right, the grey trousers are a tiny bit dullsville, but at least I'm wearing good shoes (totally impractical pale-pink wedges, a recent find at Kurt Geiger), and my fake-vintage duster coat livens things up a bit. From the photographs I saw in *Atelier*, Nancy Tavistock is a bit of a vintage queen herself. Anyway, she's a Muse, not a designer. A black Uniform isn't necessary.

With fifteen minutes to go, I jump in a cab on Great

Portland Street, and direct it straight to the Mediart Magazines building on distinctly un-fashion-fabulous High Holborn.

After the disappointments of Central St Martins, I'm all geared up for *Atelier*'s offices to be a bit on the grotty side, too. And the grey exterior of the Mediart building isn't all that promising. But from the moment I walk through the revolving doors, I can see I was wrong. Black marble floors gleam beneath my feet as I walk towards the reception desk, which is shaped like an artist's palette, and made of thick, glossy cherrywood. Two exceptionally handsome security guards greet me with toothy smiles, then phone up to *Atelier* to let them know I'm here. I get into a lift that's panelled with gleaming mirrors and more of that gorgeous cherrywood, and head, as directed, to the eighth floor.

The lift doors open up on to a bright white wall, where the word *ATELIER* is spelled out in large, black art-deco-style letters. A very-serious-looking girl with John Lennon glasses and brown corkscrew curls is waiting for me.

'Isabel?'

'Yes! That's me!' I extend a hand. 'You must be Lilian! We spoke on the phone.' Oh, God. No, we didn't. 'I mean, no, we didn't. *Ellie* told me she spoke to you on the phone.'

'That's right.' Lilian gives me a cool, firm handshake. 'I don't think I've seen you around the building before.'

Oh, yes. This is because 'Ellie' told Lilian on the phone that I'd been working on one of the other Mediart magazines. 'No, well, I haven't been here long.'

'Well, you've obviously made quite an impression on Ellie. She spoke very highly of you indeed.'

'That was nice of her.'

'Completely brilliant in every conceivable way, she said,' Lilian goes on, with the slightest raise of an eyebrow, as she starts to lead me down a corridor. 'A total fashion obsessive.'

'That's me!' I give a nervous laugh.

'Hmmm. You know, it *is* only a PA job. If you're a fashion obsessive, maybe you'd be better off waiting for one of the fashion assistant's jobs to open up.'

'Oh, no, no! No, I'm perfectly happy just being a PA!'

'Hmmm.' It's even more disapproving this time. 'There's no *just* about it. The admin staff work just as hard on this magazine as the creatives do, you know.'

'I'm sure you do!' God, I'm glad my interview isn't with Lilian. '*Harder*, probably . . .'

We come to a halt at the end of the corridor, in front of a wooden door with Nancy Tavistock's name on it. Right outside is a small open-plan area, with a big glass-topped desk and an easy chair. The desk is almost like a little shrine to Ruby. Photographs of Ruby with a similar-looking older woman, both of them on horseback; Ruby with a lantern-jawed man in a wedding dress (Ruby, not the lantern-jawed man);

Ruby gazing mistily into the middle distance on a beach at sunset. There's also a stack of old magazines, a couple of Beanie Babies, a lot of manicure paraphernalia, a magnifying mirror, and several pairs of tweezers. There's also a very untidy in-tray, in which I can see a pile of paper with a Post-it note stuck on the top.

The Post-it reads *PA APPLICATIONS.*

'So, this is where Nancy's assistant sits.' Lilian nods at the desk, unable to disguise her distress at the sight of such wanton messiness. 'Ruby. Of course, she's out at lunch at the moment,' she adds, not even bothering to hide the contempt in her voice. 'Actually, lunch is what Ruby's best at. If you want to do well in your interview with Nancy, I'd tell her you never eat lunch at all. She'll be thrilled.'

'Well, thanks for the tip!'

'I have several matters I need to get on with. Technical Support are *not* being supportive today. Can you sit here and wait for Nancy? She shouldn't be long.' Lilian nods at the pile of magazines on Ruby's desk. 'Read a magazine while you wait.'

'Will do!' I give her a little wave as she shoots off down the corridor.

Actually, though, I've got something far more important to do than sit around reading a magazine.

I've watched enough *CSI* to know that when it comes to an expectation of privacy, anything you leave *in plain sight* is pretty much fair game. I mean, how many times do you see Gil Grissom and that gorgeous one with the Afro getting the bad guy's DNA off a Coke can he's swigged from a couple of times and then left out, *in plain sight*, on the interview-room table? And then it's no good the bad guy's shyster lawyer coming over all outraged about the Constitution, because Grissom and the gorgeous one haven't, in fact, done anything unConstitutional.

So if I hang about in the vicinity of Ruby's desk and have a teeny little peek at the other applicants' letters, which have been left out *in plain sight* in that in-tray, I won't, in fact, have done anything unConstitutional either.

I'm sure it must be a British Constitutional right as well as an American one. I mean, we had Constitutional rights *first*, didn't we? It's bound to be something they borrowed from us.

And really, I think it's only fair I know who my competition is. After the debacle at Central St Martins yesterday, it's pretty vital. And after my little chat with Lilian, I'm feeling slightly underprepared. What if all the other applicants are career PAs who can type a zillion words a minute and know how to do clever things like spreadsheets and PowerPoint?

I'll hear footsteps from the corridor if anyone suddenly starts to head this way, so I think it's perfectly safe to j-u-s-t sidle towards the desk and reach for the in-tray.

I swivel the top piece of paper round as far as it will go without actually lifting it out of the tray, then swivel my head round as far as *it* will go and try to read what's written. It's from someone called Tilly Prentice-Hall, and it's handwritten in loopy green handwriting.

Dear Nancy, It's been ages since I've seen you! Mummy told me how much she enjoyed lunch with you today, and she also mentioned that you were looking for someone to replace Ruby.

Well, it isn't the most traditional of application letters. Diana Pettigrew wouldn't approve at all.

I think I'd be perfect for the job. Remember all that time I spent hanging around with Mummy on her photo shoots when I was little . . .

Oh, great. I just *knew* it.

I'm up against that kind of super-posh bohemian you always see as Babe of the Month in *Tatler*. In fact, I think I even remember someone called Tilly Prentice-Hall as Babe of the Month in *Tatler* a few months back. All blonde and bee-stung, wittering on about her ex-model mother's fabulous 1970s vintage wardrobe, which she and her equally bee-stung sisters (Milly and . . . Billie?) raided at every possible Boujis-visiting opportunity.

I haven't got a hope in hell, have I?

I lift up Tilly's letter by the corner to have a peek at the one beneath it. It's not handwritten, at least, which gets my hopes up that it's actually from a girl called Jane who goes to secretarial college in Northampton.

Dear Mrs Tavistock, My name is Lulabell Davenport. My brother and sister, David and Dee-Dee, tell me you are looking for a new assistant . . .

OK. Now I really do give up. I mean, she's the sister of the Davenports! *You* know the Davenports – that kooky-looking brother and sister who have that fabulous *D+D* label, with all those floaty, boho-luxe dresses, a bit like Alice Temperley. A lot like Alice Temperley, actually, because the Davenports hang out in Somerset on some fabulously bohemian-sounding family-run organic fruit farm only a few miles down the road from Alice Temperley's fabulously bohemian family-run cider farm.

God, *I* come from Somerset. Why couldn't *my* parents have taken the trouble to set up a fabulously bohemian farm? Then I could have given Lulabell Davenport a run for her money! As it is, growing up with a headmaster and a housewife in Ilkley Close, Shepton Mallet, isn't going to stand me in awfully good stead for this job.

You know, I was hoping to be able to get right back to the whole-truth-and-nothing-but-the-truth vow around now. But I think I might need to extend the time-out just a little bit longer.

I'm just sliding Lulabell's application sideways to have a look at the next one on the pile – a *Flopsie Cavendish*, if I've read it correctly – when all of a sudden I hear footsteps behind me.

I spin round guiltily, all ready to explain ('it's completely fine, it was *in plain sight*'), but it's just a DHL delivery man.

'Package for Nancy Tavistock?' he says, shoving a clipboard under my nose and tapping it with his pen.

'Oh, but I'm not Nancy . . .'

'Don't mind who you are, love, all you have to do is sign!'

'Oh, well . . . I suppose that's OK.' After all, I might as well impress Nancy by clocking up a couple of PA-type tasks, gratis, before I've even had my interview. I sign on the clipboard and take the small Jiffy bag from the courier before he hurries away.

Which is when the sender's name catches my eye. *GRETA BONNEVILLE.*

So *this* is the delivery that Ruby was talking about on the phone.

If this Jiffy bag is from Greta Bonneville, then it must be filled with crystal meth.

The thing is, I know I'm meant to be all cool about this. If I'm going to be a Top International Fashion Designer, or even (please, God) a Top International Fashion Muse, I'm probably going to have to start taking all kinds of banned substances myself. I mean, I do want to ensure I fit in, and make friends.

But having Class A drugs here, actually in my hands . . . *in plain sight*, if you want to get all legal about it . . .

It's making me quite anxious.

I'm racking my brains to think of any episodes of *CSI* where *completely innocent people* might accidentally have been convicted of drug dealing just because they were the muggins who got caught with the envelope, when suddenly I hear footsteps again.

Quick as a flash, I shove the incriminating Jiffy envelope into my handbag.

And then Nancy Tavistock comes round the corner towards me.

Chapter 7

Close up, she's even more fabulous than she looked in her photograph. She's incredibly tall for someone with a Chinese background – nearly six foot, I'd say, in her tan peep-toe Christian Louboutins. She's wearing a vintage Pucci-print kaftan over endless bare legs, with Lucien Black chandelier earrings dangling from her lobes and – surprise, surprise – a completely amazing, one-of-a-kind *pink suede* Tavistock bag hanging from one elbow. Her thick, black hair is exquisitely shiny, but left slightly shaggy and uncombed, which Mum would disapprove of but just makes Nancy Tavistock look devil-may-care, and heart-stoppingly stylish.

You know, she doesn't *look* like she's afflicted by a dangerous addiction to crystal meth. I mean, obviously, I don't have all that much idea what a dangerous crystal meth addiction would do to your appearance. But somehow I doubt you'd look this fantastic.

'Are you my one fifteen?' she asks briskly. Her American accent, considerably anglicised after so many years on this side of the Atlantic, makes her sound a bit like recent Madonna. 'For the PA job?'

'Yes! I'm Isabel . . .'

'Well, hi, Isabel.' She gives me a quick, firm hand-

90

shake, then shoves her office door open with a Louboutined foot. 'Come on in. Grab a seat.'

Wow.

Now *this* is my dream office.

Actually, it doesn't look much like an office at all. Which is a large part of the attraction. It's painted pure white and filled with natural light, and the floor is covered with thick, pure white carpet. There's a pure white sofa, too, one of the low-slung Scandinavian kind, and an equally low-slung glass coffee table, displaying overflowing ashtrays (so Nancy's a nicotine addict as well as a meth-head) and empty Starbucks cups. But what makes it really great is the huge fitted wardrobe filling one wall. Sliding doors are open to display rows and rows of fabulous-looking clothing, and shelves stuffed with red-soled Christian Louboutins.

'Sorry about the mess,' Nancy says, striding over to a small desk in the corner and standing over it while she checks her email on a snazzy-looking super-slim MacBook. 'I was here till late last night, and my lame-ass assistant Ruby was too busy plucking her damn eyebrows to ask the cleaners to come earlier today . . .' She looks up at me with a brief smile. 'I guess you can see why I want a new assistant.'

Is this a test? Am I meant to join in the slagging-off of the old assistant before I can be trusted to become the new one? Or is it like family, where you can bitch about your own to the high heavens, but woe betide anyone else who joins in?

'Er . . . well, I'm sure a change will be nice for everyone,' I say, rather lamely.

'Anyway, have a seat.' She waves a hand towards the Scandinavian couch, looking at her computer screen again. 'I just have a couple of urgent emails to respond to. Make yourself comfortable.'

I perch on the edge of one of the deep seat cushions and carry on looking around the office, trying to acclimatise myself. There's a kind of tribute corner to It Bags of the World – a red Birkin, a silver Baguette, and a couple of shabby black Paddingtons, all slung in a heap by the window. Oh! And look at that, on the wall opposite! A big piece of corkboard, displaying photographs of angry-looking women in floaty maxi-dresses, some snippets of chiffony material, and, in the middle of it all, in large black letters, the words SHEER, AIRY and DIAPHANOUS.

'You've got a Mood Board!'

Nancy glances up at me, then at the Mood Board. 'Oh, yes. That was a few ideas I was putting together for Lucien's last collection. You know I'm Lucien Black's Creative Director, I guess.'

'Oh, absolutely.' Doesn't *Creative Director* sound great? So much more official than *Muse*. God, if I was a *Creative Director*, I think I could even convince Dad I was doing a proper job. 'I'm just really excited to see a Mood Board . . . you know . . . in action.'

'Yeah, well . . .' Nancy casts another glance at the Mood Board. Is it my imagination, or did she just *wince* a little bit? 'Lucien usually likes to start with a word or two, whatever we're feeling at the moment, and then we see where it takes us.'

If only Diana 'standard artist's portfolio' Pettigrew were here right now!

'So!' Nancy finishes with her email, picks up a pad of paper, then comes over and flings herself down on the sofa next to me. She curls up her long, light brown legs beneath her, like an exotic cat. 'Isabel . . . Bookbinder, right?'

'Right.'

She notes this down on her pad. 'And you're . . . twenty-five?'

I *love* this woman. 'Almost twenty-eight.'

She notes this down, too. 'And you've come here from heaven?'

I study the carpet modestly. 'Well, that's very nice of you to say so.'

She looks up, confused. 'Or was it *Brides Boutique*?'

Oh, I get it. *Heaven* and *Brides Boutique* are the other Mediart magazines I'm meant to have been working on.

'Oh, well, I've actually been at several different magazines. *Heaven* and *Brides Boutique* are just two of them. Of course,' I add hastily, 'I probably haven't spent long enough at any single one to really be *remembered* by anyone who works there.' Just in case Nancy gets any ideas into her head about calling people up and checking me out. 'I tend to just keep my head down, get on with my work.'

'Oh-kay . . .' Nancy makes another couple of notes

on her pad, while I stare, mesmerised, at the diamonds on her ring finger. The smug-looking husband must certainly have a bob or two. Her wedding band is set with dozens of little sparklers, and her engagement ring is a huge emerald-cut diamond with baguette side stones. It's just like one of the styles I was picturing on my own left hand yesterday. 'Everything all right?' she suddenly asks, glancing up.

'Yes, sorry . . . I was just admiring your jewellery. I mean,' I correct myself, in case she thinks I'm here to secretly case the joint, 'I've developed an interest in engagement rings recently. I just moved in with my boyfriend.'

'Oh . . . well, that's nice. But if you're planning a wedding, maybe this isn't the best time for you to be starting a new job with me . . .'

'No, no! I mean, I'm not planning a wedding! We're not officially engaged yet.' *And my unofficial fiancé is currently in the Cayman Islands with a girl called Julia.* 'No, I'd be giving a hundred per cent to this job! More, probably. *Two* hundred!' I give her my best driven, committed look, softened with a friendly, easy-to-work-with smile, which is a lot harder than you'd think.

'That's great. Because this job can get pretty busy at times. And things are going to get a little hectic around here for the next coupla weeks.' Nancy puts her pad down on the sofa arm and reaches for a cigarette pack on the coffee table. 'So, have you done any PA work before?'

'Yes, I've worked for Katriona de Montfort.'

'The writer? Wow. How was that?'

Thank God I've still got this time-out on my truth vow. 'Wonderful. Fantastic. I really *learned* things from Katriona.'

'Well, it's good to know you've had some experience. A lot of the girls I've been seeing haven't done anything like that before.'

Ha, Lulabell Davenport and Tilly Fosbury-Flop! Ha!

'But my requirements are probably quite different from what you did for Katriona.' Nancy lights her cigarette and blows out a mouthful of smoke. 'Obviously, I need someone who can handle my schedule, take my calls, run things for me here at the office . . . You know, generally control the chaos.'

I nod. 'One of my greatest skills.'

'But that's just my *Atelier* work. Actually, I'd really like someone who could help me out with my other commitments, too.'

'You mean your commitments with Lucien Black?' I ask, ever so casually, to disguise the fact that I feel like punching the air with excitement. I *knew* this job would get me a foot in the door.

'Yeah.' Nancy pulls a wry face. 'I'm sure I don't have to tell you, Isabel, that things have gone a little crazy on that front right now.'

I need to try and sound knowledgeable here, as I'm obviously meant to. Didn't Ruby say something about Nancy being extra stressed after Fashion Week? 'Well, obviously, what with everything that happened at Fashion Week.'

'Tell me about it.' Nancy does that funny little wince again, as though there's something she can hardly bear to think about. 'There's been a lot of fallout. I'm still mopping most of it up.'

'Right,' I say sympathetically, even though I've no idea what she's talking about. 'I'm sure.'

'Anyway . . .' she plasters on a sudden, bright smile. 'I don't want to put you off! Because once things have settled down on that front, there'll be plenty of fun things for you to help me with for Lucien, too.'

'You mean *Museing*?'

'Er . . .' Nancy looks a little bit confused, just for a moment. 'Well, I suppose you could put it like that. I mean, there's going to be a *lot* of catch-up to do on his next collection, obviously. I do a lot of vintage-hunting when we're working on new ideas, so I could really use a dogsbody for that!'

Probably not the time to mention I'm terrified of going into vintage stores, then.

'Oh, well, I just *love* rooting around in vintage stores!' I beam at her.

'Yeah, I thought so.' Nancy nods at my fake-vintage duster coat. 'I just adore that Jackie Kennedy, prom-queen aesthetic, don't you?'

I nod vigorously. 'It's one of my very favourite aesthetics.'

'Fabulous shoes, too. Whose are they?'

I'm not really sure how to answer this. 'Well . . . they're *mine*.'

'You make your own shoes?'

Oh.

God, I'm an idiot. *Now* I see what she was asking. Members of the Fashion Aristocracy don't ask you where you bought your clothes – they ask *who you're wearing*.

'Oh, no, no, I misheard you. Um . . . these are vintage, too, of course.'

Wrong answer. Nancy pulls a face. 'Ugh. Now that's where I draw the line. You wouldn't catch me dead in a stranger's old shoes.'

'Oh, God, no, I didn't mean *vintage-store* vintage. These belonged to my mother. Probably something she picked up during her modelling days.' Well, I'm not having Tilly Thingy-Whatsit beat me to this job by shamelessly exploiting an ex-model mother. Not when I'm doing so well.

'Your mom was a model?'

I nod. 'In the 1970s.'

'Oh, really?' Nancy looks interested. 'What's her name?'

'She was great chums with Bianca Jagger, Edie Sedgwick . . .' I say smoothly, as though I haven't really heard the question. 'All the really top 1970s people. You know, the ones who hung out at Studio 64.'

Nancy blinks. 'Studio 54, surely?'

Shit. 'Oh, well, I think Mum and . . . er . . . Auntie

Bianca were probably a bit too drug-addled to get the address right.'

Nancy is staring at me. 'Wow. Tough childhood.'

'Oh, Mum's fine now,' I say hastily. 'She's cleaned up and now her and my dad run their own organic farm in Somerset. Making . . . er . . . mead.' Sounds just the kind of thing bohemian organic farmers *might* make in Somerset. 'Yes! Mead.'

'Mead?' Nancy's eyebrows have vanished behind her fringe. 'This all sounds quite incredible.'

'Incredible,' I nod, 'and yet completely true. I'm heading off there this weekend, in fact, for a big bohemian family gathering.' I rack my brains to think of things I've read about parties chez Temperley and Davenport. 'You know, fancy dress . . . yoga at sunrise . . . organic cotton wigwams . . .'

'Jeez!' Nancy's dark eyes are really wide now. 'Well, it's certainly a wonderfully creative background . . . but I can't help feeling you might find being my PA a little bit dull in comparison.'

'God, no.' I lean towards her. 'This is my dream job, Ms Tavistock. Honestly. If you just give me a chance, I'll be the best PA you've ever had.'

'We-e-ll . . . You're obviously passionate about fashion . . .'

I put a hand over my heart. 'Obsessive.'

'Yes, you mentioned that . . . And if you survived Katriona de Montfort, I'm sure you can cope with me. Probably even with Lucien,' she adds, as an afterthought. 'All right. Why don't we give you a month's trial, and then see where we are?'

'That's fantastic!' I want to kiss her.

'Now, Ruby is leaving – hallelujah – this coming week. I guess it would be good for her to show you the ropes before she leaves.'

'God, no!' I interrupt. 'No, I mean, there's no need for that! Besides, if Ruby is as useless as you say, she'll probably only pass on all her bad habits to me, anyway.'

'Well, maybe you're right. And you're pretty competent, aren't you?'

I just beam extra brightly, and ignore her question. '*So* exciting!'

'Well, OK. Why don't you pop your details down on here,' she shoves her pad at me, 'and I'll give you a call over the weekend to let you know what time I'll want you to start on Monday morning. Now, you're an in-house candidate, so I won't need your whole CV . . .'

'Fantastic.'

'But if you could just drop a reference in the post . . .'

My heart skips an entire beat. 'Er . . . reference?'

'Yeah, I just need a personal reference for my records. From anyone you think is suitable. Katriona de Montfort, perhaps.'

'Oh, I think Katriona's too busy for that kind of thing.'

'Well, maybe a fashion person would be more appropriate, anyway. Just someone who knows you well. Hey, your Auntie Bianca would be great!'

I've got no idea who she's talking about for a moment – I mean, I don't *have* an Auntie Bianca – then I realise she means my ex-model mother's old pal.

'Well, I'll try . . . I think she spends a lot of time in Nigeria these days, though . . .'

'What on earth is Bianca Jagger doing in Nigeria?' Nancy looks astonished.

Oh. Maybe she's not from Nigeria. I'm going to have to look that up.

'Anyway, I'll see you next week, Isabel.' Nancy shakes my hand again and opens her door to show me out.

'Thank you so much, Nancy. I'm really looking forward to working with you.'

'Oh, me too, hon.' She's already starting to close the door behind me. 'Me too.'

Bianca Jagger
Nicaragua (NOT Nigeria)

13 September

Dear Ms Jagger,

~~You don't know me, but~~

~~You won't remember my mother~~

Let me begin by saying that I have always been a great admirer of yours. From your era-defining moment photographed in that white trouser suit, to ~~your that time you your tireless~~ everything else you have ever done, it has long been my ambition to follow in your footsteps (without having to marry Mick Jagger, obviously).

Having recently been given the chance (of a lifetime) to take my first steps into the fabulous world of fashion, I was wondering if you might ~~do me a massive favour~~ oblige by signing the attached character reference. I wouldn't waste your time reading it too closely – probably you have extremely important era-defining work to be getting on with – but your signature at the bottom will do very nicely.

If it is all right with you, I have supplied the phone number of a friend in place of yours. Rest assured that she will not impersonate you for any reason other than the necessity of getting me this job. She is a qualified psychologist, and so therefore an upstanding member of the community.

While I'm at it, I wonder if you happen to have any of

those white trouser suits ~~knocking abou~~ archived in your fabulous 1970s wardrobe? For reasons too complex to go into here, I am in urgent need of a fabulous 1970s wardrobe myself, and

CHARACTER REFERENCE FOR ISABEL BOOKBINDER

As an old friend of the family, I have known Isabel ever since she was born. Even as a baby, she showed exceptional devotion to glamour, choosing head-to-toe white as her Signature Colour (like me). Maturing into ~~an exceptional~~ a teenager, she consistently performed sterling work resisting the sartorial influence of her mother, who even in her Studio ~~64~~ 54 days had a worrying tendency to do matchy-matchy.

I cannot think of anyone more suited to take the position of your Personal Assistant, and recommend most strongly that you hire her.

As requested, I am giving you my phone number (07700 910103) but would ~~politely ask~~ insist that you *only call if you really, really have to.* My ~~charity work business~~ life keeps me extremely busy, and I am often out of the country, quite often in Nicaragua, where I was born in the capital city of Managua on May 2nd 1945.

Yours ~~stylishly~~

Bianca

Chapter 8

Even though I can't actually think of a time when I haven't dreaded the Bookbinder Family Barbecue, this year is completely different.

I mean, all right, I don't get the satisfaction, for once in my life, of being able to turn up with a proper boyfriend. I think, right now, I'm almost more disappointed in Will about that than anything.

But now that I've got this amazing new job, I can at least hold my head up high on the career front. And if you knew how big Dad's family are on careers, you'd know how important that really is. By my count, at last year's barbecue there were three medical doctors, two academic doctors, one headmaster, two deputy headmasters, no less than five assorted schoolteachers, an investment banker and a tax inspector. Given that I was 'between jobs' (and between crap jobs, at that) at the time, I wasn't exactly flavour of the month, except with Auntie Clem, Dad's older sister, who likes to use me as a kind of bogeyman to terrify her grandchildren with. You know – *if you don't work hard and pass all your exams, you'll end up like silly Cousin Isabel* . . . My nineteen-year-old cousin Robert is the only bigger black sheep of the family than I am, and he's got blond dreadlocks, was expelled from two schools for dealing pot, and has already spent time in a private borstal for a higher class of young offender.

But think of the looks on everyone's faces today, when I turn up looking like a Top Fashionista and tell them all about my brand-new, *highly prestigious* internship! Let's see how much they can patronise and belittle me then.

Anyway, to really nail the Top Fashionista effect, I've spent most of yesterday working on the perfect outfit. I really put some effort into it, not to mention the last dregs of my bank account. Still, it was worth every penny. Because the Vintage/Designer/High-Street combo that so impressed Nancy could be a little bit out-there for today's audience, I've decided to go for fashiony, intimidating, head-to-toe black. And not that boring V-neck and trousers uniform, either. Oh, no. I'm wearing:

1) Just-above-the-knee black shift dress from Reiss, cinched in at the waist (or what passes for my waist, which is the bit that goes inwards by about a millimetre between my hips and my ribcage) with a wide black patent belt;

2) The most enormous black sunglasses Topshop had to offer;

3) A huge black straw hat, with picture brim and black chiffon hatband; and

4) Black patent peep-toe court shoes, with five-inch chunky heel, only thirty quid from this great little vintage shop on Kensington Church Street.

All right. A hundred and thirty quid from Kurt Geiger on Kensington High Street. I'm definitely with Nancy T on the whole stranger's shoes thing.

I give a final twirl in front of the full-length mirror just as the doorbell rings.

I assume it's my brother Matthew, who's due to pick me up any minute, but it isn't. It's Lara.

'Lars, hi!' I let her in. 'What are you doing all the way down here?'

For a moment, I wonder if she's received a call from Nancy Tavistock – which reminds me, I must instruct Lara to answer her phone as Bianca Jagger all weekend, just in case Nancy calls the number on my reference – but she doesn't *look* furious. She's just staring at me in bewilderment.

'What are you *wearing*?'

'Like it?'

'You look like Maria Callas in mourning,' says Lara.

'Thank you,' I say.

'That wasn't a compliment.' Lara comes into the hallway. 'I mean, don't get me wrong, Iz, you look incredibly glam.'

'And thin?'

'Very thin. But is it really suitable for a barbecue?'

'It is suitable for *this* barbecue,' I tell her, going to get my new black clutch bag from the Dune bag in the kitchen, and transferring my phone, my bank card, my final fiver and some lip gloss. 'Frankly, I'd wear a straitjacket if I thought it would prevent me from having to race around traffic cones with a tennis ball under my chin.'

Lara looks at me like I really ought to be in a straitjacket.

'Uncle Michael's obstacle course,' I remind her. 'Anyway, you're hardly one to talk about sartorial suitability.' I eye up Lara's own outfit. She's looking impossibly gorgeous in some fantastic knee-length shorts, a sexy racer-back vest, and espadrille wedges to add several of the inches she craves. Her hair looks fantastic, too – all mussed-up and baby-blonde from her two weeks of Florida sun – and she definitely wasn't making it up about the tan. 'Doesn't that kind of outfit distract your patients?'

'Oh, I'm not seeing clients today.' Lara starts to busy herself with finding a glass for some water. She's not meeting my eye. 'I had a few cancellations.'

'Cancellations? On a Saturday morning?'

Saturday morning is one of Lara's busiest work days of the week. Despite (or because of?) their barminess, a lot of her patients – sorry, *clients* – have extremely demanding jobs from Monday to Friday, so it's the only time they can see her. It's often been a bit of a gripe of mine, in fact, that she's never able to do anything fun on a Saturday.

'Yes, well, people are away on holidays . . . and stuff . . . Anyway, I was wondering, Iz, since I've got nothing to do today, why don't I come along to the barbecue with you?'

I say nothing.

'It's for moral support!' she says, finally looking up at me, with her most sympathetic professional expression. 'I know how difficult your dad can be.'

I remain silent.

'I knew it would be hard for you to go without Will . . .' She tries one last, desperate attempt at justification. 'And don't forget how good I was at standing up to your Auntie Clem when she asked if you and I were lesbians at Marley's engagement party.'

Not a word leaves my lips.

'All right!' Lara slams down her water glass and lets out something very like an animal howl. 'I'll admit it!'

'Admit what?' I say, adopting the kind of encouraging voice I imagine professional alcohol counsellors use when a lifetime drunk is about to make an enormous personal breakthrough. 'Admit what, Lara?'

'I just want to see Matthew,' Lara chokes out.

Actually, I don't feel all that triumphant now she's said it. She looks so forlorn, all dressed up in her sexy outfit in the hope that he'll notice her, that it makes my heart hurt. Her fourteen-year-long crush on my brother doesn't seem to be diminishing. If anything, the older and wiser she gets in every other area of her life, the madder and more desperate she gets about this. And she's completely immune, it seems, to all the clever psychologist's tricks she pulls on other people all the time. I've tried all different kinds of Cognitive Restructuring – reasoning with her, arguing with her – but to no avail. I've tried Challenging her

Assumptions, but no matter what I say I can't shake loose her erroneous Assumption that Matthewness is next to godliness. I've even tried my own brand of Aversion Therapy, by accidentally-on-purpose locking them in Mum's garden shed together for an afternoon, but that only made the problem much, much worse. So I'm basically at a loss. Unless Matthew wakes his ideas up any time in the future, I'm not all that sure what there is for me to do.

I mean, any red-blooded male with half a brain would be gagging to get their hands on Lara. But no – my stupid brother persists in being besotted, instead, with his sweet-natured voluptuous blonde girlfriend, Annie.

'But Lars, you know he'll spend the entire journey to Mum and Dad's groping Annie's knee while you have to sit in the back feeling murderous . . .'

'No! I won't!' Lara is looking triumphant. Actually, a tiny bit manic, but I'm hoping that's just the way the spotlighting is hitting her pupils. 'Because Annie *isn't coming* in the car. She's been packing up things at their old place in Dorset and she's coming up to Shepton Mallet by train!'

I stare at her. 'How do you know this?'

Lara suddenly feels a need to busy herself with water and glass again. 'Oh, well, I had a little chat with Matthew on the phone yesterday . . .'

'So you've been *planning* this? *Lara*!'

Suddenly, the doorbell rings again, the knocker knocks, and a booming male voice shouts 'Hel-*LOH*-

HO!' on the street outside. This is Matthew, never one to make a quiet, unassuming arrival.

'We'd better go!' Lara is already turning pink, and trying to barge past me to get to the front door.

'Lara, no.' I block her expertly. Well, I have had fourteen years of practice. 'You can't come with me.'

Lara's eyes go all wide and innocent. 'Won't there be room?'

'Of course there'll be room! But you know exactly what I mean.' God, it scares me when Lara makes me act like the sane one. 'You can't keep torturing yourself this way, Lars . . .'

Matthew's car horn hoots. 'Girls!' he yells. 'Double *pah-arked*!'

Abandoning all pretence of dignity, Lara dodges past me – well, she's had fourteen years of practice, too – then grabs my hand and pulls me to the front door.

Matthew is standing next to his red Polo a little way along Prince of Wales Drive, causing passing old ladies to stare and people walking their dogs to crash into lamp posts and birds to fall out of the sky, etc. etc. Tall, chiselled demigods like Matthew have this effect. It's not something I mind any more, especially. I mean, all right, having a brother who looks like this can make life tough for the first, say . . . fifteen or sixteen years. But once you've grown up a bit and got over the fact that when you're in a room/school/family home with him, nobody seems to notice you even exist, it really isn't that much of a problem.

'Girls!' He strides towards us and ruffles my hair before leaning down – a long way down – to give Lara a hearty kiss on the cheek. 'Hello, Wizzy! And looking even more gorgeous than ever, Lara. So tanned! My God! A vision!'

Oh, God. This journey's going to be agony, isn't it? With Annie temporarily absent, Matthew is going to turn the considerable power of his charm on Lara, like he's done so many times before. I'd haul him up on it if it weren't for the fact I can't possibly let on anything about Lara's feelings. And anyway, Matthew really *is* only flirting with Lara because he likes her, and he flirts with everyone he likes – male, female, it's just the way he is. I've seen him flirt with the captain of his cricket team, for God's sake. I've seen him flirt with the opposition's front-row forwards on the rugby pitch. I've seen him . . .

Hold on just one moment.

Who's that getting out of the passenger seat of Matthew's car?

It looks a lot like Ben Loxley, Matthew's oldest friend and the object of my teenage obsession.

Oh, my God. It *is* Ben Loxley.

Despite the fact we grew up on the same street – sometimes practically in the same *house*, the amount of time he and Matthew used to spend together, when Ben wasn't away at his posh boarding school – I don't think I've seen him since I was about seventeen.

OK. Scratch that. I know exactly how old I was when I last saw him. I was seventeen years and one month, and Ben would have been eighteen years and a couple of days. I remember the exact date. If pushed, I could probably produce the prevailing weather conditions. If *really* pushed, I could probably still remember most of the handful – all right, *volume* – of love poems I wrote about him in the summer after my GCSEs. And I can definitely remember the delicious aroma of the Nirvana T-shirt that me and Lara pinched off his mum's washing line so that I could cuddle up to it in bed at night and imagine that he was there with me, in all his Persil ColourCare-scented gorgeousness.

ColourCare: The new men's fragrance, from Isabel Bookbinder.

Anyway, the last I heard of Ben Loxley, he'd gone to work in New York, where I'm pretty certain he's been living for the last four or five years.

But now he's back.

'You've seen the stowaway, then?' Matthew laughs merrily at his own joke, and turns to wave Ben towards us. 'Good to have him back, isn't it? Benjy and I hooked up for some beers last night, and when he found out where we were heading off to today he asked if he could hitch a lift, see his own folks. Apparently he's only been down there twice since he came back!'

Well, the first thing I'm thinking is – thank *God* I'm looking thin today.

Because Ben Loxley is not the kind of person around whom you'd feel comfortable being a little bit porky.

I mean, just *look* at the man! (And he is a man now, not just a boy, I note, with a lurchy feeling in my stomach.) A solid six foot, he's broadened out nicely across the chest and shoulders, and where his skin was once baby-smooth, he's now got a day's worth of stubble on his chin and faint, sexy crinkles around his smoky green eyes. His dirty-blond hair is sticking up in slightly startled, just-out-of-bed tufts. His smile is still slightly crooked, the way I remember it, and he's wearing grey jeans, a faded blue shirt, nicely battered Oliver Sweeneys and an expensive, antique-looking leather-strapped watch on one tanned wrist.

You see what I mean? Not the kind of man you'd want to share a bathroom mirror with.

Though, ironically, absolutely the kind of man you'd want to share a *bath* with.

Preferably one with lots and lots of strategically placed bubbles at your end. And extremely low lighting.

OK, just stop it. I really, really shouldn't be thinking about him like this. I mean, all right, I did have this huge crush on him when I was younger, and it's not like he's got any less good-looking in the intervening decade. But I'm attached. Firmly attached. All right, maybe not actually *engaged*, lest we forget, but certainly one half of a Mature, Adult Relationship, and that means I can't just go around imagining candlelit baths with men who aren't my boyfriend.

'Little Lara Alliston! And Isabel. Of course.' Ben's got that lopsided smile on his lips as he leans in to give us both a kiss on the cheek and me a tiny pat on the small of the back. He smells of delicious, masculine things, like . . . like autumn mornings, and . . . newly dug earth . . . you know, I think there might even be a hint of Persil ColourCare in there as well. 'My God. How long has it been?'

'More than ten years!' Lara announces perkily. She's still all aglow from Matthew's compliments barrage. 'Carolyn Duffie's Christmas party! *You* remember, Isabel?' she turns to me excitedly, before being silenced by the stony look I'm giving her.

Because, I mean, really. Would I do this to her? If she were suddenly reunited with the object of her teenage lust?

Hang on – what am I saying? I'm standing *right here* with her and the object of her teenage lust, and my behaviour has been a model of decorum and discretion. I'm not reminding her of the (many) excruciating occasions when she was all geared up to throw herself at Matthew, only to be devastated when he spent the evening snogging someone else. Like Ben snogged Carolyn Duffie at her Christmas party. Just for example.

'God, Carolyn Duffie! There's a blast from the past.' Ben chuckles. 'Whatever happened to her?'

'She's married, I think,' I say hastily. 'With at least three kids.' I've actually no idea if this is true, but it might at least shatter Ben's dreamy teenage memories of sexy blonde Carolyn, with her lithe, hockey-player's figure and penchant for flicking her fringe and giggling breathlessly at everything he said. 'A *brood*, you might say.'

'Shouldn't we do some of this catching-up malarkey in the car?' Matthew says, pointedly bashing his watch.

Lara flicks her fringe and giggles breathlessly.

We all troop along to the car, where Matthew absolutely insists that Lara takes the front passenger seat, ostensibly because she gets carsick, but actually so that he can charm and flirt and shamelessly lead her on all the way down the M4. Which means that I get to sit in the back with Ben.

It's not exactly a hardship.

'You're looking amazing, Iz,' he tells me softly, as Matthew starts to shoot at high speed towards Battersea Park Road. 'Now, what is it you're doing these days? Last time I saw you, you were all set on being . . . a civil-rights campaigner, wasn't it?'

'Er . . . no.' That was when I was *fourteen*. And if Ethics teachers will insist on showing you *Mississippi Burning*, what does anyone really expect?

'Oh, no, I remember what it was – a paediatric cardiologist.'

My burning ambition when I was sixteen, in fact. Well, Dr Anna Del Amico in *ER* made the job seem so glamorous and exciting, and looked so pretty while she was doing it, that it was only when I realised it would take me seven years to qualify that I was finally put off.

'Um, no, not that either.'

Ben frowns. 'In that case . . . do I recall you wanting to be a fashion designer?'

'Yes!' I could kiss him. And not only because he looks a little bit like a young Daniel Craig. He's the only one who seems to have remembered my burning childhood ambition! Remembered several of them, in fact. Maybe he thought about me more in the old days than I imagined. 'It's what I'm doing now, actually!'

'Hey!' He reaches over and gives my hand a squeeze. 'That's fantastic! What kind of thing are you designing?'

'Er . . . well, I'm exploring a kind of *draped* effect . . .'

'Iz-Wiz has got a place at some fancy-schwancy fashion school.' Matthew breaks off complimenting Lara to tune into our conversation. 'St Martin-in-the-Fields, isn't it, Wizkins?'

'You mean Central St Martins?' Ben's eyebrows go up. 'Wow.'

'Er . . . yes . . .' I don't meet Lara's eyes, even though she's turned round to give me a *look*. 'But I'm actually starting this really important internship next week, at a Top Fashion magazine. It's highly prestigious . . .'

'Well, I'm really impressed! Isabel Bookbinder – fashionista!' Ben pulls a face. 'So much more fun than my job.'

I can't believe I've been so rude not to ask. 'I'm sorry – what is it you do?'

'Ben's a professional Midas,' Matthew says, recklessly overtaking some naive soul who's only

116

going ten miles an hour over the speed limit. 'Everything he touches turns to gold.' He falls about with mirth, which means of course that Lara does, too.

'Very amusing.' Ben leans forward and flicks the back of Matthew's head affectionately. 'I'm a venture capitalist,' he says, turning back to me. 'If you know what that is . . . ?'

Stonkingly rich, is what I know venture capitalists are. 'But I thought you'd gone into law? In New York? At Randall and Ginsberg . . .' I stop myself, just in time, before Ben puts two and two together and realises I'm the infamous Nirvana T-shirt Stalker of Ilkley Close.

'Yeah, well, I defy anyone with half a personality to stay in that job for very long!'

'Careful! Her boyfriend is a lawyer!' announces Matthew chirpily. 'And a very nice bloke he is, too,' he adds loyally. 'Fully functioning personality.'

'Oh!' Ben stares at me, and I think he's about to apologise for the lawyer crack until he goes on, 'Oh, I thought you were single.'

Is it just me, or is there something . . . *disappointed* about the way he's just said that?

'No, no . . . er . . . Will's away for work at the moment. We've been together for about eight months.'

Ben's eyes lock on to mine. 'Lucky old Will.'

My heart's pounding so hard that I'm suddenly glad Matthew's revving the engine so loudly. Surely everyone would be able to hear it otherwise.

117

'Well, at least the poor chap's got you to liven his life up a bit, hey?' Ben breaks the eye contact, and pushes me playfully on the shoulder. 'He'd probably die of boredom otherwise!'

I think of Will, most probably sipping Planter's Punch with Julia on Grand Cayman even as we speak.

Actually, I don't want to think about that. I don't want to think about it at all.

It's already nearly eleven thirty by the time we finally pull into the driveway at Mum and Dad's.

Dad is outside on the front drive with Uncle Midge, cleaning his Volvo, for no other reason than to compete with his brother-in-law about whose car is the newest and shiniest. If I know Dad, it's a contest he'll win hands down. He gives Matthew a pat on the back, shakes Ben's hand, grunts an unconvincing 'Hello-Lara-I-didn't-know-you-were-joining-us-how-nice' at Lara, and barely acknowledges my arrival at all, apart from telling me Mum needs help with the salads in the kitchen.

While Matthew and Ben roll up their sleeves and start to help Dad with the car wash, Lara and I head into the house to find Mum.

'So? How do you think it went?' Lara says, out of the side of her mouth, as we go through the hallway to the kitchen.

'Oh, same as normal.' I shrug. 'The day Dad looks glad to see me, the snowploughs will be needed in hell.'

I'm rather pleased with this, but Lara just stares at me blankly. 'No! I meant the car journey. Me and Matthew!'

'Oh. Well, it seemed fine.' I don't want to be any more committal than that.

'*Fine?*' Lara hisses. 'Didn't you think he was being nice to me?'

'He was perfectly nice.'

'More perfectly nice than usual?'

'Perhaps a little more.'

'How much more?' She's got that manic look again. 'Twenty per cent? Thirty per cent?'

'Oh, God, Lars, I don't know . . .'

'Forty? Fifty?'

'Twenty-six point four,' I say, hoping this will shock her into realising how insane this sounds.

'Twenty-six point four . . .' she echoes, putting her head on one side, deep in thought. 'Yes. That's roughly what I was thinking, too . . . Well, that's good, isn't it?' She grabs my arm all of a sudden. 'And what about you and Ben Loxley? *How* pleased was he to see you?'

'Twenty-six point four per cent pleased, I should think,' I say, but only because I don't want Lara making a great big fuss.

'Just imagine!' Lara actually clasps her hands, like she's in *Little Women*, or something. 'I could end up with Matthew, and you could end up with Ben, and we could all go on weekends away together . . . Oooh, we could go to Cornwall! And the boys could surf, and you and me could walk along the coast and go to Rick Stein and have spa treatments . . .'

There's only one slight problem with Lara's vision. And it isn't just that I wouldn't let High-Speed Matthew drive me all the way to Cornwall if my life depended on it. 'Well, that's all very nice, Lars, but I'm with Will, remember?'

'Oh. Yes. Well . . .' Lara looks as though she's about to make a suggestion. But then she remembers she's actually supposed to be a highly trained psychologist, who can't just go around advising me to dump my partner simply to satisfy her own desire to wander the Cornish coast as a cosy foursome. 'Well, I thought you'd be pleased Ben looked so happy to see you, anyway. You know I always said he liked you almost as much as you liked him. Without the stalking and the volume of love poetry, obviously.'

'Wizbit!' This is Matthew, calling from the driveway. 'Can you bring out another couple of buckets?'

'I'll do it!' Lara gasps breathlessly, shoving me out of the way to open the cupboard under the stairs and get to the buckets.

She's done a runner back out on to the driveway before I can stop her. I head for the kitchen.

The first thing I notice is that there are avocados *everywhere*. There are avocados ripening in heaps in the conservatory area of the kitchen. There are avocados in both fruit bowls in the eating area of the kitchen. There are avocados in a colander in the sink, pointlessly having their skins rinsed. And there are avocados spilling out of the hanging baskety thing where Mum usually keeps the onions.

Forget Delia Smith and her cranberries. When my mother decides to monopolise an ingredient, the supermarkets of Shepton Mallet have to start limiting all the other shoppers to only one of said item each, and bringing in riot police.

Sadly, though, it isn't only avocados in the kitchen. Auntie Clem is here, too, straining the fabric of some quite revolting denim shorts and – does she have any idea what this means? – a *Frankie Says Relax* T-shirt. She's sitting at the kitchen table with a large glass of Pimm's, holding forth about her newest grandchild's amazing ability to open its eyes *and* breathe all at the same time, or something. And Mum is at the counter, pulverising industrial quantities of avocado with a potato masher. She's all decked out in her barbecue finest – lemon-yellow Capri pants, a lemon-yellow twinset and spanking white plimsolls with a lemon-yellow trim.

'Isabel!' Mum abandons her mashing and comes across the kitchen to give me a hug, holding me a fraction tighter and longer than necessary. 'How *are* you?'

I'm not sure what she means for a second. Then I remember. Last time we spoke properly, she was getting all excited about Will proposing. And now here I am, proposal-less. And Will-less, for that matter.

'Oh, darling,' she adds, standing back and looking

at my hat and sunglasses. 'You shouldn't take this so badly. Nobody's died.'

'Mum, this is fashion black, not funeral black,' I say patiently. 'And I'm *fine*. Hi, Auntie Clem.'

'Hello, Isabel.' Auntie Clem waves over at me, but doesn't bother to get up. 'Nice to see you. Your mum was just telling me all about how you've been . . . let down.'

I shoot Mum a look of pure evil, and I'm gratified when she actually looks sheepish.

'I've not been *let down*,' I tell Auntie Clem, with great dignity. 'You can only be let down when you're expecting something. And I don't need a man to make me feel good,' I add, shaking my hair back and feeling a bit like Beyoncé.

Oh, actually, that might have been the wrong thing to say. Auntie Clem's eyebrows have just about shot right off her head.

'I've got a *career* for that,' I say hastily, denying her the thrill of having me come out as a lesbian right in the middle of her little brother's kitchen.

'Oh, yes. Your career.' Auntie Clem doesn't actually do the little quotation-marks thing with her fingers, but she might as well have. 'Moira was telling me all about Central St Martins. How nice that you're going to be there at the same time as my Portia!'

'Well, in a manner of speaking. I mean, obviously I've just been awarded this *highly prestigious* intern-ship,' I say casually, as though I've mentioned the possibility of this a million times before. 'Starting on

Monday. So, of course, Portia probably won't see me around very much. If at all!'

'Internship?' Mum glances over sharply from the hanging baskety thing. 'What internship?'

'At *Atelier* magazine! I'll be doing all kinds of highly prestigious things . . . meeting all the top fashion designers . . . making important industry contacts . . .'

'Oh, well, that sounds good.' Mum is still looking worried, though, and I think I know why. 'Does . . . er . . . your father know about this yet?'

'No, but like I said, Mum, it's highly prestigious.' I look her right in the eyes. 'I don't see why Dad should have a problem with it.'

'Well, no . . . and anyway,' Mum brightens, 'it's still part of your course, isn't it? I mean, it's not like you're dropping out, or anything!'

'And what is it you're going to be studying?' Auntie Clem takes a large sip from her glass of Pimm's and fixes me with a beady eye. 'Dressmaking?'

'Fashion design, actually,' I say, through gritted teeth.

'Oh!' But Auntie Clem isn't defeated for long. She's not a Bookbinder for nothing. 'So what will you do with that? Teach?'

'Why don't you help me with the guacamole?' Mum suddenly asks, ushering me towards the pile of mushed avocado before I can say anything to Auntie Clem. She hands me her potato masher, then thinks better of it – probably because she's had a sudden vision of the damage a carefully wielded potato masher could do to Auntie Clem's head – and exchanges it for a tiny little teaspoon. 'All these avocados are terribly hard work,' she goes on, mopping her perspiring face with the corner of a tea towel. 'I should never have picked a Mexican theme . . .'

All of a sudden, there's an awful lot of noise from the hallway – loud voices, booming laughter. Matthew – of course – barges through the door first, leading his girlfriend Annie by the hand. She must have just got out of a taxi, because she's putting her purse away in her bag (a battered old Kipling rucksack – I do despair of Annie). She's all kitted out for a barbecue, too, in tiny gingham hot pants that look like her old school gym kit and a faded tie-dye top that she probably bought for tuppence ha'penny from Oxfam. And she still looks breathtaking.

Dad's following them, looking all pleased and smug about something, and I can see Ben lurking in the hallway, as if he's not sure whether his presence is welcome or not.

There's no sign whatsoever of Lara.

'Everyone, everyone,' Matthew is saying, flapping his hands up and down to shush people, even though the only ones making all the noise are him and Annie. 'We were going to wait until the whole family was here, but *someone*,' he pulls Annie to his side and makes a *grrr* noise as he kisses her, 'has managed to blow our cover!'

We all just stare at them. Frankly I don't think any of us have a clue what he's talking about.

Then Annie lets out an excited shriek, and holds out her left hand.

Oh, my God.

There's a diamond solitaire ring glittering on her third finger.

So this explains psychic Jenni's wedding prediction.

And it also explains why there's no sign of Lara.

Chapter 9

I manage to extricate myself from all the shrieking, and the tears, and Mum telling me, with the smallest hint of remorse, that Jenni *was* right after all, followed by Auntie Clem saying in a very loud voice, 'Your turn soon, perhaps, Isabel,' and head out of the kitchen to try to find Lara.

She's not out on the driveway, though I can see Uncle Michael's Saab turning into the close, so I beat a quick retreat back into the house. She's not in my bedroom, or in the bathroom, and I can't see anyone in the garden from the bathroom window apart from my cousin Robert, vanishing into the New Zealand flax bushes with a furtive air.

I sneak back down the stairs to the hallway, though there's far too much noise and general celebration in the kitchen for anyone to notice me, and extricate my mobile from my clutch bag.

I'm just scrolling through recent calls to get to Lara's number when my phone rings. It's a mobile number I don't recognise. Normally I'm not in the habit of picking up if I don't know the number, but a sudden fear chills my heart. What if Lara's gone out on to the main road and thrown herself under a lorry?

And this is the lorry driver calling the last number that came up in her phone, to tell me to come and claim her horribly mangled body . . .

'Hello?' I can hardly breathe. 'Who's this?'

'Isabel?' It's a woman's voice.

A *woman* lorry driver.

'It's me, hon. Nancy.'

'Oh, Nancy!' I'm so relieved, I sit down, suddenly, on the stairs. 'I thought you were . . . never mind. How can I help?'

'Well, I'm really sorry to disturb during your family party. I'm sure you're having a wild time!'

'Oh, God, yes. Completely mental.' Actually, the noise from the kitchen backs me up on this one. All the laughter and champagne corks popping sound as though it could easily be a party on a bohemian mead farm. But I don't want anyone to overhear too much of my conversation with Nancy. 'Let me just go and find a nice quiet . . . er . . . wigwam,' I add, scrabbling up the stairs to my old bedroom, and closing the door. 'How can I help?'

'Well, it's a little bit of an emergency, actually, hon.'

I'm just wondering what qualifies as an emergency in top-flight fashion circles when she goes on.

'I've been trying to track down this package that I was meant to get the other day.'

Oh, my God! The drug-stuffed Jiffy envelope.

'I've just been speaking to the courier company,' Nancy continues, 'and they've told me the delivery was signed for by an Isabel Bookbinder.'

Denial is looking completely pointless. 'Oh! Yes, I remember now . . .'

'Right.' She sounds just a tiny bit put out. 'Are you always that proactive when you haven't even been given a job yet?'

'I'm sorry, Nancy.' I don't want to say that I was desperately trying to show her what a super-capable PA I could be. 'But there was nobody else there to sign for it.'

'Well, it's OK. You were taking initiative, I guess. So, where is my envelope?'

This is the sixty-four thousand dollar question.

Where *is* her envelope?

'Oh, God. *Please* don't tell me you've lost it.' Her voice sounds a little tense.

'Of course not!' Which is true. I mean, this envelope may not actually be *lost*. But I'd be a lot more confident about that if I could remember where I'd put it.

OK. I had it in my bag when I was in Nancy's office. So it must be in my bag now, right?

Except that I didn't bring that bag with me today.

Right, well, I'm not about to tell Nancy that. She'll only panic that I've gone and lost the stuff, and it would hardly be the best start to my career as her super-capable PA. 'It's right here! I'm looking at it right now, in fact!' I say, hoping my confident tone will reassure her. 'I'll get it back to you first thing Monday morning . . .'

'No, no, Izzie, I need it sooner than that. Lucien has loads of work to be getting on with, so he really needs the stuff.'

My God. Lucien Black is on the crystal meth, too? It's a Fashion Aristocracy drugs orgy.

'I'm sending a courier to you right now, OK?' Nancy goes on. 'Your folks are in Somerset, right?'

I glance in my dressing-table mirror. My face has drained of colour. 'A courier? To my parents'?'

'Oh, don't worry, he won't intrude! Now, it shouldn't take him much more than two hours,' Nancy goes on. 'If you just give me the postcode so I can let him have it for the satnav. I know farms can be tricky to find.'

Yes. My parents' organic mead farm is going to be spectacularly hard to find. Mostly due to the fact that it doesn't actually exist.

'Look, Nancy, there's no need for you to go to all this trouble, all the expense of a courier . . . I'll just get in my brother's car, head back up to London . . .'

'No, no, I won't hear of it.' Nancy sounds as though she isn't going to brook the slightest bit of argument. 'This is your family time. Now, just that postcode, please, Isabel.'

I can't even speak.

'Isabel?'

'Er . . . yes, the postcode is . . . um . . . BA4 6PQ,' I say, bunging together any old Shepton Mallet area-code numbers I can think of. Anything to avoid giving Nancy the actual postcode, to plain old number 16 Ilkley Close.

'Great . . . so call me when they get there, OK? Bye now!'

'Wait, Nancy . . .' I try one last time, but she's gone.

OK. Let's not panic here. Chances are the courier won't even find me, not with that fabricated postcode, which will give me the chance to get back to town tonight and ransack Will's flat for that envelope. Which is probably perfectly safe. And if it isn't, and I have mislaid it, well then, I'll just have to replace it, won't I? Not *actually* replace it – I mean, I don't exactly have a meth dealer on speed dial. But if I really have to, I'll just come clean to Nancy, and offer to cough up for what I've lost . . .

'Isabel?' Mum's voice is floating up through my open bedroom window. I lean out slightly, to see her standing on the scruffy bit of side patio. Her arms are folded and she's looking up at me. 'We're all moving into the garden. Aren't you going to come out and have a glass of champagne for your brother?'

'I . . . yes, look, I'm just right in the middle of something . . .'

'Something more important than Matthew getting engaged?'

'I'll be down in a minute, OK?'

'Iz-Wiz, I know you're upset about . . . well, I'm sorry, all right, darling. When Jenni gave me her psychic prediction about the family wedding, I suppose I just sort of jumped to the conclusion that it would be you. I mean, you are older than Matthew, after all – by rights it really ought to be you getting married before him.'

All right, so maybe I won't be down in a minute.

Maybe I'll be down in two and a half seconds, after I hurl myself out of the window on to the patio below.

'Mum, I really do have something to sort out . . .'

'Please, darling, come and have a drink.' She lowers her voice to a loud hiss. 'Look, people have already noticed you've disappeared. Clem's asking if you have some kind of issue with heterosexual marriage in general. And your father . . .'

'All right. All *right*! I'm coming.'

I stamp down the stairs and head out of the conservatory and into the garden. Since I've been upstairs, more and more of Dad's family have arrived. Everybody's milling about on the lawn, chinking glasses and cooing over Annie's engagement ring, which suddenly makes me glad Lara's gone AWOL. I grab the first drink that's shoved at me, say an ostentatious 'Cheers!' for Dad and Auntie Clem's benefit, and then I head for the quietest part of the garden just so that I can sit down and think about what the hell I'm going to do about the Nancy situation. Mum's New Zealand flax bushes are away from prying Bookbinder eyes, so that's probably a good bet for relative privacy. Or, more to the point, privacy from the relatives.

'Fuck!' There's a loud splutter as I make my way round the back of the flax bushes, where I'm just in time to see my cousin Robert chucking something on the lawn, grinding it with his foot, and frantically wafting a cloud of faintly green-tinged smoke away from his face.

'Oh, calm down, Robert, it's only me.'

'Isabel. Thank God.' Robert's dilated eyes roll with relief, and he reaches down for his still-smouldering joint with his free hand. There's a half-empty ramekin of guacamole in the other. 'I thought you were my mum.'

The fact he mistook me for Auntie Clem says, I hope, far more about his hallucinogen habit than it does about me.

'Good to see you,' he adds, not forgetting his expensive public school manners, and smiling at me in a fuzzy sort of way before holding out his joint. 'You look nice. I haven't seen you since . . . God, was I about ten or something?'

'No,' I say firmly. 'It was eight months ago. At Marley's wedding?' I'm surprised he's forgotten this. To the best of my own recollection, Robert distinguished himself at the wedding by joyriding in (and denting) the string quartet's van, and by asking the registrar loudly and repeatedly if it was legal to marry your first cousin because he'd always thought I was very attractive 'for an older woman that you're kind of related to'. And Dad thinks *I'm* the black sheep of this family.

Robert looks as if he hasn't the faintest memory of Marley's wedding, or, come to that, Marley himself, but he nods nostalgically nonetheless. 'Come here to chill?'

'Yes. I mean, no. Not like that.' I wave the mangy-looking stub away. 'I need a *clear* head. And to be

132

perfectly honest with you, I've had my absolute fill of drugs in the last ten minutes.'

Robert's mouth falls open slightly.

'Not like that! I just mean . . . look, Robert, you wouldn't happen to know the . . . um . . . street value of a package of . . .' I lower my voice, even though we're the only ones in the flax bushes, '. . . crystal meth? About so big?'

'Woah.' Robert's eyes actually manage to register shock. 'That's some serious shit.'

I really don't have time to stand around having Tarantino-esque discussions in Mum's New Zealand flax. 'Yes, look, can you just tell me how much something like that might actually cost? If I had to go out and buy it, say?'

Robert gives me a reproachful look, blowing out an elegant ribbon of compost-scented smoke. 'Meth's not my scene. Not five hundred quid's worth of it, anyway.'

'*Five hundred quid? That's* how much it could cost me?'

'Why? Are you in trouble with your dealer, or something?'

'No! I don't have a dealer! I've just screwed something up with my boss.' I grab the guacamole from him and scoop up a comforting pile of it on the tip of my finger. 'I signed for this parcel of drugs for her, and now I can't be sure where it is, and she's sending someone down here right now to come and get it from me . . .'

'You mean, like, an enforcer?'

'No, I mean like a DHL delivery man.'

'Ohhh.' He nods again, sagely. 'Multinational conglomerates. They're always out to get the little people.'

I give up. I'm not going to sort anything out sitting around here with dreadlocked, druggie Robert. And to be honest, given that I have neither Nancy's actual package of drugs, nor the funds or ability to purchase a replacement, I'm not sure there's very much I actually *can* sort out. All I'm going to have to hope for is that the DHL man won't actually be able to track me down with that non-existent postcode and that he eventually gives up and heads back to town.

'Well, nice chatting to you, Robert.' I'm going to have to go back to the party before my absence is noted, commented on, and disapproved of. 'And don't worry – I won't tell Auntie Clem you're back here.'

'Thanks, Isabel.' His fist comes lurching towards me, to give me one of his favoured fist bumps. 'Black sheep of the family unite, hey?'

'Yes. Black sheep unite.'

It could just be my imagination, but the Bookbinder Family Barbecue seems more ghastly this year than ever.

An unidentified child gets guacamole-covered handprints all over my brand-new dress. When I refuse to smile and coo or behave as though she's just created a priceless work of art, the entire Auntie Clem branch of the family starts cold-shouldering me as though I'm some kind of convicted child molester.

A man called Roland from DHL has left four messages on my mobile in the last hour telling me he's driving round and round in circles near Leigh Upon Mendip, but he can't locate BA4 6PQ anywhere, and can I *call him please!!!*

Uncle Michael keeps passing by with an ominous look in his eye, saying, 'Quiz begins in one hour . . . quiz begins in one hour . . . don't forget to warm up . . .'

And Dad still hasn't bothered to say anything to me at all, beyond snapping, when I refused a charred Mexican-chicken wing, 'Oh, Lord, you've not gone *veggie* now you're off to *art school*, have you, Isabel?'

It doesn't help that I still can't get hold of Lara. I'm working on the principle that, if she'd been crushed under the wheels of a lorry nearby, we'd probably have heard the police sirens by now. But it doesn't mean I'm any happier about her absence.

I'm just trying her mobile for about the eighteenth time when I hear a voice behind me.

'Isabel?'

It's Ben.

I've not had much chance to talk to him since we arrived – well, I've been busy with elaborately lying to my boss – but now that he's here, looking at me with those smoky eyes and that lopsided grin, I'm kicking myself that I haven't prioritised him.

I mean, not that I'm going to *do* anything about the

fact that I fancy the pants off him. I'm in a Mature, Adult Relationship, and all that, and flinging yourself at sexually magnetic venture capitalists isn't the done thing. And anyway, even if it *were* the done thing, or if there was some sort of loophole you could exploit while your boyfriend is rubbing coconut oil into a bikini-clad Russian, Ben's not going to want to do anything either. Just look at the man! With those genes, and that bank balance, he's probably spent the last five years fighting off an endless line of stunning Manhattan socialites. He's hardly going to be interested in me.

Except . . . well, is it normal for a guy to be looking that way at someone he's not interested in? Like he wants to . . . accompany them to the rhododendrons . . . and ravish them?

'I've hardly seen you,' he says softly. 'Been busy, Izzie?'

I laugh as heartily as possible, to let him know that being ravished in the rhododendrons is absolutely the last thing on my mind. 'Oh, you know . . .' I waggle my phone at him. 'People to call. Things to do.'

'You're calling . . . sorry, I forget his name . . . Will?'

'Oh, no, no . . . just my boss!'

He frowns. 'On a weekend? And I thought *my* hours were insane.'

'Well, this internship is very important . . .' I *wish* he'd stop looking at me like that. It makes it incredibly hard to concentrate. And breathe. 'Um . . . foot in the door . . . fashion aristocracy . . .'

'You know, I know a few people in the fashion world. In fact,' Ben takes a step closer, 'there's actually a party I'm meant to go to on Monday night. A private viewing at this boutique in Chelsea. A colleague's wife part-owns it.' His eyes fix on to mine again. 'You could join me if you liked.'

Hang on. Is he asking me out?

Like, *out*, out?

'I mean, if you're looking to make a few contacts, it could be a good opportunity for you.'

Oh, OK. So it's just a favour. A work-related favour. Not a date.

'And we could grab a bite to eat afterwards,' he adds. 'Have a proper chance to catch up on the last ten years.'

Oh!

So it *is* a date?

Frankly, I'm not sure I know. And I don't want to embarrass myself by reminding him that actually, I have a boyfriend, in case he didn't mean it to sound like a date at all.

God, this is where it would be really, really good to be a Manhattan socialite. I mean, dating rules are crystal clear over there. They practically run classes on it in high school, don't they?

'Isabel? Is everything OK?'

'Oh, yes . . . sorry, Ben . . . I, er . . .' Fudge it, Isabel. Fudging is the only option. 'Gosh, I really don't know. I mean, Mondays are often very busy for me . . . who knows what I might be doing that day . . .'

Ben reaches out. For a moment I think he's going to put a finger across my lips, and say, 'Don't speak, my darling. Don't say another word with that sensuous mouth, or I'm afraid I won't be able to stop myself from kissing you.' But he doesn't. He's reaching out for my mobile phone.

'I'll put my number in here,' he says, tapping the digits. 'Then if you change your mind on Monday, you can call me.' He hands the phone back, with another of his lopsided grins. 'No pressure. I just thought you might enjoy it.'

'Oh, well, I'm sure I would! It's just . . .'

'Iz-Wiz!'

The sudden shriek from across the garden makes both of us jump. It's Ron and Barbara, my god-parents and Mum's oldest friends, hurrying across the lawn towards us. They're both in full-on barbecue mode, like everyone else: voluminous shorts, T-shirts and, for Barbara, a broderie anglaise headscarf and giant white sunglasses, like Thelma and Louise on their road trip.

'Hi, Ron. Hi, Barbara.' I give them each a kiss. Frankly it's just nice to be greeted by someone at this godawful event who actually looks pleased to see me. 'It's been far too long.'

'Far too long!' says Barbara, unable to tear her eyes off Ben. 'So, is this the Will we've heard so much about?'

'Oh, no, no. This is Ben. Remember – Matthew's old friend? Cathy Loxley's son?'

'Oh, *yes*.' Barbara is turning slightly pink. '*Well*. How lovely to see you again, Ben!'

'And you,' Ben says, dutifully, before turning to me. 'I'm just going to go and get myself something to eat, Iz. Can I fetch you anything?'

'No, thank you, I'm fine.' All those smouldering looks have completely taken the edge off my appetite.

'He always was a handsome boy,' Barbara murmurs, as we watch Ben stride off towards the smoking barbecue. 'I'm sure all the girls are wild about him.'

'Well, you know how it is with Manhattan socialites!' Thinking about other girls being wild about Ben is giving me a burning sensation in my solar plexus.

'So!' Ron, clearly feeling a little bit excluded from the conversation, nudges me in the ribs. 'Can we call you *pard'ner*?'

'Er . . . if that's what you'd like.'

'Oh, Ron! Don't be silly! We'll call you Iz-Wiz, as normal – though not in public, of course,' Barbara adds, suddenly looking serious. 'Then we'd call you Miss Bookbinder.'

I'm starting to wonder if Ron and Barbara have got their hands on one of Robert's home-made cigarettes.

'And looking wonderful!' Barbara exclaims, admiring me in my guacamole-stained dress. 'Fabulous hat!'

Trust lovely Barbara to be the one person who understands that this is fashion black.

'Oooh, maybe you could do a line of hats for me as well,' she suddenly adds. 'We'd do ever so well when Ascot comes round.'

I stare at her. 'I'm sorry?'

'Isabel B for Underpinnings!' Barbara beams back. 'Your diversification line! Now, there's no real rush, but I've got several ladies *very* interested already, and I don't want to lose them to any of those snooty boutiques in Bath. There's a couple of new ones opened up this last year, you know, biting into our profit margins . . .' She sighs. 'Anyway, this is really going to help us differentiate ourselves!'

'She's started up a waiting list,' Ron adds proudly. 'All the top stores do it, apparently.'

'Five names already!' Barbara says, taking a Moleskine notebook out of her handbag. 'And with the Christmas party season coming up, I'm very confident there'll soon be more!'

Over their diminutive shoulders, I can see Mum. She's standing on the patio with a large platter of guacamole, pretending to chat to my cousin Felicity. But actually she's looking over here, at me and Ron and Barbara, with an expression of extreme sheepishness on her face.

'So Mum told you I'd make some clothes for you, did she?'

'Oh!' Barbara looks taken aback at my tone of voice. 'No, no, if you're too busy with really important stuff, Iz-Wiz . . . We'd never want to impinge, would we, Ron?'

'Heavens, no!'

Barbara starts to shove her Moleskine back into her bag, flapping her other hand at me in an embarrassed sort of way. 'Really, it was silly of us to assume . . .'

'No, it wasn't.' I grab the notebook before it vanishes into the depths of Barbara's capacious Jane Shilton for ever. 'I'd love to design some clothes for you, Barbara.'

'Really?' Her eyes light up. 'So you do have time?'

'Yes, I have time.' Well, I can't let Ron and Barbara down, can I? Not when they've got their hopes up that this is going to help them fight off the Bath boutique peril. And really, it's sweet of Barbara to have so much faith in me. I'll have to get a bit of a move on with learning a few of those rudimentaries of garment-making, though – unless, of course, Barbara's ladies are a fashion-forward bunch who really appreciate the artistry of my Grecian-style toga dress . . .

'Marvellous!' Barbara is already reaching across to me for the notebook and opening it at the first page. 'Now, Mrs Stedman, she's a real regular of mine, she was wondering if you could do her something . . .' she squints to read her own writing, '. . . *jazzy and modern* for her husband's 70th. She looks ever so nice in soft pastels, Iz-Wiz, so if you can think in terms of powder blue or warm peach, that would work very nicely. And then there's Margaret Huntley-Chambers and her Christmas ball . . . now, she's a huge fan of *Strictly Come Dancing*, so she'd like something a little bit like Gloria Hunniford wore in Season Three. Plenty of corsetry and a few nice ruffles. But I'd go a bit easy on the spangles, if I were you, Iz, because she's a lady of a certain girth, and you know how . . . well, you know how a turkey looks so much bigger once you've wrapped it in the foil . . .'

I'm too appalled to speak. I mean, this isn't Isabel B for Underpinnings! This is a dressmaking service for pensioners!

Pensioners of a certain girth, at that. Who need things like corsetry. And ruffles. Somehow I don't think my one-shouldered toga dresses are going to cut it.

'Um, Barbara . . .'

I'm interrupted by a noise from over by the barbecue. It's Dad, tinkling a fork against a wine glass as he clambers up on to a garden chair. He's wearing his best pompous, I'm-about-to-make-a-speech-maybe-someone-should-record-this-for-posterity face.

'Quiet please, everyone!' he says. 'I hope you're all having a fun day – especially those of you who are shareholders in avocado futures!'

There's a ripple of laughter from Dad's relatives. Mum stares down at her feet and turns pink.

Right. I don't care if I get humongous – I'm going to devour every last bite of that guacamole once Dad's got down off his chair and shut up.

'It's wonderful to be able to welcome you all again this year – and what a year it's been.' Dad is actually pulling a piece of paper out of his shorts pocket. 'Of course, Marley and Daria's wedding back in January was a great start . . .'

Oh, for crying out loud. It's Dad's rehearsal for his Christmas-card round robin. A heart-warming list of Marley and Matthew's assorted achievements, Dad's extensive school news, a tiny mention of Mum's successes in the kitchen or garden, and almost nothing at all about me. I think last year's card simply said, *'Isabel is still living in London.'*

Suddenly, my mobile vibrates with a text message. I'm praying that it's Lara. But it's actually from Nancy.

DHL can't find you!!! Please call Roland back asap. Is v important, Izzie. Lucien can't make any progress w/out the crystal mesh!!!

I look at the message more closely.

Yes, it does say *mesh*.

I'd think it was just a typing error. But *s* isn't even on the same key as *t* on the phone keypad.

And there were all those floaty, lacy, sort of . . . *mesh*-like fabrics on the Mood Board in Nancy's office.

My heart has started to race quite unpleasantly as I step away from Ron and Barbara, dialling Nancy's number. 'Oh, hello, Nancy?'

'Isabel! Thank God! Has the DHL guy found you?'

'No, not yet . . .'

'But he's been calling you! He says he's tried you four times!'

'Yes, sorry, my signal is really variable out here . . . Just one thing, Nancy – this envelope he's coming to get . . . um . . . what's it for?'

143

'For? What do you think it's for?' Nancy sounds pretty irritated; I really think I'm starting to push my luck here. 'A dress! Lucien's making something for Eve Alexander to wear in a couple of weeks, and he wants to put mesh panels in it, so I had Greta Bonneville from One of a Kind send me some terrific black mesh fabric from a damaged Chanel evening coat.'

'Mesh fabric,' I repeat faintly. 'For a dress.'

'Well, what else do you think it'd be for? Christ, Isabel, I'm really starting to have a sense of humour failure here . . .'

'Oh, thank God.'

'Sorry?'

'I mean, thank God you have a sense of humour to lose . . . my old boss didn't have one at all . . . OK, well, see you on Monday, Nancy! Bye!'

This is nowhere near as bad as I thought! I mean, obviously it's not ideal that Roland from DHL is still hunting me down, and I still have to pray that I can find that envelope at Will's. But at least if the worst comes to the worst it'll only be some black lace fabric I have to replace, not five hundred quid's worth of illegal narcotics.

'. . . the imminent arrival of my first grandchild,' Dad is saying, up on his chair. 'Not to mention the wonderful news that I'm about to gain another new daughter-in-law . . .'

There's a ripple of applause, which starts to die away as everyone suddenly turns to stare towards me, Ron and Barbara.

Or, to be more precise, at something happening just behind me, Ron and Barbara.

'Is there a Miss Isabel Bookbinder present?'

I spin round to see who's just spoken. For a split second I think it's going to be Roland, but in fact it's a uniformed police officer. Actually, it's three of them.

'Oh, God,' I croak. 'Lara . . .'

'Who's Lara?' the same policeman says, raising a ginger eyebrow. 'One of your dealers?'

'Sorry?'

He steps forward. 'Isabel Bookbinder, I'm here to arrest you under the Misuse of Drugs Act, 1971. Section four, subsection three b, being concerned in a supply.'

There's a collective gasp from the patio behind me.

'But . . . I haven't done anything . . .'

'A young man called Robert tells us very differently,' the policeman says, in that smug, self-satisfied way the police have. 'We picked him up in the act of buying an extremely large quantity of crystal methamphetamine – a quantity I'm afraid he claims to have been purchasing for you, Miss Bookbinder. He's down at the station now.'

Well, then of course, all hell breaks loose. Auntie Clem starts screeching that I've corrupted her Robert, and Mum starts sobbing incoherent things about addictive personalities and Naomi Campbell. Dad comes over and starts yelling at me until eventually one of the policemen threatens to charge *him* under the Public Order Act, and then Ben and Matthew step in and start trying to calm everyone down. The unidentified child sicks lumpy green stuff all over Uncle Michael's trainers.

And eventually I'm led to the police car on the driveway, and the entire congregation of the Bookbinder Family Barbecue watches as I'm driven away.

Chapter 10

All right. I won't say I actually enjoyed getting arrested. But the reality, at least in practical terms, isn't half as bad as you'd think.

All the way to the police station, I couldn't stop thinking that the moment we arrived I was going to be bundled out with a jacket over my head, while a baying crowd of protesters called for my blood. Followed, obviously, by a terrifying two hours in a stinking, windowless cell while brutish policemen in their shirtsleeves inflicted all kinds of invisible agonies so that, before I knew it, I'd confessed to multiple counts of murder, serious sexual assault and conspiracy to commit terrorism. I mean, you read about that kind of thing all the time – the Guildford Four, the Birmingham . . . Twelve?

Because I'm not sure I'm really cut out for the role of the Shepton Mallet One.

OK, you get to do that glamorous bit on the court steps, when you come out of your trial raising a clenched fist in triumph, quoting a few juicy bits from the Human Rights Act and wearing something sober but beautifully tailored (by Armani?). But I think there's an awful lot of pretty dismal stuff you have to go through before you get to that part – the long years unjustly incarcerated, the tireless campaigning for a retrial – so it's not something I'm in any particular hurry to try out.

Still, I can't help feeling a tiny bit underwhelmed by the reality.

There were no baying protesters calling for my blood, for starters. Which, OK, I was relieved about at first, but after a little while you do start to wonder if anyone even cares that you're here. There's no windowless cell, just a slightly shabby interview room with more of those plastic chairs that make my bottom go all sweaty. Nor are there any invisible agonies. In fact, the worst thing that's been inflicted on me (apart from the plastic chairs) is this ancient copy of *Woman and Home* and this slightly melted KitKat.

And anyway, to be completely fair, the magazine and the KitKat are actually the Shepton Mallet's police force's way of being nice to me. Because the minute I arrived, the desk sergeant took one look at me, turned pale, and said, 'You're Mr Bookbinder's girl, aren't you?'

Well, having the local headmaster as your dad has to give you an advantage sometime. God knows, it didn't exactly make my school years a blast.

Then lots of police constables went into a bit of a huddle, and I heard the desk sergeant saying he hadn't moved hell and high water to get into this catchment area only to have his kid rejected from the best school in the county next May because he'd been the one to charge the headmaster's daughter. And then the stroppy ginger one who arrested me started saying he didn't care if I was the headmaster's daughter; frankly, he didn't care if I was Nelson Mandela's daughter, because I was quite obviously also an evil, drug-pushing criminal mastermind who had laughed in the face of justice for far too long. And then the desk sergeant pointed out that I didn't look so much like I was laughing in the face of justice as quivering in the waiting area of a small-town police station. At which point, the stroppy ginger one got even stroppier and flounced off (probably) to get his fix of inflicting invisible agonies by beating up Robert in a stinking, windowless cell down the hall.

Anyway, once he'd gone off to crack his narcotics ring, everybody else relaxed a bit. The desk sergeant went all kindly and told me his name was Martin, and started asking how I'd got myself into this bit of trouble, then. Which obviously made me go all gulpy and tearful, because that's exactly what happens when somebody is suddenly nice to you in the middle of a horrible situation. And once I'd gone gulpy and tearful, there was no stopping me. I blurted out the whole stupid mix-up with the crystal meth and the crystal-mesh fabric. I gave them a full and frank account of my chat with Robert behind the New Zealand flax bushes. I think I was even contemplating throwing myself at their feet and begging them to *take me, take me instead* when they obviously took pity on me and shut me up.

Then they all huddled a bit more before deciding that the best thing to do was to store me in one of the spare interview rooms and wait for DCI Vernon to get in so he could be the one to decide what to do with me.

DCI Vernon, by the way, just happens to be chairman of the school governors and one of Dad's golfing buddies. Let him be the one who decides whether to incarcerate a Bookbinder or not, you could see them all thinking. We're washing our hands of the whole situation.

So here I am, waiting in an interview room, trying to Cognitively Restructure all this to make it feel less hideously mortifying. All right, so I've just been dragged away by the police at the annual family barbecue in front of all Dad's disapproving relatives. All right, Robert's in trouble, too, only three months after his most recent release from posho borstal, which means that Auntie Clem is going to find a way to blame me, and then, probably, kill me. All right, Ben Loxley now thinks I'm nothing but a sleazy meth-head.

But if I'm forced to look on the bright side, at least I got out of Uncle Michael's Obstacle Quiz.

My phone is ringing for at least the tenth time in the last half-hour, so now that I'm finally alone I can slide it out of my bag and have a look at it. Because the police have rapidly backtracked on the actual arrest thing, they've left me with my personal effects – though in fact, in some ways, I'd rather they hadn't. Because now I can see exactly who it is that's been trying to get hold of me. Roland the DHL man: seventeen missed calls and twenty-three new text messages. Oh, and a very recent text from Nancy herself.

Getting a little concerned, Izzie. Lucien has 2 start work so am making other arrangements for fabric but Roland (DHL) says you have gone totally AWOL. Is there some kind of problem?

OK, I'm going to have to come up with something seriously good here.

Nancy am so sorry!!! I text. *Been dealing with a bit of a*

A what?

disaster.

Now all I need is a convincing disaster that might happen at a boho family barbecue on an organic mead farm.

Oh, I've got it!

Several organic cotton yurts accidentally ignited by spliff-smoking cousin. Only just got inferno under control. Relieved to hear you can make new arrangements for necessary fabric. Again, am very, very sorry. Will personally apologise to Roland.

I check it over and change the word *inferno* to *fire*, in case Nancy thinks it all sounds a bit OTT, before adding a cheery *See you on Monday!* and sending it. Well, Lara always says the way to make people do what you want is just to pretend you're already assuming they're going to do it. If I pretend there's no chance I'm going to get fired for this, hopefully Nancy will believe me.

Which reminds me. Lara. I scan through the barrage of texts to see if any of them are from her, and I'm relieved when I see that one of them is. It was sent a couple of hours after she vanished from the barbecue.

On train

That's *it*? I mean, obviously, I'm incredibly relieved that it's not *hurling myself under train*, but I'd have appreciated a little bit more detail!

R u ok? I text back.

Her reply is almost instant.

Fine. How is Obstacle Quiz?

Fine, she tells me? How is Obstacle Quiz?

Lars am not asking how r u 2 b polite, am asking becos M (love of your life, no?) just got engaged and you did a runner from BBQ!!!

Her reply is slightly less speedy this time.

Told u. Am fine. How is Obstacle Quiz?

Oh, *terrific*. I should have known.

Despite making a professional career out of telling people they shouldn't bottle up their feelings, and that it's OK to admit they're upset, Lara has decided to bottle up her feelings, and refuse to admit she's upset. This is exactly the way she behaved when her parents got divorced (the first time – by the time they'd each moved on to their fourth respective marriage, she was handling it like an old pro). I remember the initial panicky phone call, with poor Lara gasping for breath like she was being throttled, so that even Dad, who answered the phone, was actually concerned enough to drive me over to her house there and then. But what followed, after that first dreadful night, were months and months of Lara pretending everything was just peachy until she suddenly lost it one afternoon in Home Ec and hurled an entire fruit and custard flan at Mrs Elton.

Well, there'll be no remonstrating with her. I'll just have to wait around, colluding with her pretence that everything's fine, until I start to see the signs that she's cracking up. And, maybe, restrict her access to fruit and custard flans while I'm at it.

Didn't make it to Obstacle Quiz I text back. *Got arrested under misuse of drugs act 1971 section four subsection three b, being concerned in a supply.*

It's another quick reply.

Ha ha v funny

Am serious. At police station ri

'Isabel?' DCI Vernon has just stuck his head around the door. His eyebrows shoot up when he sees me. 'It *is* you.'

'Hello, Mr Vernon.' I give him a sheepish wave. 'Yes, it's me.'

'Martin told me John Bookbinder's daughter was in here, but I just couldn't believe it!' He comes further into the room. 'What *have* you been up to, Isabel?'

'Really, Mr Vernon, I haven't done anything wrong. It's my fault Robert got arrested, kind of, but I haven't done anything illegal . . .'

'Yes, I've heard this story about this dressmaking fabric of yours . . .' He gives me a disapproving look over the top of his glasses, but actually, you can tell his heart's not really in it. He's always been a bit of a teddy bear. 'Honestly, Isabel, you do get yourself into some scrapes.'

This is a tiny bit unfair, seeing as the last scrape he actually knows about was the time Dad caught me and Eddie Vernon, the best-looking of DCI Vernon's five sons, sharing a single bottle of Diamond White outside the sports hall during the Christmas disco. Almost thirteen years ago.

'I'm really sorry,' I say, just as my phone bleeps with a text message. 'But you mustn't blame this on Robert,' I add, in a louder voice, to cover up the bleeping. 'He just thought he was doing me a favour.'

Jack Vernon's eyebrows go up once more. 'A favour that also required him to be in possession of six ounces of cannabis, a dealer's quantity of Ecstasy tablets and five stolen credit cards that he was trying to flog for a hundred quid each?'

Shit. 'I didn't know that. But . . . er . . . Robert wouldn't have been out in Shepton Mallet with all that stuff if he hadn't been trying to help me out in the first place.'

'And seeing as how he's on probation, he shouldn't have been carrying all that stuff in the first place. We're going to have to charge him, I'm afraid.'

I bury my head in my hands. Auntie Clem is definitely going to kill me.

'But in your case, I think we can let you go with an informal warning.' Jack Vernon gives me another of his half-hearted disapproving looks over his glasses. 'I'm sure you've learned your lesson.'

'I have. I really have. But Mr Vernon, about Rob . . .'

'I think the best place for you is back at home, Isabel,' he goes on, speaking over me. 'God knows, your dad's been waiting out here long enough.'

'Dad? He's here?'

'Well, of course he is! He's hardly going to sit around enjoying a barbecue when his daughter's been carted off by us lot!' Jack Vernon backs out of the interview room and calls in the direction of the waiting area. 'John? She's free to go.'

'No, really, I think it would be best if I just got a taxi . . .'

But it's too late. Dad's here. Walking up behind Jack Vernon with his arms folded, and his black thundercloud face on.

We drive to Castle Cary station in complete, total silence.

It's the longest eight miles of my life.

Dad floors the accelerator the whole way, which he only does when he's really, really angry, and he shoves the gearstick around like he wishes it was my head.

And I have absolutely no idea what to say. With anybody else, I'd be apologising by now. But I just know that the minute I show the tiniest sign of weakness, he'll leap on it like a dog with a bone. Then before I know it, every single misdemeanour I've committed in my entire life will be paraded in front of me as though all I've done, all I've ever done, is work tirelessly towards the moment when I could be arrested at the Bookbinder Family Barbecue, just to spite my father.

Let's face it, he couldn't be making the whole You Have Shamed Us thing any more obvious. If the stony silence weren't enough, there's also the fact that he's driving me straight to the train station without me even having to ask, a clear message that I'm Not Welcome Over His Threshold. I mean, I'm glad, obviously, that I don't have to go anywhere near his Threshold, to get yelled at for the rest of the evening while Mum weeps and tries to fit leftover avocados into the freezer. But I wouldn't mind *seeing* Mum, just to make sure she's OK.

And I sort of wouldn't mind somebody making sure I'm OK, too.

The stony silence finally breaks as we pull into the deserted car park at Castle Cary train station.

'When you get back to London,' Dad says, in a terse, tight voice that sounds like his vocal cords have been replaced with elastic bands, 'there are some phone calls you need to make.'

'Phone calls?'

'To Auntie Clem, to offer to pay for Robert's solicitor.' Dad ticks this one off on his fingers. 'To Uncle Michael and Auntie Geri, and Uncle Midge and Auntie Aileen, to apologise for ruining the barbecue.'

I'm not sure I'm hearing this right. I've just spent three hours in a police station, and the first thing Dad cares about is making everything OK with his relatives?

'To Matthew and Annie, for overshadowing their big news. I've already told them that I'm sure you'd be happy to pay for their engagement announcement in the *Telegraph*.'

OK. As Lara has told me a million times, I can't control Dad's behaviour; I am only responsible for my own. So I'm not going to do the obvious thing, the thing I'd dearly love to do, and strop off into the night, slamming the car door behind me for good measure. I am going to stay calm, and reasonable, and stick to the facts.

'Dad. Look. I'm really sorry about Robert. But I didn't ask him to go and buy me the drugs. And if he hadn't been caught with stolen credit cards and half a pharmacy in his pocket, he'd have left the police station when I did.'

Dad shoots me a look of intense dislike. After twenty years as a headmaster (and fifty-nine as John Anthony Bookbinder), he can't stand being proven wrong. Which is why it's such a good idea to stick to the facts, because then he can't even fall back on his age-old accusation that I'm being *hysterical* or *childish*.

'And,' I carry on, calmly and reasonably, even though my heart is racing, 'I'm sorry if I embarrassed you. Obviously I didn't intend . . .'

'Embarrassed me? *Embarrassed me?*'

That's done it. I knew I shouldn't have given him an inch.

'I'm *embarrassed*, Isabel, by the fact that every year at the barbecue I have to tell my family that you've started another new career.' He adds a thick layer of derision to the word *career* in pretty much the same way he's added it to *embarrassed*. 'I'm *embarrassed* by the fact that people are still asking me when your novel is coming out, and I have to tell them you've changed your mind about writing, and this week you're trying your hand at some other pointless nonsense, until you get tired of failing at that, too, and flounce off to fail at something else!'

'I don't *fail* at things . . .'

But Dad's on a roll. 'I'm *embarrassed* by the fact that you're nearly twenty-eight, and you haven't got a mortgage, or savings, or any hint of proper financial security,' he carries on, in his iciest voice. 'I'm *embarrassed* by the fact that Marley is married, and Matthew is engaged, but you can't even hold on to a boyfriend for long enough to bring him to a family barbecue.'

'Will had to work,' I manage to mumble. 'That wasn't my fault.'

'So you see, Isabel, I'm quite accustomed to being embarrassed by you. But as for what happened today . . . I mean, *look* at yourself, Isabel. Are *you* proud of yourself? Are *you* proud of where your life is headed?'

'Actually, Dad, I'm really making a go of my fashion career . . .'

Quite suddenly, and with no warning at all, Dad bangs his hand very hard against the steering wheel. 'That's enough!'

We both sit, in complete silence, for a very long moment.

Then I undo my seat belt. 'I've got to get the train,' I say, shakily.

'Isabel . . .'

I open my door and clamber out. 'Tell Mum I'm sorry.'

'Isabel!'

I turn back. I'm sure he's just going to take a final pop at me and all my many failings, but I can't help myself.

He's standing half outside the car himself, now, one foot still in the vehicle, as if he can't quite commit to doing one thing or the other. 'I . . . well . . .' For once in his life, he doesn't seem to know what to say. 'Do you even have enough money for the train?'

I was right. It's a final pop. He thinks I can't even afford a lousy fucking train fare.

I turn away. 'Yes. Of course I can pay for the train.'

But blatantly he has so little faith in me that he doesn't even believe that. Because even after I've bought my ticket, and I'm heading out of the station house on to the platform, his stupid, shiny Volvo is still sitting out there in the car park. Just waiting to see me screw something up again.

*

159

The next train to London is a fifteen-minute wait. It could be a lot worse. I sit down on the deserted platform with a slightly soft, soggy-tasting Boost from the vending machine and start scrolling through the text messages on my mobile.

There's a reply from Nancy: *Thanks 4 message. Like I said, am making other arrangements re fabric but can u bring envelope 2 work on Monday anyway? Glad 2 hear you're OK, despite tragic loss of yurts.*

Does that sound as though she doesn't believe me? *Tragic loss of yurts* sounds sarky to me, but then it's very hard to tell from reading a text message. And at least she's still expecting to see me at work on Monday, so even if she's dubious about my cover story, it hasn't actually compelled her to fire me. I should be grateful for small mercies.

There are also about fifteen text messages from Lara, ranging from *Oh God, you're not joking, are you* to *FFS call me!!! Do I need to come back to SM to bail you out??? Should I try to get hold of Will?*

Will.

Oh, my God, Will.

It's been such a hideous and hectic afternoon that I haven't even thought about him. Which is stupid, apart from anything else, because he's a lawyer, and he could probably have had me out of the police station in about three minutes. Not to mention the fact that he'd cheer me up. I mean, I know things haven't been exactly brilliant between us these last few weeks, but he'd know how to make me feel better about all this.

I glance at the clock on my phone. Seven thirty. The middle of the day in the Cayman Islands. Probably Will's in the middle of a big, important meeting. And I know how much he hates me interrupting him in the middle of big, important meetings. I learned that the first day I tried calling him on his mobile when he was at the office. He picked up all in a panic on my third call in as many minutes, and then got really arsey with me when he found out the reason I was calling was to ask him whether he thought I should have the Pret Super Club for lunch, or the No-Bread Wild Crayfish and Avocado. Which was reasonable, in retrospect, even though the subtext of my question was, quite obviously, to find out whether he thinks I'm a tiny bit fat or not.

But this is different. This isn't about sandwiches, no-bread or otherwise. It's about the fact that I've just been arrested. And the fact that my own father thinks I'm a total failure.

The thing is, I don't remember a single occasion in my life when Dad's actually called me that before. When he caught me drinking that Diamond White with Eddie Vernon at the fifth-form Christmas disco, he just bandied about terms like *disappointed* and *let down*. When he found out that me and Lara had gone clubbing in Bristol when he and Mum thought we were revising for our French oral at Carolyn Duffie's house, he almost went into orbit, but that was more about me being *silly* and *thoughtless*. Even when I pranged Mum's Corsa on the way back from getting my university final results, and he alternated between hollering about the dented bumper and my terrible, shameful 2.2 for most of the next fortnight, he never actually said I'd failed at anything.

Which is why, I think, I suddenly need to hear the sound of Will's voice. So that he can tell me I'm not a failure at all.

I dial his mobile. Straight to voicemail. Damn. *That's* not the way I want to hear the sound of his voice.

I scrabble in my bag for my diary, where I've written down the number of Will's hotel in the Cayman Islands. I dial the huge number of digits, and wait for a receptionist to answer.

'Grand Cayman Courtyard, how may I help you?'

'Oh, could you put me through to Mr Will Madison's room, please? I don't know if he's there . . . or if I could leave a message . . .'

'Certainly, madam. One moment.'

There's a click, then light classical music starts playing, and then another click as the phone is picked up again.

'Hello?'

Hang on a moment. This isn't Will.

It's a woman's voice.

'Oh, I'm sorry, I think I've been put through to the wrong room . . .'

'Who isz thisz?' she asks, in a foreign sort of way.

A *Russian* sort of way?

'I . . . I was trying to get through to Will Madison's room.'

'Yesz, thisz isz Will's room,' she says. 'Can I take message?'

Thisz *isz* Will's room? I mean, this *is* Will's room?

Then what is a Russian-sounding woman doing answering his phone?

'Are you . . . the cleaner?'

'Cleaner?' She sounds offended now, as well as Russian. 'No, I am not cleaner. I am Julia Smirnova. I am colleague.'

Well, OK. Maybe she's just using his room to get some work done, or something. Maybe her own room has been . . . infested by ants. Or maybe she's been disturbed by workmen building the hotel next door. Or . . .

'Will isz asleep juszt now,' she adds, in a lower voice. 'But isz right here. I can wake him if it isz emergency.'

'He's . . . asleep? Right there? With . . . beside . . . you?'

In the middle of the day?

But Will never sleeps in the middle of the day. Not even, as I so often urge him to do, for a power nap. The only time he's ever slept in the middle of the day is . . . well . . .

Post . . .

I can hardly even say it.

Coitally.

'Yesz, he isz asleep. And I wasz asleep, too,' Julia adds, slightly shirtily, I have to say, for a woman who's asleep next to someone else's boyfriend.

163

'So you're just there, in bed . . . *together*?'

'Of course we are!' She sounds really irritated now. 'We are on working trip! What elsze do we do in afternoon?'

I can't speak.

'If you give me name and number, I tell Will to phone you back. If he hasz time,' Julia is going on, in a hushed tone, as if Will is the President of the United States, or something, and mustn't have his precious sleep disturbed at all costs.

'Right.' Somehow, I manage to control my voice. 'Well, *if he has time*, can you let him know that Isabel called?'

'Iszabel, OK. And will he know who you are?'

That's it. I hang up.

Then I start to cry. Great big shuddery tears. Making my Boost bar soggier than ever.

~~Dear Will~~
~~Dear Lying, Cheating~~

Will,

When you return from your 'business trip' to the Cayman Islands, it probably won't take you very long to notice that I don't seem to be living in your flat any more. It probably also won't take you very long to notice that I have put several of your favourite blue shirts in the bath and spritzed them liberally with Flash Bleach Spray. You see – I *did* know where we kept the household cleaning products all along.

Still, I'm sure you and Julia will easily be able to afford an entire new wardrobe of blue shirts, so I wouldn't worry too much about it. The pair of you can sit around, toasting each other with fine wine and congratulating yourselves on your enormous salaries and your world-shattering tax-law prowess – that's absolutely fine by me. If I could just put in one small request, ~~as I think is the right of a wronged woman~~ *please do not do all this while wearing fur.* Countless small, adorable creatures should not have to die in agony simply to satisfy ~~that brazen hussy's~~ your new girlfriend's desire to congratulate herself on her genius while wearing mink-trimmed lingerie. ~~I can always set PETA on you, you know. And then bleached shirts will be the least of your troubles~~. Please, Will. Think of the animals.

I will be staying at Lara's until I find a new flat, so please forward my post there.

I know you think I'm just a silly little fool, Will.

Everybody thinks it. But I'm not. And I can't believe
you've tried to treat me like one.

~~Yours, furiously~~

~~Yours, in disgust and~~

No longer Yours,

Isabel

THE *SUNDAY TIMES* MAGAZINE

THE BEST OF TIMES, THE WORST OF TIMES

This week, Top International Fashion Designer Isabel Bookbinder talks about the Darkest Day of her life, and how it spurred her on to new heights of success far beyond ~~that which anybody else thought her capable~~ her wildest dreams.

I thought I'd had Dark Days before, but that particular Saturday in September was the Darkest. Having been arrested for a crime I did not commit, then told by my father in no uncertain terms just what a useless waste of space he really thinks I am, the last thing I needed to happen was to find out that my boyfriend, Will [Madison, one of the infamous Cayman Two, now serving ten years in a Caribbean jail for Crimes Against Tax], had been cheating on me.

When Julia [Smirnova, ringleader of the Cayman Two, now ~~also serving ten~~ serving life in a Caribbean jail for Crimes Against Tax and Crimes Against Minks] answered the phone in Will's hotel room, I felt like my entire world was falling apart. My Boost bar did, in fact, actually fall apart, leaving a soggy, messy chocolate stain on my black dress, not to be discovered until later. Somehow, I managed to make it back to the flat Will and I had shared in Battersea, where I ~~shovelled all my worldly goods into fifteen black bin-liners~~ packed up my things in a quiet and dignified manner before calling a taxi to take me to my best friend Lara's, near Westbourne Grove.

At this point, the Dark Day became a Dark Night. I think this might have been something to do with the quantity of brandy we drank (I would have preferred wine, but Lara insisted on brandy, and as she's the one burying all her feelings and storing them up for some sort of flan-flinging incident along the line, I didn't like to disagree) as we sat out on her undemised roof terrace. Although this started out well, with positive declarations along the lines of men being the real wastes of space, and plans made to find some kind of local Feminist group to channel all our new-found anti-male anger, things swiftly degenerated. I believe the Darkest Point came some time before two in the morning, when I dimly recall, through a haze of unstoppable tears, finding the melted Boost stain on my dress. At that point, I am ashamed to say, ending it all really felt like the only viable option.

In the cold light of day, and with one of those horrible sick-feeling hangovers that makes you need to eat vast quantities of toast, I sat in Lara's spare 'room' and thought hard about my life. Arrested, belittled, and cheated on, I knew that something had to change. I think it was there and then that I made the decision that has spurred me on ever since: to Show Them All.

I threw myself into my new job with a passion and fire I'd never experienced before. From humble beginnings, as PA to Top International Muse Nancy Tavistock, I soon rose to become her right-hand woman. After that, it was only a matter of time before I was also to become Lucien Black's right-hand woman. The day that Lucien Black offered me the job of creating his diffusion line, I seized the chance. Only a few months after that, and after glowing reviews from the fashion press, including Scary Anna Wintour ~~and that one with the big quiff~~, I left Lucien Black with the full support of both him and Nancy, to set up my own label. The rest is history.

(Isabel Bookbinder's new fragrances, ~~Dark Day, by Isabel Bookbinder, and Dark Night For Men, by Isa~~ Jour Noir, d'Isabel Bookbinder, and Nuit Noir (Pour Homme), d'Isabel Bookbinder, are available now.)

Chapter 11

You know what they say, that what doesn't kill you makes you stronger? Well, that's probably the reason I was up and about with the lark this morning. Channelling all my efforts into putting together that all-important Signature Look for my first day on the job as a fully-fledged *Atelier* girl and Top Fashionista.

I mean, this is a whole new league I'm playing in. These are girls – *women*, Isabel, *women*; you're a feminist now – who think nothing of blowing three months' salary on a Zagliani python-skin handbag. Women who would sell their grandmother for a vintage YSL 'smoking' (I must remember to look up what a 'smoking' actually *is*). Women who regularly use a dozen different words for *brown*.

So my Signature Look now consists of:

1) Indigo denim straight-leg trousers (NOT jeans) from Paper Denim & Cloth that make me look almost half a size smaller than I really am, *and* make my bottom look a little bit like Jessica Alba's;

2) A crisp white shirt, unbuttoned as far as is decent, to draw attention *towards* my nice, slim collarbones, and *away from* the evidence that I

might actually have eaten anything this calendar month;

3) My brand-new black blazer from Reiss that's going to make me swelter in this Indian summer heat, but will display to my new colleagues that I'm aware of the fact that you don't just keep wearing summer clothes because it feels like summer, you get right on the A/W horse and to hell with any sweltering;

4) Brown (chocolate? mocha? raw umber?) platform loafers from LK Bennett that are loafery enough to make me look as though I'm not making too much of an effort, but platformy enough that I don't think I'll fall foul of any Anna Wintour-esque rules about minimum heel heights in the office; and

5) My emerald-green Mikkel Borgessen clutch bag that may barely have room for my mobile, credit card and lipstick, but is the only Top Designer handbag I own, and is so beautiful that it can introduce dangerous frenzies of lust in even the most die-hard Zagliani owner.

I think it works.

I hope it works.

Because it's almost nine, and I'm due at the office in ten minutes, and I haven't got time to change anything now.

I'm just queuing up for my coffee at Starbucks on High Holborn (sorry, Barney) when my mobile starts ringing. I snap open my clutch, not missing the little sigh of envy from the woman standing behind me, and see who it is calling.

It's Mum.

She called me several times yesterday, but I didn't answer. Then Lara pointed out that she might well be working herself into a panic about me OD-ing somewhere in a needle-riddled squat, so I sent her a quick text, telling her that everything was fine and we'd speak tomorrow.

'Mum?'

'Oh, *Isabel*. Oh, *darling*.'

I let her hiccup and sniffle for a minute, before saying, as I pick up my coffee and hurry out into the street, 'Mum, you really don't need to react like this, honestly. This whole drugs thing was all just a big mistake.'

'Oh, I'm so glad you realise that, darling!'

'No, I mean it was all a big misunderstanding. The police let me go without charge!'

'That's good,' says Mum, in a way that suggests she's not really listening. 'Now, I do want you to know, darling, that I'm not angry with you.'

'Great, but look, Mum, I'm actually in a bit of a rush . . .'

'Well, I suppose I *am* angry with you, just a little bit,' she goes on, 'but that doesn't change the fact that you have . . . wait a moment . . . my *total and unconditional love and support* over these next difficult few weeks.'

Why should the next few weeks be difficult? 'Mum,

I don't know what Dad told you, but I have absolutely *not* agreed to pay Auntie Clem's solicitor's bills. Now, I will apologise to Matthew and Annie, but . . .'

'I'm so glad, Iz-Wiz. It's very important that you start making amends.'

'Amends?'

'Yes, darling. It's a critical part of the process, I gather.'

'Process?' I'm starting to feel like a parrot, but I really have no idea what Mum is wittering on about.

'The rehab process, Isabel! What on earth do you think I mean? Now, I don't know if you'll be wanting to find yourself somewhere in London, or whether you'd prefer to come back down to Somerset . . . I was on the Internet all day yesterday, and there are quite a few nice-looking treatment centres around here, actually – I was surprised, but then Barbara reminded me about all those druggie types who hang out near Glastonbury – so why don't I pop a few of the brochures in the post when they get here and you can see if anywhere takes your fancy?'

'Mum! I don't need rehab!'

'Are you sure, darling? You know, there's no stigma in it these days. Especially not in your profession. And apparently an awful lot of really productive networking gets done at the Priory . . .'

'No, Mum! Not even the Priory!' I'm right outside the Mediart building now, which means I'm getting all kinds of funny looks from people going in. Well, funny looks from some, *knowing* looks from others. I think Mum could be right about the networking. 'Look, for the millionth time, this was a misunderstanding. Now, I've got a really big day today, so can I just please go to work without you worrying about me?'

'Work?'

'Yes, work. My internship. I told you about it on Saturday, remember?'

'Oh, yes, I'd forgotten . . . Oh, Iz-Wiz, does this internship mean you'll still have time to do that range for Underpinnings that Barbara suggested?'

'That *you* suggested, surely, Mum.'

'Well, forgive me for trying to give your career a push in the right direction!'

'My career is already going in the right direction! This job . . . I mean, internship . . . could lead to really big things for me, you know.'

'Oh.' Mum is sounding worried. 'So you *won't* have time to do the range for Underpinnings?'

I sigh. 'I'll have time, Mum, OK?'

Because despite the fact that Barbara and Ron's selection of 'ladies' may not exactly be the ideal Women I'd Design For, I can hardly let them down now, can I? I'll just have to make sure I get around to mugging up on a few of those rudimentaries of garment-making beforehand, so that I can at least stitch a good strong seam or two, even if I can't actually produce a full-blown corset.

'That's good, darling. Because . . . well, I wouldn't normally say something like this to you, but I really

174

think it's important that you see this Underpinnings range through. Your father . . .'

'Yes, Mum, I already know that Dad thinks I fail at everything I turn my hand to. He told me on Saturday.'

'What? Oh, no, no, darling, he doesn't think that! No, all I meant was that I think it would be nice to be able to have something . . . well, something *concrete*, to prove . . . I mean, to show . . .' She's sounding flustered. 'But I don't want you to feel any pressure, darling! Not when you've been having these substance-abuse problems . . .'

I give up. 'Look, Mum, I really have to go. Call me later, OK?'

'All right. At home?'

'No! No, I mean, not at home . . .' I think, perhaps, it's best not to tell her about Will just at the moment. 'On my mobile. Or I'll call you. Oh, and lovely barbecue, thanks, Mum. Fantastic guacamole.'

'Really, Iz-Wiz?'

'Really, Mum. Bye!'

Walking through the revolving doors of the Mediart building was one of the best experiences of my life. I mean, it felt just like I was in a shower-gel commercial, or something advertising daily disposable contact lenses. There were all these incredibly stylish, fabulous people hurrying through the lobby, more bouncy blow-dries than you could shake a stick at, and the world's best-looking security guards flirting with me as they gave me my temporary security pass. It was completely brilliant!

But that was over an hour ago. And ever since then . . . well, I won't lie. It hasn't been especially brilliant. Not very brilliant at all.

First of all, it took me about three minutes to realise that I've managed to wear completely the wrong outfit. Everybody else has shot ahead of the seasons and is wearing next year's Spring/Summer – evidently, vintagey tea dresses and pastel capri pants (that'll be something to look forward to). In my straight-leg trousers and my black jacket, I feel like a hopeless fashion civilian, not to mention slightly sweaty.

But that isn't the only reason that things haven't been quite as much fun as I'd hoped. It's Lilian. I'd been hoping that maybe I'd just caught her on a bit of an off day when I came for my interview last week, but it turns out that I didn't. For the last hour and a half, while I wait for Nancy to get in, she's been doing my office induction. I've had office inductions before, and obviously they're pretty dull at the best of times, but Lilian has really raised (or lowered?) the bar.

I mean, you'd think that an office induction at *Atelier* would take in a tour around the fashion cupboard and a brief rundown of the best local sushi retailers. But no. Since nine fifteen this morning, I have learned that:

1) Documents of less than twenty pages can be stapled with my small, black stapler, whereas

documents of more than twenty pages must be stapled with my large, red stapler;

2) Phone messages of low importance should be recorded on the plain white message pad, whereas phone messages of high importance must be recorded on the pink message pad;

3) The key to the stationery cupboard is held by Lilian, who will die under torture rather than reveal its whereabouts (I embellish, but not much), and requests for items from said cupboard must be made in writing no less than three hours in advance, and countersigned by Nancy;

4) Technical Support is on extension 312, Maintenance on extension 213, the post room on extension 123; and

5) Any mistake I make in contacting one of the above when I was meant to be contacting another of the above will cause my phone to spontaneously combust and blow us all to kingdom come (OK, OK, I embellish big-time, but I'm starting to crack here).

To be perfectly honest, right now the only thing I want to use the stapler for is to staple my own earlobes up over my ears, to block out the sound of Lilian's voice.

'. . . now, let me run you through the procedure for using the photocopiers,' she's saying, leading me to a small, walled-in area featuring a couple of large photocopiers and an annoying electronic hum. 'The smaller photocopier is fine for ordinary black-and-white copies, but you'll need to use the larger one if you're photocopying in colour. Now, when you want to photocopy in colour, come and find me at my desk, and ask me for the start-up code for the colour photocopier . . .'

OK. This is my limit.

I mean, I need to know about far more than photocopiers, if I'm going to cut it as a Top Fashionista! Nancy will be here any minute now, and my office induction won't have taught me any of the things I really need to know!

'Wow, Lilian, you know, this has all been really great!' I beam at her, so as not to look negative. 'But actually, I'm already pretty good with photocopiers. I've used them at all my jobs before!'

Lilian stares at me. 'But you haven't used one here.'

'Yes, I know, but a photocopier is a photocopier, isn't it?' I give a little laugh. 'And I'm sure there are a lot more things I'm going to need to know about this job that only a *real insider* like you can tell me!'

'Like what?' she asks suspiciously.

'Well, like what heel height the editor prefers us to wear around the office. I mean, is there some kind of minimum-height requirement? Or is it just OK as long as you're not wearing actual flats?'

Lilian frowns. 'I . . . don't think Claudia has any kind of rule about shoes.'

'Well, not an *actual* rule, perhaps. More like an unspoken one.'

'Not even that.'

OK. Clearly poor Lilian is so busy with her stapler etiquette and her photocopier protocols that she's not had time to pick up all the really important details about working here. 'Carbohydrates, then. Are they completely banned, or is it OK to get away with the occasional sandwich?'

'Isabel, I honestly have no idea what you're talking about.' Lilian pushes her glasses back up her nose. 'Have you worked at some seriously weird places before, or something?'

I give up. I'll just have to find all this stuff out from somebody a bit more clued-up later. 'Yes. I've worked at some weird places. That's it.'

She gives a small smile of triumph. 'Ah! Then probably you *don't* know all that much about the correct way to use the photocopier! Now, our system lives or dies on people remembering to report a worn-out ink cartridge, so . . .'

Oh, thank God. Her mobile is going.

'It's Claudia. I need to take this.'

'Oh,' I flap a hand, 'please do.'

'Why don't you go and settle yourself down at your desk? Familiarise yourself with a few of the things I was talking to you about earlier?'

'Absolutely! Those staplers won't work themselves!'

Chapter 12

As Lilian dashes off to her (no doubt) stationery-related emergency, I escape from the photocopy area, looking as if I'm heading back to my desk over by Nancy's office. But I've got no intention of doing anything of the sort. This is my very first morning, for heaven's sake! I don't want to get a reputation for being the office saddo, sitting at my desk with my brace of staplers and my message pad, in the wrong height heels with the wrong choice of lunch food. I'm never going to work my way up in the fashion industry if I make a start like that!

I stride out, as confidently as I can, into the main open-plan area of the office. It's filled up since I first arrived, with lots of people sitting at their desks, on the phone or glued to their computer screens. Obviously, this all looks a tiny bit boring from the outside. But they're probably on the phone *to Kate Moss*, to book her for a bikini shoot in Mexico. And glued to their computers *emailing Stella McCartney*, to ask for a rush delivery of her latest ethical stilettos, and wasn't it nice to run into her at Zuma the other night.

There are a couple of girls standing very close by.

One of them, dressed in her own version of a vintage tea dress (thigh-high and teamed, inexplicably, with a kind of nurse's cape) is packing up an extremely large suitcase. The other, wearing pale pink capri pants and a vest top, with toweringly high wedges (yeah, right, Lilian, there isn't a rule about heels!), is ticking things off on a clipboard. She glances up and gives me a quick smile as I approach. 'Hi. Wow. I love your bag.'

Now, this is more like it. I beam at her. 'Thank you! And I love your . . . vest!'

Oh. Actually, that sounds a bit weird. *Shoes*, Isabel. Next time, say *shoes*.

'Um . . . is it vintage?'

'Nope.' She's looking at me strangely. 'Topshop.'

'Ah.' I nod knowledgeably. 'Topshop. Of course. I never buy my vests anywhere else.'

'Oh. Right.'

Oh, God, have I just committed some terrible fashionista faux pas? Has this marked me out as an imbecile? Or worse – a *civilian*?

'Except for the ones I buy at C&C California, of course,' I go on hastily. 'And . . . um . . . American Apparel.' Oh, Christ, where are the cool places to buy vests from? 'Rick Owens!' I suddenly yelp. 'Brilliant vests at Rick Owens . . .'

Now she's just staring at me like I'm completely insane. 'Do you *collect* vests, or something?'

'Oh, no, no! I just take an interest. In vests. As in all matters of fashion.'

'So are you work experience?' the girl asks, the

181

unspoken question *or do I need to call security?* lingering in the air between us.

'Oh, no, I'm Nancy's new PA. I'm Isabel!'

'Ohhh. So you're the one who's replacing Ruby?'

'That's right!'

'We've heard all about you!' she says. 'Is Bianca Jagger really your godmother?'

Shit.

'Godmother . . . style inspiration . . . humanitarian,' I say vaguely, flapping a hand. 'Sorry, I didn't catch your names?'

'Oh, sorry – I'm Cassie, and this is Elektra.'

'Cassie. Elektra,' I say, repeating their names in that way you're meant to when you first meet new people, so you don't forget them. (As if I'm ever going to forget a name like Elektra.) 'Looking forward to working with you!'

'Oh, you probably won't, much,' says Cassie. 'You'll be with Nancy most of the time, and we're the fashion assistants, so we're out of the office a lot.' She nods at the suitcase. 'We're just packing things for a shoot in the Nevada desert.'

'Wow. Lucky you!'

'Yeah, right.' Cassie rolls her eyes. 'Eighteen hours' travelling with five heavy suitcases, just to stand around for two days in the blazing heat trying to squeeze Eve Alexander into size-six hot pants. Lucky us.'

Eve Alexander? So is this what the crystal-mesh-panel dress is for?

'Will the Lucien Black dress be finished in time for the shoot, do you know?' I ask casually.

Cassie frowns. 'I don't think we're taking anything by Lucien Black. Are we, Elektra?'

'Oh, fuck.' Elektra stands up, red in the face, and pushes a sweaty strand of black hair out of her eyes. 'Are there meant to be Lucien Black things in here? Didn't you check with Tania that all the samples were in?'

'Yes, I checked with Tania! She didn't say a word about any Lucien Black stuff!' Cassie looks like she's about to start crying. 'Oh, God, I'm going to have to wake Tania again. What time is it in Vegas now?'

'No, hang on! Don't call Tania!' God, I seem to have accidentally caused an international incident here. 'I was only asking because I thought Lucien Black was making something special for Eve Alexander. I'm sure it's not for this photo shoot.'

Cassie stares at me. 'Something special?'

'Yes. A cocktail dress, I think. With crystal-mesh panels.' I enunciate very clearly, just so there's no silly confusion.

'Oh. Well, our shoot is based around a kind of Rollergirl Lolita look.'

'Right,' I nod, as though I know what she's talking about. 'Rollergirl Lolita. Fabulous.'

'Hot pants, sun visors . . . A cocktail dress sounds much more like something Eve needs for an event.' Cassie looks at Elektra for confirmation. 'Doesn't it?'

Elektra nods. 'Yeah. I think so. And come on, Cass,

how likely do you think it is that Tania would've agreed to have a single piece of new-season Lucien Black in this shoot?'

Cassie pulls a face. 'You're right. Or that Eve would agree to wear it.'

Well, this is a bit weird. What does this Tania woman have against Lucien Black's clothes? And why on earth would Eve Alexander refuse to wear them? She's the face of Lucien Black. She's starred in his ad campaigns for the last two years!

'Is Eve Alexander really difficult, then?' I ask the two girls, hoping for a juicy bit of top celebrity gossip.

'Oh, no, she's a total sweetheart,' Cassie begins. '*So* much nicer than most people we work with. Like . . .'

'Cassie? Elektra?'

Oh, God, it's Lilian, heading our way.

'Claudia wants to start the fashion meeting fifteen minutes early this morning,' she announces. 'Can you head in there now?'

Cassie and Elektra both look incredibly stressed again. 'Does she want to see the inventory?'

'Just take what you've already done,' Lilian tells them. 'But really, girls, shouldn't you have finished it by now?'

I'm slightly thrilled to see Cassie and Elektra shooting Lilian evil glances as they scurry off towards the editor's office at one end of the room, especially when Lilian turns to me, folding her arms in an officious manner.

'Isabel, you should be at your desk! I've had two

calls come through for Nancy already, and I'm the one who's had to take them!'

'I'm sorry, Lilian. I'll call them right back after the fashion meeting.'

'You don't need to come to the fashion meeting.'

'Well, that's nice of you, but I really do want to try to do all the extras, at least in my first few days . . .'

Lilian puts her hands on her hips. 'I *mean*, you don't come to the meeting. You're just a PA, Isabel. PAs don't attend fashion meetings.'

'Oh.' This is a big disappointment. 'But Nancy's not here yet. I mean, what if she needs me to take notes for her, or something?'

'She won't.' Lilian hands me two message slips (white, not pink, so clearly far from urgent). 'Can you just deal with these two calls, Isabel? Please?'

'Of course. I'm sorry. I'll deal with them both right away.'

Back at my desk outside Nancy's office, I look at the two slips she's given me. OK, what's this first one? Jasmine? Oh, God, isn't *Jasmine* the name of the girl I heard Ruby chatting to on the phone the other day? Something to do with letting her know when the crystal-mesh delivery came in? Well, seeing as all she's asking for, according to Lilian's note, is for Nancy to call her back as soon as she's in the office, I think I'll just pass that message on.

Besides, the next message is much more exciting!

Lucien Black. Time of call: 10.32 a.m. Please call him back at studio.

Well, obviously, I have to call him right back. He's trying to get hold of Nancy, his business partner, and despite Lilian's choice of the white message pad, it could very well be urgent. Some emergency Museing, perhaps.

I glance down the list of numbers Blu-tacked to the side of the computer until I see the number for Lucien's studio in Spitalfields.

Somebody picks up at his end after about eight rings. 'Nance?'

'No, actually, this is Nancy's assistant. My name's Isabel. Am I speaking to Lucien Black?'

'Yes, but . . . sorry? Who did you say you were?'

I've heard him speak once before, a quick sound bite backstage at a fashion show on some Sky News London Fashion Week special. But now the cameras are off, his Belfast accent sounds a lot rougher around the edges. It makes him sound quite sexy, actually.

'Isabel Bookbinder. Nancy's new assistant.'

'But where's Nancy?'

'Nancy's not here just yet, Mr Black. But if there's anything . . .'

The noise that comes next is so violent that I wonder, for a split second, if my phone *can* self-combust after all. *'How is that even possible?'*

'I . . . er . . .'

'She left here almost an hour ago!'

I adopt my most soothing tone of voice. 'Well, it can take longer than that to get across London, sometimes, on a Monday morning.'

Now there's an icy silence. 'Are you some kind of traffic reporter?'

'No, I'm not . . .'

'Are you the eye in the sky? Do you have permanent access to satellite signals?'

OK. I can handle this. So he's sounding a lot less like an *enfant terrible* and more like . . . well, more plain old terrible. But he's just being temperamental. All creative geniuses are temperamental. 'No, Mr Black, I just meant . . . look, is there anything I could help you with?'

'I doubt it, darling.' The *darling* isn't a term of endearment. 'I need Nancy.'

I'm going to give this another shot. 'Well, I may not be Nancy, Mr Black, but if it's some kind of . . . er . . . inspiration you're after, maybe I can help?'

'Inspiration?'

'Well, like an inspirational word for your Mood Board, perhaps? Because actually, I've got quite a lot of those, if you'd be interested in borrowing one.'

This is the point at which he's supposed to say, *really? You're a designer, too?* But he doesn't. He doesn't say anything.

'For example, a word I've used quite recently is *Pretty*.' He doesn't need to know how disparaging Diana Pettigrew was about that one. 'Or *City*, perhaps – I don't know if you're interested in microfibre T-shirts and combat trousers . . . um . . .' I'm loath to give up *Slinky*. 'Hang on, I'm sure I have more . . .'

'Toaster.'

'Sorry?'

'Toaster,' he repeats. 'I don't know what all this *city* nonsense is you're wittering about, but the only word I'm interested in right now is toaster.'

The Toaster Collection?

But what kind of clothes would that involve? Things that . . . give you muffin tops?

Well, he's the creative genius.

'I *think* that could work,' I begin.

'It doesn't work! That's the whole fucking point!' He's exploded again. 'That's why I'm trying to get hold of Nancy, you stupid wench! Because the fucking toaster doesn't work, and nobody else is around yet to go and get me anything, and I'm bloody starving, and there's nothing to eat here but a loaf of bread, and I can't even fucking toast it!'

Ohhh.

OK. This is embarrassing.

Though I have to say, not quite as embarrassing as a grown man throwing a temper tantrum because he can't work the office toaster. Or calling up his business partner to have a go at her about it.

But, thank God, not a moment too soon, Nancy is walking along the corridor towards me.

Actually, make that stalking.

And it's not just an ex-supermodel, hips-front, hand-on-hip kind of stalk, which I suspect is her default movement style, even up and down the aisles of Tesco. It's also an incredibly bad-tempered, had-enough-of-all-this-and-it's-not-even-lunchtime-

188

yet kind of stalk.' Her shoulders, broad and bony in a rather stunning halter-neck gingham prom dress, are hunched up so far they're actually touching her signature chandelier earrings, and a deep frown is clearly visible behind her Oliver Peoples sunglasses. In addition to her peacock-blue Tavistock bag, a black garment bag is slung over one shoulder like it's something foul she's taking out to put in the rubbish.

She looks gorgeously Amazonian, and absolutely terrifying.

Oh, *God*. Is she going to turn out like my last boss, Katriona de Montfort – all sweetness and light when you first meet her, only to turn into a raving madwoman the moment you start work? Was that nice text message she sent on Saturday just a ruse to lure me into the office so she could rail at me about the crystal-mesh bugger-up after all?

Feeling a little bit sick, I jump to my feet. 'Nancy! I've got Lucien on the phone . . .'

'Oh, God.' She whips off her sunglasses and stares at me with sunken eyes. She looks like she hasn't slept all weekend. 'Has he just heard, too?'

'I don't think he's . . . um . . . *heard* anything. He's calling about his toaster.'

Nancy blinks. 'About his what?'

'Well, I think he's trying to make breakfast, and . . .'

Nancy suddenly swoops in, very, very close. 'Is he *drunk*?' she hisses.

'I don't know,' I hiss back, feeling a bit like I've ended up in a wartime spy movie rather than a glamorous magazine office. 'He doesn't sound drunk.'

'Is he slurry?' Nancy demands, seemingly forgetting I've got the receiver *right here* in my hand, about four inches away from her mouth. 'Incoherent?'

'No, no, he's . . .' I lower my own voice to a whisper, 'more, well, snappy. And impatient.'

'Oh, thank God.' Nancy stalks past me and into her office. 'That means he's sober. Put him through.'

Put him through? I stare down at my large, multi-buttoned phone, trying to remember what Lilian might have mentioned about transferring calls. 'Nancy has just arrived, Mr Black,' I say into the receiver, stabbing hopefully at my Line 2 button. 'I'm putting you through!'

Or, in fact, cutting him off.

'Where's he gone?' Nancy stares at me through the open door, waggling her phone.

'I'm really sorry . . . my fault . . .'

'Don't worry about it,' Nancy sighs, but kindly, already starting to dial herself. 'I'll call him back. Can you just come in here and hang this up?' She holds up the garment bag.

'Of course!' I spring into action. 'Where should I put it?'

'Just on the back of the door there . . . Lucien?' she suddenly says into the phone. 'Hi, it's me . . . Jesus, Lucien, am I not even allowed to stop off for a coffee en route? . . . Oh, come on, Lucien, it's her first day, be reasonable . . . *No*, she's not an idiot . . .'

I deliberately turn away from Nancy and hang the

garment bag up on the back of the wardrobe, so that she doesn't see my burning cheeks.

'. . . *that's* what you're calling about? Jeez, Lucien, don't you think we have bigger things to worry about than your breakfast? . . . All right, all right . . .' Nancy is speaking patiently enough, but the hammering of her fingers against her desktop gives her away. 'Well, have you plugged it in? . . . Well, have you switched it on at the wall? . . . *There* we go.'

Keen to look useful now after my poor start, I start making all kinds of elaborate *shall-I-go-and-get-you-a-coffee* mimes at Nancy, but she shakes her head and performs her own, more minimalist mime. I think it's an instruction for me to come in and have a seat on the sofa.

'Anyway, Lucien, we need to talk about something else,' Nancy is going on, starting to chew her top lip with her bottom teeth. 'Debs called me just after I left you . . . no, it's not good news, Selfridges have come back with a definite no, too . . . no, they don't want to order a single piece . . . not even the jacket . . .'

I pick up a copy of the most recent *Atelier* that's sitting on the glass coffee table and start to flick through it, just to show Nancy that I'm not earwigging on what sounds to me like a very private conversation.

I mean, am I understanding this right? That Selfridges aren't stocking any new-season Lucien Black?

But they've got a whole area especially for Lucien Black! In the SuperBrands section, next to Alexander

McQueen. A big one, too – I know, because it's big enough to hide behind racks of clothing to prevent the assistant spotting you, decreeing you too hopelessly uncool even to browse there, and dispatching you unceremoniously up the nearby escalators to Jigsaw, where you really belong.

'Yes, Lucien, I know you have to be true to your vision . . . well, yes, I do think they're going to have something to say about it at the meeting today . . . well, would *you* want to invest in us at the moment?' She lets out a long, heavy sigh. 'No, it's OK, I'll find a way to make it sound better than it really is . . . you go and have your toast . . . speak later.' Nancy hangs up.

And then she picks up her Tavistock bag and hurls it against the wall.

We both stare at it, and its strewn contents, in a slightly startled silence.

Well, I have absolutely no idea what to say at this point. What would a proper PA do? Suggest a nice, soothing cup of tea? Make reassuring noises, and rub Nancy's shoulders? Go and pick up the nine-hundred-pound handbag and start putting things back in it?

Yes. That feels right. I mean, Tavistock bags are like works of art, practically. You can't just leave them lying about on the floor.

I get up from the sofa and crouch down next to the bag, picking up the scattered lipsticks, Polo mints, a Vertu phone, worry beads . . .

'No, Izzie, let me do that,' Nancy suddenly says, coming over to help. 'I apologise. What must you

192

think of me? And on your first morning, too!'

'Oh, don't worry about it! I told you, I used to work for Katriona de Montfort! She did *much* barmier things than . . .' I stop myself, just in time. 'I mean . . . I didn't mean . . .'

'Hey, it's OK.' Fortunately, Nancy has raised a smile. 'I *am* acting a little crazy. It's been a bad morning.' She stands up and slings the bag, more gently this time, to land on the sofa. 'You've probably gathered that Selfridges have decided not to stock anything from the new collection. I mean, it's just disaster after disaster after disaster right now.' She throws her head back, unleashing her impressive cascade of raven-black hair, and rubs her temples with her fingers. 'Fashion Week, the aftershow party, clients pulling out . . .'

I feel like I should say something upbeat and supportive. 'I'm sure things will get better soon!'

'Yeah, but will they get better soon *enough*?' Nancy lets out a weary sigh. 'OK. This has to stay confidential for the moment, Izzie, but now you're working for me, I should tell you about this deal I'm working on.'

'Deal?' Oh, I remember Ruby saying something about a big deal to her mother on the phone. Clearly she didn't take the confidentiality bit all that seriously.

Nancy reaches for her cigarettes. 'We're in the middle of negotiations to sell the majority of our shares to this investment group.' She lights her cigarette and offers one to me, but I refuse. 'Yeah,

yeah, I know, no smoking indoors, but it helps with the stress. Shut the door, will you, hon, and then it can be our little secret.'

'It does sound incredibly stressful,' I say, pushing the door shut. I mean, what is wrong with the woman? Hasn't she got the best job in the entire world without having to go around setting up investment deals? It sounds almost as boring as tax law, for heaven's sake!

'Tell me about it.' Nancy blows out a long puff of smoke. 'It's been almost a year since Redwood came to us with their offer of investment, and it's just been one long headache ever since. Believe me, if we could afford to turn down this amount of money . . . and the expansion opportunities it's going to give us . . . I mean, we could have a Lucien Black fragrance line, Izzie! We can open up stores in America!'

'Ohhhh.' Well, now it's making a lot more sense. 'It sounds like a completely brilliant idea!'

'You'd think,' she says, with a raised eyebrow, 'wouldn't you? It's just a pity Lucien doesn't seem to see it that way any more.'

'He's changed his mind? About a fragrance line? But isn't that . . . like . . . the pinnacle of fashion design achievement?'

Nancy gives me a slightly odd look. 'Well, it would certainly be a useful money-spinner. And like I keep trying to tell Lucien, if we just have a little bit of fucking *money*, then he can indulge his creative vision any fucking way he likes!' Her voice has shot upwards. 'God, I just want things to be normal again! You know, I don't think a single thing has gone right for us in the last three weeks.'

This is a bit of an opening. 'Oh, Nancy, I just want to say again how sorry I am about what happened on Saturday. I have the fabric safely stored at home,' – well, safely stored in one of my bin liners – 'so I can take it to Lucien, if you need me to.'

'What?' Nancy stares at me for a moment. 'Ohhh, the mesh fabric!'

'Yes.' For God's sake, why couldn't everyone just have called it *the mesh fabric* right from the start?

'How *are* things at the farm, by the way? Was there an awful lot of damage?'

'Oh, we got it under control in the end.' I don't especially want to talk about the fake fire on the fake mead farm. 'The main thing is that I'm sorry I let you down. Was Lucien able to finish the dress?'

'Actually, yeah. He used the lace from an old evening gown of mine. I think it worked pretty well.' She goes over to the garment bag and unzips it, taking out a black dress. 'What do you think?'

At a quick glance nothing more than a simply cut LBD, it's actually a masterpiece. It's made from this wispy, chiffony fabric that's been hand-embroidered with thousands of tiny jet beads, apart from panels down each side of the short skirt that are made from delicate black lace, giving it a sexy, semi-sheer effect. It's got a high neckline at the front, but the back is deeply plunging, finishing in a crisp, sharp V. And there's a pleated panel of hot-pink silk concealed in the length of skirt beneath the V-back, which will flash out while the wearer moves, drawing attention to a shapely behind.

'Wow. It's amazing.'

Nancy turns the dress round to admire it from the back herself. 'God, I wish he'd shown pieces like this at Fashion Week. Maybe then we wouldn't be in this mess.'

I nod sympathetically, even though I've no idea what this Fashion Week debacle actually was. But then, it does fit in with what Cassie and Elektra were talking about earlier. About Tania not wanting to have a single piece of new-season Lucien Black in her Nevada photo shoot. And Eve Alexander not agreeing to wear it. I mean, I'm dying to ask what the problem with the new collection is, but I don't want to seem like a total ignoramus.

Nancy is pulling the garment bag back over the dress. 'I need you to take this to Eve's stylist for me, OK? Eve is going to wear it to the *Mimi* Style Awards in a couple of weeks, so we need to know how it fits, if we need to make any changes . . . Her stylist is coming to pick it up from the store in about half an hour.'

'The store?'

'Lucien's store. On Conduit Street. You know where it is, right?'

Well, of course I know where it is! I've walked past it hundreds of times, drooling, but being far too scared to go in. I mean, the Lucien Black concession in

196

Selfridges is intimidating enough, but the stand-alone boutique on Conduit Street is utterly terrifying. When it first opened a couple of years ago, I read this whole article in the *Sunday Times Style* section about how it wasn't so much a shop as a *concept store*. Not so much a place to buy clothes, as a *multi-sensory retail experience*.

'Isabel? You know where it is?'

'Oh, yes, absolutely.'

'Well, take a cab, anyway.' Nancy drapes the garment bag over my arm before handing me a twenty-pound note. 'The dress is worth a fortune. I mean, one good photo of Eve Alexander in it, and everything could start turning around for us.'

I grip the garment bag a little tighter. 'Oh. Well, then I'll be really, *really*, careful.'

'Thanks, hon. Appreciate it. Now, I've got a meeting with Redwood at my lawyers'.' Nancy opens the door and stalks through it, shoving her sunglasses back on as she goes. 'Time to explain why I'd really appreciate it if they didn't pull out of their investment deal just now.'

Chapter 13

Just as I'm getting into my taxi, and draping the precious dress carefully on the back seat, my phone rings.

It's Will.

I'm going to reject the call, but then I change my mind. I mean, if I can't take a call from him now, when I'm on my way to meet a top celebrity stylist at the swankiest boutique in Mayfair with a staggeringly beautiful dress for an A-list client, then frankly, when can I?

I pick up. 'Will.'

'Isabel!' He sounds astonished. 'I . . . I assumed you wouldn't answer.'

'Then I assume you've got my email.'

'Yes, I got it. And I'm sorry, Iz. I'm so, so, *so* sorry.'

I stare at my feet on the cab floor. 'You're . . . sorry?'

'Yes, look, it was just a one-time thing! I promise you, Iz. It's never happened before, and it won't happen again.'

This is not good.

I mean, I'm not exactly sure what I expected. But I think there was a tiny part of me, even though I'd never have admitted it to Lara (maybe not even to myself), that had been assuming Will was going to call all incomprehension and befuddlement. Because maybe nothing was really happening with him and Julia after all.

But apologies? Assurances that it won't happen again?

Not good. Very, very not good indeed.

'We've just been working so hard out here,' Will is carrying on. 'The clients are being difficult . . . we're running into all kinds of problems . . . Look, Julia's just a friend. Now, obviously I'm not offering excuses, and I'm sorry you had to find out the way you did . . .'

'And if I hadn't found out? Would you even have told me?'

'Well . . . no, probably not. Because I probably wouldn't have thought it was a big enough deal.'

'Not a big enough deal?' I yelp, causing the taxi driver to shoot me a nervous look in his rear-view mirror.

'Isabel, listen to me. I don't think you've got any idea how much stress I'm under out here! Honestly, I could really do without having to worry about you slinging everything you own into an entire roll of bin liners and threatening to move out . . .'

'I'm not threatening! I've done it! I've moved in with Lara. And for your information,' I add shakily, 'there wasn't a single bin liner involved.'

'I don't believe it . . .'

'It's true! I packed proper big suitcases and everything,' I fib.

'No, I didn't mean I don't believe it about the bin liners . . . though I didn't know you actually *had* any proper big suitcases . . . I meant I don't believe you've just moved out! One little error of judgement, and you do a runner?'

I love the way he's trying to make it sound like this is just as much my fault as his. It's the same even-handedness that makes him a terrific lawyer. Just a pity it also makes him a terrible boyfriend. Who thinks that shagging his colleague is classified as an *error of judgement*.

'I got arrested this weekend, Will, and Dad called me a failure, and I couldn't even speak to you about any of it because you were in bed with Julia! I wouldn't call that a little mistake!'

Now the taxi driver is looking really alarmed.

'Isabel, I've tried to exp . . .' Will stops. 'You were *arrested*? What the hell did you get yourself arrested for?'

What the hell did you get yourself arrested for? As though I'm always getting arrested! As though I'm nothing but a hopeless case.

'Will, I don't want to talk to you.' My voice is threatening to wobble out of control. 'I just want you to leave me alone.'

'Look, you've got to be reasonable about all this! Now, I don't think I can get home for at least the rest of the week, but . . .'

'I said I don't want to talk!'

'Isabel, please . . .'

I hang up and shove my phone into my Mikkel Borgessen bag. My hands are shaking so much I catch the tips of my fingers in the clasp as I try to snap it shut. I yelp in pain.

'You all right, love?'

'Fine.' I don't sound fine. 'Just hurt my fingers . . .'

Tears are stabbing my eyes as I watch Regent Street roll by. It's even worse than it was on Saturday, when Julia picked up the phone. Because now it's real. He really has slept with another woman. A more attractive, more successful woman. A colleague. An equal.

I should be feeling disgusted. But actually, what I feel is disgusting. Too short, too fat, too ugly, too stupid. Too gullible.

With my stinging fingers I snap open my bag, and take out my phone. If Will calls . . . maybe he'll call back . . . I'll give him a couple of minutes . . . a text, even . . .

I don't know what it is about the radio silence from Will's end, but I want to fill it. I scroll through my phone for Ben Loxley's number.

Hi Ben, I find myself texting, which is tricky when my hands still won't stop shaking. *If you're still free tonight, I'd love to go to the party with you . . .*

A reply comes quickly. Gratifyingly quickly.

Pick u up @ 8. Let me know address. B xx

Well, here I am, at the Lucien Black concept store.

Though exactly what the concept is, I couldn't honestly tell you.

It's this large open space, painted entirely white. The floor is painted white, the ceiling is white, and the white walls are displaying giant white pieces of artwork. In fact, if the concept is 'Life Inside a Giant Sugar Cube', then they've got it absolutely bang-on. In addition to all the bright white, which is already deeply unflattering to anyone who hasn't got Christy Turlington's skin tone, there are these huge, industrial-style overhead lamps beaming out the kind of light you normally find in supermarkets, that makes your eyes go all fuzzy if you stay there too long. Perhaps that's what the *Sunday Times Style* meant by *multi-sensory retail experience*. As for the clothes, they're not displayed out on racks like in a normal shop, but kind of flung over various Perspex surfaces, as though an escaped lunatic has got undressed in a really big hurry.

I mean, it's hardly French Connection.

But how amazing is it to be able to walk into this place with a real purpose, and sent by none other than Lucien's Muse herself? I almost wish there was someone around to witness this colossal personal breakthrough. But actually, the shop is completely empty. There are no customers, which isn't exactly a surprise, given how scary the place is. But it's a bit weird that there aren't any sales assistants either. I mean, what am I meant to do – leave a frighteningly expensive designer dress on the counter for someone to pick up when they're back from their coffee break?

Oh, wait a moment. There *is* someone in the shop. I

couldn't tell at first because they were hidden behind one of the Perspex screens with a jacket and a T-shirt flung over it, but now I can distinctly see a moving shape. Two moving shapes, actually. As I sidle round to get a better look behind the Perspex, I can see that it's a man and a woman. The woman has a lot of honey-blonde hair, and is so skinny she's practically see-through – which, by the way, doesn't seem to be preventing the man she's with from having a good old fondle of her non-existent bottom . . .

Wait a minute. I've seen him before somewhere, haven't I? He's extremely tall – at least six foot three, I imagine. And there's something about his demeanour – the pink shirt, the carefully coiffed greying hair, the large hand proprietorially on the blonde's bottom – that looks . . . well, looks *what*? Distinguished? No, wait, I've got it – *smug*.

It's Hugo Tavistock! Nancy's husband. I recognise him from that Fashion Aristocracy piece I read in *Grazia*.

Well, what's he doing fondling this girl's bottom? My God, men are utter pigs, aren't they? Bad enough that my boyfriend has it away with other women – at least I'm not actually *married* to him.

I clear my throat pointedly. 'Um . . . hello?'

They spring apart so fast it's like they're on pogo sticks. Hugo Tavistock starts pretending to take an interest in the huge white abstract painting on the nearest wall, and the rail-thin girl hurries to come and meet me around the other side of the Perspex screen, smoothing her pencil skirt over her thighs as if she's trying to get rid of any telltale handprints.

'Can I help?' she asks, in about the snootiest, most *un*helpful way you could imagine.

'I'm here to meet Eve Alexander's stylist.'

She does a visible double take. '*You're* here to meet Eve's stylist?'

'That's right. I'm bringing her a dress. Nancy sent me.'

'Ohhhh.' She casts a slightly nervous glance over her shoulder. 'You work for *Nancy* . . .'

Hugo must have his ears pricked up, because the moment he hears this he abandons his faux-interest in the abstract painting and starts coming over. He's obviously realised he's got a certain amount of damage limitation to do here, although his face would never betray that. He's smiling (smugly), and extending the same hand that was just fondling the blonde's bottom.

'Hel*loh*,' he says. 'You must be Nancy's new assistant . . . Isabella, was it?'

'Isabel.'

'Yes, that's right. She's told me all about you. I'm Hugo. Her husband.' He puts a lot of emphasis on the *husband*, which is ironic, given what I've just seen. 'I just stopped by the store to have a word with Marina here about changing some of the artwork. Art is my *thing*, you see.'

'How nice,' I say, not commenting on the fact that skinny blondes seem to be his thing as well.

His smile broadens. 'Of course, it would be in the order of *une petite surprise* for Nancy if we did put some new art up, so you really shouldn't say anything to her. About seeing me here, I mean.'

I look him right in the eyes. 'Of course.'

'Good! Well, I'm glad we've got that sorted!' He glances over to where Marina is ostentatiously fanning out a pleated skirt. 'So, I'll call you, Marina. To talk about that Rothko, yes?'

'Roth what?' Marina stares at him before cottoning on to her role. 'Ohhhhh. Yahhhh. I seeee.'

'Well, I really must make tracks. But it was lovely to meet you, Isabel. I'm sure we'll have *le plaisir* at some point again in the near future.'

I have no intention of having any kind of *plaisir* with this sleazy charmer at any point in the future, near, distant, or otherwise.

'Cheerio, ladies!' Hugo heads for the doors. 'I'll leave you two to get on with my wife's bidding!'

Marina turns back to me, a tiny bit pink in the cheeks, but clearly determined to pretend none of this has just happened. 'Soooo. What can I do for you?'

'Is Eve's stylist here yet?'

'Nooooo, nooo, I'm sorry, she's noooot.' Marina's vowels seem to go on for ever. 'But I do know she's also coming to drop off a Tavistock bag she used on a shoot a couple of months ago, so I'm sure she won't forget.' She puts a hand on my arm. 'So, how *is* Nancy this morning? I just heard from Debs myself. *Awful* news about Selfridges, yuh?'

Marina's sympathy for the woman who is, after all, her fancy man's wife, strikes me as just a little hypocritical. 'Awful.'

'I mean, next thing we know, it'll be Harvey Nicks and Harrods, too, yuh?'

I stare at her. 'You mean, they might refuse to stock Lucien Black, too?'

Marina rolls her eyes, with the air of someone who quite enjoys a bit of drama. 'Well, can you see anyone being thick enough to spend six hundred pounds on a pair of see-through trousers or a pervy-looking transparent T-shirt?'

See-through trousers? Pervy-looking transparent T-shirts?

Hold on a moment. *Those* were by Lucien Black? Those horrible, creepy-looking cling-film things I saw in the copy of *anothermagazine* I was reading in Central St Martins' waiting room?

But I assumed they were designed by some unorthodox headline-grabber straight out of art school. Either that or it was all a clever fashiony joke that I just didn't understand.

Jesus! No wonder there've been all these dark mutterings from Nancy about things going wrong at Fashion Week. I mean, how the hell did Lucien Black get from SHEER, AIRY and DIAPHANOUS to see-through, plastic and pervy? And it's not exactly surprising that Selfridges isn't placing any orders, either. The photo in *anothermagazine* made it pretty clear that, no matter how bad you'd imagine dressing in cling film would look on a stick-insect body, doing that to a normal, everyday, slightly fleshy body is positively stomach-churning. Even if you did fancy walking about the place with all your bits and pieces on display.

'Oh, my *Gooood*, he's not done a see-through outfit for Eve Alexander, has he?' Marina suddenly gasps, grabbing my arm in the overfamiliar, no-boundaries way that people often have when they've grown up at boarding school.

'No, no, it's a little black dress. Just a couple of sheer lace panels.'

'Oh, well, that's a relief!' She lowers her voice, even though we're the only people in the shop. Sorry – the concept store. 'I mean, I know she's not as bad as those porkers Lucien used in his show, but she's *not* the skinniest, yuh?'

God, it's at times like this that I start to doubt if I can really work in the fashion industry after all. I mean, forget body fascism, this is body Nazism! I've always thought Eve Alexander is a vision of utter loveliness, and this mean-spirited hag is laying into her for daring to carry more than an ounce of spare flesh on her bones. It's the kind of attitude I intend to revolutionise the moment I'm in a position of authority in this business. I'll . . . oooh, I know – I'll ban size zeros from my catwalk! Thereby not only sending out a message that we must celebrate the ordinary body, but also helping myself out when I have to walk down the catwalk arm in arm with two of my models at the end of my show. In fact, the larger the model the better! A nice, voluptuous 36-32-38, and I'll look all tiny and delicate in comparison!

Ordinary Bodies: The new fragrance from Isabel Bookbinder.

I'll still try to get Keira Knightley and Daniel Craig for the ad campaign, though. I mean, my revolution can only go so far.

'Oh, look who's here!' Marina brays into my thoughts as she suddenly skips towards the sliding doors.

It's a gaunt-looking woman with an incredibly chic blonde crop, outlandishly dressed in a high-waisted pinstripe pencil skirt with an original Clash T-shirt and City-boy red braces, and dominatrix-style high-heeled gladiator sandals in an amazingly shiny black patent. Her lips are a deep, Gothic purple, and she's carrying a completely swoonsome purple Celine Boogie bag, as well as the large taupe (camel? fawn?) Tavistock bag she's returning.

This has to be Eve Alexander's stylist.

'Hiiiii!' Marina leans in to air-kiss her on both cheeks. 'We were just talking about you! This girl . . .' I notice she doesn't even bother to pretend to remember my name, '. . . has brought you a dress for Eve.'

The stylist stares at me. 'What?'

'Hi!' I give her a friendly smile, which isn't reciprocated. 'I'm Isabel.'

'I'm Jasmine,' she snaps.

So Jasmine is Eve's stylist? Ah. That must have been why she wanted to see what the crystal-mesh fabric looked like, before Lucien used it in her client's dress.

'For fuck's sake!' Jasmine puts a hand on her hip in a slightly posed, angular fashion. 'This is why I wanted to speak to Nancy this morning. God, I *knew* Lilian would fuck it all up. Ruby always made sure I got called back.'

I feel strangely defensive towards Lilian. Partly because I know that, actually, not passing on the message is my fault. And partly because this girl seems to be the only person who thinks horrible old Ruby was some sort of organisational colossus in comparison.

'I think Lilian was extremely busy this morning,' I say.

'Yeah, well, it doesn't bother me. You're the one who's had the wasted trip.' Jasmine runs a hand through her crop. 'Evie won't be needing the dress after all. She's going to wear Marchesa to the Style Awards instead.'

I stare at her. 'But . . . didn't you ask Lucien Black to make it specially?'

'I did not. *Evie* asked Lucien to make it specially. And that was before he turned into a raving lunatic and sent fat people down the catwalk dressed in giant condoms. *And* turned up to his aftershow party completely off his head, wearing a pair of his horrible transparent trousers, and chucking champagne at Anna Wintour.'

What?

'Well who *hasn't* done that?' I wave a hand. 'I don't think that's a good reason to refuse to wear a dress! Not when someone's made it specially for you!'

Jasmine snorts. 'You think I'm not turning down calls from people begging me to let them make something *specially for* Evie? I've got Mr Armani offering a couture gown for the Golden Globes, constant badgering from Carolina Herrera, John Galliano sending me sketches of Oscar dresses . . .'

'Ooooh, John Galliano,' breathes Marina. 'He's *fabulous*.'

'And believe me,' Jasmine carries on, 'Evie's agent doesn't want her associated with Lucien any more, either. In fact, he's the one who's finally persuaded her to listen to reason about Lucien. Her career is about to hit the stratosphere, and the last thing she needs in the run-up to awards season is to be seen out and about wearing gowns by an embarrassing old has-been.'

'Yuh.' Marina is nodding sympathetically. 'I mean, Lucien Black is, like, just really *over*.'

There's a slightly awkward silence, as we all ponder what Marina, *the Lucien Black concept-store manager*, has just said.

'Anyway, look, just tell Nancy I'll call her sometime,' Jasmine says.

I can't let this happen! Not when Nancy's entire year's work on this deal might depend on it! 'But you haven't even seen what Lucien's done! It's not see-through, or anything. In fact, it's gorgeous . . .'

Jasmine scowls at me. 'I don't care if it's gorgeous. We're not interested.'

'But Eve Alexander *always* wears Lucien Black! Isn't it a little bit mean to drop him like a hot potato now, just because he's having a rather tough time of it?'

'Well, when I'm running a benevolent fund for down-and-out fashion designers, I'll let you know.' Jasmine hands the Tavistock bag to Marina, and gives her a kiss on both cheeks. 'Thanks, darling. We'll do lunch one day soon, yeah? Maybe a bite at Zuma? I hear Dior are looking for a new manager at Sloane Street.'

'Ooooh, no, really?'

I don't really want to stick around for this. I put the garment bag over my arm and walk out of the concept store.

Chapter 14

It's a slightly dull afternoon back at the office. I hate to say it, but *Atelier* seems to have accidentally employed a load of workaholics. In fact, if it weren't for the inescapable evidence that they all work on a fashion magazine (bouncy blow-dries, great accessories, etc.), you might be concerned you'd ended up working in a mortgage broker's office, or something. There's no gathering around the water cooler, discussing what Gwyneth was wearing last night at Locanda Locatelli, or whether or not Sarah Jessica Parker should have scraped her hair back so tightly in those new photos in this week's *Grazia*. There's no popping out for a bite of sushi and a skinny cappuccino, followed by a lunch-hour dash to Marylebone High Street to check out what's new in Day Birger and Mikkelsen at Matches. There's no hanging out in the fashion cupboard, trying on all the shoes to see which pair you might wear if you ever got invited to a film premiere, say, or the Met Costume Institute Gala, or an oyster supper at Scott's of Mayfair with Daniel Craig.

Anyway, by the third time Lilian's caught me in the cupboard with the jewel-toned Brian Atwood satin slingbacks, I'm starting to realise that it might just be a bit more sensible to sit at my desk, keep my head down, and look as if I'm getting on with mountains of work like everybody else.

The trouble is, though, that there isn't a mountain of work. Not a single phone call comes through for Nancy the entire afternoon. Not even an update from Lucien Black on how things are going with the toaster. I staple a few things, which keeps me occupied for a little while. I go on Net-a-Porter for a couple of hours, which is good because it's basically important research. I'm taking out my Mood Book to jot down a few notes when, just after five o'clock, Nancy reappears.

This time she's no longer looking bad-tempered. She's looking exhausted.

'Hi,' she says, slumping into the chair opposite my desk. 'You dropped the dress off OK?'

'Well, actually, there was a little bit of a snafu with that.'

'Snafu? What do you mean, snafu?'

'Um, well, it seems that Eve has decided not to wear Lucien Black to the Style Awards after all.'

'She *what*? You have to be fucking *kidding* me.'

'No, I'm not. Jasmine said . . .'

'What? What did that jumped-up personal shopper say? Tell me word for word!'

So I do. Well, leaving out the really nasty bits where Jasmine said Lucien was an embarrassment and a has-been, obviously. I know how much that kind of stuff can hurt.

'John Galliano? *John Galliano?*' Nancy shrieks, when I get to the bit about . . . well, about John Galliano. 'Eve Alexander wouldn't even be in a position to *wear* John Galliano if it weren't for me and Lucien! Nobody would ever even have known who she was if we hadn't put her in that backless metallic at Cannes three years ago! But a couple of little blips, and all that history, all that *loyalty* . . .' She pauses to gather herself. 'All right. Anything else happen today that I need to know about?'

I don't think she needs to know that her husband was groping the manager at the concept store. 'No.'

'Any important calls?'

'Um . . . no.'

'Not a single one?'

'I'm sorry.'

She sighs. 'Great. People are avoiding me. I guess they think failure is catching.'

'Oh, I'm sure no one thinks you're a failure!'

'I'm not sure you'd think that if you'd just come from that meeting.'

'Did it go badly?'

Nancy lets out a bitter bark of laughter. 'Let me see. Apparently, ever since my business partner decided to lose the plot at London Fashion Week, Lucien Black Associates has become – how did they put it? – a *riskier investment.*'

I stare at her. 'Does that mean they're not going to give you the money any more?'

'Yes. No. Sort of.' Nancy pinches the bridge of her

nose between her thumb and forefinger. 'It means they're getting cold feet. My lawyers think they're going to reduce the amount they're willing to offer us. Try to get us to give them our shares in the company for half what they were worth a month ago.'

I really don't know what to say to this. 'God. I'm sorry.'

'And they know full well we've put too much into this deal to walk away from it now,' she adds angrily. 'God, if I didn't know better, I'd think they knew . . .' She stops. 'Anyway, Izzie, thanks for facing that horrible little bitch Jasmine. Had plenty of little barbs about Lucien, I'm sure.'

I squirm slightly. 'She did . . . er . . . mention something about an aftershow party . . . Lucien throwing a glass of champagne at Anna Wintour . . . ?'

'Oh, *that*!' Nancy starts to laugh. There's a slightly hysterical edge. 'Not a glass, actually. A bottle. Unopened. With the champagne still in it.'

'Ah.'

'And he didn't throw it *at* Anna Wintour. He threw it *near* Anna Wintour. It wasn't his fault everyone suddenly started running and she got in the way.'

Jesus. He's even madder than he sounded on the phone.

'It's partly my fault,' Nancy adds, suddenly losing the smile. 'I should've known he was starting to crack. And I should've stopped him from going to the party after I realised what people were going to be saying about him after that show.' She stares at her feet, now looking ten years older than she did first thing this morning. Then she gets up. 'Anyway, you don't need to hear all my problems! You should go home, Izzie. Back to that fiancé of yours.'

'Oh, he isn't my fiancé.'

'Oh, I'm sorry, honey. Boyfriend.'

'Actually,' I say, with a little laugh, 'he's not that any more, either!'

'Then I'm *really* sorry.'

'Don't be!' I'm not going to tell her any sob story about catching him cheating on me. Not when I've witnessed what her husband gets up to. 'In fact, I'm even going on a date tonight!'

'Really? Wow.' Nancy's eyes widen. 'That's kind of sudden, isn't it?'

'Oh, well, not a *date*, as such . . .' I say hastily. 'He's just an old friend, really.'

Nancy gets up and heads back into her office. 'Well, either way, have a fabulous time. Hey,' she adds, pointing at her cupboards, 'you know you can borrow stuff from me? If there's anything you'd like to wear this evening, I mean.'

'Oh, Nancy, that's so kind!' It really is. 'But I think I might be a little bit . . . er . . . too big for your clothes.'

She eyes me for a moment, rather professionally, clearly trying to imagine what I'd look like shoe-horned into one of her size-six dresses. 'Borrow the crystal-mesh dress if you like, then. Eve's a size ten. You should be able to fit into that.'

'*Really?*' I stare at her.

216

'Well, as long as you're not planning to eat anything tonight.'

'No, no, I mean, really I can borrow it?'

'Why not?' Nancy shrugs. 'Eve's never going to put the thing on. And it's too big for me. I mean, you can go and leave it in the fashion cupboard if you like, but one of the other girls will only get her grubby mitts on it. Borrow some of my shoes to go with it, too, if you like.'

I'm feeling a bit dizzy. 'You mean – some of your Christian Louboutins?'

Nancy nods over at her collection of shoes. 'If you can fit a size seven, you can take your pick.'

Actually, I'm a six, but I'd wear a pair of shoes three sizes too big if it meant being able to dip into Nancy's amazing Louboutin collection. 'Thank you so much, Nancy!'

'Oh, honey, you're welcome.' She sits down at her desk and hauls a huge stack of legal-looking documents out of her Tavistock bag, evidently settling in for a long night. 'If working for someone as fabulous as me doesn't get you the occasional perk, then what's the point of it all?'

Isabel Bookbinder
Atelier Magazine
High Holborn
London

John Galliano
An airy Parisian studio
Paris
France

18 September

Dear Mr Galliano,

Please don't worry that you have not yet found the time to reply to my previous letter! In the absence of a response, I have forged ahead with my Mood Book anyway, and am finding it an enormously effective part of my Process.

~~John, unless you have been hiding under a rock~~ I'm sure you must be aware of the troubles that are currently afflicting a fellow member of the Fashion Aristocracy, Lucien Black. His recent eccentricity has sent ripples through the fashion world – though which of us, John, has not turned up to a party in transparent trousers, or sent models down a catwalk wrapped in clingfilm?!

Sadly, many of Mr Black's clients do not see things this way, and have begun to abandon him in favour of other, less ~~obviously insane~~ risky designers: Eve Alexander is one such client, and, apparently, has expressed a desire to start wearing You, amongst others. I do not know if there is actually some kind of unwritten Code of Honour amongst Top International Fashion Designers, but I do know how enormously everyone at Lucien Black would appreciate it if you were to withdraw your interest in this particular actress. I'd concentrate on Nicole and Charlize instead, if I were you – they, unlike Ms Alexander, will at least reward you with their loyalty, and wouldn't just strop off to another designer if you suddenly went a little bit bonkers.

In addition, I wonder if I could possibly prevail upon you not to hire ~~snooty old~~ Marina as your new manager at Dior on Sloane Street. Not only would this be a further twist of the knife for my beleaguered boss, Nancy Tavistock, but I also wish to warn you that I think she'd do an absolutely atrocious job. Unless you actually want your customers scared off before they've even set foot inside, of course: this is entirely up to you.

Yours in admiration,

Isabel Bookbinder

PS - Just to clarify, I am in no way suggesting that you have ever turned up to a party in transparent trousers, or sent models down a catwalk wrapped in clingfilm!!!

PPS – I haven't either, by the way. Just in case you were wondering.

IBx

TIMETABLE: PRE-HOT DATE (WITH SEXUALLY MAGNETIC VENTURE CAPITALIST)

5.45 p.m. – Peruse Nancy Tavistock's world-class collection of Christian Louboutin shoes; make selection

5.55 p.m. – Make selection

6.08 p.m. – *Make selection*

6.10 p.m. – Too late for tube – taxi home

6.16 p.m. – In taxi, plan time-honoured soothing pre-date rituals: glass of chilled champagne, energising self-heating face mask, uplifting aromatherapy bath while listening to inspirational CD (Mozart arias? Gregorian plainsong? Take That?), calmly put together Signature Look for the evening

6.46 p.m. – In taxi, panicking

6.56 p.m. – Still in taxi, still panicking

7.07 p.m. – See above; also cursing London Mayor for digging up every water main in city, causing traffic chaos and (deliberately?) sabotaging time-honoured soothing pre-date rituals

7.14 p.m. – Get out of taxi and run final half-mile home – good exercise, will bring attractive glow to cheeks (Cognitive Restructuring)

7.29 p.m. – Water! Water!

7.31 p.m. – No time for face mask (thank God already have attractive glow); non-uplifting non-aromatherapy shower while listening to sound of heart thudding alarmingly, start upending bin bags in quest for suitable tights and accessories for Signature Look for evening

7.43 p.m. – Lie on bed, weeping

7.44 p.m. – Pull self together, stop weeping
7.49 p.m. – Squeeze into dress, apply light make-up, go into battle with hair
7.59 p.m. – Take deep, calming, yoga-style breaths; pay no attention to bin-bag chaos, and wait for sound of doorbell

Chapter 15

The moment I'm finally dressed, I hurry into the kitchen to get Lara's opinion. 'Ta-da!'

She turns round from cooking her mangetout-and-chicken stir-fry. This is the thing about Lara. A mere forty-eight hours after having her heart squished underfoot, she's back from a constructive day's work helping barmy people, and preparing herself a nutritious supper with a single glass of red wine. Not, oh, I don't know, refusing to shower for three days and curling up under her duvet with a large tin of Fox's Creations, like a normal person. Or heading out on a date, far, *far* too soon, with a sexually magnetic venture capitalist. Nope, Lara's all smiles. A ticking, flan-chucking time bomb.

'Oh,' she says, scrutinising my outfit. '*Very* feminist.'

'What do you mean?'

'Well, I thought we'd decided the other night. That we were going to take a more feminist approach to life. Not just do things to please men any more.'

'And?'

Lara stares at me. 'And you're going out on a date in a short, see-through dress and pink peep-toes.'

'It's not see-through! Well, not where it counts. And

anyway, what are feminists *meant* to wear? Baggy dungarees and Doc Martens?'

'I think so, Isabel, yes.'

I roll my eyes. 'Then is it any wonder they all hate men? I mean, if you go about the place looking like a bricklayer, men *are* going to be horrible to you.'

Lara returns to her stir-fry.

'Anyway, just because I want to look nice doesn't mean I'm not a feminist.' I rack my brains to think of any articles I might have ever read about feminism. 'Feminism has moved on a lot recently, you know. We don't all have to chain ourselves to railings or hurl ourselves beneath racehorses every five minutes.'

'The rail-chaining and the racehorse-hurling was the suffragettes, not feminists.'

'What's the difference?'

Lara sighs. 'About seventy years.'

Well, this just proves my point. 'Exactly! Things move on. They *advance*. First it was all the violent, uncomfortable stuff, then seventy years later it was just a bit of light bra-burning and protest-marching, and these days you're positively *encouraged* to go about in see-through dresses and pink peep-toes. Just as long as you're doing it in an *empowered* way. Standing on your own two feet.'

Which, I think most feminists would find if they'd only bother to try, is a lot more fun in pink peep-toe Christian Louboutin shoes.

'So is that why you're going out on a date with Ben Loxley two days after splitting up with Will?'

I avoid Lara's beady gaze. 'It's not a date. Not really.'

'You're wearing Wild Fig and Cassis.'

'I just want to smell nice!'

'It's your pulling perfume.'

My face flares. 'All right. I want him to find me attractive.'

'Isabel . . .'

'There's no harm in that, is there?'

'Of course not. And look, I understand you need to feel better about yourself after what Will did, but . . .'

'Lara. It's just an evening out. I'm not one of your patients.'

'Clients,' she corrects me automatically. 'I know, Iz, but . . .' She stops, and glances at the floor for a moment. 'Oh, I don't know. I'm being silly. I was just looking forward to an evening in with you, E4 and a nice glass of wine, that's all.'

Instantly, I feel terrible. I mean, how insensitive is this – me prancing out for the evening while she has to sit in alone and torture herself with images of Matthew and Annie walking down the aisle together? 'I'll call Ben right now and cancel . . .'

'No, no, I didn't mean that . . .'

'Lara, I'm not going to leave you here by yourself with nothing to do but think about Matthew and Annie!'

'*Isabel!*'

Ow. That was shrill.

'I'm not thinking about Matthew and Annie *at all*, as

224

it happens! Let alone doing *nothing but* thinking about them! In case you hadn't noticed, I'm planning a very nice, civilised evening in with my chicken stir-fry and some good TV! I absolutely do not need you to cancel your date! Don't need you to, don't want you to.'

The doorbell rings.

Lara pushes me towards the front door. 'You deserve a nice evening out. I'm completely fine! And you look amazing, by the way.'

'Really?' I mean really, is she completely fine, not really, do I look amazing, but she misunderstands. Either that, or dodges the question.

'Oh, totally amazing! That dress is fabulous. Ben won't be able to keep his hands off you.'

This is exactly what I want to hear, but I have to pretend to be all disapproving and feministic, which Lara doesn't really seem to be convinced by. I try to make her promise to phone me if she's suddenly not completely fine, but she starts looking as though she might get all shrill again, so I just grab my clutch bag, and open the front door.

'Wow.' Ben is grinning at me. 'You look fantastic!'

'So do you!' He does, of course. I mean, not that I didn't like him in his casual weekend get-up, but Ben's a man who can *seriously* work a suit. And this is quite a suit. It looks like one of those swanky Brioni ones that cost the price of a small car – mid-grey, lustrous material with the faintest blue pinstripe, and tailored to emphasise his broad shoulders and tapering torso. He's wearing it with a light blue shirt and a blue-and-grey striped tie, which would be a little bit boring, and just a fraction too painfully reminiscent of Will, if it weren't for the fact that he's accessorised the shirt with a pair of Georg Jensen cufflinks (Will never wears cufflinks; he struggles to do them up) and that the tie is sexily pulled loose at the throat (Will either wears a tie properly, or not at all – mostly properly).

Anyway, the combined effect of all this loose-tied, broad-shouldered, Italian-fabric'd gorgeousness is that my heart has started to pound like I'm eighteen again, and I can't think of anything more grown-up to say next than, 'Well. This is brilliant.'

Ben gives me his sexy, lopsided grin as he leans in to kiss me on the cheek. He smells delicious (Persil ColourCare?). 'Couldn't agree more. And I'm especially relieved to see you haven't suffered from your stay at Her Majesty's Pleasure.'

I don't know what he's talking about for a moment, and then it dawns on me. 'Look, Ben, that trouble with the police was a huge misunderstanding.'

'Really?' He leads the way on to the pavement. 'I was kind of looking forward to an evening with a hot fugitive.'

'Oh, well, then I'm sorry to disappoint.'

Ben turns to give me a look that would melt a polar ice cap. 'I'm not disappointed. You're still hot.'

God, he's smooth.

It's pretty effective, though.

'So,' he goes on, 'time for you to meet the other woman in my life!'

Other woman? What does he mean, other woman?

'In fact, I'm really looking forward to having you both here at the same time.'

Oh, for the love of God, what have I got myself into?

Is he expecting some kind of *threesome*? On our *first date*? Is he *insane*?

Actually, forget the fact it's a first date. I'm not even sure that's my scene at all! I mean, it's always sounded like twice the work for half the fun to me. Not to mention the fact that I'm not very good at . . . logistics.

OK. I don't want to sound like a fusty old prude. Probably this is the kind of thing he did all the time back in Manhattan with all those *Sex and the City*-type socialites. So I'm not going to let London down by getting all prissy and horrified.

I'm just going to make my excuses and flee.

'Ben, you know, it's been a really long day . . . I'm actually feeling very tired all of a sudden . . .'

To my amazement, Ben bursts out laughing. 'I'm sorry, Iz. I shouldn't tease you.'

'No, look, it's fine!' I try to sound laid-back. 'You have a right to your proclivities. Everyone's a consenting adult.' Apart from me, that is.

'Look.' Ben points over the road, to where an extremely shiny dark green vintage sports car is parked. '*That* is my other woman.'

Ohhh.

Such a relief.

And if it's a teeny tiny bit annoying of Ben to have

wound me up like that, and a teeny tiny bit grating that he's one of those men who talk about their cars like they're women, well, I'll manage. Because the car is *gorgeous*.

'It's a 1972 E-type.' Ben opens the passenger door for me. 'My gift to myself when I moved back to London.'

'It's very nice,' I say, trying to sound like the kind of girl who is completely accustomed to driving about town in gorgeous vintage sports cars. 'Of course, E-type make the very best cars,' I add, knowledgeably. 'Built to last!'

Ben frowns as he gets into the driver's side. 'Isabel, E-type is the model. It's *made* by Jaguar. You do realise that, don't you?'

Damn. I wish I'd paid more attention when Will was watching *Top Gear* on a Sunday evening. But all it ever looks like to me is an excuse for Jeremy Clarkson to be rude about the French and the Germans. 'Of course I realise it's a Jaguar! I mean, Jaguar are the very best, aren't they? None of that French or German rubbish!'

Ben looks completely bewildered. Then he starts the engine, which I must say does purr ever so nicely, and we drive off towards the King's Road.

And I have to say, if you've never driven around town in a vintage E-type thingy with a sexually magnetic venture capitalist on a Indian summer's evening, wearing a custom-made designer dress, I can thoroughly recommend it. It feels just like you're in a car advert! All you're really missing is the soft-rock backing track and the gravelly voiced man saying things like 'seamless handling' and 'the drive of your life'.

'So,' Ben asks, once we've whizzed down Kensington Church Street and turned towards the park, 'am I allowed to ask why you've moved in with Lara?'

I don't say anything for a moment.

'OK, OK. Sorry. None of my business.'

'No, I didn't mean that! I just mean . . . it's just a bit recent. That's all.'

Ben glances sideways at me. 'Well. Obviously I've never met this boyfriend of yours . . .'

'Ex-boyfriend,' I say quietly.

'Ah. Right.' Ben nods. 'Well, what I was about to say was, clearly he doesn't deserve you. But you must have realised that already, if you've kicked him to the kerb!'

I don't think I'll go into detail about the fact that, even though I'm the one who moved out, Will is the one, technically, who's been doing the kicking to the kerb. I don't want Ben to think I'm the kind of person who gets cheated on.

'And to be honest,' Ben shifts into fourth gear (seamless handling), 'my opinion of him was pretty low even before I knew you'd dumped him.'

I glance at him, surprised. I mean, doesn't he realise that *I'm* allowed to criticise Will, but that doesn't mean *he* is?

229

'Letting his girlfriend go out to a party with another guy?' Ben raises his eyebrows. 'He's either very confident or very stupid.'

'Oh, come on!' I laugh, before I can stop myself. '*Letting* me?'

The slightly stilted silence that follows makes me realise that Ben wasn't joking.

Oh.

So on top of being one of those men who talk about cars like they're women, Ben is obviously also one of those men who go about operating on the assumption that every other human being with a Y chromosome is after their girlfriend, and so a constant alert must be maintained at all times.

Well, after Will's utterly unchivalrous behaviour, maybe it'll be nice to feel appreciated.

Probably I won't include this little nugget in the review of the evening I give Lara later, though.

'Anyway, the point is . . .' Ben moves his left hand from the gearstick and places it, very lightly, on my right knee, 'I don't care whether he was confident, or stupid, or both. I'm just glad he's out of the picture.'

I'd be happy to sit here enjoying this new knee-touching development for quite some time longer, but we're pulling up in a parking space on a side street just off the King's Road.

Chapter 16

Ben, who really is turning out to have old-fashioned manners, comes round to open my door for me, and then reaches for my hand as we walk past the side of Bluebird and up towards the main road.

'Oh, my God!' I see the lights on up ahead, and the glamorous people spilling out of the doors with Bellini glasses in their hands. 'I didn't realise the party was at Anais!'

'You like this shop?'

'I *love* this shop!'

Well, I would, if I could pluck up the courage to come here more often. Anais is this magpie's nest of a boutique that sells all kinds of fabulous bits and pieces – one-off T-shirts, luxury lingerie, the hottest new LA denim imports – that kind of thing. One of those deceptive places where you pick up a little bead bracelet that looks like a nicer version of something you'd find in Accessorize, and then when you take it to the counter to pay it turns out to cost two hundred and fifty quid, and you have to pretend you've forgotten to refill your parking meter so you can flee without too much embarrassment. A shop for true fashionistas, with large bank balances. And now I'm here, out of hours, for a glamorous private party! This is completely brilliant.

God, how great would it be if Isabel B was stocked here someday? Alongside the William Rast jeans and the Milly cashmere, and the QFW mini-kaftans. I mean, if things don't work out with Lucien Black – and after today, I won't deny I have a few doubts – there are far worse ways I could start out in my design career. OK, it's only a small store, but when people like Kate Moss and Keira Knightley come here, your stuff would be all over *Grazia* before you knew it . . .

'So, you get quite a lot of things here, then?' Ben opens the shop door for me. It's extremely noisy and packed with more of those glam people drinking their Bellinis and nibbling at tiny portions of tuna tartare served in white porcelain spoons.

'Oh, God, yes – I come here all the time,' I fib.

Ben looks pleased. 'You must tell Queenie – I'm sure she could arrange some kind of discount for you.'

'Queenie?'

'Queenie Forbes-Wilkinson?' Ben accepts two Bellinis from a waiter and nods across the crowded room in the direction of a tall, glacial-looking girl in a DvF wrap, with stunning red hair in a retro peekaboo wave. 'She co-owns the place.'

'Oh, yes, of course! Queenie Forbes-Wilkinson!' Even if I didn't vaguely recognise Queenie herself from the society pages of *ES* magazine, I know her name. She's the former It girl turned designer whose signature pieces are the QFW mini-kaftans hanging on the rack right over there. Gorgeous though they are, I've never actually fancied splashing out on one myself. They're really for the kind of girl who spends the entire summer in Antibes lying motionless on sun loungers all day long without burning, or getting bored, or spilling Caipirinha all over her emergency sarong. Actually, the kind of girl who doesn't even *need* an emergency sarong because she's so willowy and tanned that she can strut about with nothing but a mini-kaftan over her bikini, without worrying what people think of her thighs. 'So she's the one married to your colleague?' I ask Ben.

'That's right . . . oh, and talk of the devil!' Ben's face breaks into a grin as a short, wiry, intense-looking man pushes his way through the crowd towards us. 'Isabel, meet Queenie's husband, Callum. Callum, Isabel.'

Callum shakes my hand in a desultory fashion, while his eyes fix firmly on my chest. 'Nice to meet you,' he informs my upper body.

Great. He's a chest-talker. 'Nice to meet you, too,' I say, looking him squarely in the eye.

'Would you mind,' he continues, looking me squarely in the nipple, 'if I stole Ben from you for just a moment?'

'Bad meeting?' Ben asks him, before I can even reply.

'Shit meeting,' grunts Callum. His accent reminds me of Uncle Midge's – heavily disguised Glasgow. 'I don't know what the bloody hell Fred is thinking, but . . .' He stops suddenly. 'Look, I'll tell you outside. Quieter there. Bring your drink.'

'No problem. I'll just introduce Isabel to Queenie first, OK?'

I weave through the crowd behind Ben until we reach our fabulous co-hostess, QFW herself. She's standing next to a large round table covered with pretty sorbet-coloured lingerie, chatting to two impeccably groomed women wearing Marni smocks over bare, sinewy legs.

'Queenie.' Ben kisses her on both cheeks.

'Oh, hello, Ben. It's been ages.' Unlike her husband, there's nothing either Glasgow or disguised about Queenie's accent. It's pure, unadulterated It girl.

'Do you mind looking after Isabel for a few minutes, while I have a chat with Cal?'

'What? Who?'

'Me. I'm Isabel,' I smile at her.

She doesn't smile back. 'Oh, hi.'

'I'm sure you two girls will have a lot to talk about. Isabel dabbles in the fashion world herself,' Ben says.

I glance sharply at him. Because is it just me, or is *dabbles in the fashion world* just a touch on the patronising side? I mean, he doesn't know that I haven't really got round to doing much actual designing yet. For all he knows, I've got fashion buyers from Harvey Nichols and that woman from Browns ringing me five times a day, and Debenhams begging me to do a diffusion line.

Dabbles, indeed.

Queenie looks down at me as Ben goes to join Callum outside. Close up, she's wearing several distinct layers of make-up – expertly applied, of course, but still slightly masklike. It's partly this that makes her look so glacial. 'So what kind of thing is it you do? Do you work in a shop?'

'I think I've seen her in Agnes B on the Fulham Road,' the older of the impeccably groomed women announces, before turning to me. 'I stocked up on T-shirts there the other week. Do you remember?'

'Er . . . no . . .'

'Yes, you do! You must do! You talked me into the round necks instead of the V-necks!'

'No, that wasn't me, I don't . . .'

'Joseph, then,' the woman says, with certainty. 'You were the one who helped me stock up on cashmere only yesterday.'

Good grief, is there anything she doesn't *stock up* on? Or are trips to Agnes B and Joseph for sixty quid T-shirts and three-ply cashmere just like popping to Tesco for these people?

Well, no wonder I look like a shopgirl to them!

It's a tiny bit humiliating, though. Does my custom-made Lucien Black dress not send out the signal that, although I'm not quite thin or perfectly groomed enough, I could belong here, too? And haven't they even noticed my Christian Louboutins? Is there any way of drawing attention to them, without also drawing attention to the fact that my own legs don't look quite so . . . well . . . sinewy?

'No, actually I don't work in a shop at all.' I take a sip of my Bellini and try very hard to look as if I belong here. 'I . . . um . . . I have my own fashion label!'

'Oh, *really*?' Queenie gives a what-a-surprise little eye-roll. 'Well, if that's why you came to the party, then I'm afraid you're barking up the wrong tree. I'm partying tonight, not networking. Anyway, we don't stock just *anyone* here, you know.'

I feel about two inches tall. 'I'm not here to network,' I say, trying to claw back some dignity. 'I don't really need to, actually. I mean, I've got fashion buyers from Harvey Nichols and . . . that woman from Browns ringing me five times a day.'

Queenie's eyes narrow – suspiciously? 'Sorry – what did you say your label was called again?'

'I didn't. But it's called Isabel B.'

'Never heard of it,' Queenie announces triumphantly.

'Oh, well, my things don't tend to stay on the shelves for very long,' I say. 'In fact, my last collection sold out within two hours at Harvey Nichols. You have to be a real . . . um . . . *fashion insider* to get your hands on anything.'

'Ohhh, Isabel *B*,' the younger impeccably groomed woman suddenly pipes up. 'I buy it all the time!'

I blink at her. 'You do?'

'Well, of *course*! I have several of your pieces,' she says, shooting a little superior glance at the other two. 'You do the most wonderful . . .' she halts, uncertain for a moment, '. . . cashmere?'

This is brilliant! Independent corroboration! 'Cashmere! Yes! That's right.'

'But I *swear* I've seen her working in Joseph,' the older woman is muttering to herself, rather plaintively.

'Well, lovely to meet you all,' I say, desperate to a) extricate myself, before things get any more complicated and b) replenish all my lost nervous energy with some of the canapés I've seen wafting past. 'If you don't mind, I think I'm going to take a little wander around, look at the new collections.'

None of them tries to stop me.

I lurk around the fringes of the party for a little while, chowing down on as much tuna tartare as I can get my hands on without arousing suspicion, and helping myself to a couple of the goody bags that have been laid out on a big table in the middle of the store (one for me, one for Lara). But I have to say, it's a relief when Ben finally makes a reappearance. He hurries over as soon as he sees me, looking concerned.

'Iz? Are you not chatting to anyone?'

'No, but I'm fine, honestly!' I give him a dazzling smile, to show that I'm the kind of secure, confident girl who he can comfortably leave alone at a party. 'Just enjoying a little bit of me-time!'

'At a party?' he frowns.

'Well, you know how hectic life is. You have to grab it wherever you can take it!'

'But I left you with Queenie.'

'Yes, I know . . . I just think . . .' I lower my voice. 'I think Queenie didn't actually like me all that much.'

'Oh, no.' He puts a hand on my shoulder. 'Was she mean to you?'

'Not *mean*, as such,' I lie. 'Just a tiny bit . . . hostile.'

He sighs. 'God, it's my fault, I'm afraid. I should've remembered how Queenie gets when she meets girls I'm dating.'

'We're *dating*?' I blurt, before managing to gather myself. 'I mean . . . um . . . why is Queenie funny with the girls you date?'

Ben leans in very close, so he can whisper in my ear. 'Well, don't say anything, Iz, but when Queenie and Callum were living out in New York a few years ago, she ended up a little bit . . . well, obsessed by me.'

'God,' I say, hoping he can't hear my heart pounding. Because I must say, having him this close, in all his ColourCare-scented deliciousness, is an extremely pleasant experience. 'How embarrassing.'

Ben nods. 'I mean, it's been years, for heaven's sake. You'd think a crush would have worn off by now.'

'You'd think!'

'Anyway, I'm so sorry she was horrible to you, Iz-Wiz. I should've realised.' Ben suddenly seems to be thinking of something. 'Look, I tell you what – why don't we just get out of here?'

'Really?' I don't want to sound too eager.

'Yes! I mean, we haven't really had the chance to catch up properly.' He reaches into his pocket for his mobile. 'I'll get us a late table at Zuma.'

'Oh, my God, Zuma?' *Please*, Isabel. A *little* less overexcited. 'I mean, yes, I love Zuma.'

Ben grins at me and reaches for my hand. 'You know, somehow I knew you would, Isabel. Somehow I knew it.'

Germaine Greer
Greenham Common?

19 September

Dear ~~Miss~~ Ms Greer,

Let me begin by saying what a great admirer I am of yours. From your seminal 1970s text *The Female Eunuch* to your later (but, I think, no less seminal) work on *Have I Got News For You*, *Celebrity Big Brother* and my personal favourite, *Grumpy Old Women*, you have brought us wit and wisdom in equal measure for many years.

So I am wondering if you might possibly be able to spare the time ~~in your busy schedule of TV appearances~~ to help my friend Lara and me resolve a difference of opinion. Although we are both deeply committed feminists, keen to make headway in your organisation, we cannot agree on the correct attire in which to do this. Lara maintains that dungarees and Doc Martens are customary, whereas I ~~am frankly appalled by the mere sugges~~ favour a less extreme approach.

Would you not agree, Germaine, that it is still possible to be a feminist while wearing a see-through dress and pink peep-toes? That, in fact, a beneficial sense of Empowerment may even result from doing so? And, more importantly, that you might even attract more women (wimmin?) to your Cause if they felt able to swish about in something pretty rather than tramp about in a horrible old boiler suit? I feel very strongly that in this day and age, there is no need to choose between Fighting Injustice and Looking Tasteful – look no further than Bianca Jagger, who manages to combine being a Top Humanitarian with wearing really sophisticated white trouser suits. A role model for us all.

Your opinion on this matter would be much appreciated. In the meantime, however, rest assured that Lara and I will continue in our feminist endeavours as best we can, Hating Men, Promoting Sisterhood, ~~and chaining ourselves to railings if we absolutely have to~~ etc. etc.

Yours in solidarity,

Isabel Bookbinder

PS Is it OK to go out with men who talk about 'letting you' do things, and if not, can exceptions be made for men who are *extremely sexually magnetic*?

PPS You don't happen to know Bianca Jagger from the 1970s, do you? If so, I'd really appreciate an introduction.

Chapter 17

So it's the end of my first week at *Atelier*, and I must admit, I'm quite glad it's over.

It's not that it's been a *bad* week. It's just that working for Nancy isn't turning out to be quite as useful as I'd hoped. I don't know whether it's because she's a total stress case, running around town like a maniac trying to convince fashion buyers and journalists alike that Lucien Black is still a force to be reckoned with, and popping off to crisis meetings about the big buyout with her lawyers every five minutes. Let alone all the meetings she has when she's actually here at *Atelier*, which mostly seem to be about which celebrity should grace the December issue's front cover and whether the festive-party-frocks photo shoot in New York should feature an attractive, smiley blonde (not very *Atelier*) or a miserable, anorexic teenager (very *Atelier* indeed). But the fact remains that a whole week has gone by and, despite my close proximity to the Fashion Aristocracy, I'm not making the headway I thought I would.

Which is why I've decided, as of this very morning, that I'm going back to basics. All right, I can't rely on being talent-spotted by Lucien Black, mostly due to the fact that he's gone completely mad. But I'm still in the heart of the fashion world, here at *Atelier*. I mean, I'm surrounded by networking opportunities left, right and centre! Maybe I could get myself in with the fashion-styling girls. Cassie seemed nice, and Elektra seemed . . . human enough.

So here's my plan: I come in next week ever so casually wearing something I've designed. One of my draped Grecian toga dresses, if I'm feeling brave, or just a witty slogan T-shirt, if I'm not. I stopped by the John Lewis haberdashery department on my way home from work last night and picked up all the equipment I might conceivably need, from some scrummy black silk (perfect for draping) to a selection of posh fabric paints that should help me avoid any *ebaB* T-shirt disasters. Anyway, whatever I decide to make, the rest of the plan is for Cassie and Elektra to fall over it in rapture and beg their boss, Tania, to use it in their next big photo shoot with Kate Moss, and then Kate Moss will fall in love with it and *she'll* beg Tania to let her keep it (actually, I'm not sure Kate Moss has to beg for clothes). Then she'll wear it to Glastonbury with Hunter wellingtons and bags of attitude, and then *heat* readers will jam the switchboards demanding to know where she got it, and Kate's agent will say, 'Oh, Kate loves this little-known label called Isabel B . . .'

Oh, my phone has started ringing. (My mobile, that is. My landline here doesn't seem to ring very much at all. It's as if Nancy was right about the stench of failure.) Anyway, I'm not going to pick up, because it's only Mum, and I know what it is she's calling about.

I mean, I know we're all meant to live in a global village nowadays, but the speed with which news of my date with Ben got from London to Shepton Mallet is truly terrifying. Mum's been leaving me messages on my phone about it since around lunchtime on Tuesday. And not just any messages. Five-Minute Specials. If it weren't bad enough, apparently, that I'd started seeing someone new without even informing Mum that I'd officially broken up with Will, and that I'd moved to Lara's without telling her, *and* that I'm making such major changes to my life when I'm in the throes of detoxification, her main reason for feeling put out seems to be that my social life is causing her huge social embarrassment.

'I mean, I haven't even *seen* Cathy Loxley since we went to her Christmas party two years ago,' she says, about a minute and a half into this morning's Five-Minute Special. 'I should've invited her and Ben's stepdad for supper eighteen months ago, but I never got around to it! And now you're seeing Ben, and, I don't know, Isabel, it makes things terribly awkward. I mean, what do you think I should do? Drop round with a plant? Ask her round for a coffee? Do you think *she'll* know you're seeing each other, or can I pretend I don't know anything about it, so it doesn't look so obvious that it's the only reason I've invited her? Honestly, Isabel, I do wish you'd think these things through a little bit better. Now, obviously I'm glad you're happy, but . . .'

Which I am, by the way. Immensely. I mean, things are going really well with Ben! Our dinner at Zuma was fantastic – lots of yummy cocktails and all these dishes that Ben ordered for us with things I've never heard of, like . . . *ponzu*, and . . . *ume bashi*. As Ben pointed out himself, it was a good thing he's so used to eating Japanese from his time in Manhattan, otherwise we wouldn't have known what to order! (Though obviously we could have just asked the waiter; but Ben seemed to be enjoying himself so much, I didn't want to point that out.) Anyway, we did loads of talking, about all kinds of things, like Ben's career, and what he likes to do with his spare time, and all these hilarious stories about his life back in New York. And the work he's been having done on his flat in Holland Park. And his loopy ex-girlfriend, Mad Saskia (his nickname, not mine).

I mean, obviously I could have talked about Will, too, but it's all a little bit too raw. And Ben didn't seem all that keen on the turn of conversation when I *did* mention Will, so I didn't bother again.

The only slightly disappointing thing was that we didn't have a bit of a kiss or anything. Just a quick peck on the lips when he dropped me back at Lara's after dinner. And he didn't even come in for a coffee. But then, as he kept pointing out, he had to be at work at seven a.m. . . . .

'Hi, Isabel!'

I've been so deep in thought that I'm not really expecting anyone to pop their head round the corner.

But when I look up I see that it's nice Cassie. She's looking faintly rumpled and hollow-eyed, but still managing to cling to her fashionista credentials in the new season's lumberjack shirt tucked into impossible-to-wear high-waisted drainpipes.

'Cassie, hello!' I smile up at her. 'Back from Nevada?' I don't know why I said that. *Obviously* she's back from Nevada.

'We just landed this morning.' She gives an exaggerated yawn. 'Jet lag's a bitch.'

'Well, you can get a nice early night tonight!'

'Actually, tonight's what I came to speak to you about. Are you free for some drinks this evening? I mean, nothing fancy, just a few end-of-the-week cocktails with me and Elektra, and some of the other girls.'

Nothing fancy? Just post-work cocktails with the *Atelier* girls, aka the most fabulous fashionistas in town? Oh, my God, it's going to be just like *Sex and the City*, isn't it? Just with even more amazing accessories.

'You don't have to.' Cassie is clearly mistaking my silence for reluctance. 'It's no biggie . . .'

'No, no, I'd love to! That sounds great, Cassie.'

'OK, cool! We usually head over to Aura, or the Light Bar, or the Glass Bar at Paper Club . . . you know, see where the wind blows us.'

'Absolutely. Well, I love all of those places.' I've never heard of *any* of those places. 'Wherever the wind blows us is fine by me!'

'Cool!' Cassie repeats. 'Well, maybe we can grab a cab together after work.'

Tempted as I am by the idea of zipping around town in a black cab with a posse of *Atelier* girls, I'm going to have to decline this part of the invitation. I mean, I'm not like them. I can't just throw on a cutting-edge hair accessory and a lick of mascara and get accepted into the coolest places in London. No – I'm going to need a full overhaul back at Lara's flat, where I can try to forge an acceptable outfit out of every single item of clothing I own.

'Actually, I have somewhere to be right after work . . . but if you leave me your mobile, I'll call you and find out where you've gone.'

'OK, sure.' She scribbles down her number on my message pad, signing with a not-very-cutting-edge smiley face. 'Oh, hey, is Nancy in right now?'

'No, she's not.'

'Oh, well, I'll send her over anyway. She can leave a message with you.'

'Who can leave a message with me?' I ask, but Cassie's already disappeared back round the corner, towards the fashion department. It's only about ten seconds before I hear more light footsteps, and another girl appears from where Cassie just vanished to.

'Hi,' she says, in a very quiet voice. 'Nancy's not around, then?'

'I'm sorry, I'm afraid she's working from home today.' I smile up at her, trying to work out where I recognise her from. 'Can I take a message?'

'Umm . . .' She fiddles nervously with the heavy fringe that hides her eyes. 'Yes, I suppose you can. Can you just tell her that . . . well, tell her that I was asking after her, and that I'm really, *really* sorry.'

'Of course!' It's a slightly unusual message, but I dutifully write it down on my telephone pad anyway. 'And can I take your name?'

She looks surprised. 'Umm . . . Eve? Eve Alexander?'

This is Eve Alexander? This slightly straggly-looking girl in saggy grey jeans and an outsize sweater, with unkempt hair and a quite distinct pimple breaking out on her chin?

'You don't recognise me,' she says ruefully. 'Great. I knew I looked like shit this morning.'

'What? No! No, you don't!' And actually, she doesn't. I mean, now that I'm looking at her more closely, her stunning looks are becoming more obvious. Yes, her fringe could do with a trim, but the eyes it's hiding are the incredible long-lashed ones I recognise from the close-ups in her mascara adverts, and her flaky lips are just as wide and plump as they appear on the screen. 'I'm just used to seeing you in a corset and a crinoline, that's all!'

'After four hours in hair and make-up, you mean,' she smiles. 'Anyway, listen, can you just give Nancy that message and ask her to . . . well, she probably won't want to call me,' Eve is going on, rather awkwardly. 'I mean, she probably hates me right now.'

I'm just about to reassure her with a whole spiel

248

about Nancy didn't mind about Eve's defection in the slightest, when it occurs to me – Nancy's the one I should be loyal to here! I mean, obviously, Eve is a top Hollywood celebrity, so I wouldn't be stupid enough to start lecturing her about abandoning Lucien Black in his hour of need. But she seems like such a nice, normal girl that I can't believe she'd take too badly to me giving her something closer to the truth.

I take a deep breath. 'Look. She's not thrilled about it. I'm sure she'll appreciate your apology, but she is pretty upset.'

'I knew it. I *knew* it. I *told* Jasmine, *I'm* going to be the one Nancy ends up annoyed with . . .'

'Oh, but she's pretty furious with Jasmine, too,' I say, to cheer her up.

But Eve isn't paying attention. 'I knew I shouldn't let myself get bullied by everyone, but I gave in.' She lets out a long, weary sigh. *'Again.'*

Well, this is interesting. I mean, if anyone can spot the long weary sigh of a person who's fed up with running around in circles trying to do what everybody else wants, it's me.

Is there any chance Eve is in the mood for making a decision for herself, for a change?

'You know,' I say, 'you really don't just have to do what everyone else tells you. I mean, if you want to wear Lucien Black, you should do it.'

'It's not that simple. Jasmine's already agreed something with the people at Marchesa.'

I ignore the fact that my phone has started ringing.

I feel I'm really on the verge of a breakthrough here. 'But you agreed to wear Lucien Black before, and you changed your mind about that.'

Eve shoots me a look from behind her fringe. 'I didn't change my mind. My stylist and my publicist changed their minds. And to be fair, I can kind of see it from their point of view. I mean, nobody wants to touch Lucien with a bargepole after that hideous collection he did the other week . . .'

'But Eve – I mean, Miss Alexander – the dress Lucien made for you is gorgeous. Honestly! You'll feel like a princess in it.' I don't tell her that I know this from experience, having worn it the other night. I mean, she's never likely to agree to wear it if she thinks it's already been worn by a total nobody, is she?

She seems to be wavering. 'What colour is it?'

'Black. But not boring black,' I add hastily. 'It has all these little details . . .'

'No, black is good. Marchesa want me to wear this pale lavender colour.' She plucks, absently, at the tops of her arms. 'Everyone's worried I'm going to look huge in it, so I won't be eating a morsel for the next two weeks.'

This is somewhat dispiriting, I have to say. Having squeezed myself – *just* – into the crystal-mesh dress that was made to fit Eve, it's not good news to hear that there's a general consensus that she's some kind of whale-woman. But then, the people at Marchesa probably have different standards from most. And Eve's figure looks pretty great to me, even if most of it is invisible beneath her giant sweater.

'Lucien does always design so well for my body shape,' she's saying now, wistfully.

'Exactly!' I lean forward, ignoring my phone as it starts ringing *again*. 'Think what a relief it'll be to know you're wearing his black dress instead of some lavender thing from Marchesa!' I try to load my voice with sufficient scorn, despite the fact that the lavender thing from Marchesa is probably exquisite. 'I mean, you'll be able to pig out for the next two weeks instead of starving yourself on lettuce leaves . . .'

'Isabel?' Lilian's sharp voice interrupts me. She's stalking down the corridor from the reception area with a frown that could curdle milk. 'Why aren't you answering your . . . oh, Miss Alexander!' she gasps, as she sees Eve. 'I'm so sorry, I didn't realise you were with Isabel.'

'No, well, I shouldn't be, really.' Eve is starting to turn away from my desk. 'It was a long flight. And I think Cassie has a car waiting for me.'

'Eve . . .'

'I'm sorry,' she says. 'I can't do it. But like I said . . . tell Nancy I'm so sorry.'

Chapter 18

I almost match Lilian glare for glare as Eve hurries away. 'I was just trying to do Nancy a favour!'

'You'll do her more of a favour by answering her calls when she tries to ring you!'

'That was Nancy ringing?'

'Yes. She needs you to pick something up from her at her flat.'

Damn. Just when I was about to start making some headway on my punky T-shirt collection.

'Her flat? On Mount Street?' Nancy doesn't exactly live above the shop (sorry – the concept store) but a couple of blocks down the road from it.

'Yes, Isabel. On Mount Street. Oh, and someone's just arrived for you at Reception,' Lilian adds, as I get up and grab my handbag. Her pinched face shows that she disapproves of personal visits even more than personal phone calls. 'Your sister-in-law, or something.'

My heart stops for a moment. 'Daria? Oh, God, is there something wrong with the baby?'

'No, I think her name is Annie. And she doesn't *look* pregnant.' Lilian folds her arms. 'Can you just come and sort her out, please?'

Annie is sitting in Reception, looking more dazzling

than ever. She's smartly dressed, for a change, in a black jacket and (nearly) matching trousers, and even a pair of proper shoes in place of her usual trainers. Still, this new sophistication is a veneer at best, because she's still trying to engage people in conversation by saying things like 'Morning!' and 'Chilly out, isn't it?' At *Atelier* magazine, for God's sake! I mean, why doesn't she just stick a piece of straw in her mouth, lean on a gatepost, say *Arrrrr* and be done with it?

'Iz-Wiz!' She jumps up when she sees me and gives me – no, not her usual rugby-player hug, but an unusually metropolitan kiss on each cheek. Maybe the sophistication is more than a veneer after all. 'I'm sorry to come by your work like this! But this is my only day off this week, and I had to come and talk to you . . .'

'Annie, I'm really sorry, but I'm just dashing out.'

'I'll come with you!' Annie's not the type to be deterred. She's a games teacher, for heaven's sake. A large part of her job is refusing to accept excuses (sore throats, period pains, broken ankles) and railroading people into doing what she tells them. 'Lovely day, walk'll do me good.'

'Actually, I was about to get a taxi . . .'

'Oooh, even better!' Annie practically pulls me towards the elevators. 'I love London taxis!'

The moment we're in a taxi, Annie turns to me. 'So! Wizbit! Loads to discuss! Are you bringing Ben as your plus one?'

'What?'

'Your plus one.' She roots in her big black bag for a notepad, and flicks through several pages. 'To the wedding. We're trying to finalise the guest list.' She turns the notepad round to show me my name, about halfway down the list – *halfway down?* I'm the groom's sister! – with *plus one?* written next to it. 'Obviously Ben will be invited anyway, so if he's your plus one . . .'

'Annie! We've only been on one date!' I eyeball her. 'Anyway, how do you know I'm . . . seeing Ben?'

'Oh, he called Matthew before your date, told him you were going out. Said he'd behave himself – isn't that sweet?'

So the source of the leak to Mum has made itself clear, at any rate.

Slightly odd to call up Matthew beforehand, though. I mean, was he asking *permission?* And as if Matthew could give two hoots whether Ben behaved himself with me or not.

'It would free up a place, you see,' Annie goes on, 'and I have so many new people I need to invite, from St Dominic's, and from my new yoga class . . .'

I can't keep up with any of this.

Least of all the fact that Annie – hearty, jolly-hockey Annie – has taken up *yoga?*

'. . . or we might even be able to squeeze Lara in,' Annie is saying. 'I know Matthew would like to have her there, if we have room.'

'Oh, well, Lara!' I say hastily, trying to put the

dampeners on this one. 'She tends to be away a lot over the summer.'

'But we're not planning a summer wedding. We're aiming for late Feb. Either the seventeenth or the twenty-fourth, depending on where we decide to have the reception. Matthew's keen on the rugby club, but – well, I haven't actually put it this way to him, obviously, Wiz, but *over my dead body*!' She gives a cheery laugh. 'Now, Amanda, this friend of mine from yoga, she's mentioned this lovely-looking hotel, Babington House . . . it's only about ten miles away from Mummy and Daddy's, and not very far from your parents either . . .'

'Babington House? Are you *sure*?'

'I know, it's expensive! But Mummy and Daddy are paying for most of it.'

'No, I didn't mean . . . it's just . . . well, Babington House is terribly *trendy*, Annie. Are you sure it's the kind of place you and Matthew, and . . . well, your friends . . . will feel comfortable?'

Annie shoots me an annoyed look. 'We live in London now! You're not the only one with trendy friends! Anyway, there's limited space, though. So I really will need to know about you and Ben sooner rather than later.'

Suddenly my mind has whooshed ahead to Annie and Matthew's wedding day . . . Ben will be looking devastating in his posh grey morning suit, perhaps striding around our Holland Park flat . . . sorry, *his* Holland Park flat . . . practising his brilliantly witty

255

best man's speech, while I put on something fabulous from my new Collection and tilt my Cozmo Jenks pillbox to a coquettish angle on my tumbling, frizz-free hair . . .

'. . . and I need your friend Barney's phone number.' Annie interrupts my thoughts. 'Do you think it's too late notice to ask him to do me some canapés for the engagement party tomorrow?'

'You mean your house-warming party?'

'Oh, no, now it's both! We've invited loads more people, Wizbit – my parents, your parents . . .'

Well, that's just great. I'd actually been looking forward to the party tomorrow night. Another chance to see Ben, have a few drinks together . . . Now I've got the prospect of Mum assuming I'm high on something and quizzing me about Cathy Loxley, and Dad continuing his You Have Shamed Us act and refusing to talk to me.

'Anyway, *house-warming* can sound a little bit studenty, don't you think? I mean, we live in London now, Iz,' Annie says, for the second time in as many minutes. 'Which is why I want Barney to do the nibbles . . . I mean canapés . . . if he can. But all this isn't really what I came to speak to you about, Wiz. Now, before you say anything, I just want to promise you I'm not going to turn into one of those . . . what do they call them . . . Bride-monsters?'

'Bridezillas,' I say warily.

Because I'm getting a nasty feeling that I know exactly what Annie is about to ask me.

She wants me to be a bridesmaid, doesn't she?

This is not good.

I mean, how in God's name could I swing it with Lara? Because even if she doesn't get invited, if I know Lara (and I think I do) she'll devote days – weeks, even – to poring over every wedding photo she can get her hands on, analysing every single facial expression of Matthew's so that she can see whether it really *is* the happiest day of his life, or whether a hasty divorce is in the offing. So how likely is it that she isn't going to notice me standing in the group shots, like Judas in flouncy lemon-yellow satin?

And it will be flouncy lemon-yellow satin. I mean, this is Annie we're talking about. I'll be lucky if I get away without a hairband made from yellow roses and a matching paper parasol.

'Oh, Annie, you're sweet to ask, but I just don't know if I can take on such a huge responsibility.'

'But it won't be a huge responsibility!' Annie grabs my hand. 'I'm really laid-back about it all!'

Well, that's clearly just a lie. 'But . . . look, being a bridesmaid is a much tougher job than people think . . .'

Why has Annie started laughing?

'I don't want you to be my bridesmaid!' she guffaws. 'I mean, no offence, but *you*? As a *bridesmaid*?'

Hold on just one moment. 'What would be so bad about that?'

'Isabel! I need people to chivvy me about and

257

organise me! If you were my bridesmaid, I wouldn't even get to the church on time! Or if I did, it'd be the wrong church, in the wrong county.'

I give her a look.

'On the wrong day,' she adds. 'In the wrong month . . .'

'Yes, yes,' I say. 'I get the point.'

'Anyway, I have to have Ginny and Fiona and Eleanor and Camilla as my bridesmaids, because I was bridesmaid for all of them. No, Wizzy, I want you to be in charge of the elderly relatives.'

'Sorry?'

'I'm delegating. Amanda told me right from the start, it's what saved her wedding and her sanity. You give everyone in the extended family a job to do, which means everybody gets to feel involved, and the stressed-out bride doesn't have quite so much to be dealing with. Oh, and the groom, obviously,' she adds, as an afterthought.

'So you're giving me care of the elderly relatives?'

'Yes. It's a *very* important job,' says Annie, in the tone of voice I'm sure she uses on the poor girl who's always picked last for netball teams. 'You'll need to keep them supplied with refreshing cups of tea, help them get taxis at the end of the evening . . . maybe it would be a nice touch for you to supply some little earplugs for them to use when the band plays. But those details are completely up to you, of course,' she adds. 'I don't want to get all control-freaky about it!'

258

I can hardly believe I'm hearing this. 'What does everybody else get to do?'

'Well, Mummy's in charge of the cake, of course. Your mum will be doing the flowers, because she's quite the expert on them, isn't she?' Annie flicks through her lists. 'I'm going to ask Marley and Daria to do the seating plan. I'm sure they've got some clever mathematical computer program that can work it all out nicely . . .'

So everyone's been given a job relevant to their talents, and I'm on Dotty Old Aunt Detail. She couldn't enlist my help to find her a wedding dress, or give her the benefit of my undoubted expertise on the shoes? She couldn't put me in charge of wedding-day make-up?

'. . . Auntie Vicky's booking the video man, my cousin Penny is sorting out the sugared-almond boxes . . .'

She couldn't even put me on *wedding favours*?

Is this what's going to happen, now that Annie's officially becoming a Bookbinder? She's going to start displaying as little faith in me as everybody else I'm related to?

Thank God, we're just turning on to Mount Street, so she doesn't have to see the embarrassment flooding my face. I start clambering out. 'Well, Annie, it was really nice having this chat with you . . .'

'Oh, absolutely! So, I'm officially putting you down for the Elderly Relatives,' says Annie in a voice that brooks no argument, closing up her notepad.

'Now don't forget to text me Barney's number later on!'

Suddenly, I hear a man's voice behind us. 'Is that . . . Isabella?'

Hugo Tavistock.

'What a splendid surprise!' He's walking towards the building with a polystyrene tray of coffees in one hand, looking suave in pink shirt and chinos. Just like the last time I saw him, he's abnormally well coiffed, as though he's either just come straight from the hairdresser or he's spent a minimum of an hour in front of the bathroom mirror with the diffuser and a bumper can of Elnett. 'You've just caught me on *le café* run, I'm afraid! Much needed. Out late last night. At Annabel's,' he adds, just in case I didn't get the point that he's a debonair man about town. 'So, what brings about this glorious visitation? Business or pleasure?'

Oh, God, *please* don't let him say anything about me just being a PA. News of my date with Ben got back to Shepton Mallet fast enough; the fact that I've lied about my highly prestigious internship could, too.

'I'm here to see Nancy,' I begin, 'to discuss something extremely important about Lucien Black's latest Collection . . .'

'And you've brought a friend!' Surprise, surprise, he's clocked the Amazonian blonde. '*Enchanté*,' he goes on, grasping Annie's hand between both of his, and looking for a moment as if he actually might raise it to his lips. 'Hugo Tavistock.'

'Annie Sinclair.'

'Annie!' he repeats rapturously. 'So, do you work for *ma femme*, too?'

'No, she doesn't.' I stare, pointedly, down at the hand he's gripping. 'She's my brother's fiancée.' Hopefully *fiancée* is a word he might recognise, given his fondness for chucking about little bits of French.

'Oh, well,' Hugo smiles at Annie. 'I didn't *think* a girl who looks like you would work for Nancy.'

What is that supposed to mean?

'Actually, I thought you must be a model,' Hugo adds.

Annie giggles, and flicks her hair over her shoulders. 'No! I'm just a games teacher.'

'Ohhhh.' Hugo is barely even bothering to hide the fact that his filthy mind is suddenly filled with images of Annie in a short pleated hockey skirt, whacking balls around with a big stick. 'Where do you teach?'

'St Dominic's.'

'I don't believe it. My daughter is at St Dominic's! Do you know Polly Tavistock-Wells?'

'She's in my Under Fifteen Lacrosse A team!'

'Well, then I must find the time to come and watch her play! My ex-wife has been badgering me about it ever since term started, but I haven't had the time to get to a game yet.' He gives Annie a dazzling smile. 'Now I know you'll be there, I'll make *un peu plus d'effort* . . .'

'Well, Annie, you should be getting along now, I'm sure!' I say. 'I know you've lots to do!'

'But it's my day off.'

I glare at her. 'Well, *I've* got lots to do. Can you let me in, Mr Tavistock? I think Nancy will be waiting for me.'

Hugo rolls his eyes at Annie, like I'm some kind of spinsterish chaperone. 'Well, it was delightful to meet you.'

'Maybe I'll see you at St Dominic's soon!' Annie gives him a smouldering look I've never seen her do before. 'Your Polly has a brilliant twenty-five-metre sprint on her.'

'Come on the reds!' says Hugo, smouldering back at her.

'Bye, Annie!' I give her a big goodbye wave. 'Got to get on now!'

Thank heavens, the pair of them take the hint. Hugo starts unlocking the front door, and Annie strides off down Mount Street.

The Tavistocks' apartment is on the fifth floor of their building. I race up the stairs as fast as I can to prevent Hugo getting five flights' worth of rear-viewing, and knock on the door. Nancy opens up a moment later.

She looks like she hasn't slept, and there's a large spot erupting on her jawline. But, fashion trouper that she is, she's still managing to work a rather fantastic 'at home' look of cashmere yoga pants, a drawstring camisole, a floor-length Missoni cardigan, Christian Louboutin flip-flops and her signature chandelier earrings.

'Hey, Izzie. Oh, hi, hon,' she adds to Hugo, arriving

a flight and a half behind me with his tray of coffees. 'Can you take those in for Magnus and Charlotte?'

Hugo pushes past us irritably. 'You know, we're paying them enough already,' he puffs. 'I still think they could supply their own bloody coffee.'

I notice he's not calling it *le café* any longer.

'They've been here all night,' Nancy hisses after him. 'I think it's the least we can do!' Once he's gone, she turns to me. 'You'd better come and wait in here, Izzie. My lawyer and accountant will be a few more minutes.'

The little sitting room she ushers me into is a bit of a surprise. I mean, don't get me wrong – it's beautifully decorated, with elegant bare floorboards, sage-coloured walls and pale sofas. But it's incredibly small – far smaller than I'd have thought, for someone in Nancy's position – and oddly spartan. There are no pictures on the walls, for one thing, and it feels like the heating hasn't been on in days.

'Thanks for coming, Iz,' Nancy says, flopping into a chair. 'I just need you to deliver a memo for me. To Redwood's lawyers.'

'Is everything all right?'

She runs a hand through her hair. 'Redwood hit us with a revised offer yesterday night. Just like I thought they would.'

'They're offering less money?'

She nods. 'Way less.'

'Oh, God. Will you have enough to do the fragrance line?'

She gives me a funny look. 'That's not really the big issue right now, Izzie. We've been going through their revised offer and seeing how we can make it work with the original plans we had for expansion.'

'Um – I'm not an expert or anything,' I begin. 'But can't you just . . . I don't know the terminology . . . play hardball? Threaten to walk away from the deal, I mean, until they offer more?'

'If it was that easy, believe me, we would.' Nancy slumps backwards. 'But we're not in a very strong position right now. Nobody's buying our stuff, God only knows when Lucien's going to be back on his feet, we're an industry joke after the last collection . . . Frankly I'm amazed they're still offering anything at all. Nobody else is going to.'

'Then why don't you *actually* walk away from the deal?' Maybe my fresh perspective on this might give them a huge breakthrough! 'You could wait until things turn a corner and look for an investor again! There's no point in selling now, is there, when things are so bad for you?'

'Oh, well, I suppose you're right. I mean, the only point being that we're broke.' Nancy's tone is savage, suddenly.

'Broke?'

She flaps a hand round at the tiny, chilly room. 'Can't you tell we're packing things up? We can't even stay in this poky little place any longer. We're looking for somewhere cheap on the outskirts of town – if we can even afford that, after what Redwood have offered.'

'But you own a top designer label!' I blurt, before I can stop myself. 'I mean . . . what I mean is . . .'

'It's all right. I'm still kind of appalled by it, too. Not that we were ever making a fortune, mind you. I mean, the overheads, the store, the cost of showing . . .' She sighs. 'But the company's still worth what Redwood originally offered for it. It's me and Lucien who are personally broke.'

'Oh.' I don't really know what to say to this. 'I'm sorry. I shouldn't have said anything.'

'You weren't to know. I don't exactly advertise it.' Nancy leans forward and rests her head in her hands. 'And I've only got myself to blame. I should probably have left Lucien two years ago – I mean, he was the only one with the debts back then.' She glances up at me. 'You can't tell anyone this, Izzie, OK? I mean, it's his habits that he's lost a fortune on. It's not exactly edifying.'

For a moment, I get a picture of Lucien Black attiring himself in the world's most expensive monk's outfit . . . then I realise that's not the kind of habit Nancy's talking about.

'Drugs,' I say, glad that Mum's not here.

'And boozing. And the horses. You can see why I couldn't just abandon him, Izzie. I bought up most of his half of the company, just to keep the wolf from his door, then I helped him pay for rehab, which burned another big hole in my pocket . . . It's why I have to sell to Redwood right now,' she adds. 'I've got nothing left. Whatever they pay me, I need.'

'I'm sorry,' I say again, just as there's a light knock at the door, and an exhausted-looking man sticks his head round it.

'Magnus!' Nancy gets up. 'Are we done?'

Magnus, clearly too shattered even to speak, just waves a thin plastic ring binder.

'Great.' Nancy hands it to me. 'Here you go, Izzie.'

'So I'm taking this to Redwood? On Brook Street?'

'Actually, they're meeting with their own lawyers this morning, so you're taking it there. Great Portland Street.'

That's brilliant! I can drop by the Coffee Messiah and have a chat with Barney.

Oooh, I can even pick his brains on what he thinks I ought to be drinking with the *Atelier* girls this evening. He may not exactly be cutting-edge about fashion, but if there's a hot new cocktail doing the rounds, Barney will almost certainly have read about it.

'You can just leave it at the front desk,' Nancy tells me, scribbling down the name and street number of the lawyers' office on a pad from a side table. 'Tell them it's for Mr Carmichael, visiting from Redwood Capital, and they'll make sure it gets to him.'

'Carmichael. No problem.'

'Oh, and just one thing,' Nancy adds, as we head into the hallway. 'Uh . . . I'm sure you won't see anyone from Redwood, but just in case you do, you should know that I'm telling them that Lucien is . . . going away for a while. That he's going somewhere nice and peaceful to work on the new collection.' She

pauses. 'Actually, he's going somewhere for . . . well
. . . treatment.'

'Well, that's good news, isn't it?' I give Nancy an
encouraging smile.

'Good news? That my best friend has to go into
rehab? *Again?*' she adds pointedly.

'Good news that he's agreed to it. Instead of being
in denial, I mean.' God, I'm starting to sound like
Mum.

Nancy snorts. 'Oh, believe me, Izzie, he's in deep
denial. But I'm putting my foot down about this. I
mean, if I can get him back on the straight and narrow,
we should be able to keep Redwood from ditching him
the moment this deal goes through.'

'They could *ditch* him?' I'm astonished. 'But . . .
Lucien *is* Lucien Black. How can they buy his company, with his name on it, and get rid of him?'

Nancy shrugs. 'It's been done before. They'll keep his
name and just hire someone else to run the label.
Someone who'll design nice, safe, commercially viable
collections. Someone who won't just chuck away eight
years of hard slog because they come up with brilliant
ideas like sending plastic bags down the catwalk and
throwing dangerous missiles at top magazine editors . . .'

'Well!' I interrupt, before she can work herself up
any further. 'I'm sure this stint in rehab will be just
what the doctor ordered!'

'I hope you're right.' Nancy opens the front door for
me. 'And thanks again, hon. It was good to talk about
this.'

Chapter 19

The lawyers' address Nancy has given me is only fifty yards away from Barney's stall, which is terrific news. Not only do I get to stop by and have a catch-up with Barney, but it's also a great opportunity for me to set up a bit of viral marketing. I'll take a Coffee Messiah cappuccino to the front desk with me and sip it orgasmically while saying, loudly, how lucky they are to have such brilliant coffee right on their doorstep. Everybody knows lawyers need a ton of coffee to get through their monumentally tedious working day, plus if there's a single group of people anally retentive enough to accept all Barney's myriad rules and regulations, it's lawyers.

And from the looks of things as I climb out of my taxi on Great Portland Street, Barney needs all the help he can get. Despite the fact I can see people swarming all over the streets with giant Starbucks and Pret A Manger cups in their hands, nobody is queuing at the tomato-red coffee cart. Barney is just standing behind it, in his baseball cap and apron, polishing an already gleaming Faema with a soft cloth.

It's a tiny bit heartbreaking.

'Iz!' He's seen me (reflected in the Faema?) and is

waving me over. 'What are you doing here?'

I give him a hug, noticing that he's squishier than ever. Well, at least all the pastries aren't going completely to waste. 'I've got to deliver something to that office over there.'

'Pritchard and Haynes?'

I peer over the road to read the lettering on the steel plaque. 'That's the one.'

'Oh, yes. I've had a few of them come over here.'

'So they're already good customers, then?'

'No, actually!' Barney is turning tomato-red with indignation, to match his uniform. 'You know, Iz, I thought you might have a bit of a point about all the antioxidants in coffee. I mean, that horrible pregnant woman seemed to like the idea. So I put this out.' He points to a small blackboard on the counter. It reads COFFEE IS GOOD FOR YOU – ASK YOUR BARISTA FOR MORE INFORMATION (please allow ten minutes).

'Er – well, that looks good, Barn . . .'

'Not when you're suddenly inundated with people coming down from their offices and asking you if you're adding guarana shots. Or using organic soy milk. I mean, organic soy milk, Iz! What the hell do people think I'm trying to do here?'

'I don't know, Barn – run a business?'

'By compromising my principles?' he demands, as if I've just suggested he open a child sweatshop in Malaysia. 'By selling out? To people who think you can put guarana shots in coffee?'

You know, maybe it's best not to ask him what he knows about the very latest in cocktail development after all. 'Well, I'd love a coffee, please,' I say soothingly.

'OK! Single espresso?'

'God, no, I'll have a . . .' I notice his stony face. 'Single espresso. Lovely.'

'So.' Barney starts the grinder. 'How's everything going?'

'Well, working at *Atelier* is fine. I mean, I don't get to do very much, but Nancy's a sweetheart. And I'm going out for drinks with some of the girls this evening, which is kind of exciting . . .'

'I meant with Will, actually.'

'Oh. Right.'

'Are you sure you're not being a bit hasty about all of this?'

'*Hasty?*' I know Barney's always been a big fan of Will's, but this is loyalty gone mad. 'Barney, I caught him in bed with a Russian tax-law genius!'

Barney pulls a face. 'That's bad, obviously. But it was less than a week ago, Iz. And Lara told me you've already started seeing someone else. Some dishy friend of Matthew's?'

'When have you been speaking to Lara?'

'Oh, she's called me a couple of times late at night – you know, when she's having trouble sleeping because she can't stop thinking about Matthew?'

'I . . . but . . . she isn't sleeping?'

'Oh, come on, Iz!' Barney puts his hands on his hips.

It makes him look rather like a friendly sugar bowl. 'She's been wildly in love with him for fourteen years! Don't you think she might be a *little* bit put out by the fact he's getting married?'

'Yes, Barney, I am aware of the situation. But she's not saying anything to me! All she's doing is . . . cooking chicken stir-fries!'

Barney frowns. 'God, I hope she's using a proper wok. Because the heat distribution of a normal frying pan is totally inadequate for . . .'

'That's not my point! Why is my best friend phoning someone else in the middle of the night rather than talking to me? I mean, I'm right next door!'

'I wouldn't take it personally, Iz. Maybe Lara doesn't feel she can say too much to you because he's your brother, and everything.'

'That's never stopped her before!'

'No, but maybe she doesn't want to go on too much now that you're going to have to have Annie as your sister-in-law, and everything. Maybe she thinks that isn't really fair on you.'

'*Maybe?*'

Barney looks flustered. 'Well, I'm only *guessing* . . . oh, and that reminds me!' He seems relieved to have found a way to change the subject. 'Talking of Annie, she actually left me a message about half an hour ago. Something about doing some canapés?'

'Yes. It's for their engagement party tomorrow.'

'Ooooh.' Barney's eyes go wide. 'I love doing canapés! And what a great opportunity for publicity for Coffee Messiah! I can serve everything on Coffee Messiah plates, with Coffee Messiah napkins . . .' Suddenly, he stops. 'Can I help you, sir?'

I'm taken aback for a moment, until I realise that he's speaking to a man who's just walked up beside me.

'Yeah, get me a coffee,' says a deep Belfast voice. 'Black, no sugar.'

I know that voice! Without making it obvious that I'm staring, I swivel my eyes sideways to get a proper look. And I'm right. It's Lucien Black.

'Certainly, sir,' Barney is saying in a stilted tone, a bit like a newly qualified actor in *The Bill* playing Man Behind Coffee Stall. 'Would that just be a double espresso, or would you like it topped up with a little hot water?'

'You mean like an Americano?'

Barney winces. 'God, no. A *little* hot water. The Italians call it a *caffè lungo*.'

'Just give me a black coffee, for Christ's sake,' Lucien growls. 'I don't care what the fecking Italians call it.'

While Barney makes the coffee, I have a closer squint at Lucien. He's dressed almost entirely in black, of course – black sweater, black jeans, black donkey jacket and a black-and-white Bedouin-style scarf wrapped round his neck. He's a bit shorter than he looked that time I saw him on the TV, and much, much rougher-looking. Which, I suppose, is hardly surprising, given the fact he's about to go into rehab for shovelling half of Colombia up his nose.

'Like what you see?' he suddenly snaps.

Oh, shit. He's caught me looking.

'No, no . . . I mean . . . I just . . . well, I know you.'

'Well, I don't know you.'

'We've spoken on the phone. I'm Nancy's assistant. Isabel.'

His mouth opens, and he blinks at me. If it weren't for the fact that it's hard to tell with pupils that dilated, I'd say he was looking a little bit startled.

'You're the eejit who was wittering on about inspiration.'

'That's right!' I beam at him. 'I'm the eejit!'

'Well. Nice to put a face to a voice.' He gropes in the pocket of his jacket for change. 'How much is that, then, mate?'

Isn't he going to say anything else to me? I mean, we're practically colleagues, for heaven's sake!

'So, I'm just taking this over to Pritchard and Haynes,' I say, waving the ring binder at him. 'Nancy asked me to drop it there.'

Now he looks at me again. 'You're here for Pritchard and Haynes?'

'Yes.'

'Oh! Well, that's why I'm here too, of course.' Lucien blinks heavy-lidded, pink-rimmed eyes at me. 'I've just been over there to tell them that I'm . . . well, going away for a little while. Nancy thought it best to tell them in person.'

The phrase 'going away' hangs in the air. I mean, just look at the state of him! Frankly, I think it was a terrible idea of Nancy's to send him to speak to Pritchard and Haynes in person. As if anyone will have been remotely convinced that he's just off to get a suntan and a little bit of R & R!

Lucien slaps a fiver down on the counter as Barney hands him his coffee. 'Keep the change, mate.'

'But it's only two twenty for a large . . .'

'I *said*, keep the change,' he repeats, already turning away. 'Grand to meet you, Isabel. I need to be running.'

'Of course. I'm sure you have a lot to pack for your . . . er . . . holiday . . .'

'Yeah. See you around.'

The airy lobby of Pritchard and Haynes is so quiet after the noise of Great Portland Street that I think for a moment that something's suddenly blocked my ears. Although the big plate-glass windows are tinted from the outside, from inside they let in streaming daylight, which makes the whole place feel ever so slightly celestial. There are two large, easel-shaped reception desks, one on each side, so I pick the one with the less-grouchy-looking man behind it, and go over.

'Hello, welcome to Pritchard and Haynes. How can I help you?'

'Hi!' I beam at him, then take a long, slow sip of my single espresso. 'Mmmm . . . this coffee is so good.'

'Right . . .'

'I'm sure you've seen the cart – I think it's called the Coffee Messiah, or some such . . . ? You really are lucky to have it right on your doorstep.'

'Is that the guy who won't make you a cappuccino unless the wind is coming from a northerly direction on the second Tuesday of the month and your middle name is Rupert?'

Damn.

'Do you have any business here?' he goes on. 'Or did you just pop by to tell me how amazing your cup of coffee is?'

'Oh, yes.' I hold up my ring binder. 'I have to leave this for a Mr Carmichael. From a company called Redwood.'

'Give it to him yourself.'

'Well, there's no need to be rude . . .'

'No, I mean, those are the Redwood guys over there.' He nods over to the sofa area that's all the way across the far side of the lobby. A stocky man in a dark suit is pacing around, muttering into a mobile phone, and another man, his back to me, is sitting in one of the plush black armchairs flicking through the *FT*. 'You might as well hand it over yourself, before they go up for their meeting.'

'Oh, thanks.' I head over to the sofas, tucking the file under my arm. 'Excuse me – Mr Carmichael?'

The stocky one, who's still on the phone, spins round at the sound of his name.

Oh, my God.

Mr Carmichael is Callum. Queenie Forbes-

Wilkinson's husband. The one Ben introduced me to at the party the other night.

Wait a moment. Ben called him *a colleague*. So does that mean . . . ?

Yes. It does.

The guy who's sitting here reading the *Financial Times* is Ben.

Now he's turned round, too, and he's staring at me. '*Isabel?* What in God's name are you doing here?'

This is a tricky question. Or rather, a perfectly reasonable question with an extremely tricky answer. Because Ben has no idea that I work for Nancy Tavistock, does he? If I hand over Nancy's ring binder to Callum like I'm meant to, it'll become fairly obvious that I'm actually just a PA, and not a fashion designer. A fact, possibly, that Ben might feel compelled to mention to Matthew the next time they speak, which will mean it gets back to Shepton Mallet faster than a speeding bullet . . .

'Isabel?' Ben repeats, getting to his feet. 'Is everything all right?'

I shove Nancy's file further up under my arm, so it's barely visible. 'Oh, I was just in the area catching up with a good friend of mine, Barney. He runs that coffee stall out there.' I nod out of the plate-glass windows, to where Barney is giving the Faema its twentieth polish of the day. 'Fabulous coffee!'

'And you . . . saw me through the windows?' Ben is frowning slightly.

'That's right!' To avoid having to explain how,

precisely, I might have seen him through windows that are tinted on the outside, I distract us both by giving Callum a little wave. 'Just saying hi!'

Callum, still talking intently into the phone as though he's only just discovered the miracle of tele-communication, doesn't wave back.

'Right.' Ben's frown deepens. 'Well, I'm here for quite an important meeting, Isabel.'

'Yes. Sorry. I didn't mean to intrude.'

'And sorry I didn't call all week. I've been horren-dously busy. I will try to call you over the weekend.'

'But you'll be at Matthew's party tomorrow, won't you?' Oh, for the love of God, Isabel, *shut up*. That sounded clingy – clingy and desperate. 'I mean,' I carry on, in the most casual, carefree, un-clingy voice I can possibly summon, 'that's if you're going . . .'

'Oh, yeah. Matt's party. Well, I'll try to make it, but I might have to play it by ear . . .'

'Ben!' Callum has finished his call and is coming over. 'That was Fred. He's just had a call from the Tavistock woman saying she's sending someone over with some memo . . .'

I shift the incriminating file even further up under my armpit. 'Callum! How nice to see you again.'

Callum blinks at my face, uncomprehending for a moment, until his eyes travel about twenty centimetres south. 'Oh, yes, I remember. Ishbel, wasn't it?'

'Isabel.' Ben gives us both a sudden, lopsided smile. 'Bloody hell, Cal, can't you even get my girlfriend's name right?'

Wait a moment. Ben's calling me his *girlfriend*?

But that's . . . amazing?

A little bit sudden?

No, no, it's amazing! Obviously! I mean, yay, and all that.

And now that Ben's warmed up by about twenty degrees, he's even putting an arm lightly around my waist. 'Sweet of you to drop in, Iz. You know I'd take you out for some lunch if I had the time, but this meeting . . . Still, as long as I see you at Matthew's party tomorrow!'

'Oh!' Now I'm really confused. 'So . . . you *are* coming, then?'

'Well, yeah! I'm busy, but I wouldn't miss it for the world!'

'Ben?' Callum is stabbing pointedly at the Rolex on his wrist. 'They'll be waiting for us up there.'

'Sure. Of course.' Ben reaches over to grab his briefcase from the sofa, then turns back to me. 'So.' He smiles again, looking sexier than ever. 'I'll see you tomorrow then, OK?'

'Yes . . . lovely.'

He leans down and very softly brushes his lips over mine. 'Can't wait,' he murmurs, before following Callum as they head towards an open lift and get in. The doors close behind them.

That was our first proper kiss!

Slightly odd, perhaps, to have your first proper kiss in a lawyers' lobby. But with kisses like that one, I'm not complaining.

I'm walking on air as I hurry back over to the reception desk and put my (hot, sweaty, armpitty) file down on the counter. 'I'm so sorry,' I say, 'but I actually forgot to give this to Mr Carmichael!'

He blinks. 'But you went over there to do just that.'

'Well, you know how it is. A million things to do and you always forget the most important one!'

'Do you need me to call someone down from the fifth floor and ask them to come and take the file back up?'

'Would you? That really would be brilliant. Thanks ever so much!'

Even as he's picking up his internal phone, I'm already hurrying back out of the revolving doors.

Chapter 20

So, as soon as I got back to the office, I really threw myself into preparation for tonight's post-work drinks. I looked up all three of the possible venues that Cassie mentioned, and found out exactly where they are, who hangs out there, and the correct choice of cocktail to order at each. I went into the main shared file on the computer and read all the articles that are going into the December issue of *Atelier*, so that I can join in any high-level fashion discussion that's likely to develop. Most crucially of all, I lurked around the fashion cupboard eavesdropping on conversations between everyone from the work experience girls to Tania Samuels, the executive fashion editor, in order to get a proper handle on the *Atelier* vernacular. Which is important, because these people do not speak about clothes the way ordinary people do. Like, trousers are not trousers. They're *pants*. Or, more often, *a pant*. Similarly, shoes are always *a shoe*; jeans are usually *a jean* (unless using the plural *denims*); you must never say 'I love your skirt' when you can say 'That's a fabulous piece' instead; and the designer rip-off jacket you might just have picked up in Hennes is not a *designer rip-off* but a *tribute to*.

And I know it sounds unimportant, but these are the kind of small details that I don't want to get wrong. I really just want to fit in, and not expose myself as a hopeless fashion civilian who can't tell the new season's Haute Hippy from last year's Boho Deluxe. (It's all to do with the amount of fringing, I think; I'm kind of hoping nobody quizzes me on it too closely.)

Anyway, as soon as I've called Cassie to find out where she's heading (the Light Bar; the St Martin's Lane Hotel; order the lavender Martini), I pull on my rigorously selected outfit (a slouchy *pant*, a strappy *shoe*, and a chiffon blouse from COS that's *a tribute to* a Stella McCartney one I saw in this week's *Grazia*) and make my way across town towards St Martin's Lane.

Inside, it's just achingly hip as I thought it was going to be. Thanks to the hours I spent Googling this afternoon, I know that the hotel's design is *a brilliant collision of influences, from the modern to the baroque, that suffuses the hotel with energy, vitality and magic*. Well. I mean, *obviously*. The lobby out front is all light and airy and filled with weird blobby sculptures (the modern?) and swirly gilt chaises longues (the baroque?), and the bar itself is breathtakingly cool-looking – a long, narrow corridor with little tables on either side, leading up to a state-of-the-art cocktail bar at one end, and all these amazing coloured lighting installations that change every few moments and turn the darkness from orangey to purplish and back again. I feel energised and vitalised already, and I've only just got here!

Through the hazy purple-tinted gloom, I can just see Cassie waving me over from the table at the back, closest to the bar, so I head towards her.

Most of the table is already full with people I recognise from the magazine – Elektra, obviously; Olivia and Shilpi from Beauty; fashion supremo Tania Samuels herself, sporting a typically bizarre Signature Look of CND T-shirt, high-waisted Levi's, shrunken Balenciaga blazer and a *Smooth Criminal*-esque fedora; several of the extremely intense girls from the Fashion Features department, who are all called wafty Victorian things like Flora and Gracie; all the fashion department interns, who spend most of their day rearranging things on rails in the airless, stuffy fashion cupboard (and look like it); and, sitting next to one of the interns, Lilian.

Yes, I'm surprised, too. I would have thought Lilian would be far happier spending Friday night doing an inventory of paper clips, or polishing the glass on the photocopiers. Actually, to be completely fair to her, *Lilian* looks as though she'd be happier spending Friday night doing an inventory of paper clips, or polishing the glass on the photocopiers. She's sipping rather sourly from a glass of wine and looking irritated by both the intern sitting next to her, and the constantly changing light feature.

'Isabel!' Cassie gives me a nice smile and a squeeze

of the arm as I reach her. 'You made it! Grab a seat and have a look at the cocktail menu.'

'Oh, no need! I always have the lavender Martini.'

'Oh, cool. I'll get you one next time the waitress comes over.'

'Thanks, Cassie!' I make my way round to the only available seat, which is between Tania Samuels and one of the wafty Victorians. Tania is deep in conversation with another of the wafty Victorians on her right, so I turn to my wafty Victorian, a milky-blonde in beatnik black, and smile. 'I don't think we've met yet. I'm Isabel. Nancy's assistant.'

'I'm Hattie.' She blinks at me curiously. 'Aren't you the one whose godmother is Bianca Jagger?'

'Um . . . yes. Yes, I am.'

'Oh, wow, I'm so pleased to meet you!' She edges forward on her seat. 'God, I only wish I'd met you three or four years ago, when I was still at Oxford. I wrote my History of Art dissertation on Andy Warhol, you see.'

'Gosh. How clever of you.'

'And as you know, Bianca Jagger was a close friend of Andy's for a time.'

'As I know. Absolutely!'

'So, does she ever speak about him?' Hattie reaches for her drink, but doesn't take her eyes off me. She seems slightly mesmerised. 'Does she tell you what it was like, you know, being there?'

'Well, not really. I mean, not with *specifics*.' I'm racking my brains for any nugget of information I may have stored away about Andy Warhol. He's Pop Art, right? Everybody being famous for fifteen minutes? Oh, and that picture of the soup can! 'Just that it was a very poppy, very artistic atmosphere . . . lots of wannabe celebrities . . . I think everybody ate a lot of soup . . .'

'*Soup?*'

'Yes, well, think about it . . . young people, living this hedonistic party life . . . they weren't likely to sit down for a proper home-cooked meal too often, were they?'

'Oh!' Hattie considers this. 'I suppose . . .'

I'm relieved to see that Cassie has caught the waitress's eye and ordered me a drink. Now I just need to find a way to get Hattie off the subject of Bianca Jagger. And Andy Warhol. And, indeed, soup. 'So! Tell me . . .'

'You see, *that's* the kind of detail I would have loved to put in my dissertation! God, if only I'd had the chance to put a few questions to Bianca.'

'And I'm sure she would have been thrilled to have answered them. Now, Hattie . . .'

'*Really?*' Hattie edges further forward on her seat. 'Because I've always thought about extending my dissertation into a book one day. I mean, I met this publisher a couple of years ago, and he said he thought there was a real *need* for some fresh perspectives on Warhol . . . Hey, Isabel, you don't think you'd be able to get me half an hour with your godmother at some point?'

'God, I'm sorry, Hattie, I really doubt that. I mean, she travels so much, you see. Back and forth from Nicaragua . . . the United Nations . . . I see her so rarely these days myself. In fact, sometimes I think she wouldn't even recognise me if she saw me!'

'Oh.' Hattie frowns, but more from disappointment, I think, than suspicion. 'Oh, well, I understand.'

Thank God for that. And thank God for the fact that my Martini is arriving.

'Still, lucky old you, having such an amazing godmother!' She's getting an even waftier look about her than usual. 'God, everything she's lived through . . . Mick Jagger, and the Sandinistas . . .'

'Actually, I think Mick Jagger was with the Rolling Stones,' I correct her politely.

'I *meant* the Sandinista revolution.'

'Ah. Of course. The Sandinista revolution.' Well, I can't admit I've never even heard of it, can I, not when it was clearly such a big deal to my alleged godmother? 'Good revolution, that one. Great, in fact . . .'

'Oh, *crap*.'

Oh, no, she's rumbled me, hasn't she? I've said something seriously stupid – I mean, *seriously* seriously stupid – and Hattie has cottoned on to the fact that I'm making this all up. 'Hattie, can I just explain . . .'

'What the hell's she doing here?' Sounding a lot less wafty now, Hattie is actually staring over my shoulder, down the bar, at someone walking towards our table. 'You might not have met her,' she adds, snatching up her drink and taking an irritable gulp. 'She used to do your job.'

'Ruby!'

'Yeah, Ruby. I didn't think I'd actually ever have to *see* her again.'

Which makes two of us.

I turn, very slightly, and cast a glance over my right-hand shoulder. Hattie is right. Ruby, and her perfectly proportioned bump, are walking towards us.

OK. It may be dark in here. And it may be that, thanks to the fact that the last time she saw me I was wearing a tomato-red Coffee Messiah baseball cap and apron, Ruby doesn't actually recognise me at all.

But that's not a risk I'm willing to take.

Can I make a dash for the bathrooms? I'm not sure there's time. Anyway, I'm hemmed in on both sides, and squeezing past three or four sets of legs will just draw Ruby's attention right to me. Elektra and Olivia-from-Beauty have jumped up to greet her, but once they stop fussing and flapping she's going to sit down in one of the vacated seats they're offering, which are directly opposite me.

Thinking quickly, I turn to my right, and smile at Tania Samuels. 'Wow – I love your hat!'

'What?'

'Sorry, I mean – that's a fabulous piece! I wonder, would you mind . . .' Before Tania can disagree I reach over, grab the fedora from her head, and place it on my own, tilting the brim forward as far as possible and hiding the top half of my face.

'Excuse me!' Tania is staring at me, her mouth open. 'What are you doing?'

'Well, I'm thinking of incorporating hats into my own Signature Look, you see.' Ruby is being drawn towards the empty seats, waving and smiling at everyone as though she's brightened their dreary lives just by being here. 'Gosh, it feels really wonderful. So natural. I mean . . .' I pick up my drink and take a couple of sips, then keep holding the Martini glass so that most of the rest of my face is hidden, too. 'It doesn't stop you from doing any of the things you can do *without* a hat, does it? You can drink, you can talk . . .'

'That's a custom-made Stephen Jones!' Tania snaps. 'Would you please give it back?'

'Isabel?' Alerted by the fact that rules are being broken somewhere, Lilian is leaning around the wan intern to see if she can get involved. 'Did you just snatch Tania's hat?'

'No! I mean, yes, but I'm going to give it back . . .'

'Well, give it back *now*! You can't just take people's things like that!'

Stickler though she is, she does have a point. Reluctantly, I take off the fedora and hand it back, making sure that, as I do so, I brush lots of my hair forward. 'Ah, yes. Now, *this* is why I worry that it's not a Look I can pull off. I'm terribly prone to hat hair.' Still clutching my glass in front of my chin, and leaning forward so that my hair hangs about my face like a heavy-metaller's, I get to my feet. 'Better go and sort myself out in the bathroom mirror . . . excuse me . . .'

It's as much of a faff to squeeze past everyone as I thought it would be, but I'm just hoping that my temporary Slash from Guns N' Roses impersonation is keeping Ruby from noticing me. Well, I mean, obviously she's noticing me, because I can distinctly hear her saying, 'Who the fuck is that, she nearly pushed the table into me?' but given that in the same breath she's back to talking about Dr Roussos and his excessive concern for her well-being, and how he's more impressed by her stoicism than any other pregnant woman he's ever treated in a twenty-year career, I think I'm getting away with it.

In fact, I think I have got away with it! I'm hurrying along the bar, past the door woman with her clipboard, out into the lobby . . .

'Isabel!'

I can hear Lilian's voice behind me. And when I turn around, the look on her face is telling me that maybe I haven't quite got away with it after all.

'Isabel, what on earth was that? Tania Samuels is the second most important person at *Atelier* magazine! You might as well have assaulted the deputy prime minister!'

Well, that's just not true, is it? I mean, for all her fury, being shouted at by Lilian is hardly the equivalent of being rugby-tackled by a police protection detail. 'I didn't assault her, Lilian. I didn't even touch her. If anything, I assaulted her hat.'

'Very funny,' she snaps.

'Look, I really didn't mean anything by it . . .'

'Well, it was very inappropriate behaviour! It may be an evening out, Isabel, but that doesn't mean you can just go around disregarding the authority of people in the office.'

'I'm sorry.' I try to look chastened. 'It was inappropriate.'

'Not *just* inappropriate! Very peculiar! I mean, it's almost like you *wanted* to create a big scene!' She folds her arms. 'Were you trying to get Tania to notice you, Isabel?'

'What? No, no, Lilian, absolutely nothing of the sort . . .'

'Because it's quite obvious that you're not comfortable in a boring old admin job at *Atelier*,' she sniffs. 'But if you want to get in as a fashion assistant, I can assure you you won't do it by acting up around Tania Samuels!'

'But Lilian. I don't want . . .' My phone is going! 'I'm sorry, I really need to get this.'

'Can't it wait?'

I pull my phone from my bag and glance at the screen. *Barbara*. 'It's Nancy. So I really should answer.'

Lilian scowls. 'All right. Fine. I'll talk to you later.'

'Sorry again . . .' I call after her, as she spins back towards the bar and I flick my phone open. 'Barbara?'

'Oh, Wiz! Thank God you've answered! I was just about to leave a message! Is this a bad time?'

'No, it's a fine time. A great time. Is everything OK?'

'Yes, Iz-Wiz, everything's great! Because you'll never guess who phoned the shop today!' She takes a deep breath. 'Lady Rutherford!'

'Lady Rutherford?' I take a seat on one of the flimsy-looking gilt-painted baroque chaises longues. 'What, you mean *the* Lady Rutherford?'

'Yes, Isabel, Lady Rutherford! From Hanley Hall!'

'But . . . what was she doing in Underpinnings?'

I'm not trying to insult Barbara. It's just that Lady Rutherford doesn't strike me as Underpinnings' most natural fit. Let's face it, she's hardly your average chinless aristo, pottering around the county towns of Somerset in tweeds and a headscarf and occasionally popping up in a Hartnell frock in the *Tatler*. In fact, you're more likely to see her on the pages of the *Sunday Times Style* supplement or even *Grazia*, in full-length Carolina Herrera at a glittering charity ball. If you don't know who I'm talking about, then you might recognise her by her name from before she was married – Abby Maynard. She was a top model about fifteen years ago, one of those amazing Amazonians who used to hang around looking glossy and toothsome with Christy Turlington and Claudia Schiffer. A couple of years back she hooked up with this slightly crusty but completely loaded lord, or knight, or peer of the realm – I'm not all that hot on titles – and now she's single-handedly propping up the whole of Somerset's economy by running a luxury organic business out of Hanley Hall, a few miles outside Taunton.

I mean, the Hanley Hall catalogues alone are enough to make you want to sprout a few apple-cheeked moppets and up sticks to the West Country for the rest of your life, to live in a gingham-trimmed paradise, milling your own stoneground flour and whittling children's playthings from sustainable oak. Oh, and looking completely fabulous while you're at it, too – because Lady Rutherford herself stars in the catalogues, posing like a pro in Jackie O-chic riding gear and Carla Bruni-esque lady-of-the-manor suits.

'Well, she wants something from Isabel B, of course!' Barbara squeaks. 'I was just closing up and I wasn't even going to take the call, but it's a good thing I did, because she told me she's up in London tomorrow and she really wants to come and see you for a fitting, and . . .'

'Hang on.' I hold up a hand, even though Barbara isn't there to see it. 'Lady Rutherford wants me to make her an outfit?'

'Yes! A party dress, she said, for some event she's got coming up, so it really is pretty important, and . . .'

'Wait. Stop.' I manage to interrupt Barbara again. Because I can really hardly believe what I'm hearing. 'You're telling me I've got a . . . a *commission* from Lady Rutherford? *The* Lady Rutherford?'

'Yes, Isabel!' Barbara actually sounds slightly impatient. '*The* Lady Rutherford. She's popped into the shop once or twice before, but she didn't buy anything – well, I'm not sure we were really her kind of thing, if you know what I mean?'

'Yes. I do.'

'Anyway, she said on the phone she'd heard about the new couture design service from a friend, and she's *extremely* keen to support local businesses, obviously . . .'

'Obviously.' Hanley Hall are big on local. Local suppliers, local farmers, local people (preferably the really smart, rich ones who have second homes on the Wiltshire/Somerset border) popping into the Hall for a biodynamic yoga workshop . . .

'. . . and she'd very much like to give us a try!'

'But . . . this is fantastic!'

'Isn't it? Who knows where this could lead?'

Barbara has hit the nail on the head. Because seriously, this could be huge.

Aside from the fact that stunning, elegant Abby Rutherford is just about the ideal Woman I'd Design For, just *think* of all her old friends from her modelling days who she can introduce to my label! God – maybe she'll end up wanting an eco-chic range in the next Hanley Hall catalogue! Biodegradable designer denim, Fairtrade evening gowns, recycled leather It bags. And then all the most right-on celebrities will start coming to me for fabulous clothing with a conscience: Cate Blanchett, Angelina Jolie, Natalie Portman . . .

Daniel Craig, who probably has to fly all over the world to appear on red carpets every five minutes, could very well be interested in a carbon-neutral tuxedo.

'Now, I've told Lady Rutherford she can come round to see you tomorrow afternoon, if that's all right? I know that's short notice, but if she comes at about four, that should give you some time to get a few things ready, see if anything takes her fancy, no?'

My heart sinks. I was hoping to have a couple of weeks' grace on this one, not least to master some of those rudimentaries of garment-making, possibly even get to grips with some sleeves. 'Tomorrow afternoon? But that's . . . really soon.'

'You can't do it?' Barbara sounds dismayed.

Well, *can't* is a very negative word.

I've got all those bits and pieces I picked up at the John Lewis haberdashery section yesterday. If I sit up all night, I've got around eighteen hours to come up with something that at least might be able to pique Abby Rutherford's interest. As for the rudimentaries of garment-making – well, I can hand-sew, can't I? And if it's a party dress that she's after, sleeves won't even need to come into it! A statuesque beauty like her is going to look amazing in one of my draped Grecian-style toga dresses. Or even an effortless body-skimming *sleeveless* tunic . . .

Plus this is a big deal for Ron and Barbara, as well as for me. Having a client as important and influential as Lady Rutherford could see off the challenge from all those boutiques in Bath that keep stealing Barbara's regular customers.

'No. I can do it. Four o'clock should be OK.'

'Oh, that's wonderful! Now, I'll send her to your friend Lara's, isn't that where you're living now?'

'Yes. Mum's got the address.' I'm already getting up and heading out of the doors on to St Martin's Lane. I'll just have to call Cassie and apologise for disappearing. Tell her I had a work emergency, which is sort of true. And it doesn't hurt, of course, that this way I get to avoid going back in and facing Ruby. *Or* angry Lilian. 'I'll expect Lady Rutherford at four tomorrow.'

'Four it is! Bye, Iz-Wiz!'

This Morning, 19 March, 11.15 a.m., ITV1

FERN BRITTON . . . and Dr Chris will be back with us later for his open surgery, so please do call in with any of your health problems, from tummy bugs to tonsillitis!

PHILLIP SCHOFIELD Now, our next guest this morning is a Top International Fashion Designer who at one point thought she was consigned to making party dresses for pensioners . . .

FERN . . . until a late-night phone call from a family friend resulted in the biggest break of her career.

PHIL Since then, she's been catapulted to global fame and fortune as the A-listers' designer of choice, and ~~the entire nation watched with pride as~~ just last month, at the Academy Awards, no less than three of the hottest actresses in Hollywood walked down the red carpet wearing her designs. She is . . .

FERN . . . Isabel Bookbinder. Isabel, darling, welcome! Lovely to meet you!

ISABEL BOOKBINDER Lovely to meet you, too!

PHIL Let's start at the beginning. A young, talented designer. Completely unconnected to the fashion world. Father a teacher, mother a local-news-round-ups journalist for the *Yeovil Express* . . .

ISABEL Actually, it's the *Central Somerset Gazette*.

PHIL Oh, my mistake! But tell us, Isabel – how did you break into the closed world of Top International Fashion Design?

ISABEL Well, Phil, fashion design was my dream ~~for yonks~~ from a very young age. Friends and colleagues had often noted how I would neglect other duties to ~~sit around flicking through~~ obsessively pore over fashion magazines. I thought about clothes in every waking moment. But doors were cruelly slammed in my face left, right and centre. Every fashion school I applied to turned me down, and [looks away, clears throat] eventually I was forced to lie to my family about winning a place at Central St Martins.

FERN Where a certain . . . Diana Pettigrew, was it? . . . not only refused to admit you to her course, but also questioned your very right to follow your dream?

ISABEL That's right. But I bear no grudges. After all, if Diana hadn't turned me down, I probably wouldn't be where I am today.

PHIL Because like Fern said in our introduction, a call from a family friend resulted in a special commission from none other than Lady Abby Rutherford of Hanley Hall, ex-model turned society hostess.

ISABEL Yes. Her first request was for me to make her something special for a party at Hanley Hall itself . . .

FERN . . . but you got on so well together that she soon began to ask you to work with her on more than just a couple of balls . . . [struggles to keep straight face] . . . I'm so sorry . . .

PHIL [covers mouth with hand, squeaks with laughter] I do apologise, viewers . . .

FERN [wheezes apoplectically] I meant, *charity* balls . . .

PHIL [hiccups] Goodness, Isabel, what must you think of us? Please, carry on.

ISABEL Well, as you say, Abby and I really clicked, and

her commissions didn't stop there. She also began to recommend my services to many of her most ~~fabulous~~ well-known friends, not to mention the range of glamorous ~~organic recycled~~ environmentally friendly eveningwear she asked me to design for her ever-growing Hanley Hall empire. That was the leap into the big time that I really needed. Requests began flooding in, and only six months later I was seeing my own-name label stocked in the finest department stores in the land. A year after that I was opening my own Bond Street boutique, and it's all just spiralled from there.

PHIL And now you're the proud owner of your very own boutique, with plans in place for your very first fragrance . . . and the word on the street is that Daniel Craig and Keira Knightley are going to star in your ad campaign.

ISABEL Yes, I really went all out for that one, ~~stalking~~ badgering Daniel Craig and Keira Knightley until they agreed to become the new faces of the label!

FERN So tell us how all this Oscars malarkey came about. Because our jolly showbiz reporter, Alison Hammond, interviewed Cate Blanchett just a couple of months ago, and she let slip that she intended to fight tooth and nail to get you to dress her for this year's Academy Awards!

ISABEL [modestly] Oh, well, that's very sweet of Cate. She and I have been real bosom buddies since . . .

FERN [splutters into script] I'm so sorry, Isabel, this is so childish!

PHIL [falls off sofa, beats floor with fist] Bosom!

ISABEL Cate and I have been *close friends* ever since the early days of my Hanley Hall collection. It was Cate, in fact, who introduced me to other ~~right on~~ environmentally aware but glamorous actresses such as Angelina Jolie and Natalie Portman.

FERN And thanks to all that, your gowns were worn by all three actresses on Oscar night this year!

ISABEL Well, I'm lucky. All three ladies are big fans of the Grecian draping effect. ~~And, thank God, they all look good in anything~~.

PHIL So what's next for you, Isabel?

ISABEL Well, after my Oscars success, the time has really come to take the Isabel B brand onwards and upwards. More boutiques, a second fragrance, perhaps an interiors line . . . It's going to be a real challenge, of course, but challenges always inspire me. There's nothing that gives me more satisfaction than starting at the bottom and doing it the hard way. [horrified pause] Oh, God, no, no, I didn't mean . . .

FERN [throws back head and howls]

PHIL [is carried from studio helpless with mirth]

FERN [mopping eyes with sleeve] Thank you, Isabel. It was lovely to have you on the show.

ISABEL Not at all, Fern. Thank *you*.

Ad break.

Isabel Bookbinder
Westbourne Grove

Daniel Craig
~~Cap Ferrat?~~
~~On location at Pinewood Studios?~~
London

Dear Daniel,

Chapter 21

God, I feel inspired.

Exhausted, yes, and extremely jittery from all the caffeine I needed to keep me up working all night. But inspired.

Because I've done it. I've actually done it. I've *made a garment*.

Two garments, in fact. Get that, Diana Pettigrew!

As soon as I got back from the Light Bar yesterday evening, I made a start. There wasn't time, unfortunately, for putting together a Mood Book, or bandying about too many Inspiring Words in my head. I just dived right into my John Lewis haberdashery bag, put on a mammoth pot of coffee, and got down to the nitty-gritty. I started out with a tunic dress – folding over a single piece of fabric and cutting a hole for the head – but I have to admit that it didn't work out quite the way I wanted it to. I mean, there was nothing terribly wrong with the actual execution: in fact, it's actually rather beautifully hand-sewn up each side, to armpit level, with an elegant running stitch that's started coming back to me from my junior-school days. But the one thing I completely forgot to think about was sizing. So while it's a perfectly pleasant tunic, it's also a perfectly pleasant *giant* tunic. Which I suspect is probably not the kind of thing that svelte, elegant Lady Rutherford is looking for.

For my second garment, my draped Grecian-style toga dress, I actually used my own body. Partly to help with the sizing issue, and partly because . . . well, have you ever tried to make a draped Grecian-style toga dress without actually draping it *on* something? I took a long length of the lovely black silk, draped it over one shoulder, looped the lengths around my waist, and then clasped it on the hip on one side with a couple of hidden safety pins. Then, once I'd eased it off, I did some more of my beautiful running stitch above and below the safety pins, so that the dress isn't actually one-sided instead of just one-shouldered. And I have to say, it's a lot more successful than the giant tunic. The silk fabric lightly skims over my tricky places – not that Abby Rutherford has tricky places – and it's gathered enough at the waist to give me . . . well, a waist. Which is no mean feat, considering the fact that I don't actually have one. The one-shouldered effect is very flattering, or it would be if I wasn't wearing it over a woolly black polo neck, and the matching asymmetric hemline is simultaneously sexy and demure.

Asymmetry: The New Fragrance for a Woman . . . Or a Man, from Isabel Bookbinder.

Now, obviously it's not perfect. I mean, I'm hoping that Abby Rutherford sees my hand-stitching as evidence of the fact that this is a truly artisanal product of the kind she's always pushing in the Hanley Hall catalogue, and not just because I don't know how to work a sewing machine yet. And I'm also hoping that she recognises that if safety pins are good enough for her chum Elizabeth Hurley, then they're good enough for her. But team this dress with, say, a fabulous pair of metallic sandals, whack a little clutch bag under the arm . . .

She's going to love it!

God, I hope that's not just the caffeine talking.

I mean, I *think* she's going to love it.

Anyway, it's not *all* about the dress. Lady Rutherford is probably going to be quite accustomed to attending dress fittings with Top International Fashion Designers, so I've done everything else I can to make myself look professional. Exhausted though I am, I've just spent a very productive half-hour throwing big white sheets all over the furniture in the living room, and dragging Lara's Chinese bamboo screen and full-length mirror through from her bedroom, to use as a private changing area. And it looks pretty good, I have to say. Not *quite* a proper studio, but not far off. I've hung both of my black silk dresses – yes, even the giant tunic one – on the back of the bamboo screen, and I've scattered about little piles of pins and old copies of *Vogue*, to add to the designer's-atelier feel. I've also just nipped to the supermarket for fresh coffee, a bottle of champagne, and every Hanley Hall product I could lay my hands on (from the yummy lemon cookies to the bleach-free toilet cleaner; I do want Lady Rutherford to feel at home), plus I've bought up virtually every white lily in West London, and arranged them in a charmingly rustic fashion in mismatching vases, old jam jars, and a couple of Lara's posh Cath Kidston coffee mugs.

And now, with an hour or so to go until Lady Rutherford's arrival, I'm just putting the finishing touches to my Uniform – black trousers with a black belt, a black T-shirt, black ballet pumps . . . Perhaps this tape measure dangling artlessly around my neck . . .

I jump, startled, as the front doorbell rings.

But it's only ten past three! If that's Abby Rutherford, she's almost an hour early. But aren't models all famously late, even ex-models?

The doorbell goes again, sounding a tiny bit impatient this time. Well, I'm going to have to go and let her in, even though I haven't had time to get the coffee ready, or put the champagne in an ice bucket. Damn it! I hastily comb my hair with my fingers, and then hurry to the front door.

'Hello!' I fling the door open wide. 'You must be . . .'

'Iz-Wiz!'

It's Mum. And Barbara. They're standing on the doorstep in the light September drizzle, like Tweedledum and Tweedledee in new-season Betty Barclay.

'What are you . . . when did you . . . *why?*'

'Well, darling, we realised we were coming up to town for Matthew's party anyway, and so we thought why not make the most of the day?' Mum kisses me on both cheeks, a new greeting for her, then squeezes past me into the hallway and starts taking off her mac, while Barbara shakes her umbrella out over the terracotta flowerpot on Lara's doorstep. 'So we did a little bit of shopping this morning, and then we had a lovely light lunch back at the hotel, and then we thought we'd pop over here and give you a bit of moral support.'

Barbara gives me a hug. 'For your first big client!'

'Oh, hasn't Lara made this place nice?' Mum is already heading for the kitchen. 'I don't think I've seen it since she first moved in. And isn't it good of her to let you stay here, darling, what with . . . well . . . everything . . .'

I try to keep my temper, so I can't be accused of Snapping (second only to Ethnic Cleansing and Genocide in the Bookbinder ledger of Crimes against Humanity. Unless you're Dad, of course, and then you can just snap with abandon whenever you want). 'Look, it's really good of you to drop by. But there isn't very much you can do here, I'm afraid.'

'Surely you can use an extra pair of hands,' Barbara says, patting my arm. 'Even if it's just tea-making!'

'Why don't I just run the Hoover round quickly? If you just show me where Lara keeps it . . . oh!' Mum has peered into the living room and is gazing in raptures at the sheet-draped furniture, the bamboo screen, and the rustic lilies. 'A proper studio! It's just like Trinny and Susannah's place!'

'And are these some of your dresses?' Barbara bustles excitedly over to the Chinese screen and picks up the toga dress for a closer look. 'Oh! Well. It's very . . . modern.'

'Yes.' I cross my arms, feeling defensive. 'Is that a problem?'

'No, no, Iz-Wiz, not at all! I mean, you're the designer! The only thing . . . a little thing . . . you are going to do some other colours, aren't you?'

'Oh, Barbara, I'm sure she is! After all, Lady Rutherford isn't going to want anything in black! She's coming here for a *party dress.*'

I take a deep, calming breath, the way Lara would tell me to. 'Mum. Barbara. I appreciate you showing your moral support, but I'm trying to do a job of work here. Lady Rutherford is accustomed to dealing with top designers all over the world, so it's very important that she thinks I'm professional.'

'Oh, I'm sure she'll think that, Iz-Wiz!' Mum gives my back a little rub. 'Really, darling, you mustn't lose your confidence, not when you've worked so hard.'

All right. That's it. 'I am not *losing my confidence . . .*'

'The only thing,' Barbara interrupts, a concerned look on her face all of a sudden, 'is that I think Lady Rutherford *might* prefer it if you didn't have all these Hanley Hall bits and bobs around.' She's pointing to the dishes of HH-stamped lemon cookies and little boxes of dark chocolate truffles in Hanley Hall recycled cardboard boxes that I've put out on the side tables. 'Not that you aren't being terribly hospitable, Iz-Wiz, of course!' she adds. 'But I just wonder if she mightn't be happier with just a simple chocolate HobNob. Or similar! Whatever you've got in stock, really.'

'You're saying Lady Rutherford will be *offended* that I've put out *Hanley Hall* products?'

'Well, I'm not sure she'll be thrilled.' Mum is unilaterally gathering up my carefully displayed organic snacks and taking them into the kitchen. 'It'll be a terrible reminder for her, after all.'

'A terrible reminder of what?'

'Of her husband dumping her for the younger model!'

'Quite literally, I gather,' Barbara adds. '*Model*, I mean. The new Lady Rutherford used to be on the catwalks, apparently.'

'Wait . . .' I hold up a hand to stop Barbara, ignoring the look Mum shoots me. 'The *new* Lady Rutherford? You mean there's an *old* Lady Rutherford?'

'Oh, don't worry, Iz-Wiz.' Barbara lays a reassuring hand on my arm. 'The right one is coming today!'

I'm getting this horrible, sinking, sick feeling. Because I have my doubts that Barbara's definition of *the right one* is the same as mine. 'Which one is that?'

'Well, the *proper* one, of course. Not *that woman* who's turned that beautiful old house into a luxury hippy commune for all her luvvie friends!'

You know, I could, quite honestly, kill Barbara.

Why couldn't she have said any of this on the phone yesterday? As far as anyone who isn't from the immediate Taunton area is concerned, there is only *one* Lady Rutherford – the gorgeous, glamorous, well-connected one who'd be any fashion designer's dream client.

And I've done all this – the champagne, the lilies, the small fortune on inappropriate Hanley Hall products – for *another* Lady Rutherford?

'Barbara! You said *the* Lady Rutherford!'

'But this is *the* Lady Rutherford,' Barbara says staunchly. 'Nobody I know will ever think of her any other way.'

'Anyway, you can't possibly mean you'd actually want to design a dress for that jumped-up little madam?' Mum is looking disapproving. 'I've heard she's horribly high-handed, with an awful manner about her . . .'

'I don't care about that!' Well, obviously I *do* care about that. It can't be much fun designing a dress for someone who's a total cow, and goes around seducing wealthy old landed aristocrats. But she's a *glamorous* total cow. Who seduces wealthy old aristocrats while wearing *fabulous outfits*. 'Look, this is just not what I was expecting . . .'

'Oh, I bet that's her now!' Mum gasps, as the doorbell rings. 'Shall I go and let her in, Iz-Wiz? Maybe when she comes in, you could be sitting by the window, sketching . . . Or flicking through a copy of *Vogue*!

'I'm getting the door.' I stamp past Mum, down the tiny hallway, and open the front door.

Standing on the doorstep is a short, plump, weary-looking woman in her mid-fifties. She's dressed in a battered green Barbour and slightly muddy cords, and she looks more like a harassed mum of four on the school run than a titled Lady of the manor – even an ex-Lady of the manor.

She frowns at me. 'Isabel?'

'Yes.'

'Of Isabel B for Underpinnings.'

I grit my teeth. 'Apparently!'

'Oh. You don't look like a fashion designer.'

Well, that's a bit rich, considering. 'Um, how should I look?'

'I don't know. Foreign, I suppose. The woman in Underpinnings told me you were just like that what's-her-name. Donna Versace.'

Did she, now? 'Well, I'm sorry to disappoint!'

'That's OK. I'm here now.' She steps into the hallway. 'I'm Sonia, by the way.'

'You don't prefer to be called Lady Rutherford?'

She actually winces. 'Obviously I'd *prefer* it. But I'm not really entitled to it any more. One of the many things my ex-husband took from me when he married a woman twenty years my junior.'

There's really nothing I can say to this. 'Sorry. Sonia. Of course. Er – won't you come on through?'

Mum and Barbara are waiting in the living room/studio, looking poised to break into curtsys.

Thank God neither of them actually does anything of the sort, but they both fuss and flap around Sonia, taking her Barbour and her handbag and ushering her on to the two-seater sofa, while I head to the fridge and get out the chilled champagne and four glasses. I mean, sod it – I may as well try and make this whole ghastly event as glamorous as possible. And having a bit of alcohol to take the edge off it all can't possibly be a bad thing.

'At half past three in the afternoon?' Sonia Rutherford – and Barbara and, of course, Mum – look at me and my champagne as though I'm offering them all fat lines of coke.

I grit my teeth. 'A cup of tea, then? Coffee?'

She accepts the offer of tea, which thrills Mum as she's allowed to bustle about making a pot, and I sit down next to Sonia on the two-seater and pick up one of my brand-new Smythson notebooks.

'So! Perhaps you can talk me through the kind of thing you're after.'

Sonia Rutherford shrugs. 'A frock.'

I shoot Barbara A Look. 'I'm sorry, I'm not being clear. What *kind* of frock? What sort of thing do you like?'

'Well, if I knew that, I wouldn't have come to you.' Sonia doesn't sound so much bad-tempered as fed up. She rakes a hand through her shaggy cropped hair and gestures down at her mud-spattered cords. 'I don't really wear dresses very often, as you can probably tell. Not particularly practical, with three kids, two smelly Labradors, and a crappy old Land Rover that's the only car my husband considers it necessary for us to have.'

There's a moment's silence. Mum clatters tea things. Barbara clears her throat.

It's up to me, then. 'Right! I see! So . . . um . . . nothing too flimsy, then . . . ?'

'Isabel!' Mum is coming back into the room with a tray. 'We told you, Lady Rutherford is here for a party dress! That is what you told Barbara, isn't it, Lady Rutherford?'

'*Sonia*. Please.' She glances sideways at me in a way that suggests she'd rather it was just the two of us as much as I would. 'And yes, that is what I told Barbara. It's my daughter's twenty-first next weekend.'

'A twenty-first! Well, then you really have to get yourself something special!'

Sonia sighs deeply, and takes a long drink from her teacup. 'That's what my friends are telling me. And Katie – that's my daughter. To be honest, I'd be happy enough bunging on an old Laura Ashley. But obviously, the new Lady Rutherford is going to be at the party, and I think I've probably got *just* enough vanity left to want to avoid looking like a total dog's dinner next to her.'

'Abby Rutherford is going to be there, too?'

Sonia shoots me a sharp smile that doesn't even begin to conceal the bitterness behind it. 'Well, my ex-husband has told Katie he won't attend if Abby isn't invited.'

There's another of those awkward pauses, while we all contemplate the utter vileness of this.

'The thing is, I just don't want to look like an idiot,' Sonia carries on. 'I'm sure Abby will show up in some fabulous outfit that costs the earth – and I don't know if you know this, but she used to be a top model . . .'

'Vaguely,' I fib.

'. . . and she's got the most condescending manner you could possibly imagine. I mean, really, she makes me feel two foot shorter, four sizes fatter, and fifty IQ points more stupid than I actually am. As if it's not enough that she's younger, and slimmer, and more successful.'

'*And* that she's got your husband.'

'Mum!'

'Oh, I don't care about that!' Sonia says. 'Let her have him, if that's what she really wants.'

'Sonia, I'm so sorry, my mum didn't really mean . . .'

'I just want her, for once, not to behave as if I don't matter. On my daughter's twenty-first birthday, in front of all her friends, I'd like to feel that I matter.'

God, I wish Lara was here. I'm not equipped to cope with this!

More to the point, I'm not equipped to provide Sonia Rutherford with the show-stopping, going-head-to-head-with-a-supermodel dress that she's obviously come here for.

I close my notebook and get to my feet. 'Look, Sonia, I have a suggestion. Why don't we have a little walk along Westbourne Grove – it's a very trendy shopping street,' I add, when she looks at me a bit blankly, 'just a few minutes from here. We can pop into some of the shops, and you can try a few things on, and maybe we can find you something for Katie's party that way.'

'Isabel!' Mum and Barbara are both looking at me in horror.

'I'm sorry, but I just don't know if I have anything that will be suitable. And you said the party is next weekend, so I really don't think . . .'

'Isabel, don't be silly!' Mum stands up, too, and grabs the Grecian-style toga and the oversized tunic from their hangers. 'You haven't even offered her one of these to try on! Now, I know they may look dreadfully plain to you, Lady Rutherford, but Isabel was talking about adding a smattering of sequins, if that's something that appeals to you . . .'

'I was not talking about adding a smattering of anything! Least of all sequins!'

'Isabel.' Barbara is trying to get my attention. 'I think Lady Ru . . . Sonia should try something on. After all, she has come all the way up from Taunton, and she was looking for a proper designer dress. I mean, that is what she came to Underpinnings for,' she adds, meaningfully.

Shit, I'm forgetting. This is Barbara's customer, too. And Underpinnings could probably really use the business.

'Well, I'm not trying *that* one on,' Sonia Rutherford

says, as I hesitate. She's pointing at the Grecian-style toga. 'I'll look like a sausage in a straitjacket. Give me the sack thing, and I'll see how it looks.'

'Yes, you know, it's the kind of piece that's really wonderful *on*,' says Barbara. 'Isn't it, Isabel?'

Well, no, actually. It's a lot more wonderful *off*. But I'm not going to say that now. 'I think you might need this, Sonia.' I pull the skinny black patent belt I'm wearing out of my belt loops, and pass it over the Chinese screen.

'A defined waist is a key part of this season's silhouette!' Mum adds helpfully, giving me a thumbs-up.

I hustle her to one side and lower my voice. 'Mum. What are you doing?'

'Helping you sell your first dress, darling!'

'But I don't need your help!'

'Isabel! Barbara is a very experienced saleswoman. And I did six months at John Lewis in Kingston before I met your father . . .'

'I don't mean that! I mean, you and Barbara shouldn't really have come today! This is *my* job, Mum. And I'm quite capable of getting on with it without your interference!'

'I don't mean to interfere!' Mum actually looks a little bit sheepish. She lowers her voice. 'Look, I was just slightly concerned, darling, that you might not be able to do a proper job of this.'

'Because of all the drugs I'm not taking?'

She's turning pink. 'Well, I know you're clean now,

Iz-Wiz, and I'm terribly proud of you, but this is such an important client for Barbara and Ron . . .'

'Ta-da!' Barbara suddenly sings out, as Sonia Rutherford emerges from behind the bamboo screen.

Well.

I wouldn't quite go so far as to say anything about a butterfly emerging from a cocoon, or a duckling becoming a swan, or any of those things that happen a lot in teen romantic comedies.

But Sonia looks . . . better.

Much better.

For starters, the nubbly black silk is wonderful against her pale, slightly freckled skin, bringing out a hint of a cheekbone and making her look ethereal rather than washed-out.

But the shape of the tunic is pretty decent on her, too. Whereas it made me look like a giant black postage stamp, on shorter, rounder Sonia Rutherford it's actually very elegant. It hits her legs at mid-calf, her slimmest part, and thanks to the belt pulling it in at the waist, it flares over her hips and thighs in an extremely flattering manner. The neckline still looks a bit ragged, obviously, but that's nothing a chunky necklace or (whisper it) a sequin scarf won't disguise.

'Sonia, you look wonderful!'

'Really?' She's turning a bit pink, and glancing in the full-length mirror. 'I must say, it's very comfortable.'

'Oh, it's fabulous, Lady Rutherford!' Says Mum. Now, what do you think, some sequins on the top half, to draw attention to your face? Or maybe dotted around the skirt; that could be very pretty . . .'

'No. No sequins.' I realise I probably ought to look as though I'm doing designery things, so I take my tape measure off my neck and measure, vaguely, up and down the sides, then blouse the fabric slightly above the belt. 'You can always try a lovely gold bag or shoes, if you want to break up the plain black a bit.'

'Oooh, yes, that'd be a nice way to jazz it up!' Barbara looks pleased.

'Well . . . if you really think it looks nice . . .' Sonia looks at herself in the mirror for a long moment, twisting this way and that. 'I'll take it!'

Then she goes and changes, while I go and call a taxi to take her back to Paddington, and Mum and Barbara to their hotel. When I come back, Sonia has written Barbara a cheque, and Barbara is trying to give me half the amount in cash, and it takes me almost ten minutes to convince her I'd feel happier just covering the cost of the silk and letting her keep the rest. And then, thank God, the taxi arrives, and I can hustle them all out of the door and wave them away.

God, that was . . . bizarre.

Nice, though, to be able to send Sonia away with a dress that, even if it's never going to put her up there with Abby Rutherford, is at least going to make her look elegant and stylish at her daughter's birthday party. I mean, exciting though it would have been to have had Abby Rutherford here this afternoon, how much satisfaction can there be, really, in making an ex-supermodel look good?

Anyway, I can still *tell* people I've made a dress for 'Lady Rutherford', can't I? People like that horrible Queenie Forbes-Wilkinson, I mean, if I ever have the misfortune to meet her again. Apart from Mum and Barbara, nobody's to know which Lady Rutherford it actually is. And I'll hang on to the Grecian-style toga dress I made for Abby, just in case (you never know) Sonia's tunic is such a hit at the party that I really *do* get a commission from her this time.

In the meantime, I need to tidy up the living room and start getting ready for Matthew's engagement party tonight. Lara will be back home any minute, and I'm setting aside at least two of the next three hours before Barney's taxi stops to collect me, to do my level best to persuade her that just because she agreed to go when it was only a house-warming, it doesn't mean she has to inflict it on herself now that it's also their engagement party.

Might do the tidying with a glass of that nice chilled champagne, though. After all, I have just sold my first ever Isabel B dress. I think I deserve it.

Chapter 22

Well, I tried. I waylaid Lara the moment she got back from her Saturday clinic. And I tried. But Lara, of course, instantly went all professional on me, and started bandying about phrases like *important part of moving on* and *necessary closure*, and getting all red-faced and huffy when I started bandying about phrases of my own like *glutton for punishment* and *are you sure you're not just going to spy on them*. Anyway, all any of that did was waste valuable time, because I utterly failed in my task. And Lara is coming.

When we finally climb into the taxi, fifteen minutes late, Barney's looking even more cranky than I am. His hair is sticking up like he's just stuck his finger in an electric socket and he's clutching a tall stack of foil-covered trays. There are even more foil-covered trays all over the back seat, and he yelps when I try to move them so I can sit down.

'Mind my soufflés!'

'But, Barn, there's no room to sit.'

'Yes, there is. There are two perfectly good seats right there.' He nods at the two flip-down seats facing the opposite way.

'But those are the uncomfortable ones!'

317

'Better you should be uncomfortable than my soufflés be annihilated.'

'Fine.' I sigh. 'At least let me shut this window so my hair doesn't get blown to pieces.'

'No!' Barney yelps again, swatting my hand away. 'I need cool air circulating to stop my puff pastry going soggy!'

This goes some way to explaining the bouffant hairdo.

'So, tell me what you think of my canapé selection,' he goes on, as the taxi pulls away. 'Now, I've focused mainly on sweet canapés, but I think people are going to find them very interesting.' He lifts up a tinfoil corner from one tray. 'These are mini coffee soufflés – remind me, I need to get these in the oven as soon as we arrive. Then we all just have to pray to the Soufflé Gods that they rise, OK?'

Lara and I both nod, taking our duty seriously.

'Now, these ones are little cappuccino crème brûlées,' he pats another tray. 'Then there are these little tartlets filled with a coffee custard . . . oh, and espresso cups with a bitter coffee cream, topped with an almond milk foam . . . You wouldn't *believe* how long it took me with the soda siphon to get that foam right. I wanted it to look a bit like a macchiato . . .'

Lara interrupts him. 'So *everything* is just coffee-flavoured?'

'*Just* coffee-flavoured?' Barney looks wounded. 'God, I was only trying to simplify it for you! But if you must know, the soufflés are made with a really

318

distinctive Jamaican Blue Mountain bean, for the custard tarts I've used an Ethiopian Sidamo that really brings out the buttery pastry . . . now, I've taken a risk with the cappuccino brûlées, because they're made with a Guatemalan Huehuetenango I'm not as familiar with as I should be . . .'

'Barney!' I stare at him. 'I don't believe this!'

'Well, you said this would be a great opportunity to get some publicity for Coffee Messiah!' He's looking at me quite indignantly. 'Anyway, Annie doesn't mind.'

'You've cleared this with her, then?'

'Oh, yes.' Barney clutches his trays for dear life as we swing on to Holland Park Avenue. 'And guess what? She's even making espresso Martinis to go with the food!' Suddenly he turns rather pale. 'God, I hope she hasn't just used a tin of Segafredo or something.'

'This is Annie we're talking about,' mutters Lara. 'You'll be lucky if she hasn't used a jar of Nescafé.'

Thanks to the Saturday traffic, it's gone eight thirty by the time we finally pull up outside Matthew and Annie's ground-floor flat, just off Putney High Street. The party looks a much bigger affair than I was expecting. There are loads of pink-shirted men spilling out on to the pavement drinking from Guinness bottles, accompanied by women in wrap dresses and kitten heels sipping revolting-looking pale brown liquid from plastic Martini glasses. These must be Annie's espresso (Nescafé?) Martinis. Armed with Barney's precious trays, we fight our way through the crowd until we finally reach the front door, where Annie, who's also wearing a wrap dress and kitten heels, is waving at us as though she's a drowning swimmer and we're manning the lifeboat.

'Guys! I thought you were never going to get here!'

'Here now,' puffs Barney dramatically, as though we are in fact manning a lifeboat. 'Can I . . . use your . . . oven?'

'Of course. Oh, and Matthew's in there making some disgusting-looking fruit punch,' Annie says, 'so he can help you if you need anything. It's about the most helpful he's been all day,' she goes on, as Barney and Lara start pushing their way through the crowded hallway towards the kitchen. 'I hate to say this about your brother, Wiz, but when he doesn't want to do something, he really won't cooperate.'

'Matthew didn't want to have the party?' This is extremely hard to believe. Sometimes I suspect that Matthew might actually have been born with a cold beer in one hand and a set of barbecue tongs in the other, wearing an embarrassing party hat and letting off a party popper. Though I'm sure Mum would have mentioned this if it had actually been the case.

'Matthew didn't want to have *this* party. He wanted to stick with the plans we had for a small, casual house-warming. But that wouldn't have made much of an engagement soirée, would it? Anyway, we've loads of new people to invite, now we're living in London.' Annie casts an arm over the assembled throng.

'Honestly, if it was up to Matthew, we'd never bother to make any new friends at all! Do you know, we've been here a month now, and for three of those weekends, all we've done is go back to Dorset and hang out in the Hind's Head. I mean, we're in *London* now!' she adds, just in case I'd forgotten. 'What was the point of moving here if we never do anything fun and glamorous? I mean, look at you, Isabel! There's never a night when you're not out on the town with one of your millionaires!'

'Er . . .' I'm not quite sure how Annie has managed to get this impression of my life, but at least I've spotted an opportunity to make my escape. 'Oh, talking of my many millionaires, ha ha, I ought to go and find Ben now. He'll be wondering if I'm here or not.'

'Get engaged to him,' suggests Annie grumpily, 'and he'll stop caring where you are at all.'

I push my way into the living room, where Elton John's Greatest Hits are playing, and more of the pink-shirted, wrap-dressed guests are bopping along to 'Crocodile Rock'. There's a sweet smell of coffee suffusing the air, which must mean Barney is in the kitchen offering up incantations over his mini soufflés. Lara is circulating with a big tomato-red Coffee Messiah paper platter bearing little coffee-custard tartlets, and deliberately ignoring Matthew, who's doling out fruit punch a few steps behind her.

I've spotted Ben across the other side of the living room, so I pick my way through the Crocodile

Rockers to let him know I'm here. I have to say, he's looking gratifyingly gorgeous. Unlike practically every other male in the room, he's eschewed the pink-shirt-and-chinos option in favour of a tobacco-coloured cotton sweater and mid-blue jeans. I can't see who it is he's talking to, but he's giving them his extra charming, lopsided smile every three seconds, which makes him look even more sexually magnetic. Oh, God, he's not talking to another girl, is he? Whoever it is must be on the short side, because he's having to look down quite a long way . . . oh. It's Mum. And Barbara. And Ron. Both Mum and Barbara have changed into (sparkly) tops and floaty trousers, and Ron is jovially sporting one of his favourite 'fun' ties (printed with little champagne bottles) that he always brings out for this kind of occasion.

'Darling!' Ben says, as he spots me.

Darling? I'm his darling?

I don't think I've ever been a darling before. I wasn't Will's darling. I'm not sure I even really *do* darling.

'Er – hello, darling,' I hazard, in reply.

OK. I was right. I don't do darling.

'Iz-Wiz!' Mum, Barbara and Ron are all beaming at me like I've just won the lottery. I think they've all had one too many espresso Martinis already.

'Madame la couturière!' adds Ron, with a wink. 'I've been hearing about your dress fitting this afternoon – clever old Iz-Wiz!'

'Oh, well, it was just nice to have a satisfied client,' I begin, before Mum interrupts me.

'And Ben's been telling us all about his wonderful new flat, in . . . where did you say it was, Ben?'

'Holland Park.'

'Holland *Park*,' she breathes. 'Doesn't that sound lovely, Isabel?'

Well, so much for her interest in my career. I don't know why she didn't just turn up to the party wearing a T-shirt saying *Daughter for Sale: Will Go Cheap to Good Home (in Posh Part of London)*.

'Lovely.' I give her a look. 'I've heard all about it.'

Ben laughs. 'I'm afraid I've already bored poor Isabel senseless talking about it!'

'Oh, I'm sure that isn't what she meant!' Mum looks panic-stricken. 'Is it, Isabel?'

'No, of course it isn't.' God, I need a drink. 'Look, can I get anyone an espresso Martini? I'm going myself.'

'No, darling, let me.' Ben puts a hand on my arm to stop me. 'You stay here. Chat to the Shepton Mallet Massive.'

Of course, Mum and Ron and Barbara all fall over themselves, shrieking with laughter, until the second he's out of earshot, when they all turn back to me, like girls in the playground. Yes, even Ron.

'What a catch, eh, Iz-Wiz?'

Especially Ron.

'Oh, I'm *so* glad I'm meeting Cathy Loxley for a coffee next week,' Mum says, rolling her eyes at us all as if she's narrowly averted some kind of natural disaster. 'I'd hate her to put her stamp of disapproval on the relationship just because she thought I'd been unfriendly!'

'Mum!'

'What, Iz-Wiz? I'm only saying! Ben's far too good a prospect for you to mess this up.'

I give her a frozen stare. 'I'm not messing anything up.'

She at least has the decency to look sheepish. 'I didn't mean that. But still, Isabel, you really will need to hang on to him. There's a houseful of girls here who'd give their eye teeth to nab themselves a rich, successful hunk like Ben!'

'He is awfully hunky,' Barbara agrees.

Oh, God. 'Actually, I think I'm going to go and help Ben with the drinks.'

'Oh, I'm sure he's not off talking to any of the other girls!' Mum gives me a concerned look. 'You know, drugs *can* make you paranoid, darling, even after you've stopped taking them.'

'I'm not paranoid, Mum. I'm just going to help him with the drinks. That's all.'

It occurs to me as I hurry away that Dad isn't with them, and I'm almost at the kitchen when I catch sight of him.

He's standing on his own near the kitchen door, holding an espresso Martini like it might be laced with strychnine and studying the Elton John CD case as though he's expecting to find the secrets of the universe in the lyrics to 'Don't Go Breaking My Heart'. Typical Dad. Always trying to turn everything, even a party, into an educational experience.

Except . . . I don't know. Is he staring quite that intently at the CD case for another reason?

Because he doesn't have anyone to talk to?

I mean, seeing him here, the very embodiment of the phrase *fish out of water*, he doesn't seem his usual scary, pompous, headmasterly self at all.

And then he looks up, and sees me looking at him.

'Isabel!'

'Dad.'

There's a silence.

'Keeping well?'

'Yes, thanks.'

'Right.'

Is this *it*? He's not going to say anything else? Like, he's sorry for yelling at me when I got out of my stressful afternoon in police custody? That he shouldn't have called me a failure?

'Oh, I spoke to Clem today. Robert's probably going to get away with community service. I thought you should be told,' he adds pointedly.

'Well, I'm very glad to hear that.'

'Yes, well . . .'

There's a silence again.

I clear my throat. 'So, Dad . . . um . . .'

'I'm Still Standing' suddenly blares out of the nearby speakers, at twice the previous volume.

'Oh, for the love of God, I can't stand this bloody racket any more!' Dad snaps, throwing down the CD case. 'Doesn't anyone listen to anything decent these days?'

And he stamps off to track down the CD player, and, no doubt, the person responsible for the CD player, to berate them for assaulting his eardrums and intimidate them into putting on something by Mozart instead.

Chapter 23

By ten o'clock, I'm seriously ready to leave. Thanks to the espresso Martinis and Barney's coffee canapés, which I'm glad to say have been a huge hit, there's a growing air of mania. I've lost Lara and Barney, I've had to spend all night avoiding Dad (and Mum, and Ron, and Barbara, who are partly responsible for the air of mania), and I've been stuck for the last hour with the most boring man in the world, a pink-shirted City boy who's talking over my head at Ben about share pricing, and dividends, and something (or someone?) called Long-Term Capital Management.

If it weren't so terminally dull, I'm sure it would be wonderfully educational. Not to mention very useful data for my hemlines.

I can't even wander off to track down Lara and Barney, or drown myself in Matthew's fruit punch, because Ben has me sort of . . . *clamped* to his side. For the first fifteen minutes or so it was great, because his arm is so nice and strong, and I felt all kind of treasured and precious and tiny. But since then, I'm sorry to say, there's been a sharp decline in my enjoyment. I'm dying to go and get a drink, and see if there are any Guatemalan Hugga-mugga-tango crème brûlées left, and neither Ben nor the City boy is talking to me. Neither of them is even talking *at* me. And now they've started comparing the amount of hours they work, a favourite topic amongst Alpha males, in my experience.

'. . . mostly sixteen-, seventeen-hour days,' the City boy is saying. 'But it's not unusual that I put in two all-nighters in a row . . .'

Actually, I think I'm going to go and get myself that drink after all.

I'm just about to begin the tricky process of extricating myself from Ben's grasp when something catches my attention over by the living-room door. Something I really, really didn't expect to see. Actually, make that some*one*.

It's Will. Will has just walked into Matthew and Annie's living room.

Oh, God. Oh God, oh God, oh God.

This is completely hideous.

Actually, Will looks pretty hideous himself. For a man who's just spent the best part of a week sunning himself in the Cayman Islands, and fornicating with a beautiful Russian, he looks pale, pasty, ever so slightly bloated, and in need of a few very good nights' sleep.

Except that being in need of a few good nights' sleep probably *is* the way you look after a week fornicating with a beautiful Russian.

He's seen me. He's seen Ben standing next to me with his arm around my shoulders. And he's coming straight over.

I try to wrest myself out of Ben's clasp, a process I

knew would be difficult. But I was wrong. It's not difficult, it's impossible.

'Isabel,' Will says, as he reaches us. 'I had to come. I . . .'

'For God's sake, Will, what on earth are you doing here?'

'Matthew and Annie invited me.'

I could kill him! 'But that was *before* . . .'

'Darling?' Ben has stopped pretending he believes City boy's frankly unconvincing tales of hundred-hour weeks and has turned his full attention to us. 'Is everything all right?'

'*Darling?*' Will's jaw falls open. I'm not sure he sees me as a person who does *darling*, either. 'Isabel, who on earth *is* this?'

'I'm her boyfriend,' announces Ben. 'Who are you?'

'Her . . . *what* did you say?' Will is looking from Ben to me, and back again, in complete bewilderment.

'Boyfriend,' Ben repeats loudly. He's clasping me, if that were possible, even closer. 'Do you have a problem with that?'

'But . . . how on earth . . .' Will pushes back his slightly-unwashed-looking hair. 'I thought I'd only been away a week . . .'

'Look, *boyfriend* is probably pushing it a bit,' I say, partly because I want to maintain the moral high ground with Will, and partly because . . . well, because it *is* a little weird that Ben's insisting he's my boyfriend after about one and a half dates together. Then I carry on, before Ben can say anything, 'But Will, you really shouldn't be here! I told you I don't want to talk to you!'

'Isabel, I really think you're overreacting to all this,' Will begins, taking a step forward, only for Ben's hand to reach up and push his shoulder.

'Hey!' Ben snaps. 'Back off!'

Oh, *Christ*, this is excruciating. If I've ever entertained a fantasy about being fought over by two men, it'd be a lot better than this. Two dashing young officers engaging in pistols at dawn, perhaps, while I peep from an upper window with my maidservant, wearing something lacy and romantic that gives me a tiny waist, and with ringlets in my hair. Not two men, one of whom is slightly unwashed, shoving each other's shoulders at a caffeine-crazed house party, with my parents somewhere in the background and lots of complete strangers in pink shirts and wrap dresses looking on.

Except Will's not shoving back. He's ignoring Ben completely.

'Isabel, look, I don't really understand what's going on here, but if you just give me a couple of minutes . . .'

'No, I won't give you a couple of minutes! This isn't the time or the place, Will!'

'But I just want to explain . . .'

'You can't explain!'

'Look,' this time it's Ben taking a step forward, 'don't you think you ought to leave, mate? I think Isabel's made it pretty clear she doesn't want to speak to you.'

The two of them stare at each other for a moment, and then just as I think it's all about to get excruciating again, Will turns away.

'Fine. I'll leave.' He glances back in my direction. 'I'll leave you two to it.'

Damn Will. Why did he have to turn up like that?

I mean, how was I supposed to enjoy the fact that Ben and I left the party together in a cab, bound for his swanky Holland Park pad, when all I could think about was the weary sadness in Will's eyes, and the dejected slump of his shoulders as he walked away?

How am I supposed to enjoy the fact that now I'm sitting in a living room that looks like something out of *Elle Decor*, while a sexually magnetic millionaire whips up a couple of proper Martinis in the stainless steel and burgundy lacquer Poggenpohl kitchen next door and something sophisticated and jazzy (not, thank God, 'Crocodile Rock') plays on an invisible stereo that seems to be hidden up in the ceiling somewhere? When all I can think about is Will mournfully staring at me, not unlike the way a Labrador regards his empty dinner bowl.

OK. This has got to stop. I am not going to let Will's surprise appearance put the dampeners on this evening.

I am going to have wild, abandoned sex with Ben Loxley in his *Elle Decor* apartment. Quite possibly even in his stainless steel and burgundy lacquer Poggenpohl kitchen.

And I am going to enjoy every single minute of it.

Every single *hour* of it, more likely. Because you just know that Ben will be quite the expert between the sheets (or on the island unit). I mean, look at his flat, his car, his clothes – everything about him just screams sophistication. So I doubt his bedroom technique is any different. Probably, ten minutes from now, he'll lead me to a champagne-filled sunken bath some-where, where we'll linger with some kind of erotic massage oil before entwining ourselves into the first of many complicated Kama Sutra-esque positions and reaching new heights of dizzying carnal pleasure.

It's going to be completely brilliant.

I sort of hope, though, that it doesn't go on *too* long. For one thing, I myself can only bring two or three complicated Kama Sutra-esque positions to the table, so I'd rather things reached a natural conclusion before I have to admit I'm all out of ideas. And for another . . . well, I wouldn't go around saying this to just anyone. But it's been an incredibly long day at the end of an incredibly long week, and while I'm all for the erotic-massage stuff in principle, I'd be just a little bit grateful if we could keep things to a respectable minimum in practice.

'Comfortable?' Ben is coming back into the living room with a drink in each hand.

'Oh, fantastically comfortable.' I sit back on the chocolate-brown leather sofa and try to cross my legs so that they look as though I spend five days a week on the cross-trainer. I read about it in *Cosmo* about a million years ago, and it's never failed to impress. 'This place is amazing.'

'Thank you.' Ben passes me my Martini and we chink glasses. 'You wouldn't believe the state the place was in when I bought it. Of course, it was a bit of a nightmare having the place remodelled from the other side of the Atlantic, but I had the most fantastic architect.'

'Mm.' I sip my Martini and arrange my face into an interested expression. Because, I mean, didn't he tell me all this already, at Zuma the other night?

'. . . and my favourite feature is my A/V system,' Ben is saying. 'Twenty-five grand, the whole thing cost me. Everything is set up on the one system – music, Internet, phones . . .'

'Mmm . . .' I say again, trying to look both interested enough not to offend him but uninterested enough that he might take the hint and start kissing me.

'. . . and obviously, the floors are all Scandinavian. I really do enjoy Scandinavian design . . .'

'Mm.' But I don't want to talk about *Scandinavian design*. I want to be taken to a sunken bath, and dizzying heights of carnal pleasure! Just so he might get the hint, I take a sultry sip from my Martini glass, then lean forward to put it down on the coffee table so I can easily shift closer to him.

A tiny muscle in Ben's forehead twitches. 'Glasses on coasters!' he says, turning round to put my glass on one of the little tiles, too.

'Oh! Sorry!'

'That's all right.' He puts a hand on my leg, and stares into my eyes, which I'm pretty sure is a prelude to the carnal pleasuring. 'So . . .'

I stare back into his eyes. 'So . . .'

'How would you like to go away next weekend?'

'What?'

'Next weekend. Would you like to go away?'

'Er . . .'

'It's a corporate golfing do with one of our clients, and I thought it'd be much more fun if you came along. Oh, and it's at Babington House,' he adds. 'Scarily close to the parents, I know, but I promise I'll keep you secreted away.'

Babington House? *The* celeb hang-out, where Madonna and Gwyneth stay, and where I've always wanted to go? Oh, and where Annie ill-advisedly wants to have her wedding?

On the other hand . . . well, a corporate golfing do? It isn't much of a third date. Not to mention the fact that it feels weirdly soon to be going away with Ben. I mean, Will and I only managed one weekend away in our entire eight-month relationship, albeit to the world's swankiest hotel with the entirely gratuitous pillow menu.

'Um, well, I have quite a lot on next weekend . . .'

'Really?' That muscle in his forehead twitches again. 'Too busy for a short break?'

'Well . . .'

'Because if you really want to get ahead in this

334

fashion business of yours, then weekends like this are just the kind of thing you're looking for. These clients are huge investors in luxury brands! You could do some serious networking.'

'Oh.' So now it's *networking* at Babington House. 'Well, I suppose I could move a few things around.'

'So it's settled!' He looks pleased as he leans in and plants the softest of kisses on my lips. 'I'll pick you up on Saturday afternoon! About one-ish, so we'll have a bit of time for relaxing before dinner.'

'Lovely.' I sit back and wait for him to start where we left off, with all the gazing and the leg-touching.

But he's getting up, and reaching into his jeans pocket for his car keys.

'So! Shall I drop you back?'

'Drop me back?'

'I don't want you getting a taxi at this time of night!'

'But . . . I thought . . .' Well, what can I say? *I thought you were going to erotically massage me in a sunken bath? I thought you were going to wear me out with pages one to twenty-seven of the Kama Sutra until the wee small hours of the morning?*

'Obviously I'd love you to stay longer,' Ben says, pushing a tendril of hair back over my ear, 'but I've got to be up at six tomorrow to get to the gym, and then I'm working at Fred's all day . . .'

'Oh, well, I have to be up at six for the gym, too!' I say, gathering up my bag and trying not to look horribly embarrassed by the fact I thought we were about to fall into bed together.

'I thought so!' Ben opens the front door for me, then holds me back for a second. 'Besides, there'll be plenty of time for all this,' he adds, dropping a soft little kiss on my lips, 'next weekend . . .'

TIMETABLE: PRE-WEEKEND AT TOP LUXURY HOTEL
(WITH SEXUALLY MAGNETIC VENTURE CAPITALIST)

Sunday, 6 a.m. – Spring out of bed. Go to gym for hour on treadmill, followed by further hour in free-weights area, incorporating lunges, squats, *tricep dips*, more lunges, and anything else it looks like very thin toned gym-bunny girls in running shorts and bra tops are doing.

Sunday, 8 a.m. – Emerge from facial, steam room and coffee bar feeling refreshed, invigorated, and all the more determined to go to the gym properly tomorrow.

Monday, 6 a.m. – Spring out of bed. Go to gym for hour on treadmill, followed by further hour in intermediate yoga class, incorporating Shoulder Stand, Half-Spinal Twist, Revolved Side Angle, Reclining Bound Angle, and Flat Back Forward Bend.

Monday, 8 a.m. – Emerge from changing room bent double, in quite considerable pain, and all the more determined not to confuse Flat Back Forward Bend with Half-Spinal Twist tomorrow.

Tuesday, 6 a.m. – Don't spring out of bed. May never go to gym (or get out of bed) again.

Tuesday, 8 a.m. – Have Lara help me into taxi, drive to *Atelier* magazine, spend morning pretending to concerned well-wishers that I have been involved in nasty traffic accident.

Tuesday, 1 p.m. – Drag hunched wreckage of body to Wax On/Wax Off for full depilation process; drag hair-free hunched wreckage of body back to office again.

Wednesday, 5 p.m. – Hit lingerie department at Selfridges.

Wednesday, 6 p.m. – Hit lingerie department at Harvey Nichols.

Wednesday, 6.14 p.m. – Hit strange man who seems to have followed me from lingerie department at Selfridges to lingerie department at Harvey Nichols.

Thursday, 1 p.m. – Agonising Swedish massage at Harrods Urban Retreat to repair ravages of Monday's overenthusiastic Half-Spinal Twisting.

Thursday, 1.45 p.m. – Visit Harrods' world-renowned sporting goods department to purchase suitable golfing outfit in mode of Catherine Zeta-Jones; leave with golfing outfit in mode of Griff Rhys Jones.

Thursday, 6 p.m. – Contouring spray tan, mani/pedi and eyebrow-threading.

Friday, 5 p.m. – Cut and blow-dry with Saint Luc, including addition of emergency fringe to disguise ravages of Thursday's overenthusiastic eyebrow-threading.

Friday, 8 p.m. – Large, nerve-stiffening gin and tonic and pre-date pep talk with Lara.

Friday, 10 p.m. – Early night, all the better to enjoy weekend at Top Luxury Hotel with Sexually Magnetic Venture Capitalist tomorrow.

Isabel Bookbinder
Her one home in
London

Catherine Zeta-Jones
One of her many homes in New York,
Barbados, Mallorca, or the scenic
Welsh valleys

29 September

Dear ~~Miss Zeta-Jones~~ ~~Mrs Zeta-Douglas~~ Catherine,
May I start by saying that I have always been a huge fan
of yours. From your early years in ITV's classic Sunday-
night serial *The Darling Buds of May*, to your later
ascension to the highest ranks of Hollywood Royalty, I
believe you have pursued your career with grace and
elegance, and a particularly nice line in va-va-voom
glamour on the red carpet.

Which brings me to my burning question – where,
Catherine, is it possible to purchase glamorous golfing
attire that does not make you look like one half of a
(male) 1980s comedy duo? I have seen pictures of you
golfing, and you always look rather fabulous, in sassy
little cropped trousers and figure-flattering tops. And
yet, despite visiting a world-renowned sporting goods
department, I have only managed to kit myself out in
quite unpleasant checked trousers and a kind of polo-
shirt thing that makes me look both very fat and
extremely pregnant.

Your expertise in this matter is all the more critical

since I have recently entered into a relationship with a ~~sexually magnetic~~ man who is, like your own partner, a keen golfer. Having spent a good deal of time and money stocking up on appealing lingerie for our first weekend away ~~(wish me luck!)~~ I obviously do not wish to negate the effect of this with some seriously unappealing golfwear.

Please advise.

Yours in admiration,

Isabel Bookbinder

PS ~~Just in case Keira isn't keen~~ Would you ever consider abandoning your megabucks contract with Elizabeth Arden and promoting an unknown designer's fragrance line instead?

PPS Oggy Oggy Oggy, Oy Oy Oy.

IB x

Chapter 24

It's a good thing, frankly, that I've not had all that much to do for Nancy this week apart from opening her post and booking her taxis, because preparations for Babington House have taken up most of my time. I mean, how do people *do* it? You only have to open *Sunday Times Style* magazine to know that, all over the country, people are throwing a handful of things into a Bill Amberg holdall and getting away for a luxury weekend at the drop of a hat. Whereas I've been getting ready all week! Tanning here, threading there, waxing pretty much everywhere . . . not to mention all the shopping I've had to do, for everything from golf clothing to erotic-massage oil. It just makes me realise how badly stocked I am on all life's essentials.

But I'm all ready now. Just popping a few final things into my holdall (not a Bill Amberg one, sadly, but a very nice faux-leather thing from M&S that *looks* a bit Bill Ambergy) and checking myself out in the mirror to make sure my outfit is perfectly pitched for an easy, breezy golfing weekend at Babington House. I'm wearing navy cigarette pants from LK Bennett, an easy, breezy Breton-striped T-shirt from (ssssh) Boden, and, for absolute maximum easy-breeziness, a little polka-dot silk scarf that I found in the bottom of one of my black bin bags.

Yes. This is perfect.

Easy-Breezy: The new unisex fragrance from Isabel Bookbinder.

Shoes have been something of a dilemma. Obviously the easiest, breeziest look for a golfing weekend would be some lovely flats – something two-tone, possibly even quilted, from Chanel. In the absence of anything quite so fabulous as this (and because I don't want Ben to realise how badly proportioned my legs really are) I'm wearing my brand-new utterly amazing beige crocodile-effect courts that look a lot like Jimmy Choo but were actually sixty quid from Kurt Geiger. And OK, some people might argue that the seven-inch heel isn't the most practical thing for a country golf weekend, but they've also, brilliantly, got a platform sole of at least an inch and a half, which make the heel height you're *actually* wearing a much more manageable five and a half.

And the point is, obviously, that when I'm actually *playing* golf, I'll probably be forced to wear the hideous lace-up golfing shoes I've just bought anyway, so it's imperative that I look even more fabulous when I'm off the golf . . . pitch?

God, I wish I had time to mug up on some of the basics of golf before I leave. Maybe I can sneak in a quick call to Lara while I'm there, get her to Google *golf basic terminology and practice*. In fact, I should probably have spent a bit more time last night Googling that myself, and a bit less time Googling *Kama Sutra basic terminology and practice*. But obviously, this weekend is about more than just golf. Obviously, this weekend is about me and Ben taking our relationship to the next level.

To that end, by the way, this is what makes up most of the contents of my faux-Bill-Amberg holdall:

1) an Elle Macpherson Intimates hot-pink lace bra and knickers with a little black bow wittily positioned at the back, in case Ben likes the cheeky look;

2) Malizia by La Perla ivory silk pyjamas, trimmed with antique-rose lace, in case Ben likes the classy look;

3) a Knickerbox white strappy vest and matching boy-shorts, in case Ben likes the sporty look;

4) an incredibly complicated Agent Provocateur ensemble, featuring a black satin corset with built-in suspender belt, an eye-watering thong studded with diamanté, fishnet stockings, and all these weird tasselly things that I was too intimidated to tell the shop assistant I didn't understand, in case Ben likes the burlesque look; and

5) a horrible cheap, slutty, bright red baby-doll nightie from H&M, in case Ben likes the horrible, cheap, slutty look.

I think that's got all my bases covered.

Anyway, whatever Ben likes (please, please don't let it be the burlesque look), I'm probably not going to be spending all that much time wearing it, once we've settled down for all that erotic massage and the sunken bathing.

There's a knock on my door at exactly the same moment that the front doorbell rings, and Lara sticks her head around it to face me. She's still in the clothes she wore to work this morning, but she's kicked off her shoes and she's clutching two cups of steaming tea.

'Oh. I thought we might have time for a quick cuppa,' she says, 'but I think that's Ben at the door already. Shall I go and let him in?'

'No, better not.' I close my holdall and pull on an easy-breezy navy Brora cardy. 'So? How do I look?'

'Very nice,' says Lara mechanically.

I give her a suspicious look. 'Really?'

'Iz, you always look nice.'

'Lara . . .'

'All right, all right. I do think you look nice . . .'

'But?'

'Well, it's just a little bit . . . easy-breezy.'

'Oh, well, that's all right!' I'm relieved. 'That's exactly the look I was after.'

'Really?' Lara's eyebrows shoot upwards for a moment, but fall back downwards again when she clocks my face and realises that I'm being completely serious. 'I mean, don't get me wrong, it's very chic, Iz-Wiz, but I'm just not sure it's very *you*.'

'Well, you're wrong. It *is* me. I *am* chic.'

'OK.' Lara holds the door open for me with her foot. 'You're the fashion expert.'

'That's right. Oh, by the way, Lars, will you be around later today? I might need to call you to get you to Google the basic rules of golf for me.'

'*Golf?*' Lara hisses, as the front doorbell rings again. '*Isabel!* You didn't tell me you were going to have to play golf! Golf is for wrinkly old men!'

'Catherine Zeta-Jones plays golf, too,' I point out, 'actually. *She's* not a wrinkly old man.'

'No, but she's married to one. God, Iz, I hope you know what you're getting into here.'

'Well, obviously the weekend isn't *all* about golf. I'm sure we'll actually be doing some fun stuff, too.'

Lara sighs. 'Well, I'm not going to be in, anyway. I took the afternoon off work to see Claudine, Marcus and Harry. And I'll be round at Barney's after that, but you can get me on my mobile if you need me.'

'Oh! Well, that'll be nice.' I try to dispel the completely unreasonable pang of jealousy that's just jabbed me in the stomach. 'So, what will you and Barney be doing?'

'Just hanging out, I think. He'll cook, obviously. He's been planning to make me his special ragu . . .'

The doorbell rings for the third time, a little more impatiently.

'Have a brilliant time,' Lara says, suddenly reaching over and giving me a hug. 'And Iz . . .' She seems to be thinking for a second, before going on. 'Just . . . be yourself, OK?'

'Well, who else would I be?'

'I just mean . . . oh, never mind.' Lara is already heading back to the kitchen with her tea. 'Give me a call later. I'll see you tomorrow.'

I usually dread this drive to Somerset with every fibre of my being. Probably something to do with the fact that I'm normally heading in the direction of a dismal Sunday lunch where Dad will belittle and disapprove of me. But today, the drive is uncharacteristically enjoyable. Probably something to do with the fact that I'm heading in the direction of a swanky country house hotel to be ravished by a gorgeous millionaire.

Nor does it hurt that Ben is on top form this afternoon, too. I mean, he looks sexier than ever, with a little hint of a tan that's set off beautifully by his pale pink shirt. He's full of praise for my outfit, agreeing that it's the perfect thing to wear for a weekend away, and he raves about my new fringe, and he's complimentary about my luggage to the point where I actually tell him it's from Bill Amberg, just to make him feel as though he's got incredible taste. Plus he's on equally top form conversationally, with loads of really great stories about all the hotels he used to stay at in the Hamptons, and the brilliant round of golf he played at Myrtle Beach, despite the fact he was feeling really under par, or something.

We're about ten minutes away from Frome when he suddenly stops telling me another hilarious story about a round of golf he once played with Callum in Arizona, and says, 'God, Iz-Wiz, I hope Queenie's a bit nicer to you this weekend than she was the last time you met!'

I glance across the E-type at him. 'Ha, ha.'

'What?' He glances back. 'I'm serious. I really hope she's a little less bitchy.'

'You mean . . . Queenie's going to be at Babington House, too?'

'Did I not mention that?' Ben indicates left to turn off the A36. 'Well, I thought you'd assume if it was a work event, she'd obviously be coming with Callum.'

He's right. I should have assumed that.

'Oh, great.' I lay my head against the car window, not even caring that it bumps. 'That'll be a fun way to go around the golf course.'

'Darling, she won't be on the golf course.'

'Why? Is she injured or something?'

Ben laughs. 'Isabel, you girls don't play golf!'

This is just outrageously sexist. Not to mention completely inaccurate. 'What about Catherine Zeta-Jones?'

'I mean you girls won't be playing any golf this weekend. The golf is really just another way of talking business with the clients. You get to go to the hotel spa with the other wives and girlfriends to be pampered!'

Hold on a moment.

How has *this* happened?

I'm a soon-to-be Top International Fashion Designer. Not some kind of . . . executive WAG.

And it doesn't matter that, obviously, it's going to be much more fun having lovely treatments in the posh CowShed spa than traipsing round a horrible windy golf course in unflattering shoes.

'But you said I'd be able to network with the clients. How am I supposed to network if I'm sitting around getting my toenails polished with Queenie Forbes-Wilkinson?'

Ben looks puzzled. '*Did* I say you could network with the clients?'

'Yes! You said they were big luxury-brand investors!'

'Isabel . . .' He pats my knee. 'They're Rotterdam-based property developers who build designer shopping malls in Dubai. Is there really anything you can network *about*?'

'There might be! And I'll never know if I don't even meet them!'

'Well, of course you'll *meet* them, darling. There's dinner tonight, and drinks beforehand . . .'

'So I can come to dinner and drinks, but I can't come to the golf?'

'Darling, I told you! Girls don't join us for the golf!'

'But what about the ones who *want* to play golf?'

Now he just looks confused. 'But none of them *do* want to play golf. They want to get massages and manicures.'

I don't say anything.

'And you know, Iz, if it's exercise you feel like, I'm sure one of the other girls will go with you to the hotel

348

gym. Queenie, perhaps. It'd be nice for you two to bond a bit. Or maybe you could book yourself a tennis lesson.'

Is it me, or has the E-type suddenly got an awful lot chillier?

I mean, if I wanted a boyfriend to treat me like a Stepford Wife, I could leave right now and go running back to Will in Battersea.

I mean, now I think about it, Will never *actually* suggested tennis lessons.

Still, there's no time to think all this through properly, because we're just pulling up outside the beautiful stone exterior of Babington House.

The car park is full nearly to bursting with the most expensive cars I've ever seen: Porsches, Ferraris, great big gas-guzzling 4x4s. Milling about, taking golf bags out of boots and meandering up the hotel steps, are the people who obviously own these fabulous vehicles. Some are the Rotterdam-based property developers, all yellow-blond hair and pastel sweaters, others are probably Ben's colleagues from Redwood, lean and hungry-looking in Aertex polo shirts. There are a few women hanging around, too, who must be the executive WAGs. On average, they look ten years younger than the men, and I'm instantly glad I spent all that time and money tanning and waxing and titivating myself for the weekend. I mean, some of them look as though they're actually *gleaming*.

Ben steers the E-type into a vacant spot next to a planet-polluting 4x4, just as Queenie and Callum clamber out of it and start making their way, with their genuine Bill Amberg luggage, towards the hotel.

The moment I see Queenie, my relief at reaching the required level of grooming dissolves. Because it's obvious that, compared to her, I've got my entire outfit strategy wrong. It's not just the Bill Amberg holdall. She's mastered weekend boho luxe in the way that only a true It girl knows how: layers of fine cashmere, blue jeans tucked into green wellington boots (complete with small mud splatters), a long, vintage-look scarf looped around her neck and a yoga mat underneath one arm. She's still wearing half a cosmetics counter, though, with some clever blending to make it look like she's not wearing any.

'Well, well, well!' says Ben, leaping out of the car like he's just turned into Tigger, and giving them both a hearty wave. 'Looking forward to getting slaughtered on the links again, Cal?'

Cal gives a hearty wave back, and calls something I don't understand about having a new iron, and Queenie sucks in her expertly contoured cheeks, death-stares in my direction, and carries on stalking indoors.

Great. Just bloody *great*. A weekend away with a girl who hates my guts. And is, while doing so, more impressively accessorised than I could ever be.

Well, at least I can safely say I'm getting my money's worth out of Babington House. The moment we arrived Ben announced that he was going straight to the gym, so I went with him. By which I mean, I walked in that direction with him. Then we parted ways so I could go to the spa, where I've just spent the last hour being pummelled, prodded, and slathered in seaweed, all in the name of detoxification. And now I'm back in our gorgeous room, retoxing most satisfactorily with a delicious late afternoon tea, complete with half a bottle of excellent pink champagne. I'm just waiting for Ben to get back.

Let the carnal pleasures begin!

Thank God I've had that half-bottle of champagne, I must say, because I'm feeling pretty nervous. There's just something so weirdly grown-up about all this. A corporate golf weekend, this super-romantic hotel room with the giant four-poster bed, all the sexy lingerie I've brought with me . . . I mean, is it just me, or is it all a tiny bit too . . . formal?

Then there's this niggling feeling that I haven't been able to shake off all day, that I really need to speak to Ben about that conversation we had in the car earlier. I'm going to have to ensure, after all the carnal pleasuring, that I make it clear that I'd appreciate it if he'd try to remember that I'm a strong, independent woman, with an important career and a mind of my own.

Now. Which lingerie set will it be most appropriate to do this in? Classy pyjamas? Sporty white vest-and-pants? Actually, both of those are more the kind of thing to wear tomorrow morning with coffee and croissants in bed. Cheeky pink bra and pants? Hmmm. Would have been a better option *before* I stuffed myself with scones, sandwiches, and little slices of fruitcake. So it's a straight choice between the cheap, nasty baby-doll nightie and the trussed-up, cantilevered corset with the inexplicable tasselly bits.

Oh, what the heck. If I need something that's really going to disguise my recent scone intake, trussed-up and cantilevered it is.

I shimmy out of my trousers, my Breton top and my faded old M&S bra before peeling off my (non-matching) faded old M&S knickers and pulling on the diamanté-studded thong.

Ow ow ow ow *ow*.

All right. First step down, two more to go.

Or it could be three more, if I can work out what it is I'm meant to do with these tassels.

It's not a very good time for my mobile to start ringing.

I grab it from the bedside table. 'Hello?'

'Darling?'

'Ben.'

'How's it going at the spa? Are you having a good time with the other girls? Queenie being OK with you?'

'Actually, I just had a quick massage. I'm back in the room.'

'Oh.' He sounds slightly put out. 'Well, I'm just about to leave the gym. But I'd really like a massage too when I get back, if that's OK?'

That's a tiny bit of a demanding way to ask, isn't it? 'Well, yes . . .'

'Good. That's settled then. I just wanted to check you wouldn't find it too off-putting.'

Off-putting? That sounds extremely . . . well . . . off-putting. Does he know something about his body that I don't?

'Er . . . no, no . . . not off-putting at all . . .'

'Great. Oh, and why don't you run a nice hot bath, too?'

God, he really likes to take charge, doesn't he? It's both completely thrilling and oddly aggravating. 'Sure, I'll run a bath . . .' My phone suddenly bleeps with another call. 'Ben, someone's trying to get hold of me. I really should go.'

'No problem. I'll see you in five!'

With slightly shaking hands, I press the button to transfer my call. 'Hello?'

'Wiz?'

'*Matthew?*'

'Hi.' Silence.

I'm forgetting: Matthew is completely hopeless on the phone. He can roar his way around a rugby field, effing and blinding like there's no tomorrow, but stick him in front of a telephone receiver and he suddenly gets all shy and retiring. It's the main reason why we haven't spoken on the phone since . . . well, since so long ago I can't even remember.

'Is everything OK?'

'Yeah, everything's fine,' he says unconvincingly. 'How's Bab House?'

'How do you know I'm here?'

'Ben, of course.'

Oh, *God*. Going out with my brother's best friend has more drawbacks than I'd have thought. Especially when my brother's best friend is a complete blabbermouth.

'He phoned to ask me if it was OK that he was taking you away for the weekend,' Matthew adds, with a snigger.

'He *didn't*.'

'He did.' Matthew sniggers again. 'But don't worry, Wiz. I told him I didn't have a problem with it as long as he didn't mind the moonlit howling and remembered to make sure you took your medication.'

I don't really have time for Matthew's hilarious jokes. Not when I'm standing here naked but for a diamanté thong, and Ben will be back for his erotic massage any minute. 'Very funny. Look, Matthew, is there something you wanted? Because I'm right in the middle of something . . .'

'Oh, sorry, Wizbit. I shouldn't have disturbed. It was just a chat, really.'

He sounds so dismal, all of a sudden, that I feel incredibly guilty. 'Tell you what, why don't I call you back in about . . .' How long will an erotic massage and several positions of the Kama Sutra take? Minimum? '. . . say three hours? We can have a chat then, if you're around?'

'Well, yeah. That'll be fine. Oh, Wiz, if you can't get me on my mobile, call me at Mum and Dad's, OK? I'll be there till later this evening.'

'You're at Mum and Dad's?' Something about the way he's said this prompts me to add, 'Annie's with you, of course?'

'Er – no. She's stayed up in town. She's shopping all day with this yoga friend of hers. Amanda.'

'Right . . . Well, I'll give you a call later. Oh! Matthew – does Mum know I'm at Babington House?'

'Don't worry, Wizkins. I haven't told her.'

'Thanks, Matthew. Speak later.'

OK. I need to get myself sorted out here. Now, what the hell are these tasselly bits? Will it help me work it out if I hoick myself into the corset?

I pick the corset up from the bed, wrap it around my waist, breathe in as far as the scones will allow, and start doing up the bazillion fiddling hooks and eyes. God, I *hate* hooks and eyes. No sooner have you got one of them fastened and made a start on another when the first one pops open again and you're back to square one . . . After ten minutes of wrestling I'm still just half-in, half-out of the damn thing.

It's only when I hear voices in the little internal hallway that I realise someone is coming into the room.

'I find I get a terrible tenderness in the sciatic area when . . . *Isabel*?'

I stare at Ben, and the man in the white spa-therapist's uniform, who's just walked in with him.

They stare at me, and my diamanté thong.

'Oh, my God!' The spa therapist backs away, and retreats out of the door covering his eyes with one hand. 'Madam, I am *so* sorry . . .'

OK. I don't know if it's possible to pass out from embarrassment. But right now, it certainly feels like it.

Then again, it could just be the corset.

'*Isabel!*' Ben repeats, looking at me in an aghast way that was absolutely *not* meant to happen when he saw me in this outfit. 'For heaven's sake, what are you wearing?'

I stumble for one of the thick towelling robes on the bathroom door, and pull it on. 'I . . . but . . . who on earth was *that*?'

'My masseur!' Ben has the nerve to look indignant. 'I told you I was arranging a massage! I slightly overdid it in the gym, and I need someone to work on my sciatic area.'

'Well, you could have *said* so!' I put my hands on my hips. 'That was seriously embarrassing!'

'Isabel, I wasn't to know you'd be all done up in . . . well, what *was* that?'

'It's a corset,' I say, in as dignified a way as possible. 'I'm afraid I don't know what the tasselly bits are.'

'Right. Well, it certainly looked interesting.' He doesn't say *interesting* as though what he means is *I know that was all a bit embarrassing but you looked completely fantastic, why don't we jump into bed so I can ravish you, please*. He says *interesting* as though he means . . . well, *interesting*. 'I presume you were too busy getting yourself into all that to start running the bath I asked you about?'

'Well, yes . . .'

'Never *mind*,' he sighs. 'I can run it myself. I really

do need some heat on this sciatic nerve, you know. Oh, darling,' he adds, going past me to the bathroom, and starting up the hot tap. 'While I'm soaking, can you make sure you take my shirt out of the dry-cleaners' packet and bring it in here on a hanger to steam. It'll save you running the iron over it before dinner.'

You know, I think I have to get out of this room before I injure someone.

'Actually, Ben, I had a bit of a worrying call from Matthew just now. He's at Mum and Dad's. Would you mind very much if I got a taxi over to Shepton Mallet to see him?'

Ben sticks his head out of the bathroom door. 'Is he all right? Should I come?'

'*No!* I mean, no, no. You should stay here. Rest your sciatic nerve.'

'Oh, well, all right, then. But you will be back in time for dinner, won't you, Isabel? All the other wives and girlfriends will be there.'

'Oh, yes, I wouldn't miss it for the world!'

'Excellent. See you later, darling!'

Chapter 25

Luckily I manage to get hold of Matthew on his mobile, and we arrange to meet at a wine bar on the High Street that I don't think I've been to since the summer after my A levels. Clearly the rest of Shepton Mallet hasn't abandoned the old place, though, because it's heaving with people all geared up for big nights out. Even so, it doesn't take me long to spot Matthew – all I have to do is follow the scent of lust and the sound of shrieky female laughter, and I've tracked him down to a table by the window, surrounded by his usual gaggle of adoring women. I get all kinds of murderous looks when he stands up to greet me, which don't even recede when he tells them I'm just his sister.

'*She's* never *his* sister,' I hear one of them saying to her friend as they repair to the other side of the wine bar to regroup their forces. 'Not unless one of them is adopted.'

Matthew pours me a glass from the bottle of red wine he's been drinking. 'This is nice of you, Wizkins. Interrupting your weekend with Ben like this.'

'Oh, please.' We chink glasses. 'You know I'll always make time for a chat.'

He shoots me a suspicious look. 'Right. So the weekend's going well, then?'

'Brilliantly!' I take a very long drink of wine. 'The hotel is wonderful . . . great spa treatments . . . excellent scones . . .' I take another drink. 'Idyllic, really.'

'Good for you, Wiz!' Matthew nudges me, grinning. 'You always had a bit of a crush on Ben, didn't you?'

'Well . . .'

'Oh, come on, Iz! I may not be as brainy as Marley, but I notice these things!'

I don't point out the fact that Lara's unrequited love has obviously slipped past his radar for the last fourteen years.

'Matthew, I'm not here to talk about Ben.' I put my glass down and give him a Serious Older Sister look. It's not one I have the opportunity to use all that often, and I have to say, I rather enjoy it. 'What's going on with Annie? You sounded a bit down on the phone.'

The smile slides off his handsome face. 'Oh, yeah. I wanted to talk to you about that. I really need your advice, Wiz.'

I'm so taken aback, I need another large gulp of wine. In the twenty-six-and-a-half years I've known him, Matthew has never come to me for advice before. Well, good-looking, sporty, wildly popular boys don't tend to have much need for advice. Hence the fact I've never had the chance to be the Serious Older Sister. It's a shame, really, because I think it's a role I'd have excelled at. But still, better late than never.

I reach across the table and put my hand on his.

'Matthew. You can ask me anything. You know that.'

'Thanks, Iz . . .'

'I mean, relationships can be difficult. Especially when you've taken huge steps like you and Annie have recently – moving to London together, getting engaged . . . And if there's anything I've learned from my own experience . . .' Oh. Actually, I've never moved to London with anyone or been engaged before. 'Well, anyone will tell you that moving to London together and getting engaged can place a tremendous toll on even the happiest couple.' Oooh, I like that. I sound just like Lara! 'So in my opinion . . .'

'The thing is, Wizbit,' Matthew interrupts, leaning forward in his chair, 'I really need you to tell me where the cool places are in London.'

That's the advice he needs me for? 'Sorry?'

'You know.' He waves a hand around the wine bar, taking in the red-and-white check tablecloths and the melted-wax-covered Frascati bottles posing as candlesticks. 'Places like this.'

'Right . . . sorry, so do you mean *places like this* or *cool places*?' I pour more wine into both our glasses. 'Because they're not one and the same thing, you know.'

Matthew groans, and buries his head in his hands. 'See? It's hopeless! No wonder Annie's had enough of me!'

'She's had enough of you?'

'Yes . . . no . . . I don't know.' He removes his head from his hands, grabs his wine glass, and empties it in one gulp. 'I think she's had enough of me being so boring. You know – watching rugby . . . playing rugby . . . going out drinking at the rugby club . . .'

'But that's not boring!' Let me rephrase that. 'But Annie doesn't find that boring! I mean, that's what she enjoys doing as well, isn't it?'

'Not since we moved to London.' Matthew stares mournfully at the bottle until I pick it up and pour what's left of it into his glass. 'She says the whole reason we moved was because we needed a change.'

'A change from what?'

'From living in the middle of nowhere, from spending Saturday nights with the pub-quiz team at the Hind's Head, from having everyone round to the cottage on a Sunday afternoon for a barbecue and a game of sevens.' Matthew looks wistful. 'But Annie was tired of that, apparently. And she's got all these friends who live in London, Ginny and Fiona, and then of course there's you, with your glamorous life . . .'

'Oh, Matthew.' I swat this away modestly. 'My life isn't so glamorous.'

'Hey.' Matthew shrugs. 'I'm not saying it is. Believe me, Isabel. I'm just letting you know what Annie thinks.'

'Right. Thanks.'

'And you know what I'm like, Iz. I wouldn't know Clarabell's from a hole in the road.'

'Clarabell's?' I'm not sure I'd know it from a hole in the road either.

'*You* know, Iz-Wiz! Some God-awful-sounding nightspot in Mayfair, or somewhere.'

'*Annabel's.*'

'Yeah, that's the one.' He pulls a face. 'Icky pink cocktails and dancing on the tables.'

'You've *been* there?'

'Christ, no. But Annie has. Keeps talking about it like it's the Holy Grail and Somewhere Over The Rainbow all rolled into one.'

Wait a moment. Annie's hanging out at Annabel's? But . . . well, is that an idea Hugo Tavistock put into her mind that day we bumped into him outside his flat? Or . . .

She hasn't actually *been* there with him, has she? Because that would just be so completely revolting . . . not to mention the fact that she's happily engaged to a man her own age . . .

'Anyway, it was all her idea to get away from Dorset. *I* wish we'd never come to London,' Matthew continues savagely. 'Horrible fucking dump.'

Illicit trips to Mayfair nightclubs or not, I don't think it's fair of Matthew to take this out on London. I mean, it would be like me blaming the issues I have with Ben on Babington House, or something.

'Are you sure you're not just going through a bit of a rocky patch? The pressure of the wedding, and everything?'

'Oh, Christ, the *wedding*.' The wine has really started to warm Matthew up. 'Now, there's another bloody great issue. I mean, what would be so wrong

362

about keeping the guest list down to just our close friends, hiring out the rugby club . . .'

I sit back and listen. Probably best just to let Matthew unburden himself. You know what men are like – they don't do this kind of thing very often, but once they get started, there's no stopping them. I sip my wine a bit more, and think about Annie (possibly) dancing on tables with Hugo at Annabel's, and then I try *not* to think about Annie dancing on tables with Hugo at Annabel's . . . then I think about Corsetgate back in the bedroom, and then I try *not* to think about Corsetgate back in the bedroom . . . and suddenly something catches my eye on the other side of the road.

Is that . . . ?

Oh, yes, it is. How weird.

It's Lucien Black. He's striding down the High Street, completely failing to blend in with Shepton Mallet's early-evening pub crowd in his Top International Fashion Designer ensemble of black roll neck, tight black jeans, that black-and-white Bedouin scarf and black Ugg boots.

Did Nancy say his rehab centre was somewhere around here?

Well, Mum did say there were lots of good treatment facilities in this area. Still, I'm not sure the rehab centre can be all that great if they just let the inhabitants (inmates?) wander the local town like this. I mean, we all know how easy it is to buy hard drugs on the streets of Shepton Mallet.

And surprise, surprise, Lucien's gone into a pub. The slightly scuzzy one with all the fruit machines, a little way along the High Street.

Well, so much for his rehab. Should I say something to Nancy? Or is it against the principles of rehab to snoop on people? Isn't it all meant to be about taking responsibility for yourself, and surrendering to a Higher Power? Not about being caught out mid-binge by someone who shops you straight to the person who's made you go for treatment in the first place.

'. . . and I know her parents are stumping up for the whole thing, but I don't see why that means I get no say in it,' Matthew is saying. 'You know, I was going to call Lara last week, see what she thought I should do about it.'

This brings my attention crashing back. 'You were going to call Lara?'

'Yes – get her professional opinion on how to handle all this. She's very good at suggesting ways that you can get people to listen to you. I remember how helpful she was when I had that dispute about the MOT with the guy who sold me his Corsa.'

'Matthew, I really, really wouldn't speak to Lara about any of this.' The last thing Lara needs is to get false hope that all is not rosy in the world of Matthew and Annie. 'She's terribly busy these days, you know.'

'Oh.' Matthew looks disappointed. 'But I like talking to Lara.'

He likes *flirting* with Lara, is what he means. 'Look, Matthew, I'm your older sister. I really think if there's anyone who you should be turning to for advice on how to handle Annie, it should be me.'

'Wiz, I appreciate the offer, but all I really needed from you were the names of those restaurants and stuff. Now, Annie said you often go to a place called Zoo-something . . . Or was it Knob-something . . . ?'

I talk Matthew through Zuma, and Nobu, and as many 'cool places' as I can possibly think of, and he writes them down dutifully on a corner of the red-and-white paper tablecloth, and then he glances at his watch and says, 'Well, I should be getting back. Mum wants to feed me before I head back to London.'

'Yes, I should go, too. I've got this dinner to get back for.' I can't help feeling slightly dismal at the prospect. 'Some important clients of Ben's.'

A broad beam breaks over Matthew's face. 'Awww. It's so sweet. You and Benjy-boy, all grown-up together!'

'Yes . . .' I smile, too, just a bit less broadly. 'Ben *is* very grown-up, isn't he?'

'God, yes. But you're used to that, aren't you? Will was pretty grown-up, too.'

'Oh, yes, of course . . . maybe not *quite* in the same league as Ben, though.'

'Tell me about it!' Matthew pulls a face that I think is meant to be funny, but actually comes out looking slightly grotesque. 'I mean, if it weren't for Ben, I'm not sure I'd ever have got round to asking Annie to marry me!'

'But what's Ben got to do with it?'

'Well, you know what he's like – so old-fashioned about a lot of things.'

'Yes. I know.'

'He's badgered me about it for the last two years by email, and then in person ever since he's been back!' Matthew lets out a slightly mirthless laugh.

'Didn't you *want* to get engaged?'

'Oh, well, you know . . . obviously *one* day . . . but Ben said probably a lot of the reason Annie wanted to move to London was her way of saying she felt our relationship needed an upgrade. He said women reach a certain point when they start taking stock of their lives, and all they want to do is get married, and that if I didn't get the ring on her finger at the double I'd end up losing her to some flash bastard and being left with the dregs. I think something happened to him with some girl he knew back in New York. Oh!' Matthew stops, looking appalled. 'Not that you're the dregs, Iz-Wiz! I'm sure Ben doesn't think that!'

I stare at him, probably looking as aghast as Ben was when he saw me in my diamanté thong; he just stood and stared at me, with that look on his face that suggested, pretty categorically, that he does, in fact, think I'm the dregs.

'I should let you get back to him, anyway,' says Matthew, pushing back his chair and standing up, a simple act that prompts his fan club on the other side of the bar to shriek a bit and clasp each other, as though he's a member of Westlife getting up from a high stool for the chord change or something. 'And

Mum's been preparing my dinner almost all day. You know how she gets when she's worried about something.'

'Worried about what?'

'About me.' Matthew holds the door open for me. 'What else would she be worried about? Now come on, Wizbit. Let's find you a taxi.'

Chapter 26

I thought I was in plenty of time to get ready for an eight o'clock dinner, but when I get back to our room at Babington House, Ben has obviously been clock-watching.

'You said you'd be back in plenty of time!'

'It's only seven-thirty. Dinner's not until eight-thirty.'

'Isabel! We can't just go *straight into dinner*!' he says, as though I've suggested that we might like to turn up stark naked and painted in bright blue body paint. 'Everyone else is already in the bar!'

'Oh, well, the bar sounds good to me!' I'm determined to make a bit more of an effort, to prove to him that I'm absolutely not the dregs. I smile, and pat his shoulder. 'You go now and I'll come along when I'm ready.'

'Well, how long will that be?'

'Oh, probably about twenty minutes, if I really get a move on . . .'

'God, no, I don't want you *rushing*.' His nostrils flare in alarm and he peers at me speculatively. 'You should go the whole hog.'

'The whole . . . hog?'

'Yes, I don't know . . .' Ben flaps a hand. 'Face mask, make-up . . . you know, all the other girls will have made a proper effort, Isabel. I really think you'll feel very out of place if you throw yourself together in twenty minutes.' He stops, watching me as I take my Lucien Black cocktail dress out of the wardrobe. 'You're wearing that?'

'Yes, I'm wearing this!' I clutch the dress to me defensively. 'It's custom-made Lucien Black!'

'Well, fine, but *again*?' He wrinkles his nose slightly. 'Didn't you wear it to the last party we were at with Queenie and Callum? I mean, people will think you don't have anything else to wear.'

I take a deep breath. 'If I'd known Queenie was going to be here before I packed for the weekend, believe me, I'd have brought something different. But right now, it's all I have. So unless you want me to come to this dinner in these trousers and a stripy T-shirt . . .'

'Oh, no, God no,' he says hastily. 'The dress will be fine. Just . . . try to make it look a bit different than the last time you wore it, perhaps?'

'Different *how*?' I ask helplessly.

'I don't know, Isabel!' He picks up his room key and his wallet. 'A new belt, a change of earrings . . . you're meant to be the fashion expert!'

The door clicks shut behind him.

Great. Now what am I supposed to do? Despite Ben's apparent belief that I've brought an entire wardrobe of accessories with me, all I've really got is the skinny tan belt I was wearing with my trousers earlier, a stripy red-and-white scarf that I brought in case it was chilly, and a couple of wooden bangles that I chucked into my overnight bag as an afterthought.

OK. What happens if I add the red-and-white scarf? Does it look like a bold, definitive Style Statement, or does it just draw attention to the fact I know I'm wearing the same dress again?

It just draws attention to the fact I know I'm wearing the same dress again.

The only thing I can do is try, at least, to make *myself* look a bit different. Instead of leaving my hair loose, or shoving it up in a deliberately messy chignon, I take almost half an hour to put it into a high, sleek ponytail. Then I raid my entire make-up bag (I did bring *that* with me) for all the expensive powders, gel crèmes and brightening potions I'm always reading about in *Grazia*, dashing out to buy, and then never actually getting around to using. No mere flick of eyeliner and a dab of Benetint this evening! This is *the whole hog*. Cream foundation, highlighting stick, three different shades of blended smoky eyeshadow, liquid eyeliner, two sorts of mascara (black undercoat, slightly sparkly topcoat), powder blusher then cream blusher – then after I panic that it's the wrong way round, an emergency local reapplication of cream blusher then powder blusher – lip liner, lipstick, and then, the cherry on the icing on the cake, a light layer of clear gloss.

Oh, and a dusting of loose powder, to 'set' everything. Whatever that means.

Well, I certainly look different.

Oddly enough, with the sleek ponytail and the full face of slap, I look a little bit like Queenie Forbes-Wilkinson. Without the incredible figure, the heirloom jewels and the permanent scowl, that is. Well, hopefully my inadvertent tribute act will prevent her from noticing (gasp!) The Return of the Previously Worn Dress, and Ben'll be happy for once.

Anyway, I remind myself, as I head for the bar, I shouldn't give two hoots what Queenie thinks. My God, are we all millionaires that can afford to go around casting aside five-figure dresses after one outing, just because snooty old fashion snobs might look down on us and think we're paupers?

Except that I'm forgetting one thing – tonight, we *are* all millionaires.

By which, of course, I really mean *they're* all millionaires.

The blond, pastel-clad property developers I saw earlier are all done up in fresh pastels for the evening, the Redwood guys in chinos and crisp shirts like Ben. To a man, practically, they're wearing chunky Rolexes, and a good half-dozen or so are waving pink fifty-pound notes at the bar staff. But it's the gleaming women who really reek of their husbands' bank balances tonight. The Redwood WAGs are all doing Babington-fabulous (*Babulous?*) in effortless sack dresses, Jimmy Choo wedges and the kind of legs you buy from five sessions a week with a personal trainer and all the Bliss Fat Girl Slim lotion you can get your hands on, and the Euro-WAGs are flaunting floaty Versace, honeyed Sardinian tans and real diamonds.

It's enough to make me feel actually quite relieved I wore the Lucien Black dress after all, repeat viewing or not. And it's certainly enough to make me glad of Ben's advice to go the whole hog with the hair and make-up. I may feel a bit like a porcelain doll, my pores may be slowly suffocating underneath the entire cosmetics counter I've applied, but at least I look like I might actually fit in.

'Isabel? Is that right?'

This is coming from a white-haired man with a smiley, pleasant face, standing at the bar. With him is a very pretty, very young girl in new-season Jonathan Saunders and a gold Jade Jagger skull pendant; also with him is a very scowly Callum, who gets even scowlier when he sees me coming.

But what am I meant to do? I don't know anybody else here, I can't see Ben, and I can't just stand about at the fringes looking slightly lost.

'Hi. Yes, I'm Isabel.'

'Here with Ben?' The white-haired man extends a hand. 'Lovely to meet you! I'm Fred. Senior partner at Redwood,' he adds, with a chuckle, 'just before you start confiding in me how much your boyfriend hates his boss!'

So this is the guy who's responsible for all Nancy's stress and tension at the moment. Though actually, he looks like a pretty nice guy. Grandfatherly, even, with that white hair and the jovial twinkle. And it was good of him to rescue me from social Siberia like he did.

'Oh, no, Ben thinks you're a great boss!' I feel simultaneously pleased with myself for winning Ben some Brownie points, and slightly uneasy that I've just behaved more like an executive WAG than ever.

'Oh, well, you can come here again!' Fred grins at me. 'How about a nice cool vodka and tonic?' He turns briefly to waggle a fifty-pound note and mouth *V and T* at the unnaturally handsome barman, before turning back to me. 'So, Isabel, you must meet my wife, Kirsty!'

'I'd love to!' I glance around. 'Is she here yet?'

'She's me.' It's the twenty-year-old in the Jonathan Saunders. '*I'm* Kirsty Elfman.'

'Oh, of course!' How can I tell her I was looking around for a woman in her fifties or sixties? Anyway, it's completely my fault. Fred is the senior partner of Redwood Capital, for heaven's sake. *Obviously* he's going to be married to a trophy blonde young enough to be his . . . yes. His granddaughter. 'Nice to meet you,' I go on hastily, taking a huge gulp of the vodka and tonic Fred has just handed me. 'And Callum . . . !'

He doesn't raise so much as a smile in greeting. 'Isabel.'

'So! Um . . .' I raise my glass. 'Great to be here!'

Fred winks and chinks his glass with mine, thawing the atmosphere by about twenty degrees. 'Had a good day, then?'

'Oh, yes, wonderful, thank you . . . terrific spa . . . fabulous massage . . .'

'Kirsty had a good massage too, didn't you, babe?' Fred puts an arm around his wife and nuzzles her neck. 'You should tell Isabel what you were just telling us – what your masseur said about one of the guests. You'll love this,' he adds, nodding at me conspiratorially. 'Hysterical story.'

'Oooh, really? Who was it about?' I lean towards Kirsty, lowering my voice in a confidential, gossipy way that I hope is going to make her bond with me. 'Madonna? Gwyneth Paltrow?'

Kirsty looks unimpressed. Despite her glossy blondeness, I think she's worked very hard indeed to cultivate the air of seriousness that being married to a man three times her age probably requires. 'Christ, no. Do you think the girls in the spa would gossip about celebrity guests?'

Seeing as one of them seems to have happily gossiped about a non-celebrity guest, I can't say I'd necessarily put it past them. 'No. Of course.'

'Apparently,' Fred says, his twinkly eyes dancing with amusement, 'one of the massage therapists got an unexpected peep show in a guest's bedroom today!'

I accidentally inhale the gulp of vodka I've just taken.

'For God's sake!' yelps Callum, as I snort most of it back into the glass, and a small proportion of it over his shirtsleeve.

'Sorry . . . sorry . . .' My throat is burning, and I'm sure my cheeks are following suit. I grab the handful of cocktail napkins Fred hands me and dab Callum's arm. 'I just found that so hilarious . . . sorry . . .'

'It *is* hilarious!' chortles Fred, like an overgrown schoolboy. 'He was booked for an in-room massage and when he went in, this girl was prancing around in diamanté knickers – a good deal of her top half on display too!'

Surreptitiously I press my glass against my neck, hoping to cool down the burning flush. 'Poor girl!'

'Poor girl nothing.' Callum knocks back his Scotch and waggles his glass imperiously at the barman for another. 'Sex-starved desperate housewife getting the staff to "accidentally" walk in on her in the buff.'

'Not in the buff,' says Kirsty, warming up enough to give a little giggle. 'Bursting out of a corset and in knickers made from diamanté. I mean, *how* tasteless?'

'Not necessarily,' I blurt. 'I mean, we don't know that the knickers were *made from diamanté*, do we? Only that diamanté was a . . . a feature . . .'

Kirsty stares at me, clearly noticing the fact that my face is practically self-combusting. 'It wasn't *you*, was it?'

'Me? God, no! I was in Shepton Mallet all afternoon. Meeting my brother. In a wine bar. On the High Street.' I feel like a criminal trying to establish a false alibi. 'We drank a bottle of Shiraz . . .'

'I think your boyfriend is trying to get your attention,' Fred interrupts me, which I assume is just an act of kindness until I look to where he's pointing and see that Ben is waving me towards him. Rather insistently, in fact. He's sitting on one of the big, squashy sofas on the other side of the bar. Queenie is with him.

I never thought I'd say it, but Queenie's company looks positively enticing right now.

'Duty calls!' I say, already starting to hurry towards them. 'Thanks so much for the drink, Fred!'

You know, I do think it's a tiny bit cruel of Ben to keep inflicting his presence on Queenie when it so obviously upsets her. I mean, look at her now, staring at the back of his head as he waves me over. It's as bad as Matthew, leading on poor Lara. Except, of course, that big, dumb Matthew doesn't realise Lara's painfully in love with him. Whereas Ben is in no doubt about Queenie's feelings.

'Darling!' Ben stands and kisses me, noisily, on the lips, before ushering me into his vacated seat on the sofa. 'You look amazing.'

'Thanks.'

'Just amazing,' he repeats, staring at me in wonderment, as though he's astonished at what an hour with a hairbrush and make-up bag can achieve.

'Hi, Queenie. I love your dress!' I smile at her, hoping she realises I'm trying to be nice, and reciprocates. Anyway, I do love her dress. She's gone maxi-length in a green and blue zigzag-stripe Missoni number that would make me look like a badly wrapped birthday present, but makes her look like she's just stepped off Valentino's yacht on the Costa Smeralda. 'You look great.'

'Oh, so do you,' she says.

I practically fall off the sofa. 'Thanks, Queenie! That's so nice of you!'

'I mean, that dress is obviously your favourite. *So* nice to find something you feel so comfortable in that you can just wear it and wear it and wear it.'

Oh. I see. My shock came too soon.

'And your hair looks great,' she adds, nodding at my ponytail and smoothing her fingers pointedly through her own. 'Doesn't her hair look great, Ben?'

'Yes, it does!' Ben beams down at the pair of us, clearly hopelessly unaware of Queenie's guerrilla assault. 'I should leave you two to have a good old gossip! Let me get you some more drinks.'

'Oh, no, I really don't need another right now,' I croak, desperate not to be left alone with Queenie.

'Well, I do.' Imperiously, Queenie holds out her empty Martini glass.

'Coming right up! Isabel, the same?'

'Actually, I'm drinking . . .'

Too late. Ben's already heading to the bar.

Queenie fixes me with a cool stare. Her own eye make-up is rather spectacular tonight, bronze and a stunning molten gold that brings out the green in her eyes. 'So. I've been meaning to ask – what was your fashion label called again?'

'Er . . . Isabel B.'

'Yes, I thought so.' Queenie smirks. 'You know, I mentioned it to a couple of my contacts at Harvey Nicks, and they'd never heard of it.'

Shit. 'Oh, well,' I say, trying not to let my cheeks flare up again, 'which branch do your friends work for?'

'London, of course.'

'Ah. That would explain it. I'm only stocked in the Leeds and Edinburgh stores.'

'But you said . . .' Queenie stops, trying to remember exactly what I said. When she realises she can't, or that she can't remember clearly enough to be able actually to use my own words against me, she scowls. 'So how's it going with you and Ben, then?' she asks sulkily. 'Bit soon for you to be going away for a weekend together, don't you think?'

'Not really,' I lie. 'Anyway, we've known each other for donkey's years . . .' Actually, that doesn't sound particularly romantic. Not to mention the fact that it makes me sound ancient. '. . . ever since we were children.' *That's* more like it. Lovely and rather Victorian, it conjures up images of the two of us frolicking in freshly mown meadows in pristine white smocks, and enjoying ham sandwiches and home-made lemonade from a wicker picnic hamper by a cool woodland lake. 'Ben is my brother's oldest friend.'

'Ohhhhhh.' Queenie's metallic-painted eyes widen. 'I didn't realise *that's* how you knew him.'

'Er . . . yes.'

'So you practically grew up together,' she adds, which ought to have more of those Victorian lemonade-drinking connotations. But actually, when she says it, just sounds a little bit creepy.

378

'I suppose so.'

'I bet you fancied him right from the start, didn't you?'

I take a deep breath. 'Queenie, look, I know this is difficult . . .'

'Difficult?' she snaps. 'What on earth would make you think that?'

'Well, I know how you feel about Ben, and . . .'

'Ladies! Drinks up!' It's Ben, returning with two Martini glasses. 'I've just been told we're drifting in for dinner,' he goes on, handing one to each of us. 'There's no formal seating plan, but I'm sure you two would like to sit together . . .'

'I'm all right, thanks.' Queenie stands up sharply, and stalks towards the dining room. 'Thanks for the drink.'

'Ben!' I hiss, as soon as she's out of earshot. 'What are you doing?'

'What?'

I haul myself up off the squashy sofa with considerably more difficulty than Queenie; I don't have the lean, strong thigh muscles. 'Trying to push me and Queenie together all the time! She hates me!'

'She doesn't hate you, darling!' Ben smiles indulgently. 'She's jealous, that's all.'

'Exactly! So jealous that she hates me!'

'Isabel . . .'

I knock back my Martini in a single swallow. 'I keep trying to be nice to her, and all she does is take swipes at me!'

'Oh, now you're just being paranoid, darling. She said how much she liked your dress, your hair . . . which looks gorgeous, by the way,' he adds. 'You should do it like this more often.'

'Well, I can't. It takes too long and it's giving me a headache. I mean, no wonder Queenie's so crotchety all the time, torturing her follicles like this . . .'

'Yes, darling.' Ben isn't listening. 'Now, I need to go and have a quick word with Niels. I'll see you in there, yes?'

And he's gone, off to the other side of the bar to shake hands with one of the Rotterdam-based property developers. Which means I have to walk into dinner on my own.

Two hours later, and I've learned more about property development than I think I'll ever need to know in a lifetime. Also, quite a lot more about Antwerp. I mean, did *you* know that Antwerp hosted the World Gymnastics Championships in 1903? Or that Antwerp's Central Station has two monumental neo-baroque facades and a 197-foot-tall dome made from metal and glass?

Actually, it might have been a 297-foot-tall dome. And it might have been *three* monumental neo-baroque facades. Or three neo-monumental baroque facades. After two cocktails and a bottle of red, you start to lose track of those kinds of details. So, if you're planning a day trip there, or anything, don't take my word for it.

Come to think of it, I'm still not sure I actually know where Antwerp is.

Oh, Belgium, that's right. It must be, because Joost, my dinner companion, and the Antwerp expert, keeps promising me that next time I'm in Antwerp – well, I couldn't admit there's never even been a *first* time for me in Antwerp; he's so sweet and chatty, and he keeps refilling my wine glass in such a generous manner – we'll go and drink yummy Belgian beer and eat chips with mayonnaise in one of the city's many fine dining establishments. Joost and I really are getting on like a house on fire. I mean, you wouldn't necessarily have thought we'd have that much in common, him being a multimillionaire Belgian property developer and me being . . . well, none of those things. But it's been non-stop chat ever since we sat down to eat. And he's not dominating the conversation with his own interests, either: we've just spent an extremely pleasant half-hour discussing, of all things, boots!

I love Joost.

Joost, Pour Homme: The new fragrance from Isabel Bookbinder.

So what, he's not the most stunningly charismatic person I've ever met. And so what, our conversation about boots is starting to take a slightly concerning turn towards the obsessive (he spent seventeen million pounds on boots last year, apparently, which either means he's a candidate for some serious Aversion Therapy, or I've got all my foreign currencies in a twist). At least he's bothering to talk to me! Unlike

Callum, on my other side, who turned his back on me the moment he sat down and hasn't uttered a word to me since. Or Ben, across the other side of the table, who's deep in conversation with Niels and Fred Elfman and only glances in my direction to shoot me a disapproving look every time Joost refills my wine glass. Or Queenie and Kirsty, who despite sitting right opposite me haven't addressed me once, doing nothing but whisper to each other behind Rouge Noired fingertips and giggle occasionally.

Well, sod them. Let them gossip about me. I don't care. Not in the slightest.

I retune myself to Joost's frequency and turn my attention to the damson and apple cobbler going cold in front of me, at which point I hear an exclamation from Queenie's side of the table.

'Isabel!' Queenie is looking at my cobbler. 'Are you sure you want to do that?'

Oh, so it's cracks about my weight now, is it? Well, she's no idea who she's dealing with. I survived Katriona de Montfort's digs on the matter; I think I can survive Queenie's. I dig my spoon defiantly into the bowl. 'I like pudding.'

'Well, we all *like* pudding, Isabel! But we need to be careful, or how will we fit into our diamanté knickers?'

Kirsty lets out a little scream of laughter, while Queenie just holds my gaze, a smile playing around the corners of her lipsticked mouth.

I could kill her.

Either that, or I could kill myself.

Because at the mere mention of the word *knickers*, every single person at the dining table stops their conversation and swivels round to stare.

'What is this joke?' Joost asks politely, tapping me on the hand. 'I do not understand it.'

'It's nothing,' I mutter.

'Oh, Isabel, don't be shy.' Queenie's smile widens; she isn't going to let this one go. 'I mean, it was your first weekend away with Ben. *Obviously* you were going to be showcasing some interesting underwear! It could happen to any of us.'

I open my mouth, but can't seem to make any words come out. I'm frozen, like an animal caught in the headlights. I'm sure everybody at the table is expecting me to say something witty, or clever, or even just ask Queenie what the hell she's talking about, but I can produce . . . nothing.

And where's Ben when I need him? Why isn't he leaping to my defence, instead of sitting there grinning like a Cheshire cat whose Christmases have all come at once? I mean, wasn't that the way he was meant to look when I was actually *wearing* the lingerie? Not when the entire dinner party is discussing it?

'I . . . er . . .'

Joost taps me on the hand again. 'Isabel, I think that your cellphone is ringing.'

God, I *love* Joost. Didn't I say I loved him? I barely know the guy, but he's trying to rescue me from this hideous tableau.

He picks my clutch bag up from the floor, and waves it at me. 'This is your bag, no?'

Oh. He wasn't trying to rescue me. My phone really is ringing.

More to the point, it's ringing twice, stopping, and then ringing twice again – the Distress Code that Lara and I have used since the sixth form.

'I have to take that,' I mumble, getting up and snatching my bag. 'It's an emergency.'

It's mercifuly cool out in the grounds. I take a couple of gulps of the chilly night air, trying to block out the nasty scene in the dining room. I mean, what the hell have I done to make Queenie hate me so much? If she's that much in love with Ben, quite frankly, she's welcome to him . . .

The Distress Code has started again, so I pick up. 'Lara?'

'Iz-Wiz?'

'Lara!' I'm so relieved to hear a friendly voice that I can actually feel sharp tears prickling the backs of my eyes. 'Is everything OK?'

'Yes, everything's good . . . amazing, actually . . . can you talk?'

'God, yes. Please talk to me!'

'Oh, no.' She sounds concerned. 'Are you having a bad time?'

'I've had better.'

'Is it the golf?'

'No, it's not the golf. God forbid I should actually play golf,' I add, under my breath. 'It's . . . too complicated to go into now. Look, why did you use the Distress Code if everything's all right?'

'Because I *had* to get hold of you, Iz!' There's a sudden car horn and Lara gives a tiny shriek. 'Sorry, sorry . . . I'm dashing home from Barney's,' she continues. 'No cabs, had to get the Tube . . .'

'Why are you heading home? I thought Barney was making his ragu.' This, I know from my own experience, is a minimum six-hour operation, culminating in a delicious bowl of posh spag bol sometime after midnight. 'You can't have eaten yet.'

'No, I left before that. Because . . . oh, Iz . . . Matthew called me!'

'Sorry?'

'*Matthew* called me! About half an hour ago! Can you believe it? He's on his way back from seeing your parents, apparently, and he asked if he could drop round for a chat!'

I'm going to kill Matthew. I swear I'm going to kill him.

After I quite specifically told him not to, and for the sake of a couple of hours of free therapy and an ego-boosting flirt, he's going to completely shatter Lara's precarious equilibrium.

'And the best part is, Westbourne Grove isn't even *on* his way back! He's making a *diversion* to see me,' Lara is going on, her feminist principles scattered to the wind. 'Can you believe it, Iz? I'm a diversion!'

'Lara . . .'

'Now, I need your fashion advice . . .' I can hear her key turning in the lock. 'Matthew likes me in grey, doesn't he? So I was thinking I'd wear my Blue Cult jeans, to look like I'm just hanging out at home on a Saturday night, all relaxed, and then that grey sweater you gave me for my birthday last year, you remember, the one Matthew said made my eyes look even more blue . . .'

'Lara!'

She stops talking.

'Have you gone completely mad?' I carry on, taking advantage of the silence. 'Have you forgotten he's engaged?'

'Obviously I haven't forgotten that. I just thought it was nice that he wants to come and see me! Because it occurred to me on the way over here, you know, that Matthew and I have never really hung out together before. By ourselves, I mean. You're always around, or that Annie . . .'

'*That Annie* is his fiancée!'

'Well, yes . . . but what if he's having doubts?'

'What do you mean?'

'People do, you know. Get engaged and then change their minds. And let's face it, they have kind of rushed into it . . .'

'They've been together for *four years*!' I'm panicking slightly. Crazed though her logic is, Lara has actually hit the nail on the head. Matthew *is* having doubts. And if he turns up and confirms what she's thinking . . .

I mean, she wouldn't *pounce* on him, or anything, obviously . . .

Would she?

'Honestly, Lars . . .' From the mutinous silence at the other end, I know I'm not getting through to her. 'You have to be sensible about this.'

'Oh, yes, I forget – you're the world expert on sensible.'

'No, but . . .'

'So tell me.' Lara's voice has gone all high. 'Was it *sensible*, do you think, to throw yourself so fast into your rebound fling with Ben Loxley that you didn't even give Will a chance to explain what happened in the Cayman Islands?'

I'm taken aback. 'Lara, Will cheated on me! I caught him in bed with someone!'

'No you didn't,' she snaps. 'You weren't *there*, Isabel. You were on the other end of a phone.'

Well, that's just complete and utter tripe! Another woman picks up the phone in his bedroom, and tells me they're sleeping together, followed two days later by Will's desperate apologies, and I'm meant to sit back and do nothing simply because I wasn't *there*?

And something has occurred to me. 'What do you know about it? Have you been *talking* to Will?'

Lara sighs. 'I don't need to talk to him to know he probably deserves the chance to explain. All I'm saying is, don't preach to me about being sensible.'

I don't have anything to say for a moment. Because to be perfectly honest, it's never actually occurred to me before. That maybe I ought to have given Will the *chance to explain.*

Except that he's a lawyer, isn't he? *Explaining* things – justifying them, rationalising them, no matter how spurious or downright untruthful – is a major part of his job.

'Look, Iz.' Lara speaks up again before I can say anything. 'I have to go now. Matthew will be here any minute.'

'Lara, no . . .'

She's gone.

I call her immediately – no answer. So I redial, this time using our Seriously, Pick Up The Bloody Phone Distress Code – three rings, followed by two rings, followed by . . . oh, Christ, I can't remember. The last time we used it must have been ten years ago, probably at that ill-fated Christmas party when Ben snogged Carolyn Duffie. And even if I could remember it, Lara's obviously planning on ignoring me.

All right. I'll get hold of Matthew. I'll just tell him he's got to come and rescue me from the world's worst dinner party, to turn the car round and drive back to Somerset *right away*. I stab his number into my mobile.

'Hello, this is Matthew Bookbinder's phone. I'm either asleep, drunk, or driving, maybe even all three! Not really, Mum!'

For the love of God. What does Lara see in him?

'Leave a message at the beep!'

I'm not going to leave a message. It's pointless. Right now, there's only one solution: I have to get back to London as fast as I possibly can, and put a whopping great spanner in the works of this ill-advised rendezvous before anyone gets hurt.

Right. Surely one of these Rotterdam-based property developers has a helicopter I can borrow. Or, come to think of it, I'm pretty sure lovely Joost said something about a private jet . . .

'Isabel?' It's Ben, striding out on to the gravel to find me. 'What the hell's taking you so long out here?'

'Ben, I'm sorry, I have to leave.'

'*Leave?* What are you talking about?'

'I really have to get back to London tonight. Now, I know you've been drinking, so you can't drive, but . . .'

'Isabel. You're being ridiculous.' Ben stares down at me, his handsome face looking more chiselled than ever in the moonlight. 'Queenie was teasing. You can't just run away because of a little joke.'

'That's not the reason I want to leave!' It was the reason I wanted to leave ten minutes ago. Right now, I've got bigger concerns. 'Honestly, Ben, I have to get back to town. Can we see if Joost can help at all?'

Ben's eyes narrow slightly. 'Joost's your new knight in shining armour, then?'

'What?'

'You know, if you want the other girls to like you, it's probably better if you *don't* spend all night flirting with a billionaire Dutch bachelor.'

Is Ben *jealous*? Despite the fact he's not shown the smallest bit of interest in me that way all day?

And is Joost a *billionaire*? *Seriously?*

'Actually,' I feel compelled to leap to Joost's defence, 'he's not Dutch, he's Belgian.'

'Dutch, Belgian, do you think I really care?' Ben is looking really annoyed now. 'And I don't care if he owns every single bloody boat in St Tropez harbour – I didn't bring you here to spend all night making eyes at other . . . at my clients!'

Ohhhhh. *Boats.*

Actually, that makes a lot more sense. I was struggling to work out how Joost could possibly have spent seventeen million on boots last year.

'Now, just come on back inside.' Ben puts a hand on my shoulder and starts to steer me towards the entrance. 'The other girls have gone for a drink in the bar again, so you should probably join them.'

'But I don't want to join them! They're not my friends, Ben! They're just a bunch of girls who are mean to me. And my best friend back at home really needs me right now . . .'

'All right, all right!' he snaps. 'I'll do you a deal – go and have a drink with Queenie and the others, and we'll see about leaving a bit early tomorrow, OK? Maybe just after lunch?'

'That's . . .' *completely useless.* '. . . not ideal . . .'

'Well, it's the best I can do. I can't drive you back tonight. You're too late for a train. Now,' he goes on crisply, steering me inside again, 'I've still got work to discuss in there. You go along and have a nice drink.'

I wait until he's gone back into the dining room

before turning away from the bar and heading straight to our bedroom.

Honestly, wild horses couldn't drag me back into that bar with Queenie and Kirsty ganging up on me. And if I'm going to be stuck here for the night, I may as well at least try to get a decent night's sleep out of it.

But once I've got ready for bed, changed into my La Perla pyjamas (I don't think I need worry too much any more about exactly which lingerie look Ben finds the most attractive) and turned out the light, I can't actually sleep at all.

I'm too worried about what's going on back at Lara's.

And I can't stop thinking about what she said about Will.

Because all I know is that if I were here with Will, he'd be helping me get back to London any way he could. I could trust him. Rely on him. So is it fair that I didn't even give him the benefit of the doubt?

Anyway, there's one thing I know for certain. Which is that even though I've been here before, lying in the dark, waiting for my boyfriend to come in from work, uneasy about the way things are going between us, this time it feels quite different.

This time I'm lonely.

Isabel Bookbinder
West London

Germaine Greer
~~Greenham Common~~

30 September

Germaine,

Well, thanks a lot. ~~A hundred years~~ ~~Forty years~~ Generations of Feminism, and this is what we have come to: two women (wimmin?) publicly humiliating another for the crime of not being able to work the world's most complicated lingerie. It's all very well going around telling everyone to Promote Sisterhood, but what if some of the Sisters are a lot less nice than the other ones? And what is the point of channelling all one's energies into Hating Men when actually some of the Men (quite often the Belgian ones; it may be something to do with their superior social security system and top-quality kinder-garten educations) are actually rather nice in comparison? I have done my best to fight the age-old cliché that we are Our Own Worst Enemies, but enough is enough.

In addition, I am sorry to say that I have found myself extremely disappointed by the speed with which Feminism seems to be dropped when good-looking men are on the scene. ~~Admittedly I may not have been whiter than white on this front myself, but~~ Where are we when attractive, intelligent professional psychologists are giddy with excitement because they may be worth a diversion en route from Shepton Mallet to Putney? How are we to Smash Glass Ceilings when we are prepared to accept crumbs from the floor? I hate to say it, Germaine, but I am increasingly concerned that your bra may have been burnt in vain.

Speaking of bra-burning, if I'm going to have one last stab at this Feminism thing, I'd appreciate a little flexibility on the matter. I have recently spent ~~an obscenely large amount~~ a considerable sum on premium-brand lingerie and have no particular desire to send it all up in smoke. Unfortunately ~~my boyfriend this man I'm seeing my boyf~~ this man I'm seeing seems to have no particular desire to see me in it, but I don't see why the lingerie should have to suffer.

I will, however, happily burn the diamanté thong and the weird tasselly bits. What good they can possibly do Womankind is nothing but a mystery to me.

Yours in ~~bitter~~ disappointment,

Isabel Bookbinder

PS It's not OK, is it, for a man you've only been on three dates with to expect you to iron his shirt and run him a bath? Just checking.

PPS And girls can play golf if they want to, can't they?

IB x

Chapter 27

I must have fallen asleep eventually, because the next thing I know, I can hear Ben moving around the bedroom. He stamps about the place like a cranky hippopotamus for a couple of moments before flooding the room with electric light.

'Sorry to wake you,' he says, in a completely unapologetic tone.

'That's all right . . .' My tongue feels a bit furry, and I've got a gritty feeling in my eyes that I think is caused by the fact that all the scrubbing on earth last night couldn't completely remove my three shades of smoky eyeshadow and the two types of mascara. Not to mention the fact that I already know, without even looking to check, that my sleek ponytail has been replaced by an acute case of scarecrow hair.

But then if he will start turning lights on at . . . what time is it? I grab my watch from the bedside table. *Half past six in the morning . . .*

Well, why the hell are we getting up at half past six in the morning?

And why is Ben throwing his clothes into his holdall?

And what's that large reddish-purple area around his left eye?

Blearily, I sit up, noticing that his side of the bed has definitely been slept in. It's a tiny bit unsettling to think of him sleeping there next to me all night, actually. Sleeping together before we've even *slept together*. I hope to God I wasn't snoring.

'Did someone *hit* you?'

He stamps towards the wardrobe and takes out a couple of his hangers. 'I was in a fight.'

'A fight?'

'Yes, Isabel, a fight.' He starts folding the clothes. 'That's what happens when you flirt with Dutchmen and they get the wrong idea.'

OK, now this is just too confusing. 'You were . . . flirting with Dutchmen?'

'No, Isabel! You! And Joost!'

'But he's Belgian . . .'

Ben shoots me a Very Cross Look. 'The fact *remains*, Isabel, that unsurprisingly, Joost got completely the wrong idea about you. And when I tried to stop him leaving the bar to come and find you last night, armed with a handful of fifty-pound notes,' he stabs a finger towards his eye, '*this* happened!'

'He thought I was *for hire*?'

'Well, really, what do you expect? Fluttering your eyelashes, all that talk about your underwear . . .'

'That wasn't my fault!' I'm mortified. 'That was Queenie!'

Ben pulls my own holdall out of the wardrobe and pointedly places it on the end of the bed. 'Come on. Get packing.'

'We're leaving?'

'Am I supposed to stay? Joost is still here, bearing a grudge, Fred is going to be furious with me, for scrapping with a potential client . . .' Ben taps these off on his fingers. 'Anyway, you wanted to leave, didn't you?'

'Yes, but . . .'

'So, you win. I'll meet you at the car in fifteen minutes.'

The journey back to London is nowhere near as jolly as the one we made down to Frome yesterday. Ben is in such a black mood that we barely speak, and the only thing filling the uncomfortable silence is more of that horrendous jangly jazz on the car stereo. He drives up the M3 at an average of ninety in the early-morning quiet, and only manages to form a coherent sentence when we're back in London and speeding down Bayswater Road towards Westbourne Grove.

'I hope you don't mind me dropping you straight back at Lara's,' he says stiffly. 'I've got quite a lot to be getting on with today.'

'Oh, absolutely!' Shit. That sounded just a touch too eager. 'I mean, that's fine. I have a lot to be doing, too.'

We sit in awkward silence again until Ben pulls up just along the road from Lara's flat. He doesn't turn the engine off.

'Well,' he says, not really turning to look at me. 'Here we are.'

'Yes.'

There's another awkward silence. We're getting rather good at these.

'Well! That was a very nice weekend,' I lie.

'Yes.' I can tell from his voice that he's lying too. And to be honest, I can't blame him. 'Sorry – you know . . .' Ben goes on, '. . . about how things turned out.'

I take a deep breath. 'Do you mean sorry about how things turned out with the weekend? Or sorry about how things turned out with us?'

He waits slightly too long before he answers. 'Look, Isabel . . . it's early. My head hurts. Can we talk some more tomorrow? Or next week, perhaps?'

'Oh. OK.'

So this is just about the most embarrassing experience of my life. Because what's *can we talk some more tomorrow . . . or next week, perhaps* if it's not a bottom-of-the-barrel fob-off? I mean, I may have started to have my doubts about this so-called relationship, but it doesn't mean I wanted this kind of dismal failure.

I turn to the back seat to reach my bag, then start getting out of the passenger seat. 'Well, thank you for the weekend away,' I say politely. 'And look, I'm really sorry if I caused you any kind of a problem with Joost . . .'

'It's fine,' he snaps. 'Don't stress about it.'

He barely even bothers to let me shut my door properly before he's roared off, back towards Holland Park.

Great. Just bloody *great*.

He's not even going to have the decency to put this little episode out of its misery himself, is he? He's going to be one of those horrible, horrible men who just get all distant and cold and nasty, and then expect you to do the dirty work . . .

Wait a moment. What's this, parked right outside Lara's flat?

Matthew's Polo.

What is his car still doing here at nine o'clock in the morning?

Oh, God, it's happened, hasn't it? Just like I thought. Lara has done it. Got what she wanted.

Except it isn't what she wants. What she wants is Matthew. Hers, in entirety. Not just the one night. And it'll only be the one night. Matthew's never going to break off the engagement. (*Do* people even 'break off' engagements any more, come to think of it, or is it something that went out with Empire-line muslins and stately quadrilles?)

I feel a surge of anger towards my stupid brother as I open the door of the flat, which is quickly replaced by a sudden horror that I'm going to see him striding out of the bathroom in his boxer shorts, or . . . worse. Thank God, though, it looks like the coast is clear. The bathroom door is actually open, so I know there aren't going to be any nasty surprises coming out of there. And Lara's bedroom door is wide open, too. So where are they? In the kitchen, sharing a lazy breakfast?

Ah. The living room. As I sidle towards the door, I

can hear a low murmuring sound coming from behind it, followed, suddenly, by the jaunty piano notes of the *Will & Grace* theme tune.

Well, then, Matthew can't be in there. He hates *Will & Grace* with a passion. Actually, not just *Will & Grace*. All the American sitcoms. *Friends*. *Frasier*. The only one he'll happily sit down and watch is *Home Improvement*. Which is just one of the many reasons why I can't seriously believe Lara's in love with him.

Tentatively, and as quietly as I can, I inch open the living-room door. The blinds are still down, but the lights are on, so I can see quite clearly that the place is a total tip. An open wine bottle, without a coaster, leaving a mark on the oak lamp table. A half-eaten bowl of Kettle Chips, surrounded by crumbs, on the floor. Most worryingly of all, two . . . no, three open packets of milk chocolate HobNobs, an upturned carton of Phish Food ice cream, and, for some reason, one of those big French hot-chocolate bowls full to the brim with what looks like Heinz cream of chicken soup. And Lara is lying on the sofa, watching the television. Her hair is matted, she's still wearing the jeans and grey sweater she said she was going to wear last night, and she looks . . . absolutely terrible.

'Lara?'

'Oh, my God!' She lets out a small scream before realising it's me. 'Isabel! You gave me the shock of my life!'

'Sorry. I should have let you know I was coming back early.'

She sits up a bit. 'What the hell happened?'

'Oh, Ben got into a fight with this really nice Belgian billionaire and we couldn't stay because his boss was going to be cross with him,' I say vaguely, flapping a hand. 'But Lara, what happened *here*?'

I think she's about to protest that everything is fine and dandy, but then she remembers she's sitting in a room in last night's clothes surrounded by empty HobNob packets. And that while this might not be an unusual start to a Sunday morning for me, for Lara it's just plain wrong.

'Nothing happened.' Her voice is flat.

'Lara, I saw Matthew's car outside . . .'

'No, I mean it. Nothing . . . *happened*. His car's only there because he drank too much to drive home and got a taxi back instead.'

'So if nothing *happened*, what did happen?'

Lara picks up one of the sofa cushions and hugs it to her stomach. 'Matthew showed up. I opened a bottle of wine. We sat on the sofa. He poured out his heart about how he was having mixed feelings about marrying Annie. We opened another bottle of wine. He started holding my hand . . .'

'Oh, God, Lars . . .'

'. . . and that's when I told him to go back home, tell Annie how much he loved her, and work a bit harder at their relationship.'

I'm not sure I can possibly have heard this right. 'What?'

'I told him to stick it out.' She glances up at me. 'I

told him if he was having doubts, it was most likely the pressure of the engagement, and moving house . . . I told him he can't just throw a four-year relationship down the drain because things have got a bit tough.'

It's a little bit like she's speaking a foreign language. I just don't understand: two bottles of wine in, he starts holding her hand, fourteen years of desperate dreams are coming true and . . . she turns psychologist on him? 'Lara, why?'

'Because that was my professional opinion.' Her face is rigid with misery. 'Because it's exactly what I'd tell one of my clients if they were in his position. Because it's the right thing to do.'

'Oh, Lara. I'm so sorry.'

'What else could I tell him? I mean, let's face it, it was only the wine that made him come over all romantic. And if we'd taken it any further . . .' Her voice wobbles. 'Well, you said it yesterday. He has a fiancée. I can't mess around with that.'

I don't know what to say. Because I'm not sure there's anything that could possibly help. 'Maybe . . . if you Cognitively Restructure it . . .'

'I can't.'

'No. I know.' I pick up her chilly, crumb-dusted hand, and stroke it. 'You're very brave.'

'I'm very stupid.'

'For turning him down?'

Lara shakes her head, and reaches for the TV remote. 'For ever getting my hopes up at all.'

Chapter 28

All right. There may not *actually* have been any fruit flan-flinging. But Lara's pretty much lost it. Yesterday was a gradually descending cycle of tears, HobNob binges, *Will & Grace* marathons and raging against the world, until I finally managed to get her into bed for a restorative nap, away from the TV screen, sometime in the early evening.

Well, *that* was a huge mistake. Because having got into bed, she won't get out of it. I was actually on my way out of the front door this morning when I realised that Lara hadn't left yet. More to the point, she hadn't even got up yet. And if you knew Lara, who hasn't taken a single day off work in *five years*, you'd realise how serious that is. Anyway, it took ten minutes to persuade her to even emerge from under the duvet, a further ten to get her to put her feet on the floor, and ten more to cajole her into the shower. Even then, the minute my back was turned, picking out a Face-The-World-With-Pride Look for her, she sneaked back into bed, pulled the duvet up over her head again and announced that she thought it was probably best if she stayed there for ever.

The thing is, with anyone else, I'd just have given in.

Lara, though, is different. I mean, look at the sheer level of the chaos that greeted me when I got back from Babington House yesterday morning – any ordinary person would have taken at least two days to get quite that bad. She's such a high achiever that she can't do anything, not even a nervous breakdown, by halves. Not to mention the fact that, thanks to years of hearing her patients' descriptions of fridge-raiding, gin-swigging and husband's-tie-chopping, all the tools of a full-scale crack-up are right at her fingertips. I mean, what else were all those HobNobs about?

Anyway, after practically manhandling her into her clothes, then accompanying her to her Tube stop, I finally jumped on the Tube myself half an hour ago. Well, hopefully Nancy won't really notice how late I am. She should still be in the Monday morning fashion meeting, so I'll be able to get settled down at my desk and look like I've been there for an hour already.

But of course, I haven't considered the Lilian factor. I thought I'd got away with it when I didn't see her at her desk as I stepped out of the lift. But I was wrong. Because she's actually standing right next to *my* desk. And when she sees me coming, she folds her arms and stares at me.

'Isabel! You're over an hour late!'

'I know. I'm sorry. I had a domestic crisis . . .'

She frowns. 'That's not *Atelier*'s problem, Isabel. It's not Nancy's problem. And it's not my problem. *I'm* the one who has to handle things for Nancy when you can't be bothered to turn up on time.'

I try to look contrite. 'It won't happen again.'

'Well, you can explain that to Nancy. She's been looking for you.'

Shit. 'But she's in the fashion meeting, surely?'

'No.' Lilian gives me a triumphant smile. 'Claudia's ill, so the meeting was cancelled.'

'Oh.'

'Yes, Isabel, *oh*. And since Claudia's ill, Nancy's been needing you to help her get organised for the *MiMi* Style Awards tonight.'

'But I thought she wasn't going to those.'

Lilian shrugs. 'Claudia's asked Nancy to attend in her place. *MiMi* will get all antsy if a senior staff member from *Atelier* isn't there, and say we're snubbing their magazine or something. Anyway, Nancy needs about half a dozen appointments set up if she's even got a chance of being ready on time, and you must know she's meeting with her lawyers this morning . . .'

'Yes. Sorry. I'll go right in and speak to her.'

Nancy is on the phone but when she sees me hovering on the other side of the half-open door, she waves me on in.

'I told you, I don't know what time I'm going to be back tonight,' she's saying tersely. 'Around eleven, I'd guess . . . no, obviously I don't want to go to the damn party either, but Claudia thinks she's got shingles . . . of course she's being a drama queen . . . look, Hugo, I have to go, OK, I'm scheduled in with Magnus in twenty minutes . . . all right, bye.'

She's already reaching for a cigarette as she puts the phone down.

'Husbands,' she grunts, lighting up. 'Never bother with one, Izzie. Far more trouble than they're worth.'

I make no comment. 'I'm sorry I was late. I had a . . .'

She flaps a smoke-trailing hand, nowhere near as interested in my excuses as Lilian implied. 'You're here now. So look, I'm being roped into this *MiMi* do tonight . . .'

'Lilian told me. It sounds like fun!'

Nancy lets out a bark of laughter. 'Yeah, well, the last thing I want to do is go to a fashion party where Eve Alexander turns up in Marchesa and everyone talks behind my back about how *teehhrrible* it is that she's dropped us, and how *sooorry* they feel for me . . .'

She sounds so much like Marina from the Lucien Black store that I have to hold in a giggle. 'I forgot about the Eve Alexander issue. I'm sorry. How can I help?'

Nancy takes a final puff of her cigarette before grinding it out, somewhat recklessly, in a messy pile of Lilian's precious message slips. 'Well, if I have to go and have everyone sneer at me behind my back, the least I can do is look fabulous while they do it. So I need you to book me a manicure, pedicure, hair, make-up . . .' She ticks them off on her fingers. 'And I need you to bring them all here to the office, because I haven't got time to go running around town.'

'Right, sure . . .'

'I need you to pick me out something to wear from the fashion cupboard and I need you to call Tammy at Christian Louboutin and get her to send me a selection of sandals. Then I'll need a car to take me to Berkeley Square at six.' She runs her fingers through her hair and grimaces as she pulls a grey out. 'Can you do all that, Izzie?'

'Of course.' I try to sound a lot more confident than I feel. Because actually, logistics like this aren't exactly my strong point. 'I'll have everything set up by the time you get back from the lawyers'.'

'Thanks, hon. Oh . . .' Nancy lowers her voice. 'One more thing. Can you call Lucien's rehab centre, and tell them to get him to call me when he gets phone access later today? There's a lot I need to go through with him before we sign on Wednesday.' She rifles through her bag and drags out a slightly dusty Post-it. 'Here's the number.'

I glance down at the red biro scrawl. 'Sorry, Nancy, I think you've given me the wrong number.'

'What?'

'00353 . . .' I read out the first few digits. 'That sounds like a foreign number, not anywhere in Somerset.'

'Why would it be in Somerset?' Nancy blinks at me. 'Lucien's in Ireland.'

'*Ireland?*'

'Yeah, well, Ireland was where he learned to drink, I figured Ireland could be the place where he learned to *stop* drinking.' She pulls a sardonic smile. 'Plus it's far away from prying eyes. The last thing I needed was for him to go into the Priory and spend most of this week featured in the *Daily Mail*.' She glances at her watch. 'Christ, I have to go. You'll get everything under control here, though, yeah?'

'Yes, sure. But Nancy . . .'

'What?'

'Um . . . it's nothing. Sorry. See you later.'

The moment she's gone, I scurry to my desk and dial the number she's just left me. Because there's something very important I want to find out.

Has Lucien *escaped* from rehab in Ireland, or . . .

'Hope and a Prayer Centre, how may I help you?'

'Oh, hello!' I say to the Irish voice on the other end of the line. 'I wonder if I could possibly leave a message for one of your . . .' Clients? Patients? Inmates? '. . . um, guests?'

'Certainly you can! Who is it you're after?'

'His name is Lucien Black.'

'Oh, the fashion designer!' The woman sounds impossibly cheery for someone whose job it is to keep liquor out of the hands of die-hard boozers all day. 'No, I'm sorry, dear, you've got the wrong place. We've not had Mr Black staying here for . . . oh, it must be two or three years now.'

'What, not at all?'

'No, dear, no.'

'So . . . he didn't turn up a few days ago and then . . . well . . . *escape*, or anything?'

407

'Escape?' She lets out a steely peal of laughter. 'Oh, no, dear, nobody escapes from Hope and a Prayer! No, take my word for it, he hasn't been here. Now, you could try the Avondale Clinic in County Wexford, because I do know he spent some time there in the past . . .'

'No, this was the number I was given. It must be a mistake, though. Thank you!' I put the phone down hastily.

Well, I was right. Lucien's not in rehab in Ireland at all. Which could be neither here nor there – I mean, clearly the man has been in and out of rehab establishments for most of his adult life. But the fact is that Nancy *thinks* he's in rehab in Ireland. So he's lying to her.

Still, I'd better keep it to myself for the time being. Nancy has enough on her plate right now.

Well, I've had a fair old amount on my plate today, too. I've been on the phone for most of the last five hours, getting all of Nancy's last-minute grooming appointments fitted in, and more importantly, fitted around each other. I feel a bit like one of those wide-boy traders you always see on the Six O'Clock News when the stock market has taken a tumble, yelling into phones and waving their hands at people in inexplicable coded signals. It takes me nearly an hour to get someone from Daniel Galvin to agree to send someone round for a blow-dry. I'm the most unpopular person in the world at the Elemis day spa, because I've insisted that their pregnant manicurist (who may be on her day off, but seems to be the only manicurist available in the whole of London) come over to tend to Nancy's fingers and toes. I've somehow persuaded Olivia in Beauty to give up the name and number of her most favoured make-up artist, who will (*should*) be here to start Nancy's make-up just as soon as Precious has finished with her blow-dry. And now I'm sitting at my desk praying that the cache of sandals arrives from Christian Louboutin in time for Nancy to team a pair with the last-season sunset-coloured Lucien Black maxi-dress I've picked out for her from the back of the fashion cupboard.

I have to say, I'm rather proud of myself. I actually didn't know I had it in me.

I'm just about to go and ask Precious if she'd like a coffee while she makes a start on Nancy's hair when my desk phone starts going. Oh, shit. If this is Tammy telling me she can't send the shoes after all . . .

'Nancy? Is that you?'

'No, this is Isabel. Is that Tammy?' It doesn't sound like Tammy. Tammy, on the five occasions that I've spoken to her already today, was softly-spoken and patient. This voice, familiar though it is, is strident and irritable.

'*Isabel*,' the voice hisses. '*You.* You're the one.'

'I'm the one what?' I feel like I've accidentally fallen into the plot of a teen horror movie. 'Who is this?'

'It's Jasmine.'

'Oh! Eve Alexander's stylist!'

409

'Am I?' Jasmine snaps. '*Am I?*'

Has she gone quite mad? 'Er . . . well, you said you were . . .'

'Because apparently,' she goes on, ignoring me, '*you* think you're Eve Alexander's stylist.'

'No, I don't.'

'Really? Then why would you take it upon yourself to pester Eve to wear Lucien Black to the Style Awards?'

'I didn't pester her! I just said . . .'

'Well, you win, Isabel!' Jasmine says viciously. 'I've just had Eve on the line telling me that she's not feeling quite confident enough to go with the lavender Marchesa, and she'd like to wear Lucien's dress tonight after all.'

'Oh, wow! That's brilliant!'

'Brilliant for Nancy and Lucien,' she snaps. 'From my point of view it's weeks of work and my hard-won reputation with Marchesa right down the fucking drain.'

I feel a pang of guilt, despite the fact she's being such a cow. 'I'm really sorry . . .'

'It's too late for sorry. I just need to come and get the dress. Is it at the store? At Nancy's?'

Oh, God. The dress is still hanging on the back of my wardrobe door. 'No, no, it's . . . well, it's elsewhere.'

'Elsewhere? *Where* elsewhere?'

Given that there's just the smallest possibility an A-lister like Eve Alexander might be slightly miffed to learn that her custom-made dress has already been worn (twice) by – well, by a total nobody – I think I'm going to have to spin a little bit of an untruth here.

'Actually, it's at my flat. You see, Nancy was very unhappy about storing it in the fashion cupboard here, and obviously her own wardrobe at home is too full already, so . . .'

'Oh, God, like I care. Just tell me where your flat is. And *please* don't tell me it's all the way out in Wimbledon, or something,' she adds, as though I might have chosen where I live just to spite her.

'No,' I say, feeling pleased that I can do something right. 'I'm near Westbourne Grove!'

'Oh, that's all right, then. I'll leave now and see you there in . . . what? Twenty-five?'

'Er . . .'

'Don't tell me you're going to be any longer than that!' she snaps. 'I've got to get the dress to Eve at Claridge's by six o'clock!'

'OK, OK, twenty-five.'

I can do it in twenty-five minutes. That is, of course, if I don't have to wait a single minute for the Central Line, if my Tube train doesn't sit, inexplicably, at Bond Street station for four minutes and if I can find a free taxi at Notting Hill to speed me the final half-mile down towards Westbourne Grove.

I give her the exact address, then hang up before darting into Nancy's office.

'Nancy!' I say, over the noise of the dryer. 'I have to

411

go round to my flat! Jasmine is coming round to collect Lucien's dress for Eve to wear tonight!'

Nancy's eyes widen, and she flaps a hand to stop the hair-stylist. 'My God! How?'

'Oh, I'll explain all that later,' I say modestly. 'But I should get over there now.'

'Yes, yes . . . go, go! Oh, Christ, Izzie, the dress is OK, isn't it? I mean, you didn't damage it that time you wore it?'

I don't tell her that actually, it was two times I wore it. 'No. It's fine. Eve will look amazing in it.'

'Good. Great. Oh, Izzie, this is terrific!' Nancy's face has fallen into the first real smile I've seen in . . . well, ever since I've known her. 'Looks like she's changing her mind about dropping Lucien after all!'

I didn't have to wait more than thirty seconds for the Central Line, but naturally, we sat for a full six minutes at Bond Street without going anywhere. By the time I jump in a cab at Notting Hill, it's already gone half an hour after Jasmine called. Great. She's going to be waiting for me outside, pacing like a caged tiger, and I'm not even going to have two minutes spare to do a blitzkrieg tidy of my 'room' before she goes in and sees the bin-liner chaos I live in.

But we've just pulled up outside, and there's no sign of her. Thank God, I seem to have beaten her to it! OK, well, this should give me enough time to clear the worst of the bin liners . . .

412

Oh. The front door isn't double-locked. Did I forget to do it when I was getting Lara out this morning?

The answer is staring me right in the face as I walk into the tiny hallway: Lara's work briefcase, her trench coat and her handbag are on the floor. She didn't go into work after all.

'Lara!' I march straight to her closed bedroom door, and rap on it sharply.

'Come in.'

I push open the door, about to have a bit of a go, but when I see that she's back in bed, surrounded by McVitie's wrappers, with the duvet pulled up around her ears, I just can't.

'Oh, Lara.'

'Sorry.' She stares at me with mascara-smudged raccoon eyes. 'I did get on the Tube this morning, Iz-Wiz. But then I realised I'd got on the Westbound line by mistake, and I just went round and round in circles, the wrong way, and then people started asking me why I was crying and I thought I'd better just come back here . . . I'm no use to my clients anyway, like this,' she sniffles. 'How am I supposed to give them professional advice when I can't even get the right Tube line?'

'Well, maybe this experience will give you great new insights!' I say encouragingly. 'Anyway you shouldn't be so hard on yourself. I mean, you're always telling me there's nothing wrong with hiding under your duvet with a twin-pack of chocolate biccies when you're feeling low!'

'No, I'm not. I say there's nothing wrong with taking a bit of time out. Recharging your batteries.'

'Yes, well, that's exactly what you're doing!'

'This isn't time out!' she wails. 'This isn't recharging my batteries! I've been in bed *all day*, Iz! I've eaten *four thousand six hundred and fifty-three calories' worth of chocolate digestives*!'

'Lars, you have to stay calm.' I put my hands on her shoulders. 'We're going to get you out of this, I promise. Whatever it takes. Now, there's this horrible stylist woman arriving any minute to get a dress, so I have to see to her, but then . . .'

Lara gulps. 'You mean Jasmine?'

I blink at her. 'How do you know about Jasmine?'

'Horrible stylist woman who came to get a dress? She was here fifteen minutes ago. I wouldn't have answered the doorbell, but she rang it about a zillion times. She took the dress and buggered off without so much as a thanks.'

Oh, *great*. Just bloody great. So Jasmine *has* seen the bin-bag-littered bomb site after all.

Not to mention the fact that I have this really awful sinking feeling that I may have left my Piglet pyjamas strewn on top of the sofa bed.

'With you in a sec . . .' I leave Lara and hurry to my 'room'. Yup – it's as bad as I thought: the Piglet pyjamas *are* in full view; the bin bags are, of course, everywhere; I'd forgotten about the small army of half-drunk Evian bottles surrounding my bed, and . . .

Hold on a moment.

Lucien's crystal-mesh cocktail dress is still here. It's hanging on the back of the wardrobe, on its posh padded hanger, exactly where it was when I left home this morning.

How did Jasmine come all the way here, with the sole purpose of getting this dress, and manage to *not* take it with her?

Did Lara *imagine* it? Like some kind of psychotic episode?

Dear God. The stress of having to tell Matthew to go ahead and marry Annie must have put so much pressure on . . . well, whatever bit of the brain those kinds of things put pressure on (cortex? synapses?) that she's lost her grip on reality, and started imagining events and conversations that haven't really happened.

I hurry back to her room, crouch down beside the bed, and adopt that gentle, slightly sing-song voice I think you're meant to use with people who've just suffered terrible trauma. 'Lars, I have an important question. It's about this Jasmine that you said came to collect the dress . . .'

'She did come to collect the dress.'

I take her hand. It's just like that moment in *The Sixth Sense* when you realise Haley Joel Whatsit is actually a ghost. 'But Lara. The dress is still here.'

Lara, who obviously hasn't seen *The Sixth Sense* recently, just pulls a face. 'No, she definitely took it.'

'Then why is it still hanging up on the back of my cupboard?'

415

'Well, I don't know, Isabel! I saw her taking a black dress.'

Suddenly, something occurs to me.

Except . . . no. It couldn't be.

'What did the dress look like?'

'I told you. Black.' Lara sketches vaguely in the air. 'One-shouldered. Safety-pinned at the hip . . .'

'She took *that* dress? But . . . it's the wrong one! That was just my toga dress! It was barely even finished!'

'Ohhh . . . Well, I wouldn't worry too much, Iz. She seemed perfectly happy with the one she took . . .'

'That's because she *thought* it was made by a proper Top International Fashion Designer!' I stand up. 'Anyway, that's not the point! Nancy thinks Eve Alexander is wearing the Lucien Black dress tonight . . .' I head for my room again. 'I have to go.'

'Wait, Iz . . .' Lara calls after me. 'Where are you going?'

I take the precious crystal-mesh dress off the wardrobe, fold it over one arm, and call back over my shoulder as I open the front door. 'Claridge's.'

Chapter 29

Obviously, I've seen *Notting Hill*. So obviously I know that all the top A-listers check into hotels under a fictional name. But Eve Alexander is an Oxford graduate, whose most famous roles have been in those corseted Jane Austen-type adaptations, so the chances are she's chosen something high-minded from one of the great classics of English literature. So I try out pretty much every single literary character I can remember from A-level English, but by the time I get to Tess of the D'Urbervilles the frosty woman on Claridge's reception desk is already manoeuvring her hand towards her phone, so I back off before she calls security.

There must be a better way of working out how to get access to Eve . . . oh, I know! The photographers! The ones lurking on the pavement on the opposite side of the road, pointing their long lenses at the revolving doors. It's their entire life's work to track down top celebrities, isn't it? Surely one of them will be able to give me a proper clue as to Eve Alexander's secret check-in name. I single out the least-scary-looking of them, a beanpole of a man in a badly fitting leather jacket, and hurry across.

'Excuse me? I'm so sorry to disturb while you're

working! I just wanted a very quick word about Eve Alexander . . .'

'Autograph, is it?' He glances down at me. 'You're too late, sweetheart. She left about five minutes ago.'

All right. Don't panic. Maybe she just nipped down to Fenwick's of Bond Street to get a pair of tights, or something. 'I don't suppose you happened to notice what she was wearing? I mean, was she all dressed up, or . . . ?'

'Oh, yeah, all dressed up.' He licks his lips. 'Little black dress, bit like a toga, very nice indeed.'

Shit. She's gone. I've missed her.

'Don't get upset, sweetheart. Lindsay Lohan's meant to be coming out any minute, maybe she'll give you an autograph.'

'I . . . don't want an autograph . . .' I drift away from the paparazzi pack and start to wander up Brook Street. My head is spinning. I mean, quite apart from the truly astonishing fact that both Jasmine and Eve seem to think my home-made, hand-stitched dress is some kind of statement of design genius, what the hell is going to happen when they realise it isn't Lucien Black after all?

And when Nancy sees Eve arrive in a black safety-pinned toga that bears no resemblance to Lucien Black's exquisite creation whatsoever?

'Oh, God,' comes a sudden, sharp voice. 'What are *you* doing here?'

Queenie Forbes-Wilkinson has just stopped on the pavement in front of me.

She's got a little less than her usual faceful of make-up and she's only wearing skinny jeans and a T-shirt, but she's carrying a full-length garment bag over one shoulder, and a Jimmy Choo carrier in one hand, which makes her look a bit like an off-duty model, dashing between fashion shows. Clearly she's caught sight of the dress over my own arm, because she pulls a face.

'Oh, Isabel, you're not wearing that *again*, are you? To the *MiMi* Style Awards? Couldn't you have made a *bit* more of an effort to find something new?'

'Oh, no, I'm not going to the Style Awards . . .'

'Well, what are you doing here, then, if you're not going?'

'Er . . . ?' I don't understand what she means.

'The hair and beauty suites? At Claridge's? Nicky Clarke? Jemma Kidd? I just picked up my dress from Callum's office and came over here to get done myself. Ohhhh,' she suddenly says. 'If you're not here for Claridge's, you must be here for Ben.'

I suppose this is as good a reason as any, given that Redwood's offices are on this street. 'Yes.'

'How's his eye, then?'

'It's . . . fine.'

'I told Callum off, you know. I mean, no matter what the provocation, he shouldn't have just thumped Ben.'

'*Callum* gave him the black eye?'

'What, did he tell you he'd walked into a door or something?'

'No, he . . .' He spun me what, in retrospect, sounds like an incredibly spurious line about defending my honour against a randy Belgian. 'But . . . why on earth did Callum hit him?'

'Oh, he finally realised about Ben's obsession with me.' She raises her eyebrows at my astonished expression. 'Don't tell me you didn't know about it either! He's mooned over me ever since we went out with each other for about a week back in the States, before I met Callum. Practically stalked me since he got back to the UK.'

'But I thought . . .' I stop. Because what Queenie's saying actually makes a lot more sense. Ben fawning over me whenever Queenie was around . . . Inviting me to places he knew she'd be . . . The speed with which he declared me to be his girlfriend, despite the fact that behind closed doors he didn't even seem to want to touch me . . .

'I assumed you knew he was just using you to try to make me jealous.' Queenie tosses her ponytail. 'God, you and Callum are a right pair! Do you always miss things that are going on right under your nose?'

'Apparently I do . . .'

'Well, I hope I haven't upset you or anything,' she says insincerely, before glancing at her watch. 'I'm running late for Jemma. See you around, Isabel.' She pushes her way past me and hurries towards Claridge's for her make-up appointment.

I could *kill* Ben Loxley.

Could he have not just *told* me why he really wanted

to go out with me? I wouldn't have ε.
thrilled, but at least I wouldn't have started get
paranoid, thinking I was the dregs. I wasn't the dreg
I just . . . wasn't Queenie. I mean, I was only going out
with Ben to make me feel desirable after the Will
debacle! Fat bloody chance there was of that, when he
had the hots for someone else all along. Well, running
into Queenie may just have been exactly what the last
vestiges of my dignity actually needed. I'm going to go
and have it out with Ben right now. Break it off with
him before he breaks it off with me.

I start striding in the direction of Park Lane, looking
at all the shiny brass plaques on the red-brick build-
ings. Butterworth Finlay Associates . . . Kleinmann,
Susskind, Lessing and Lomas . . . God, imagine
answering *their* telephones all day long . . . Newton
Capital . . .

Oh, hang on – is that Ben I can see right now? Just
a little way up the street, on the other side, stepping
out of a rather beautiful building with those neatly
trimmed bay trees shaped like lollipops on either side
of the entrance? Yes . . . it is him, looking undeniably
gorgeous in a dark grey suit, white shirt, and no tie.
That shiny black eye is almost visible from here, too,
turning a traffic-stopping shade of purple. In fact,
traffic is actually stopping – a taxi he's just hailed, so
that he and a couple of other men can get into it. One
of them is Fred Elfman, similarly smartly clad, and the
other . . . I can't quite see him behind Ben . . . probably
not Callum, I shouldn't think, after the recent fist

ght . . . Oh, now I can see a bit better, as they start climbing into the taxi.

It's Lucien Black.

He's clapping Ben on the shoulder as he gets into the taxi, before turning round to laugh at something Fred's saying. One of them pulls the door shut, and the taxi moves off, heading in the direction of Grosvenor Square. I'm about to dart behind a parked car so they don't see me as they go past, but then I realise they're all far too deep in animated conversation to take any notice of me at all.

So Lucien's definitely not in rehab. And now he's back in London. Hanging out, cheerful as you like, with the very people who are just about to buy his company.

I'm no expert, but this doesn't seem right.

This doesn't seem right at all.

Chapter 30

So the good news is, there was no shouty phone call in the middle of the night from Nancy, demanding to know why Eve Alexander's promised appearance in glorious, elegant Lucien Black was actually an appearance in unidentifiable, safety-pinned Isabel Bookbinder.

Still, it didn't mean I got a decent night's sleep, though. I just lay awake, trying to work out what I should do about Lucien Black. Anyway, after all the tossing and turning, I've made up my mind: I have to say something to Nancy. I mean, the deal is being signed tomorrow morning! If Lucien *is* getting up to anything dodgy, it's probably better that Nancy finds out about it sooner rather than later. However upset she's going to be. Which is why I'm already at the office at eight fifteen this morning, so I can speak to Nancy on this delicate matter in a certain amount of privacy.

Actually, I should come in this early more often: it's lovely and quiet, and there's no Lilian on the front desk to make me feel I'm on the back foot before the day's even started. I make my way along the corridor towards Nancy's office, and I'm not surprised to see she's already sitting at her desk. Actually, more kind of hunched over it – she's draped in a huge shahtoosh scarf, smoking a cigarette and sipping from a poly-styrene cup of coffee. *And* she's wearing sunglasses indoors.

Wow. It must have been a seriously big night at the Style Awards.

I knock on her door, and she turns, briefly, to see who it is. 'Oh. It's you.'

Now that I'm in her office, I can see that beneath her shahtoosh she's still wearing last night's sunset-coloured dress. Her hair is half up, half down, in a way that suggests she's started taking out a rather swanky up-do but been interrupted in the middle, and I can see smudged eye make-up behind the huge sunglasses.

'Did you come straight from the party?'

'I slept here.'

'Oh! Was it a very late night?'

'Not really. I left early, in fact. Went home about an hour after it all started.' She isn't looking at me. 'Which was certainly a surprise for my husband and the extremely athletic young lady he was entertaining in our bed.'

'You're joking . . .'

'What on earth makes you think I'm joking?' There's a flash of anger. 'My husband making an utter fool of himself – and me – with another of his slutty blondes is not a particularly amusing matter.'

Oh, God. The slutty blonde must be horrible Marina from the Lucien Black boutique. 'Nancy, I'm so sorry. I should have told you when I saw them in the concept store together . . .'

'Concept store? What do you mean, the concept store? This girl is some gym teacher from his daughter Polly's school. Teaches field hockey, or lacrosse, or some such clichéd fantasy of my husband's.'

What did she just say?

'Annie,' I blurt.

'Yeah, that was the name.' Nancy glances at me sharply. 'Know her or something?'

I have to sit down, very suddenly, on the white sofa. 'I think . . . she's my brother's fiancée . . .'

Nancy's face twists. 'Well, you might want to tell your brother to cancel the cake order. She didn't look the most devoted of brides-to-be.'

Annie cheating on *Matthew*? But they're the Bookbinder family golden couple, for God's sake! Even Dad has never found a bad word to say about Annie. It's why I've spent much of the last four years trying to convince Lara to abandon hope. Because Matthew and Annie were completely indivisible.

But now, it turns out, only indivisible until a smooth-talking lech like Hugo Tavistock came along.

God, was this the real reason Annie was busy all day Saturday? Not so much shopping with Amanda as bed-hopping with Hugo? And it looks like Annie's mysterious trips to Annabel's weren't just drinking pink cocktails and dancing on the tables after all . . .

'But you know, the evening was already pretty

much a write-off by then anyway.' Nancy takes off her sunglasses and looks right at me with red, swollen eyes. 'I'm sure you'll understand, after my excitement about Eve Alexander deciding to wear Lucien's dress after all, what a nasty shock it was to see her arriving in something else entirely.'

Oh, God. 'Nancy, I can explain about that. It was an awful mix-up, and I take full responsibility . . .'

'Followed,' Nancy continues, as though I haven't spoken at all, 'by the rather unexpected revelation from my fellow guest Miss Queenie Forbes-Wilkinson that you, Isabel, just *happen* to be dating a leading light at Redwood Capital.'

Wait – Queenie knows I work for Nancy? But how on earth did she find that out?

Nancy must sense my confusion. 'Apparently she ran into a certain stylist friend of hers in the Claridge's makeover suites who was griping about this wretched girl called Isabel Bookbinder who'd made Eve change her mind about wearing Marchesa.'

'Jasmine,' I croak.

'Jasmine.' Nancy nods. 'Queenie was somewhat surprised, of course, given that as far as she knew, you're a fashion designer, not my PA. But then, of course, it is perfectly possible to be both. A real bonus, even, if what you really want to do is steal your boss's clients *and* find out all the inside info on her company to feed back to your boyfriend at the same time.'

What? No, wait . . . 'Nancy, you've got this all

completely wrong! I wasn't trying to steal Eve from you! She wore that dress by mistake. Anyway, I'm not a fashion designer at all!'

'*Really?*' Nancy's voice drips with disbelief. 'You somehow manage to get Eve Alexander into a dress of yours for an awards do, but you're *not a fashion designer at all?*'

'No! Honestly!' I twist my hands desperately. 'I don't have a fashion business. It was just this one dress I made, for a family friend. It was hanging next to Lucien's dress in my bedroom, and Jasmine obviously thought it was the right one . . .'

'Well, I'm not surprised. It was brilliant.'

I stare at her. 'Brilliant?'

'Yes, brilliant, Isabel. That asymmetric cut, the draping, the hand-stitching . . . Eve looked like a fucking angel.' Nancy picks up the *Daily Mail* from the stack of newspapers on her desk, the ones that are delivered to Claudia's office every morning, and chucks it across at me. 'Here.'

I pick it up from where it's fallen on the floor, and stare at the front page. Eve is on the cover, looking, as Nancy put it, like an angel. *In my dress*. She's posing with a half-smile, and a hand on one hip, and she looks cool, and elegant, and funky. And *thin*, too – something about the drape of the silk . . . the way *I've* draped the silk . . . has shaved off just a couple of those extra pounds her critics in papers like the *Mail* are always talking about. The one-shouldered effect shows off her creamy collarbones to perfection, and

427

the asymmetric hemline finishes high above her knee, giving a flash of leg that's both demure and sexy.

I did this?

'So . . .' Nancy is staring at me. 'Was that Ben Loxley's idea, too? Or was stealing my client just an added bonus for you while you spied on me on Redwood's behalf?'

Well, I hope Queenie is happy. Whether the notion that I'm spying for Redwood has actually been planted in Nancy's head by Queenie herself, or whether it's been entirely formed by Nancy once Queenie told her I was dating Ben, this is a seriously huge misunderstanding. Especially when I've got news about Redwood that Nancy really needs to listen to.

I put the paper down. My hands are shaking. 'Nancy, please. I'm not spying on you, I swear. And there's something you need to know about Redwood. I think they're up to something with Lucien behind your back. I saw him in Shepton Mallet at the weekend, and I thought he was just going round the pubs, but now I think he was down there to meet Redwood, because then I saw him again yesterday, with Ben, and Fred Elfman . . .'

'How *dare* you try to deflect attention off yourself by turning this all around on Lucien?'

'No, no, that's not what I'm trying to do!'

'I mean, who do you think you are? Lucien's been my best friend for fifteen years, and I've known you barely fifteen days!'

'Look, just call the rehab centre! They'll tell you he's

428

not there, and then you can call him on his mobile, and ask him to expl . . .'

Very suddenly, Nancy slams a hand down on her desk. 'You want me to *grill* my best friend? On the say-so of a proven liar?'

'I've not lied,' I mumble, 'not exactly . . .'

'Oh, *please*. I just wish I'd stopped you from the very start. I mean, all that crap about Bianca Jagger . . . I thought you were lying then, but I just thought that's how badly you wanted to work with me. That's what I get for being easily flattered.'

'But I really did want to work with you . . .'

She stands up, walks to the door, and holds it open. 'Get out, Isabel.'

'Nancy, please . . .'

'Just get out, right now, or I'll call security.'

I'm not going to argue any more. Getting thrown out by security would be so heinously embarrassing, I'd rather just leave with a fragment of dignity intact. I stand up and walk to the door.

'You know,' Nancy says, as I reach her, 'the thing that really gets to me, Isabel, is how much I liked you. I was really starting to depend on you.'

'But you can depend on me still. I promise . . .'

'No. I can't. So go, Isabel. Just . . . go.'

Chapter 31

When Ben opens his apartment door to me this evening, I can tell from the expression on his face how very little he expected it to be me standing there. He's holding a large glass of red wine in one hand, and a sheaf of papers and a biro in the other. The bruise on his eye is even more lurid now, showcasing a mottled rainbow of colours from beetroot to blackberry, and one side of his nose still looks slightly swollen.

'Ben. Do you mind if I come in?'

His eyebrows shoot upwards and he glances pointedly at his watch. 'Isabel, it's nine o'clock at night. To be perfectly honest, I'm right in the thick of it. The Lucien Black deal is completing tomorrow, I've got a ton of paperwork . . .'

'I'll only be a few minutes. Please. We really need to talk.'

He sighs, and shoves his papers under one arm to put a hand on my shoulder. 'Look, I know how you feel about me, but I think you've allowed yourself to become too attached too quickly. This intensity – it's just too much.'

I knew it! He's trying to turn it all around on me, make it seem like I'm the source of the problem! God, it's a good thing Queenie did tell me the truth. Otherwise I'd be a weeping wreck right now.

I force a sad little smile on to my face. 'I do understand that, Ben.'

'You do?' He looks surprised. I think he would have rather liked a bit of weeping and gnashing of teeth.

'Yes. But I'd still really like a few minutes to talk, Ben. Clear up any awkwardness. I mean, we're never going to be able to avoid each other completely. Not with you being Matthew's best friend and everything.'

He thinks about this. 'I suppose with his wedding coming up . . .'

Or not, if Hugo Tavistock has anything to do with it.

'Exactly,' I say. 'I just want to clear the air.'

Ben shoots me one last suspicious look. 'Just as friends, yes?'

Unbelievable. 'Just as friends.'

'Well, all right then.' Magnanimous now, he lets me past him and ushers me towards the living room. 'I'm working in here, so you'll have to excuse the mess.'

It's hardly a mess. Compared to the pigsty Lara's been making of her flat for the past forty-eight hours, it's positively pristine. There's a laptop on the coffee table, a plate half-filled with cut-up carrot and celery sticks next to the Bang and Olufsen phone on the lamp table, and . . . oh, good. His iPhone is on the sofa. Which is perfect, because that's exactly what I'm here for.

Well, not the *actual phone*, of course – I'm not

about to go adding charges of property theft to all the trouble I'm already in today. But I need something *from* the phone. I need proof that Ben is in private contact with Lucien Black.

Evidence of calls to Lucien's mobile would be good; a sneaky text message even better. Just something I can show to Nancy that might make her stop for a moment, before the deal goes ahead, and question whether her so-called partner is really operating in the company's best interests after all.

'Quick glass of wine?' Ben is asking, in a tone of voice that suggests he's only being polite, and is desperate for me to say no.

'Yes, I'd love one, please.' The longer I can stick around, the better. I just need to work out a way to get him out of the room for a couple of minutes.

Ben goes over to the sleek chrome sideboard, picks up a wine bottle and pours me what I'd describe as a generous thimbleful. So he really did mean *quick*. Damn. Sticking around could be harder than I thought.

'So,' he says, in a brisk and businesslike manner, as he hands me my glass. 'Let me just say, Isabel, that I really don't want you to feel too awkward about all this.' He sips his own large glass of wine. 'I mean, we had a few dates, it didn't work out . . . no harm, no foul.'

No harm no foul?

I can't help the bubble of anger that rises up in me. 'Actually, Ben, it isn't *quite* no harm, no foul. I

432

mean, if you thought it was just a *few dates*, then why did you go around telling everyone I was your girlfriend?'

'Sorry?'

'Because you've put me in a pretty embarrassing situation,' I carry on, before I can stop myself. 'I mean, my family already think I'm a walking disaster. They're going to be really disappointed it's all over between us.'

I didn't intend to say any of this right now, but there's something about Ben's extreme smugness, not to mention the fact that he's trying to dump responsibility on me, that has really got under my skin.

Now he's nodding sagely. 'I understand that. When I split up with Saskia, her mother was just devastated . . .'

'Oh, for crying out loud, Ben, it's not because you're the catch of the century!' I say. I'm exasperated beyond belief. 'I'm just saying it's another reason for them to think I've screwed up at something! And while we're on the subject of Saskia,' I carry on, unable to stop myself now I've started, 'does she really even exist, or is she just another relationship you've fabricated?'

Ben's whole face shuts down. He slams his glass of wine angrily on to the coffee table. *'Fabricated?'*

OK. I need to be careful here. I can't have him throwing me out.

And anyway, I don't mean to rile him like this. To be honest, I'm feeling a little bit sorry for him. All right, he's been selfish, and he's used me, but being helplessly in love with Queenie isn't a crime. A mystery, yes. But not a crime.

'Sorry. I don't mean anything. I just . . . look, you know how critical Dad always is of the way I live my life, and now I've got another failed relationship . . .' I sniff. 'God, I'm sorry. The last thing I wanted to do was cry . . .'

'That's all right,' he says irritably.

'Do you have a tissue?'

He peers at me, clearly seeing no sign of tears whatsoever. 'Do you *need* a tissue?'

'Well, my mascara could run . . . I don't want to get any messy black stains on your beautiful cream couch . . .'

That does it. He's practically hurdling the furniture to get to the bathroom. 'I'll fetch you some!'

The minute he's out of the room, I grab his iPhone and turn the screen on. My hands have started to shake, which is hopeless, and my brain has suddenly gone all foggy, which is even worse. Focus, Isabel, focus . . . All right, let's see if I can find Ben's recent calls . . . no, *not* a useless weather report that's telling me it's going to be fifteen degrees and cloudy tomorrow . . .

'Here you go.'

I jump, and actually drop the phone back on to the sofa as I hear Ben come back into the room. He's carrying a box of tissues and wearing a scowl.

'You haven't got anything on the cushions, have you?'

'No, no . . . er . . . you know, though, what I really think I need?'

He hands over the tissues. 'What?'

'A cup of tea!' Yes! That's it. Making me a cup of tea has to take him a couple of minutes, doesn't it? 'A cup of hot, sweet tea.'

'*Tea?*'

'Well, you know, this whole thing has been a dreadful shock to me, Ben.' I make my voice go shaky – which, actually, isn't that difficult – and mop at my non-existent tears with a trembling tissue.

'But you said you understood. That all you wanted to do was clear up any awkwardness.'

'Yes, but now that I'm actually *here*,' I glance around the flat, 'I think I'm beginning to realise just how badly I'm handling it all.'

He looks torn, for a moment, between irritation and vanity. It's not much surprise when vanity wins.

'All right. I'll make you some tea.'

'Oh, thank you!' I say in a quavering voice, as he marches towards the kitchen and disappears out of my sight behind the tall Poggenpohl cabinets. There's a clatter of a kettle, and then water running, before the sound of cupboards being opened and mugs chinked.

Right. Back to square one. I grab the iPhone again. Recent calls, recent calls . . . I press the 'phone' button . . . got them! OK, so, calls to Fred Elfman . . . Matthew Bookbinder . . . and Lucien Black. *Lucien B mobile.* Showing his most recent call as being at 19.57 today.

This is just what I need! I fumble in my bag for my own phone, switch it to the camera function, and take a hasty snapshot of the iPhone screen.

'Earl Grey all right?' calls Ben's voice from the kitchen.

'Oh, yes, Earl Grey is perfect . . .' I press the central button to go back to the main screen, and click on the SMS icon. Again, there's a list of names of all the people who've texted Ben in the course of the day – one from Queenie saying *Never in a million years* that makes me wish I had time to read the rest of the exchange, a few from various Venture-Capitalist-sounding people called things like Bradley and Mitch and Lachlan, and then, right at the bottom, the Holy Grail.

Lucien B mobile – 19.46

With NT right now. Give it ten and I'll call

I don't know why I'm surprised – after all, I have seen them swanning off in a taxi together looking like the best of chums – but seeing the confirmation, in print, that they're in communication with each other is rather unnerving. Because I was right. And I'm never usually right.

Lightly tapping on this message brings up a screenful of more of them. I scan the little speech bubbles as quickly as I can, starting with one from Ben.

Time for quick drink tomorrow? Need last-minute chat

Yeah is there a problem?

Don't think so but Fred agrees NT's lawyers getting jumpy. U sure she's not realised anything?

Of course am sure. Have delib blown my entire reputation 4 this, it's not a fucking game

Lucien's done *what*?

Delib blown his entire reputation? I mean, *deliberately*?

But does that mean . . . all this transparent-clothing nonsense, the chucking of champagne bottles at top fashion editors . . . all that was done on purpose? But why would Lucien do that?

Except . . . now I think about it, it's kind of convenient for Redwood Capital that Lucien's nervous breakdown, his first-ever major commercial flop, should happen only weeks before they're about to buy out his company. They can offer a lot less money, for starters . . .

I switch my phone to the camera function again, aim it at the iPhone and take the best photo I can. It's a little bit blurry, and you have to squint to read it, but it's legible, from Lucien's name at the top of the screen to his inadvertent admission of guilt at the bottom of it.

I switch the iPhone back to its neutral screen and slip my own phone safely into my bag just as Ben appears with a china mug in his hand.

'Oh, lovely!' I stand up and take the mug, then drink in a scalding sip. 'God, thanks, Ben, that was just what I needed.' I take another glug. 'Well! I'm so glad we had this chance to talk, Ben. I really feel the air has been cleared between us.'

'You're going?' He stares, astonished, as I hand

back the mug of tea and slip my bag over my shoulder. *'Already?'*

'Of course!' I reach up and give him a kiss on each cheek, before heading for the front door. 'You did say you had a lot to be getting on with.'

'But . . . the tea . . . and I thought you wanted to talk more about *us*.'

'Well, what's there to say, really? All I wanted was a little bit of closure. And I think we've achieved that, don't you?' I open the door and start off down the steps towards the street.

'I suppose . . .'

'Oh, and thank you for the tea! Thanks for everything.' I glance back up the stairs just before I turn the corner. 'I'll see you around, Ben.'

He just shrugs and lifts a hand that I think is about to wave me off. But all it does is close the door behind me.

This Morning, 11 January, 11.15 a.m., ITV1

FERN BRITTON . . . so keep your calls coming for agony aunt Denise Robertson, who wants to hear from you in our phone-in this morning if you're struggling to come to terms with the menopause.

PHILLIP SCHOFIELD Now, our next guest is a Top International Fashion Designer, owner of twenty worldwide ~~concept stores~~ boutiques, and the go-to girl for the rich and famous whenever they need a frock for the Oscars.

FERN Not only that, but she's written a candid new biography that blows the lid open on the dirt behind the glamorous facade of the fashion world . . .

PHIL . . . and she's an old friend of the show, so we're very pleased to welcome back . . . Isabel Bookbinder. Isabel, how are you?

ISABEL BOOKBINDER I'm well, Phil. It's lovely to see you.

FERN This book, *Isabel – My Struggle* [holds up large coffee-table book, containing more photographs than actual wordage], it's fascinating stuff. Was it terribly painful for you to produce?

ISABEL In some ways, Fern, it was. It certainly brought back a lot of memories from a very turbulent time in my life.

PHIL Yes, let's talk about that time, first of all. You admit in the book that your very first job in fashion was not, in fact, as a designer at all, but actually that you were ~~nothing more than~~ a lowly PA to professional Muse Nancy Tavistock. And more to the point, you also admit

439

that you, shall we say, stretched the truth somewhat in order to get that job.

ISABEL That's right. [looks down, dabs eyes] I've never admitted the truth until now, but I did ~~tell a few porkies~~ fudge my CV a little to break into the business in the first place. In fact, I'd like to take this opportunity to apologise to several people I inadvertently dragged into this ~~mess~~ situation: Nancy Tavistock, who was my extremely good-willed and generous boss, Bianca Jagger, who wasn't my godmother . . .

FERN And there was a terrible falling-out with Nancy Tavistock, wasn't there, when she accused you of deliberately sabotaging her attempts to put top actress Eve Alexander in a Lucien Black frock, when her company was crumbling around her?

ISABEL There was, Fern, yes. But that simply wasn't true. ~~If anyone was to blame for that it was this awful stylist called Jas~~ In fact, that's one of the many reasons I wrote this book – to try to set the record straight. I should never have lied to get the job, but I didn't deceive her in the way she thought I did.

PHIL And you do very much regret that first big whopper, don't you? [struggling to keep a straight face] I mean . . .

FERN [covering her mouth with her script] Oh, Phil, really . . .

PHIL [wheezing with poorly suppressed hysterics] I'm so sorry . . .

FERN [stifling a giggle] I do apologise, Isabel. Now, there were other people you worked with who carried out deceptions far worse than yours, weren't there?

ISABEL Yes. Obviously I haven't really been able to reveal names, but I was shocked to my very core when I discovered that a certain Top International Fashion Designer was deceiving his business partner and lifelong friend. I observed him having clandestine meetings with their investors, lying about his whereabouts, and in the end I was able to produce text messages that proved he had deliberately staged a nervous breakdown, possibly to allow the investors to offer less money for his company.

PHIL That was very resourceful of you, Isabel.

ISABEL Well, he was cheating Nancy Tavistock, my good-willed and generous boss, out of money she desperately needed. It was really the least I could do.

FERN So, a rocky start to your fashion career, but one that spurred you on to succeed, isn't that right?

ISABEL Exactly. ~~Having seriously pissed off one of the most important people in the industry~~ It made me decide it was probably best to take a more traditional route into the fashion world. I realised I needed to knuckle down to some kind of proper design course, even if it wasn't the prestigious Fashion Master's at Central St Martins, and learn some of the rudimentaries of garment-making for a change.

PHIL This despite the fact you'd already enjoyed some astonishing success as the creator of the now-famous Toga Dress that catapulted Eve Alexander into world-wide best-dressed lists and, insiders say, to the notice of Martin Scorsese, in whose next film she won her first Oscar only months later?

ISABEL [modestly] Well, Eve is a very beautiful woman. I'm sure any designer she asked to make her a dress would be thrilled to give her one. [sighs] Let me rephrase that . . .

FERN [shrieks with laughter]

PHIL [bends double]

FERN [mascara runs down face]

PHIL [mops eyes with sleeve] Thank you, Isabel. It was lovely to have you on the show.

ISABEL Not at all, Phil. Thank *you*.

Ad break.

Chapter 32

I wouldn't have thought anyone could look more surprised to see me than Ben did earlier this evening, but when Will opens the front door of his – our – Battersea Park flat, you could probably knock him down with a feather.

'Isabel!'

'Hi.'

'What . . .' He clears his throat. 'What are you doing here?'

'I don't know.'

For God's sake. Where did that come from? Of course I know what I'm doing here. I even had my opening lines all worked out! But Will, damn him, standing here looking brooding and rather gorgeous in the jeans I made him buy in Harvey Nichols, and one of his half-million near-identical blue shirts, is putting me off my stride.

I start again. 'I mean, I *do* know, obviously. Um – I had something I wanted to ask you about. Something work-related. But . . .'

'Oh.' In an instant he's erased the astonished expression from his face, and replaced it with a cool, careful blankness. 'Work. Of course.' He pulls the door behind him so it's nearly closed. 'Nothing your new boyfriend can help you with?'

'He's not my new boyfriend.'

Will's left eyebrow arches. It's a trick I know he uses when he's dealing with difficult clients, or hot-air-filled barristers, and it's pretty effective. 'Really? Because *he* certainly seemed to think he was.'

'Well, all right, he was. Sort of. But he isn't any more . . .' I take a deep breath. 'It's complicated. It was a mistake. And I'm sorry about that night at the party. It was inexcusable.'

Will shrugs awkwardly. 'That's all right. I should never have come in the first place. I don't know what I was thinking.'

We stand there in silence, both of us shivering slightly in the night air.

'So,' Will says, after a moment or two. 'You said you had a work problem?'

'Oh, yes, sorry . . . um, it's a legal matter.'

This is Will's cue to hold up a hand, smiling, and say *whoa, a legal matter? In that case, we could be here all night! You'd better come in and I'll open a bottle.*

But he doesn't say anything. No joke. No invitation inside. Nothing. He just folds his arms, patiently, and waits.

'Right. So – er – from a legal point of view, is it actually *illegal* for people to conspire together to make a company less valuable?'

'*What?*'

'You know, so they can buy it on the cheap, say?'

'Oh, good God.' Will's eyes widen in alarm. 'What have you got yourself into, Isabel?'

'Nothing! It's not *me*!' Suddenly, anger flares up inside me. Because it's the same old story, isn't it? – *silly old Isabel, what's she up to now?* I turn away. 'Oh, just forget about it. I'm sorry I even came . . .'

'Iz, no – wait!' Will grabs my arm. 'I didn't mean anything by that. It's just that, well, what you're describing sounds dangerously close to corporate fraud. And that's an extremely serious matter.' His forehead creases. 'I just don't understand. I mean, I thought you were working in fashion.'

'I am. But there's been a development.'

His hand is still on my arm. 'Please, Iz – tell me. I'd really like to help if I can.'

I look up at him. His face is still set in that cool, careful expression, but his eyes have softened. At least, I *think* his eyes have softened. 'All right. It could be nothing. And you have to keep it all confidential.'

'Of course.' He nods gravely. 'I promise I won't run off to my stockbroker with inside information first thing in the morning.'

I shoot him a look. 'Ha ha. OK, I've been working for this woman called Nancy Tavistock, who co-owns Lucien Black – you know, the designer?'

'Wow.' Will's eyebrows shoot upwards. 'That sounds great, Isabel.'

'I'm only a PA.' I can suddenly feel my cheeks flame. 'Nothing special. It was just meant to be a foot in the door.'

'Well, it sounds like a big foot. In . . . er . . . a big door.' Now he looks embarrassed. 'I mean . . . oh, you know what I mean.'

I carry on, slightly buoyed up by the fact that I'm not the only one saying stupid things round here. 'Anyway, Nancy and Lucien are just about to sell the company to these big venture capitalists, Redwood. But I think Lucien has been in league with Redwood behind Nancy's back.'

'In league to do what?'

'I'm not sure, exactly. But I've seen him meeting people from Redwood when he's meant to be in rehab, and now I've got evidence of these texts between him and Be . . .' I stop myself just in time. '. . . er, someone from Redwood . . .'

'It's all right. I know this ex-non-boyfriend of yours works for Redwood Capital.'

'You do?'

Will stares at the doorstep tiles. 'I asked one of Matthew and Annie's friends what his name was and Googled him the day after the party,' he mumbles.

This is, believe it or not, about the best piece of news I've had for a week. Will Googled Ben! Which surely he wouldn't have done if he'd stopped caring about me.

'Anyway,' I go on, 'Lucien is meant to have had this big breakdown, and he produced this disastrous collection, and Redwood have ended up offering less than half what they originally offered . . .'

'And you're thinking maybe they've got together to engineer it all, and they're . . . what? Paying Lucien a chunk of what they're saving by buying the company for less than it's really worth?'

I blink. 'Er – yes. I suppose that is what I'm thinking.'

'So, can I see these texts?' he asks.

I locate the blurry photo, hand over my phone, and watch Will's frown deepen as he reads them.

'So?' I chew my lip. 'What do you think? I mean, I don't need it to be enough to stand up in court or anything. I just need Nancy to take it seriously enough to put a stop to the deal.'

'Well, you're right, it wouldn't stand up in court.'

'Oh.' I can't help feeling a tiny bit crushed, despite what I just said. Because I've had these visions of Lucien, Ben and Fred in the dock, heads bowed in shame, while a velvet-robed judge lists their many misdemeanours before thanking me for taking dangerous fraudsters off the streets.

'But I have to say, Isabel, if Nancy was a client of mine, and I saw these text messages, I'd be advising her to pull out of the deal immediately.'

'Really?'

'Yes. The whole thing stinks. This Nancy Tavistock of yours needs to run a mile.'

I pull a face. 'Yes, but that's part of the problem. She's spent months working on this deal, and she really needs the money . . .'

'So, she can use what you know to force Redwood to renegotiate. I'm sure the prospect of an investigation by the Financial Services Authority would be enough to bring about a new spirit of generosity. Look, she must have lawyers, right? Would you like me to have a word with them, tell them what you've found out, and then they can decide how best to proceed?'

I'm tempted. But actually, I think this is going to be better coming to Nancy straight from me. And it's about time I saw something through for once. 'No, it's fine. I'll try to make her listen.'

He shrugs. 'Well, if you need a hand, just let me know. I'll give you a good rate.'

I can't prevent the grin that suddenly stretches across my face. Because it's one of his lawyer jokes. His hackneyed, crappy lawyer jokes. The ones I always used to tell him were the least funny things I'd ever heard, but that actually sometimes – all right, often – used to make me smile.

'Will . . .'

'Will?' Somebody else is saying his name, too. It's a man's voice, suddenly calling from behind the door, from the top of the stairs that lead up to the flat. 'Did you say we should open the red Planeta or the white?'

I start to back away. 'I'm disturbing. I'm sorry . . .'

'No, no!' Will practically yelps. 'It's just a couple of work colleagues.'

Work colleagues. Typical. 'Oh, well, then it's a good thing you didn't invite me in,' I say stiffly. 'I wouldn't want to embarrass you.'

'I *would* have invited you in!' Will snaps. 'But I know how you feel . . . used to feel, I mean . . . about people from Thomson Tibble . . .'

'William? Red or white?' The man who's been calling out pulls the door open behind us. He's short, white-blond, and distinctly portly. 'Oh, sorry,' he says, with a cheery smile, in one of those all-purpose Euro-American accents you so often hear when tennis players are interviewed in Wimbledon fortnight. 'I am interrupting.'

'It's fine, I'm just leaving.'

'No you're not!' Will sounds exasperated, and he's turning slightly pink, though whether through frustration or embarrassment, it's hard to tell. 'Open whichever you prefer, Erik,' he says, turning to the portly man. 'I'll be up in a minute.'

'Well, I think, then, perhaps the red,' Erik says. 'Julia, of course, prefers it that I drink white . . .'

'*Julia?*' I don't believe this. 'She's here?'

'Of course!' Erik says, before Will can speak. 'We are just having a little dinner!'

I know how you feel about people from Thomson Tibble, my arse! It's nothing to do with me feeling uncomfortable around his colleagues, and everything to do with me feeling uncomfortable around his . . . his fancy woman! I bet they're all having the most wonderful cosy little supper party – sitting around sipping expensive wines, and chewing the fat about oil prices, no doubt, or the government's education and social housing policies, or how *War and Peace* is just *so* superior to *Anna Karenina*. And Julia's probably whipped up a nine-course molecular gastronomy menu wearing nothing but her fur-trimmed bikini and a sexy little apron, using *my* old saucepans and . . . and other cooking equipment . . .

I start to stumble into the street. 'I'll leave you to it . . .'

'Isabel . . .'

'This is *Isabel*?' Erik's beam widens. 'Well, how nice to meet you! You and I have so much to talk about!'

'We do?'

'Erik . . .'

'Yes!' Erik interrupts Will. 'We are both Thomson Tibble Telford widows!' He laughs, and claps Will on the back. 'Every time I telephoned my wife in the Cayman Islands, she was with your boyfriend!' He lowers his voice conspiratorially. 'You know, once I am pretty sure I even *caught them in bed* together!'

Wait a minute. Julia is Erik's *wife*?

And . . . and he didn't *mind* the fact that they were in bed together?

'Oh, I do not mean to alarm you!' says Erik. 'I only mean in bed *asleep* together! Will is a true gentleman, to let my wife take a nap in his room when the air conditioning was broken in hers.'

'Air conditioning?' I mumble.

'Of course, now the twelve-week stage is passed, there is less to worry about, but I still do not like Julia working so hard on these overseas trips . . .'

So Julia is not only married, she's pregnant? And she *still* lay around sipping planter's punch in a fur-trimmed bikini?

450

Except that I never *actually saw* Julia in a fur bikini with a cocktail in her hand.

And as Lara observed, I never *actually saw* her in flagrante with Will either. She just picked up the phone in his bedroom and said they were both sleeping . . .

'Erik, can I just have a moment with Isabel alone, please?' Will's saying tersely.

'Oh, of course.' Erik smiles at us both. 'Nice to meet you, Isabel. You and Will must come round to our place and have some dinner. Don't worry,' he adds, with a wink, 'I will not inflict Julia's cooking on you!'

Once he's gone, back up the stairs to open the wine, Will and I look at each other. Neither of us speaks for a moment.

'So,' I eventually say. 'Broken air conditioning?'

Will runs a hand through his hair, which makes it stick up in sexy little tufts. 'It had been a *thirty-hour* working day, Isabel. We were gearing up for another five- or six-hour meeting. When I knew Julia's air con was down, I offered to let her have a nap in my room.'

'But . . . you kept apologising . . .'

'Because I felt so terrible! I knew I should never really have just gone to sleep right next to Julia. It was inappropriate, considering. But, Isabel . . .' He starts to rub his forehead with his hands, and I notice that they're shaking slightly. 'I didn't realise what you thought I was apologising *for*! Did you seriously think I was actually sleeping with her?'

'I . . . didn't know.'

451

'But, Iz, you know that's not me! Why couldn't you just have trusted me?'

'That's not fair.' I feel a little stab of anger. 'You were thousands of miles away. She was in your bedroom. She didn't even know who I was.'

Will is looking shamefaced. 'I was sorry about that, too, Isabel. I hadn't really ever talked about you to people at work, you see. Talking too much about your personal life is sort of . . . frowned upon.'

'It's not *talking too much* to let people know I even exist! Look, I know you're probably ashamed of me, and everything, because I'm not a bazillion-quid-an-hour lawyer . . .'

'Ashamed of you?' Will's eyes widen. 'What on earth makes you think that?'

'Oh, please. Your colleagues didn't know about me, your parents didn't know about me . . .'

'Wait – you think I didn't introduce you to my parents because I was ashamed of you?' Will grabs both my hands. 'Isabel. The reason – the *only* reason – that I didn't introduce you to my parents was because I didn't want them to know how serious I was about you.'

I blink at him. Is this meant to be making me feel *better*?

'You don't know what my mother is like,' he goes on. 'The minute she met you, and realised how I felt, she'd have been on our cases 24–7, badgering us – badgering *you*, most likely – about engagements, and weddings, and grandchildren . . .'

'Will, I have a mother of my own, remember?'

He almost smiles. 'Yeah, well, I was working on the principle you could do without getting it from both sides. Maybe I shouldn't have taken that decision for you. But as for feeling ashamed of you . . . nothing could have been further from the truth.'

I open my mouth to speak, before realising that I have no idea what to say. Because I'm just realising how badly I – *we* – have screwed this up.

But then, he's still holding my hands. And it still feels as perfectly right as it ever did.

Will takes a deep breath. 'I tried to explain it all to you, Isabel. I did. But you just ran, without so much as a backward glance.' He looks down at the floor. 'Straight to Ben bloody Loxley.'

'I . . . I'm sorry.'

'I am, too.' Will is still staring at the floor. 'There's just been so much going on with work, I didn't have time to think what it must all look like to you.'

'You were always busy with work.'

'Isabel,' he sighs, 'I love what I do. I'd have thought you of all people would understand that.'

'Me of all people?'

'Well, yes – because you're like me. Passionate about succeeding. I always thought that was partly why we worked so well together . . .'

'You think I'm . . . passionate about succeeding?'

He blinks. 'Aren't you?'

'Yes! But I didn't think *you* thought that. I thought you just assumed I was sitting around the flat all day . . . twiddling my thumbs and booking manicures . . .'

Now Will is looking truly astonished. 'I'll admit, I didn't really understand your – er – working process, but that's because I'm not a creative person like you. I never thought you were just sitting around!'

'Well,' I mumble, 'some of the time I was. A bit.'

'Maybe, but in the end it got you where you wanted to be, didn't it? I mean, you're working for Nancy Tavistock now. Even I know what a big deal that is.'

I don't think now is the time to admit to Will that Nancy has fired me. Not when I'm just beginning to realise that he doesn't think I'm a waster after all.

'Isabel . . .' He stops. 'Look. It sounds like you have a lot to do right now. The last thing I want is to get in your way.'

But you wouldn't be in my way.

Except . . . well, he's right, in one sense. I *have* got a lot to do. And not just with Nancy. Because I've made this decision, ever since seeing my dress on the cover of the newspaper this morning, that I'm going to make a proper go of my design career after all. No more faffing around trying to get in the back door, fooling people into giving me an opening and then winging it. I'm going to do something the right way, for once. Start an evening class in those rudimentaries of garment-making that Diana Pettigrew went on about. Take a course in fashion drawing. Build up my portfolio – and a proper one this time, not just a silly little Mood Book. If I've really got a trace of genuine talent for this, I'm going to do whatever it takes to get Isabel B up and running.

And I'm not sure I'm going to be able to do that if I'm putting all my energy into getting this relationship back up and running too.

'You wouldn't be in my way,' I say, honestly. 'It's just . . . well, you're right about the other thing. I do have a lot to do . . .'

'Listen.' Will holds up a hand. 'Call me. That's all. Just . . . call me. I'll be here.'

'Really?'

'Well, either that, or at the office.' His chocolate-coloured eyes crinkle slightly, the way they do when he's about to smile.

It's the crap joke, again, that does it. I reach up and kiss him. I only intend it to be a brief brush of the lips, but once we're both there it turns into a longer brush. And then . . . well, if I'm honest, that really wasn't a brush at all.

When we pull away from each other, he's definitely smiling. He clears his throat. 'It's late. Let me help you get a cab . . .'

'Don't worry.' I smile back as I step off the doorstep and out on to the pavement. 'I'll do it on my own.'

The taxi gods are obviously feeling generous tonight, because a free one comes trundling round the corner about half a minute after I've started looking. As I get in, and sink back on the seat, I glance back in the direction of Will's flat. He's still standing there, silhouetted in the bright electric light, watching out for me.

I really just want to turn the taxi round and go home.

But I have something extremely important to do, and it can't wait. I take out my phone and dial Nancy's number. I'm not exactly astonished when, after a couple of rings, it cuts straight to voicemail.

I take a deep breath. 'Nancy, it's Isabel. Please – don't delete this. All I want to say is, I can prove what I said earlier. About Lucien, I mean. So . . . look, please just call me back. I need to talk to you.'

I'm not even over Battersea Bridge before my phone starts ringing.

Chapter 33

It's really, really strange seeing Nancy Tavistock, queen bee of the fashion world, sitting at Lara's kitchen table this morning, sipping tea from the *If You're OCD And You Know It, Wash Your Hands* mug that I bought Lara one Christmas, which she won't take into the office.

Even more strange because Nancy herself doesn't seem to realise how surreal it actually is. She's slipped off her towering black Louboutins, slung her white jacket over the back of one of the kitchen chairs, turned the pink Roberts radio to a nerve-jangling breakfast show, and has just this minute volunteered to make Lara some toast.

'It's the least I can do, honey,' she's telling Lara, who's standing wide-eyed in her truly ancient Dangermouse pyjamas, watching Nancy bustle about at the bread bin and the Dualit. 'Surprise visitors taking over your kitchen at eight in the morning ought to damn well make themselves useful, don't you agree?'

'Well, it's very nice of you . . .'

'Nice nothing.' Nancy shoots Lara a dazzling grin and then, unable to prevent herself, peers more closely at Lara's pyjamas. 'You know, that's a really interesting T-shirt you're wearing . . . Dangermouse. I haven't heard of that. Is it vintage?'

'Lars, maybe just a quick word,' I interrupt, doing my *One Man and His Dog* bit and herding her, sheepdog-style, out of the kitchen and back towards the bathroom. I close the door behind us. 'Look, I'm really sorry about this . . .'

'Well, it is a little bit out of the blue. And if I'd known Nancy Tavistock was going to be standing in my kitchen when I got up this morning, I'd probably have made sure I brushed my hair and put on some non-vintage pyjamas first . . .'

'I know. I would have warned you, but I only got her text saying she wanted to come over about an hour ago.'

It took me by surprise, too, I can tell you. I mean, I already stayed up with Nancy until after midnight last night. As soon as she heard about my discovery of Lucien's text messages, she summoned me to the hotel she's staying at and insisted I tell her, in painstaking detail, every single thing I could remember about where I'd spotted Lucien, and when . . . Then she called Magnus, her solicitor, and he came over, too, and we went through it all about five more times, while Nancy worked her way around the minibar and Magnus and I nibbled on room-service club sandwiches. Anyway, I thought we'd gone through it quite enough, so the last thing I expected to wake me at half six this morning was a text from Nancy saying she needed to talk some more and could she 'swing by' on the way to this morning's big meeting with Redwood at Pritchard and Haynes.

'But Iz – and I hate to sound inhospitable here – couldn't she have asked you to go to her place?'

I don't have the time just now to give Lara any details about precisely why we can't meet at Nancy's place. The pertinent information – that Nancy's staying at a hotel because her husband has been bedding Annie – is probably not the kind of thing I want to be hitting Lara with at half seven on a workday morning. 'That's a bit complicated.'

'But what's going on, Iz? I don't get why you have to meet at this hour at all.' Lara sits down on the edge of the toilet seat and stares up at me. 'You left a message for me at work barely twenty-four hours ago telling me you'd been fired. Then you didn't answer your phone all day . . .'

'I'm sorry. I had a lot to think about.'

'. . . you get back in the early hours, and now I wake up this morning to find the woman who fired you making me toast in my kitchen.' She rubs her eyes blearily. 'I know I'm a hideously anal control freak, Iz, but none of it makes any real sense.'

'Look, things have got a bit . . . unexpected. Nancy was meant to be signing a deal with these investors this morning, but I found something out last night that's kind of put a spanner in the works.'

'Oh, Isabel.' Lara puts her hands to her face. 'Not a spanner.'

'No, no, it's a good spanner! In shoddy, fraudulent works! So Nancy's talked it through with her lawyer, and she's going to go to the meeting this morning and tell the investors she isn't going to sell at the price they're offering.'

'She's backing out of an investment deal? Isn't whatshisname . . . Lucien Black . . . going to be a bit pissed off about that?'

'Oh, no, she's not going to back out. She's just going to demand the price they originally agreed. And anyway, Lucien's the one who tried to cheat her in the first place, so he shouldn't really get to have too much of a say . . .'

'Izzie! Laura!' Nancy's voice floats down the hallway. 'Toast's up!'

'Look.' I hand Lara her towel and shower cap, and my special L'Occitane lavender shower gel – anything for Brownie points right now. 'You should get ready for work. I'll go and keep Nancy under control. I'll explain all this properly this evening, I promise.'

In the kitchen, Nancy is buttering toast and taking sips from a freshly made mug of tea. She grins at me as I come in. 'What does your friend like? Honey? Jam? That disgusting Bovril stuff you Brits are always spreading on your toast?'

'Marmite. Yes, actually.' I open the cupboard and pull out the jar. 'This is really nice of you, Nancy. Making breakfast and everything.'

Nancy flaps a hand. 'Like I said, it's the least I could do. Invading your home like this.' She digs a buttery knife into the Marmite in a way that would make Lara wince if she could see it. 'Oh, listen, Izzie, will you come along with me to Pritchard and Haynes this morning?'

'Into your meeting with Redwood?'

I must look completely horrified at this prospect, because Nancy laughs. 'Christ, no. Just come along in the cab with me. I could do with the moral support.'

'Absolutely!' This is great. I can hang out with Barney at Coffee Messiah while the meeting goes ahead, and then . . .

Well, then what? Does this mean Nancy is thinking of hiring me back again? I daren't really ask. I mean, obviously, I have to ask. Because if I'm going to start any kind of fashion design course, I'm going to need a job to fund my way through it, and I'd still rather work for Nancy than anyone. But it will be hideously embarrassing if she says no.

'Um, Nancy . . .'

'Thanks, Izzie. I appreciate it. This meeting's going to be horrible for me. Ugh.' She pulls a face, but I think it's more about the Marmite than the prospect of confronting Lucien with the fact that she knows he's been swindling her. For some reason – relief? hysteria? – Nancy's whole demeanour is spelling out a woman who's more excited by this morning's schedule than daunted by it. 'I don't know why you don't just snack on creosote and be done with it.'

I laugh politely. 'Nancy, I have something to speak to you about . . .'

'Oh, God, I'm forgetting! I mean, why I came round

in the first place. *I* need to speak to *you*, Isabel. I think I can rely on you to tell me the truth. After everything that's happened, I mean. As long as you're not planning on spinning me any more lines about your close personal friendships with any more of Mick Jagger's exes!' She hoots with laughter for a moment, while I squirm and pray for Lara's kitchen floor to swallow me whole. 'Anyway, hon, I want you to be honest with me now, about something important.' She points the Marmitey knife in my direction. 'Do you think I should set up on my own?'

'Sorry?'

'On my own. My own fashion label.' Nancy glances at her watch and starts to slip her shoes back on, making her seem more toweringly tall than ever in the small room. 'I mean, face it, I practically ran Lucien's label single-handed for the last five years, and I know I can find a fabulous production team to actually put together any collection I envisage. Hopefully once I've split from Lucien, all the rats who've been avoiding me will welcome me back into the fashion fold with great big open arms, and I'll have my pay-off from Redwood to get things set up . . .' She shrugs. 'Do you think I can make a go of something like that?'

'I think it's a fantastic idea!' Because it is. I mean, people would pay a small fortune to get their hands on a piece of Nancy Tavistock style. 'God, you could start with your very own rival to the Tavistock bag . . . Signature dangly earrings . . . oh, and kaftans! A whole range of mini-kaftans . . .'

'Great. OK.' Nancy cuts me off with a thumbs-up, then dusts her hands of toast crumbs, pulls on her jacket, and picks up the Celine Boogie bag she's carrying this morning in place of her usual Tavistock. 'Well, it's good to hear you've got a little faith in me. Let's see how this meeting goes and then I can sit down and think it all through. Now, we should be thinking about finding a taxi . . .'

'Right. Sure. Um, just give me a minute to grab my bag.' I can't help feeling pretty disappointed as I hurry to my 'room' and start gathering everything I need. I mean, it was nice of Nancy to ask my opinion, obviously. But it isn't like she actually wants any of my suggestions. And I still haven't had the chance to ask her about whether or not I'm still fired. Well, maybe I'll pluck up the courage on the way over to her meeting. Or maybe after, fortified by one of Barney's strongest espressos.

Outside, Nancy is already on her way out of the front door, simultaneously thanking a towel-clad Lara for her hospitality, cheerily accepting my post from a dazzled postman, and dialling up Magnus to let him know she's on her way.

'I'll call you,' I mouth to Lara, as I follow Nancy out into the street. 'I'll explain everything. I promise.'

I don't know how I'd be managing without Coffee Messiah, that's for sure. I've been outside Pritchard and Haynes for hours, and Nancy's still inside. There's an extremely chilly breeze, and the only thing that's kept me from turning blue is regular injections of caffeine from Barney's glittering Faema machine.

Mind you, I've been waiting for my most recent coffee for a good twenty minutes. Because there's actually a queue at the stall! Six or seven deep, all happily waiting for the single espressos Barney will allow them (it's just gone eleven o'clock). It's the longest line I've witnessed so far this morning, but in fact there's been a pretty steady stream of customers the whole time I've been here.

'You're doing brilliantly, Barn!' I tell him, once the rush clears, and he's rewarding himself with half a pain au chocolat from his dwindling supplies.

'I know!' Generously, he hands me the other half of the pain au chocolat. 'One of the big ad agencies has just merged with an Italian agency and sent some of their guys over to train here. Now they're spreading the word around, and I'm getting most of them coming down here at least once a day!' He sighs happily. 'You know, one of the Italians called me an oasis in the desert?'

I grin at him. 'That's fantastic. Just keep up the good work, and you should be able to open up another branch outside Central St Martins. Then we can hang out whenever I'm there!'

'You know, I'm really impressed, Iz.' Barney starts making my espresso. 'I mean, I don't want to sound like your dad, but doing this evening course sounds like a really sensible idea.'

'You don't sound like my dad.' Dad would be calling it a really sensible idea *for once*. And that would only

464

happen after several consecutive hours of yelling about the fact I'd lied about getting on the full-time course in the first place. Which, by the way, is another reason why doing this evening course is such a very sensible idea: it'll give me access to Central St Martins so I can probably manage to convince Cousin Portia, and therefore the rest of the family, that I'm studying there full-time! 'Anyway,' I go on, 'we shouldn't speak too soon. I might not even get accepted.'

Though actually, I'm only saying this to make sure I don't jinx anything. From the look of the application pack I picked up yesterday afternoon, getting on the Introduction to Fashion Design course is pretty easy. You don't need a portfolio of previous work, you don't need previous fashion-related degrees or relevant work experience. You just need to show that you have an interest in the fashion industry. Which, let's face it, I have. In spades.

And if I really have to, I can always pull out my little selection of newspaper clippings where some of the most respected names in the fashion industry are raving on and on about the dress I made for Eve Alexander. Plus, perhaps, a little note attached from Nancy saying that these may *say* it's a Lucien Black dress, but actually, I'm the one responsible. Just in case I'm unlucky enough to be interviewed by Diana Pettigrew who, let's face it, isn't going to believe a word I say . . .

'Iz?' Barney is waggling my coffee at me, trying to get my attention. 'Your phone?'

I scrabble for it in my bag, expecting to see Nancy's number come up, but it's a mobile number I don't recognise.

'Hello, Isabel speaking.'

'Isabel? This is your father.'

I almost drop my phone into my espresso cup. No wonder I didn't recognise the number. *Dad?*

'Yes,' he says, rather irritably. 'Am I disturbing?'

'Er . . . no . . .'

'It's about Matthew.'

My heart plummets. Now I know why he's calling me.

'Look, Dad . . .'

'I don't know if you know this yet, but Annie has broken things off with him.' Dad's voice is clipped and careful. 'He telephoned us first thing this morning.'

Well, yes, I do know. And I know it's probably to do with the fact that I called her yesterday afternoon, told her I knew about her and Hugo, and that if she didn't come clean to Matthew, then I would. The question is, how does Dad know? Because the only reason he'd be calling me about this would be to have a go at me about interfering.

'Yes, look, Dad, I couldn't just sit back and watch while . . .'

'I know you're very busy,' he interrupts, 'but I'd appreciate it if you'd try to have a word with Matthew. Maybe take him out for a bite to eat.' He clears his throat. 'I'll reimburse you for whatever it costs.'

466

I stare at the pavement, too shocked to speak for a moment. 'Sorry?'

'He's just been chucked, Isabel,' Dad says, uncomfortable as ever with the slang. 'I would have thought you'd be the perfect person to speak to him.'

I get it. 'Because I'm always getting dumped, you mean?'

'No.' He clears his throat again. 'Because you're his sister. And because people seem to like talking to you. You . . . ah . . . seem to make them feel better.'

Barney is looking at me like I'm about to fall down dead. 'Are you *all right*?' he hisses, in alarm.

I nod, returning my attention to the phone. 'Of course I'll talk to him. Anything I can do . . .'

'Well. Good. Thank you, Isabel. Your mother will appreciate it.'

'OK. Consider it done.'

'Oh, and one more thing . . .'

Here we go. I knew this was never going to be an entirely uncritical phone call.

'I had a very pleasant chat with Lady Rutherford a couple of days ago. Nice woman, we sit on the tennis club fund-raising committee together.'

'*Sonia* Rutherford?'

'Well, obviously. Do you think that ghastly moppet who replaced her would have anything to do with something so lowly as the Mid-Somerset Tennis Club?' Dad's voice is packed with his most withering scorn. I have to say, it's refreshing not to have it directed at me for a change. 'Anyway, she told me how

467

much she'd enjoyed having you make her a dress.'

'She did?'

'Yes. She said you were very professional, and that you offered an excellent service . . .'

I can just hear Dad actually putting the questions to her across watery coffee and pink wafers at a tennis club committee meeting. *Did she behave professionally, Lady Rutherford? Were you impressed with her level of service?*

Still, at least he got affirmative answers. That must have made a nice change for him.

'. . . and apparently, the dress was a big success. Really stole the show, she told me. I reminded her of your address, in fact, because she even wanted to send you a little thank-you note!'

I'm about to say something about there being no need for him to sound so astonished. But then I realise – he doesn't sound astonished. He just sounds kind of pleased.

'Well, I'm glad. That the dress was a success, I mean.'

'Yes.' Dad clears his throat. 'So. Well done, Isabel.'

'Thank you . . .'

'And good luck with Matthew. Bye.'

'Bye, Dad.'

OK. Did that just really happen?

Did Dad just . . . well, what was that? A compliment? Congratulations? Praise?

Because I can't help but think I imagined it. I mean, I have been under a lot of stress lately.

Except . . . didn't Dad say Sonia Rutherford told him she was sending me a thank-you note? Because I think . . . yes, I'm right. A quick scrabble through my bag has produced a pale pink handwritten envelope that Nancy snatched from the postman back at Lara's this morning.

'Iz? Who was that?'

'That was my dad,' I tell Barney, tearing open the envelope and opening the little flowery card inside. 'I just need to check something . . .'

Dear Miss Bookbinder,

Just a note to say what a stellar success your dress was at Katie's 21st! Photo enclosed, for your records – and thank you!

Best wishes, Sonia Rutherford

PS How could I not have realised your father is John Bookbinder of my tennis club committee? What a nice man – and how proud he must be of you!

So I didn't imagine it. It's not some kind of alternate reality.

Though looking at the photo Sonia Rutherford has very nicely enclosed is kind of making me wish that this *were* an alternate reality. It's of a pretty, ruddy girl, who must be Katie, with her arm around a shyly smiling Sonia herself. Katie is wearing a navy-blue satin puff-ball. And Sonia is wearing my black tunic dress, which is almost completely obscured behind . . . I'd guess . . . approximately . . . eight bazillion silver sequins.

'Jesus.' Barney is looking at the photo over my shoulder. 'What happened to her?'

'Mum and Barbara happened to her.'

I mean, no wonder Sonia told Dad her dress *stole the show*! But then, she seems to like it. Katie, too. Though Katie Rutherford is, seemingly unironically, attending her own twenty-first in a navy satin puffball, so I'm not sure how much faith we can have in her judgement. I suppose, though, that as long as they were both happy . . .

'Have you been blinded by all those spangles, Iz? Isn't that your boss coming?'

Barney's right. The revolving doors to Pritchard and Haynes have just spun round and disgorged Nancy and Magnus, her solicitor, on to Great Portland Street.

'I'd better go.' I start to hurry towards them.

Nancy spots me coming and waves. 'God, I'm sorry,' she says, as I reach them. 'We've really kept you waiting!'

'That's all right.' I've got butterflies in my stomach. If the meeting went badly, if Redwood had some big explanation for their contact with Lucien after all, I'm going to feel horribly responsible. 'So? How did it go?'

A huge smile spreads across Nancy's face. 'We did it. They're offering the original level of investment. Well, minus a buck or two, but we're not going to quibble, are we, Magnus?'

Magnus, who's trying to hail a taxi, looks like he's about to pass out from exhaustion. 'We're certainly not.'

'Nancy, that's fantastic!'

'Tell me about it!' She hugs me, very tightly, before turning back to Magnus. 'You grab a cab, Mags. I've got a few things to do.'

'So did they admit anything?' I ask, as Magnus collapses into a taxi and heads off down Great Portland Street. 'Did they call Lucien? Does he know you know?'

Nancy holds up both hands. 'Whoa. One at a time. No, they've not actually admitted to anything, of course, but seeing those text messages soon put the wind up them. They're claiming they're just returning to their original offer *out of goodwill*.' She snorts. 'And yes, they called Lucien. And yes, he knows I know.' She shoves on her sunglasses with sudden force. 'And now he knows I'm leaving the company, too.'

'So you've decided? To set up on your own, I mean?'

'Yes, Isabel, I think I have. Lucien's furious about it, of course. Can't live without me, and all that crap. Can't live without me running his life, he means. Well, he'll get over it. He might have lost whatever fabulous little sum I'm sure Fred Elfman was slipping him, but he's getting a decent amount now that Redwood are paying the full price.' Her face is cold and hard now. 'Anyhow, he's really not my problem any more.'

Wow. Hell hath no fury like a Nancy nearly swindled.

'Now,' she continues, 'I should get back to Hugo, let him know what happened . . .'

471

'You're . . .' I stop, just before I can say *you're staying with him?* 'Um . . . so you're going back home, then?'

She shrugs. 'Yeah. Well. You know, I'm gonna be really busy setting up the new business. We'll barely even see each other for the next few months. That'll make it easier.'

'But . . . what you saw . . . I mean, you actually caught him red-handed . . .'

'Isabel.' Nancy takes her sunglasses off for a moment and looks right at me. Her eyes are suddenly terribly weary. 'I've caught him before. I'll catch him again. Like I say, I have far too much work on right now to waste my time punishing a leopard for not changing its spots.'

So all that chirpiness back at Lara's flat this morning wasn't because she's leaving Hugo. It was despite the fact she's staying with him.

'Nancy . . .'

'And talking of work,' she adds, deliberately switching the subject, 'you and I have a lot of it to do.'

'Sorry?'

Nancy prods me in the shoulder with a long finger. 'I only fired you from *Atelier*, you know. And I need a creative assistant for my new company. Obviously it has to be someone I can bounce ideas off . . . maybe even someone who can give me a hand with some of the designs for my first collection . . .'

I stare at her. 'You want to hire me? To do that?'

'Yes, Isabel, I do. You did a terrific job with that

472

dress for Eve Alexander. You've already given me my first big idea for the new label – a rival to the Tavistock bag. So if you think you've got a few more tricks like that up your sleeve, then you're the first person I want to hire. Not to mention the fact that I need someone I can trust.'

I'm lost for words.

Me – creative assistant on what's surely going to be the hottest new fashion label in London a few months from now? A paying job with the rejuvenated queen of the Fashion Aristocracy, while I spend my spare time working towards setting up my own label? With all the contacts and influence that Nancy Tavistock can give me? This is going to be incredible!

And if she liked my idea about the handbags, then she's sure to like some of my other ideas, too. A Nancy Tavistock fragrance, for example. I mean, how brilliant would it be to work on something like that? I could help her design the bottle, and pick out the name . . . maybe even head up the whole campaign, from scouting out the tropical island where the adverts will be shot to picking out the A-list actors and actresses to star in them.

'Well? Will you take the job?'

I clear my throat, and try to sound calm, level-headed and sensible. 'Well, I'd need to keep Tuesday and Thursday evenings clear. I mean, I have this course I'm hoping to do . . .'

'Fine. Whatever. Are you going to come work with me or not?'

'I'd love to.' I smile at her. 'I'd be honoured.'

Nancy lets out a little whoop and grabs my hand. 'Fabulous! God, we should celebrate! Can I take you out to lunch, Izzie? I could try Scott's . . . Cipriani . . .'

'Actually,' I say, glancing over the road, 'I'm more in the mood for just a cup of coffee right now.'

Nancy shoves her sunglasses back on. 'Suits me. Know anywhere good round here?'

'Yes.' I'm already leading the way towards Coffee Messiah. 'As a matter of fact, I do.'

In the End

God, I feel inspired.

I've been flat-hunting all day, and I've found the perfect place! It's approximately the size of a shoebox, but it's bright and airy, and it's at the very top of a teetering Victorian town house, which makes it feel a little bit like a proper artist's garret. But within walking distance of the lovely shops on Westbourne Grove, which probably makes it a cut above the average garret. Anyway, the moment I saw it with the rental agent, I signed on the dotted line. With what Nancy's paying me, of course, I'm barely going to be able to furnish it, but then I've always been a huge fan of the minimalist look. After all, all I really need is a place to lay my head. Oh, and room for my clothing mannequin, sewing machine, bolts of fabric, fashion-design textbooks, and all the other bits and pieces I seem to be accumulating ever since I started my course at Central St Martins a couple of weeks ago. OK, so it'll be a bit crowded. It'll still be totally amazing to have a place I can call my own.

I mean, Lara hasn't said anything, obviously, but I think it's going to be best for me to get out of her hair as quickly as possible. She hasn't actually been on a proper date with Matthew yet, but from the increasing amount of giggly phone calls, flirty text messages, and the looks they were giving each other across the kitchen table when he came round for an endless Sunday lunch last weekend, it's only going to be a matter of time. Obviously my first thought was that I'd just have to stick it out, live with the awkwardness and stay there to pick up the pieces when Matthew backed off again. But the thing is, I don't think there's going to be any backing off. It may only have been a few weeks since everything ended with Annie, but I should recognise a rebound relationship when I see one, and this isn't it. Despite the fact they blatantly fancy the pants off each other, they're just like best friends. Thick as thieves. And if this is going to work out the way I want it to, I need to give them some time alone together.

So we're off. Me and my bin liners. Which, obviously, I'm not going to just leave lying around my lovely new place. I mean, I don't want Will to tease me about it. You know, if he should happen to pop round for a flat-warming drink, or something. We've agreed to take things slowly for the next couple of months, but that doesn't mean he can't come over and see where I'm living. And you know, if we decide to stop taking things slowly, and I end up back in his lovely, cosy Battersea Park flat, then this place is going to be a brilliant studio space for me to focus on my work. My work, by the way, being helping Nancy set up Tavistock, Inc, which is already being talked about in

Grazia and the *Sunday Times Style* as the most exciting prospect on the fashion horizon since Kate Moss launched her own range at Topshop! And starting to put together my own ideas for Isabel B, which . . . well, it isn't being talked about by anyone just yet. But I'm giving it time, this time.

And I'm starting with a totally clean slate. Because Isabel B for Underpinnings, thank God, has been officially disbanded. To boil down Barbara's extremely long, endlessly apologetic Dear John phone call to its essential points, she had such a terrific time blinging up the tunic I made for Sonia Rutherford that she's decided to branch out into a little bit of fashion design herself. She's calling her label Lady Barbara, and (heaven help us) Mum is going to be her very own creative consultant. I've seen a few of the pieces they're getting together for their inaugural collection, and all I can say is, if you've ever thought about investing in sequin futures, do it now. Still, I'm quite sure that Lady Barbara will find plenty of die-hard fans amongst Underpinnings' core clientele in a way that my Grecian-style toga dresses and plain tunics were never going to.

Not that I think I'm ever going to be making a toga or a tunic again, by the way. Because things are coming on leaps and bounds in my Introduction to Fashion Design classes. Rudimentaries of garment-making left, right and centre! I can sew a proper hem! I can make a proper seam! And I'm sure if I do enough practice on my little sewing machine, the basics of sleeve-making can't be too far off either! Which I can hardly wait for, because I'm just *bursting* with all these ideas that I want to try out the moment I'm capable. Ever since the mini-triumph of my Eve Alexander dress, I'm filling more Mood Books than I know what to do with. But with serious ideas this time, of course. Designs, sketches, little swatches of material. In fact, they're so very serious-looking that the whole idea of the Mood Book has started to catch on with other people in my evening class. I think I'm regarded as a bit of a professional, which is thoroughly refreshing.

Thoroughly Refreshing: *The new fragrance from Isabel Bookbinder.*

Oooh, now *that* sounds like something Daniel Craig would advertise. Him and Eve Alexander, perhaps – she owes me a favour – bathing in some moonlit lake, looking bronzed and lithe and thoroughly refreshed. And then the launch party could take place at . . . at the Ice Hotel in Sweden! The guests could be pulled across the snow on sledges by teams of huskies, and Barney could serve vodka granitas and slivers of sashimi, and Eve and Daniel could appear on the stroke of midnight in fur cloaks – not real fur, of course, I'd have to speak to the party planners about that – before pulling them off and executing perfect dives into some kind of steaming outdoor pool . . .

God, I have to get all this down in a Mood Book, quick! Not one of the serious, professional-looking ones I take into college. The secret, private one I keep tucked away in a safe place in my handbag, should a moment of inspiration like this suddenly arise.

In fact, the more I come to think of it, I'm really *feeling* cloaks for Autumn/Winter. Great big swishy ones, as an exciting alternative to boring winter coats, and sexy little capelets to pop over a fancy frock for the Christmas party season! I could even try a kind of Little Red Riding Hood theme, but tastefully rather than tackily – I think The Woman I Design For would be quite amenable if I did, say, skating skirts and button boots to go with the capes. And called them *crimson* and *carmine* instead of plain old red.

Come to think of it, cloaks don't even have sleeves . . .

God, I feel inspired.

I mean, really, really inspired.

Now all I need is a Debut Collection.

The Glamorous (Double) Life of Isabel Bookbinder

Holly McQueen

'A marvellously funny debut' Jilly Cooper

Isabel Bookbinder might not be leading the most glamorous life ever – measuring column inches at the *Saturday Mercury* isn't exactly the job of her dreams – but luckily she's developed a foolproof plan to change all that.

Reasons to become a bestselling author:
- Plentiful opportunities to swish new Super-hair
- Sophisticated launch parties (with smoked salmon blinis)
- Am bound to captivate the delicious Joe Madison
- Can finally prove to father that Really Am Not a Waster

Potential setbacks:
- Don't yet have 'Yoko' bag, as carried by arch rival Gina D
- Hmm. Am inadvertently at the centre of a major political sex scandal
- Paparazzi are doorstepping my parents and boring boyfriend Russell
- Haven't *actually* got round to putting pen to paper yet

Admittedly some of the setbacks are a little daunting, but Isabel's sure that a woman of her ingenuity – and creativity – can find a way . . .

'I quite fell in love with Isabel. Funny, charming and accident prone, she is the perfect heroine for today' Penny Vincenzi

The Secret Life of a Slummy Mummy

Fiona Neill

For Lucy Sweeney, motherhood isn't all astanga yoga and Cath Kidston prints. It's been years since the dirty laundry pile was less than a metre high, months since Lucy remembered to have sex with her husband, and a week since she last did the school run wearing pyjamas.

Motherhood, it seems, has more pitfalls than she might have expected. Caught between perfectionist Yummy Mummy No 1 and hypercompetitive Alpha Mum, Lucy is in danger of losing the parenting plot. And worst of all, she's alarmingly distracted by Sexy Domesticated Dad. It's only a matter of time before the dirty laundry quite literally blows up in her face . . .

'This slice of angst and affluenza is several cuts above the rest . . . witty, observant and supremely intelligent.' *The Times*

'There is something of Bridget Jones's hopeless-but-adorable quality about Lucy . . . Neill's hilarious depiction of the manifold daily perils of stay-at-home motherhood is so convincing that it soon looks like the most challenging job in the world – and Lucy is all the more sympathetic simply for staying afloat.'
Daily Telegraph

arrow books

THE POWER OF READING

Visit the Random House website and get connected with information on all our books and authors

EXTRACTS from our recently published books and selected backlist titles

COMPETITIONS AND PRIZE DRAWS Win signed books, audiobooks and more

AUTHOR EVENTS Find out which of our authors are on tour and where you can meet them

LATEST NEWS on bestsellers, awards and new publications

MINISITES with exclusive special features dedicated to our authors and their titles

READING GROUPS Reading guides, special features and all the information you need for your reading group

LISTEN to extracts from the latest audiobook publications

WATCH video clips of interviews and readings with our authors

RANDOM HOUSE INFORMATION including advice for writers, job vacancies and all your general queries answered

Come home to Random House

www.rbooks.co.uk

The Love Academy

Belinda Jones

Do you have enough romance in your life?

Journalist Kirsty Bailey would have to answer no. She has the essential starter kit – a boyfriend – but somehow Joe seems to have skipped the vows of for better/for worse and gone straight to for granted.

But then just as she's on the verge of settling for a swoon-free existence, Kirsty's magazine sends her to a majestic Venetian palazzo to attend the much gossiped-about Love Academy . . . Her undercover mission? To prove her editor's theory that this 'school for singles' is nothing more than an escort agency with a sexy accent and fancy glass chandeliers.

But what if her editor is wrong and their promise of true amore is for real? Will Kirsty be able to resist the kind of moonlit temptations she's been dreaming of for years, or is her relationship with Joe going, going, *gondola*?

If you think Casanova was a bad boy, just wait until you see what Cupid has in store for Kirsty . . .

arrow books

Diary of a Hapless Househusband

Sam Holden

One man's encounter with domesticity . . .

When father-of-two Sam loses his job, he reluctantly agrees to stay at home while his wife returns to work. Secretly thinking this whole parenthood thing a breeze of leisurely jaunts to the park, reading the paper while the children play quietly and occasionally attending a civilised play date or two, Sam quickly realises just what exactly it means to be a stay-at-home parent.

Inevitably, domestic mayhem ensues. Just trying to get dressed in the morning and out of the house without going to A&E is a feat, as is managing the children's complicated play-date schedule while fending off the unwelcome advances of Jodhpur Mum at the playground. And Sam's foolproof 72-step Childcare Programme doesn't seem remotely up to the task.

Desperate to get his life back on track, Sam seizes upon a variety of mad schemes, but just as things look like they're beginning to fall into place, he makes a very surprising discovery . . .

'A very, very funny and often touching account of one man's struggle to try and run Planet Home.' Allison Pearson, author of *I Don't Know How She Does It*

arrow books

Wedding Season

Katie Fforde

All you need is love . . .?

Sarah Stratford is a wedding planner hiding a rather inconvenient truth – she doesn't believe in love. Or not for herself, anyway. But as the confetti flutters away on the June breeze of yet another successful wedding she somehow finds herself agreeing to organise two more, on the same day and only two months away. And whilst her celebrity bride is all sweetness and light, her own sister soon starts driving her mad with her high expectations but very limited budget.

Luckily Sarah has two tried and tested friends on hand to help her. Elsa, an accomplished dress designer who likes to keep a very low profile, and Bron, a multi-talented hairdresser who lives with her unreconstructed boyfriend and who'd like to go solo in more ways than one. They may be very good at their work but romance doesn't feature very highly in any of their lives.

As the big day draws near all three women find that patience is definitely a virtue in the marriage game. And as all their working hours are spent preparing for the wedding of the year plus one, they certainly haven't got any time to even think about love. Or have they?

'A funny, fresh and lively read' *heat*

arrow books

Going Dutch

Katie Fforde

Love isn't always plain sailing . . .

Jo Edwards never planned to live on a barge. She's not even sure she likes boats. But when her husband trades her in for a younger model, she finds her options alarmingly limited.

Dora Hamilton never planned to run out on her own wedding. But as The Big Day approaches, her cold feet show no signs of warming up – and accepting Jo's offer of refuge aboard *The Three Sisters* seems the only alternative.

As Jo and Dora embark on reorganising their muddled lives, they realise they both need a practical way to keep themselves afloat. But, despite their certainty that they've sworn off men for good, they haven't bargained for the persistent intervention of attractive but enigmatic Marcus, and laid-back, charming Tom, who both seem determined to help them whether they like it or not . . .

arrow books

ALSO AVAILABLE IN ARROW

The Accidental Wife

Rowan Coleman

How do you know if your life has taken a wrong turn?

Alison James thinks she might be living the wrong life. She loves
her husband Marc and their three children but somehow, in the
process of building a perfect life for her family, she seems to have
lost herself. And sometimes she worries that she's being punished
for how it all started – for the day she ran away with her best
friend's boyfriend.

Catherine Ashley knows she's living the wrong life. She adores her
two daughters, but she'd always thought that at thirty-one she'd be
more than a near-divorcee with a dead-end job. In those dark
middle-of-the-night moments that come all too often these days,
her mind still flicks back to the love of her life: Marc James. And she
still wonders whether Alison stole her life as well as her boyfriend.

Alison and Catherine have been living separate lives, a hundred
miles apart, for fifteen years – since Alison and Marc ran away. But
now Alison's moving back to Farmington, the town in which they
both grew up. And they're about to find out just how different both
their lives could still be . . .

arrow books